A Dog Called Jack

Center Point
Large Print

**This Large Print Book carries the
Seal of Approval of N.A.V.H.**

A Dog Called Jack

Ivy Pembroke

CENTER POINT LARGE PRINT
THORNDIKE, MAINE

Library of Congress Cataloging-in-Publication Data

Names: Pembroke, Ivy, author.
Title: A dog called Jack / Ivy Pembroke.
Description: Center Point Large Print edition. | Thorndike, Maine :
    Center Point Large Print, 2019.
Identifiers: LCCN 2018057273 | ISBN 9781643581279 (hardcover :
    alk. paper)
Subjects: LCSH: Large type books. | Domestic fiction.
Classification: LCC PS3616.E444 D64 2019 | DDC 813/.6—dc23
LC record available at https://lccn.loc.gov/2018057273

For Jordan, Isabella, Gabriella and Audrey—with all my love

Prologue

If Jack had to tell you this story, he'd tell you:

This is a story about the things you think you'll never lose in life, the things you do lose, the things that get left behind, either accidentally or on purpose.

But it's also a story about the things you think you'll never find in life, the things you do find, the things that get left behind by others that you pick up and make into yours.

Jack had a family, until the day when he didn't, and then what Jack had was a street.

Jack lost one family but gained many more.

Christmas is a very special time.

Jack's a very special dog.

Chapter 1

THREE-BEDROOM MID-TERRACE
HOUSE FOR SALE

A delightful three-bedroom, three-story house with many original features and a bright and airy reception. The kitchen/dining area provides access to a private garden planted with shrubbery. Upstairs contains three bedrooms and a main bathroom off the landing. A lovely family home situated on a quiet and charming residential street, close to transport links.

When Bill Hammersley first moved to Christmas Street, it was full of tidy, well-kept, quiet houses where everybody knew each other. Where, more importantly, everybody *understood* each other. Everybody spoke the same language and worked in the same places and ate the same things and listened to the same music. Nobody drove down the street with obnoxious music blaring or wanted to put up weirdly patterned curtains in the windows. Everybody kept neat gardens with beautiful roses and exchanged pleasantries and shared cups of sugar or milk when necessary. It was only *friendly*.

Bill had no idea if any of the people around him would have sugar or milk these days, if he were to ask them. Lord only knew what these people considered food. They would have weird spices Bill had never heard of before, or maybe some kind of "organic" sugar—like normal sugar hadn't been good enough all those years—or milk that came from nuts. As if nuts could produce milk. Any idiot could look at a nut and see that there was no way milk was coming out of it. The world had gone absolutely mad all around him.

The flamingo, though. The flamingo was the last straw.

Bill told Jack as much. "Would you look at that plastic flamingo? Where do they think this is? Have you ever seen a flamingo round here? I mean, things have changed around here—Lord knows things have changed—but they haven't changed that much, Jack. Not yet. Have they?"

Jack wagged his tail.

"You're right," Bill sighed. "Maybe they *have* changed that much." He scratched Jack behind the ears as a reward for Jack's steady wisdom. As far as Bill could tell, Jack was the most intelligent neighbor he had these days. Certainly Jack didn't have teenagers traipsing through everybody's gardens as if they owned all of them, and maybe he went running along the street sometimes in pursuit of a squirrel or two, but he didn't carry a weird sludgy green drink while he did it. Jack had water after a run. Water had always been good enough after a run. Nothing natural about a green drink.

In the house next door, where the offending flamingo had been erected, a family was moving in: a man, a woman, a little boy. It was the little boy who had stuck the flamingo right in the middle of Dolores's prized rosebushes. As if a flamingo should be in a proper British garden in the middle of beautiful heritage roses. As if it made any sense at all for that flamingo to be the first thing to be unpacked.

"As if it hasn't been enough that we've had to deal with all the hammering going on over there," Bill said to Jack, "all the strangers in and out of the street. You've had to keep an eye on all of them and you've been tip-top at it, but that's not the point, is it? The point is people these days just can't be happy with the way things *are*."

Bill warmed to his topic and Jack looked receptive to Bill's pronouncements. "No, people these days, before they move into a place they have to knock everything down and then replace it all with plastic flamingos. A fake pink bird, right there in the front garden, right there in the middle of Dolores's roses." Bill jabbed a finger toward Dolores's roses, in front of which were standing people who were not Dolores. The new neighbors. *New* new neighbors, because Dolores hadn't lived in that house for years now, having sold it to Jack's former owners, who in turn had sold it again, because nobody could ever stay put these days. More new people. There were just so many *new people* these days.

Bill lowered his finger and regarded the new neighbors, sighing again. "Remember when this place felt like home instead of . . . a place belonging to someone else? I almost forget what that felt like."

Jack wagged his tail.

Which made Bill think. "You're right," he agreed, shaking his head briskly. "No need to sit here moping. When did moping ever accomplish anything?"

Jack followed behind Bill as he walked across to where one of the new neighbors was struggling with another box.

"You're not lifting that correctly," Bill barked at the man, because really, people these days knew *nothing*. "You need to lift from your knees, don't you know that?"

The man gave up struggling with the box, straightening and pushing his floppy hair off his forehead. If he cut his hair shorter, he wouldn't have to worry about that, thought Bill.

The man said, "Yeah, you're right, I'm tempting

fate." He smiled easily, and then he held out his hand. "I'm Sam."

"So, the flamingo." Bill ignored the hand in favor of pointing to the flamingo, in case this new neighbor named Sam was too daft to know what Bill was referring to.

The man glanced at it. "Oh. Yeah. Bob."

Bill blinked at him. He had not expected that reaction. "What?"

"The flamingo's name is Bob."

Bill boggled. Blimey, he was gaining lunatics for neighbors.

"Hello there, buddy," said the new neighbor.

Bill turned back from staring at the flamingo to find that Sam had crouched down and was scratching behind Jack's ears, just the way Jack liked. Jack was wagging his tail, but Bill understood that. Jack had to infiltrate all of the barmy neighbors in order to keep a closer eye on them. Bill approved of this solid strategy.

"You made an awful lot of racket over here, you know," said Bill, because he didn't want Sam to think that had been acceptable. "Constant hammering. Could barely hear my telly over them banging away on the lounge wall hanging all of your modern art or whatever it was."

"The electrics had to be fixed," Sam said. "They were a fire hazard."

Like that was an explanation. Bill scoffed, "The

13

old electrics weren't good enough for you? It was never a fire hazard in the old days."

Sam said, "And there was damp in the bedrooms, so we had to take care of that."

"Damp. A little damp never killed anyone."

"It can make you really sick," said Sam.

"You lot don't even know what 'really sick' is," said Bill. "In my day, a little thing like damp didn't stop us. Where are you moving here from?"

"America," said Sam.

"Oh," said Bill. "Well, that explains that. Try to remember to drive on the proper side of the road." Bill decided that was all he needed to say, turning on his heel and marching determinedly back to his house.

"I'm from here originally," Sam called after him.

As if living in America for however many years didn't have an effect on *that*.

Bill, back in his kitchen, decided to make a cuppa and looked for Jack to see if he might want a biscuit. He was mildly surprised to find that Jack wasn't anywhere in the house, but he supposed it was only wise for Jack to perform reconnaissance on the new lot next door. Couldn't be too careful.

Teddy Bishop was not sitting in the back garden by *choice*. But choice was not a big part of

Teddy's life these days. Teddy wasn't even in this *country* by choice.

Inside, Dad and Aunt Ellen were stacking a stupid amount of boxes and pretending like unpacking was going to be easy and Teddy hadn't even wanted to move here in the first place, so he wasn't interested in helping with any of that. So he was in the back garden.

The problem was he wasn't interested in the back garden, either. He didn't think anything about it was a "garden." It was small and messy. A lot of it had been paved. At the back was a tiny amount of grass definitely not big enough to play baseball on, and a few ugly bushes, and a single stupid tree. And on either side were high fences separating it from the houses right next door. This "garden" was basically a cage.

There was shouting from the yard next door, someone calling for someone a couple of times and then a resulting whining *Mum* in response and then a door slamming shut somewhere.

Teddy got up to investigate, just to see, but he could barely see anything at all from peering through the fence.

And then he turned from the fence to find a dog sitting in the spot he had just vacated. It came up about as high as Teddy's waist, and was slightly shaggy, with floppy ears and mostly black fur except for white along its chest and stomach.

"Who are you?" Teddy asked without thinking,

and then realized the dog wasn't going to answer him.

The dog didn't answer him. It just stood up and wagged its tail.

Teddy walked over to it and looked at it and wondered if it was going to bite him.

It didn't look like it was going to bite him.

Teddy reached a hand out cautiously and patted the dog's head. It wagged its tail more furiously.

Teddy realized he was smiling and admitted, "Well. I guess *you're* not so bad."

The dog tipped its head so it could lick Teddy's hand.

"Everything else here is stupid, though," Teddy said, just to make sure the dog understood that. "Like that stupid tree. I don't even think that tree is big enough for a treehouse. Mom built me such a great treehouse back home. We couldn't build one in that tree even if Dad wasn't totally useless when it comes to that stuff."

The dog nudged its head against Teddy's hand, and Teddy realized he'd stopped petting it, so he started up again.

He looked down at this strange dog in this strange place and thought about how he didn't know anyone or anything—not the people next door, not this dog in his very own garden, not even what the view from one of the upper tree branches looked like—and he said, because the dog was easy to talk to and it wasn't like Teddy had anyone else around, "Everything just keeps changing. I don't know why things have to keep changing. Why can't things just . . . stay the same? I really liked the way things were, but I couldn't keep it that way. Everything had to change. And I just don't get why."

The dog whined a little, as if to say, *I don't know why things can't stay the same, either.*

Teddy sighed. It would be nice if strange British dogs had answers to questions like that. But Teddy was pretty sure no one had answers to questions like that. He'd learned that a while ago.

"I just miss having a place that feels like home," Teddy confessed to the dog. "Instead of a place that . . . belongs to other people. I almost forget what that felt like."

The dog put its head on Teddy's knee.

And then the dog lifted its head and barked at a squirrel leaping from one tree to the next.

And then the dog put its head back down.

Sam Bishop watched his new neighbor walk back to the house next door. He walked with the careful gingerness of someone his age, which Sam estimated to be nearing eighty. But he kept his shoulders back and his head high in a way that Sam recognized as being pride and stubbornness all wrapped up in a crotchety package.

"That went well," remarked Sam to Bob the flamingo.

Who neither agreed nor disagreed. That was the thing about Bob: very nonjudgmental. In comparison to new neighbors, for instance.

Sam lifted the box the wrong way and struggled his way through the entrance hall and all the way back to the kitchen. They'd already filled the front rooms with boxes, and they were well on their way to filling the kitchen, too. Sam was beginning to question all of his life choices, especially the decision to move across an ocean. Even if this place across the ocean had been his original home.

His sister Ellen was perched on the kitchen counter eating crisps, which was not exactly the most helpful thing she could have been doing.

Sam put the box down on the counter next to her and said, "I have met one of the neighbors."

"Excellent. Did you make a good impression?"

"He doesn't approve of Bob."

"How sad for Bob," said Ellen. "Who's Bob?"

"The flamingo."

"The flamingo's name is Bob?"

Sam ignored her. "He doesn't approve of my replacing the electrics and he thinks I should have a heartier constitution when it comes to damp."

"Bob the flamingo?"

Sam scowled and stole some crisps from her in punishment. "No, my new neighbor. He wanted to know why I had workmen in here making a racket."

Ellen snorted. "I guess that throws a spanner in the works. How will you throw wild parties now?"

"I think my eight-year-old son is probably a bigger spanner with regard to wild parties than my crotchety old neighbor," said Sam.

"I can babysit your eight-year-old son, though," Ellen pointed out. "But I probably won't be babysitting your neighbor. You might have to just invite him to the parties. If he's a guest at the party, he can't complain about it."

"Something tells me he'd find a way to complain about anything," remarked Sam drily.

"Ah, he was that sort?" said Ellen knowingly.

"Yes. So." Sam put his hands on the small of his back and leaned back just a bit and refused to acknowledge that maybe his back was starting to bother him from carrying boxes wrong. "Just a few more boxes and we'll be done." He was fantasizing about being done lugging in the boxes. Of course, that then meant he was going to have to *unpack* all of the boxes. But in between he was going to have a few pints.

"Are you sure?" said Ellen. "I thought we'd never reach the end. I thought the boxes would keep multiplying endlessly. Have you introduced effective box birth control? Handed out moving-box condoms?"

"Do you hear the level of nonsense that comes out of your mouth?" asked Sam.

"No," said Ellen seriously. "I am a constant surprise to myself."

Sam laughed, because sometimes you couldn't help but laugh at Ellen.

Ellen responded by dropping the packet of crisps to take his hand and say earnestly, "I want to say something completely clichéd, but I mean it, from the bottom of my loving big sister heart. And this is not nonsense."

Sam braced himself, regarding Ellen warily. "This can't be good. . . ."

Ellen's blue eyes were solemn and inescapable. "She would have wanted you to find someone, Sam. She wouldn't have wanted you to live your life in some lonely, perpetual memorial for her."

"That's not what I'm doing," Sam denied. "I packed everything up and moved an entire ocean away. Nothing in England is a memorial to Sara."

"Except her plastic flamingo Bob. Literally the only thing you knew the location of in this sea of boxes." Ellen nudged a box at her feet with one trainer-clad toe, as if that proved her point.

"That was for Teddy," Sam defended himself. "I wanted to make sure he had something here right away that would make it feel like home."

"She wouldn't want you to be alone, Sam."

"I am not alone. I have Teddy. I have you now, as dubious a circumstance as that might turn out to be. I have your girls."

"None of that is what I'm talking about," said Ellen, "and you know it."

"Trust me, Ellen, I know precious little these days. I just made my little boy leave every single familiar thing in his life to come live in a completely different country where he doesn't know anyone or anything."

"He knows the girls and me," said Ellen.

"And none of *that* is what I'm talking about," said Sam, echoing her words, "and you know it."

Ellen, after a moment of studying him, said, "You did it with the best of intentions, Sam."

"Standing in the middle of a sea of boxes with a child outside who's barely speaking to me, it's hard to remember what those were," said Sam, and *hated* that he said it, because it sounded so pathetic.

But Sam had forgotten, in all the years he had lived in the States: you could be pathetic in front of your big sister. Ellen just slid off the counter and pulled him into a hug and Sam was not in a mood capable of refusing a hug. He squeezed a little tighter and thought how this was part of the reason he was here in the first place: to have someone around who gave him a moment to be the huggee instead of the hugger. Sam had moved Teddy and himself home for a lot of reasons, but right now this seemed like a most vitally important one.

Ellen said, "You're a good dad—I know you

know that. You're just having a moment. But you are a really good dad, and he loves you a lot, and he's going to be okay. He's resilient."

"Yeah," Sam said. "I've noticed." Sam really wished he hadn't had cause to notice how resilient his son was.

"He'll make friends and he'll get settled and he'll be fine."

"Yeah," Sam said, and took a deep breath. "Yeah, you're right." He released Ellen from the hug and went to turn back to the all-consuming task of moving.

Except that Ellen took his arm and said, "Wait, I have one more really important thing to tell you," and pulled him back into the hug. "You're going to be okay, too," she said.

And Sam would not have said that he'd needed to hear that out loud—Sam would have said, in fact, that he'd been okay for a very long time now—but he suddenly found himself so very grateful that Ellen was there.

Pari Basak was spying through the fence on the goings-on next door.

Pari was a *very* good spy.

"Pari!" her mother shouted. "Come inside for a second!"

Pari frowned, leaning closer to the fence. The new boy was sitting outside, looking very unhappy for some reason, and Pari could swear that she'd seen Jack making his way through the garden next door.

Her Jack.

"Pari!" Mum shouted more insistently.

"Ugh," Pari muttered. "Mum!" She raced inside just so she could protest being called inside. "I was *doing something.*"

"What could you have been doing outside?" asked Mum vaguely, because she was distracted by what she was doing, which was packing up pakoras.

"I was . . . looking at the new boy." Pari's mum didn't like the word *spy*.

Mum looked up. "What new boy?"

"The one who moved in next door," Pari said.

"Leave him alone," Mum said automatically. "Do you want to come with me to your uncle's?"

Pari had zero interest in going to her uncle's. She wanted to stay here and spy on the new boy and figure out where Jack was. Jack's whereabouts were very important. She said, "No."

"You can stay here then and wait for Sai to come home from the library," said Mum.

Sai, Pari's older brother, was not at the library. Sai was at the Pachutas', two doors down, with his girlfriend Emilia. But if their mother knew that, it would be, as Sai had put it, an *epic freak-out*. Sai wasn't supposed to be dating anyone. Sai was supposed to be spending all-day-every-day studying at the library so he could get into a good university and have an excellent career. Even though it was the summer vacation.

"Yeah," said Pari, who was nothing but united with Sai in her desire to Keep Mum From Freaking Out, and who also felt kind of bad for Sai, because how boring was spending all-day-every-day at the library for your summer vacation? "I'll wait for Sai to come home."

Mum gathered up her pakoras and tried to juggle them all while also pointing a Mum Finger in Pari's direction. "Don't bother the new boy next door."

"Got it," Pari said, nodding.

And then Mum paused and looked at her and smiled.

Pari knew that smile. She knew what came next.

"You're just so beautiful," Mum said, and then dropped a kiss on the top of Pari's head. "See you soon!" she called.

Pari went to the front window and watched Mum until she couldn't see her anymore.

Then she immediately slipped out the back door, walked over to the fence, and peered through it. At *Jack. Jack. With the new boy.*

"We were busy," Sai informed Pari, when he let her into Emilia's house.

"You were just snogging," Pari said. "That's not important. *This* is important."

"Hiya, Pari," Emilia said, coming into the kitchen and pulling her blond hair into a ponytail as she came. "Can I make you a cuppa?"

"No," said Pari, marveling at how Emilia could worry about tea at a time like this. "There's an emergency."

"What's the emergency?" asked Sai, sliding onto a chair at the kitchen counter, not looking appropriately alarmed.

"A new family is moving in."

"I saw that," Emilia said, where she was now pulling biscuits down from the cupboard. "Want some?" she offered in Sai's and Pari's direction. Again: *like there was no emergency going on.*

"Thanks, babe," Sai said.

Emilia gave him a playful whack on the back of the head.

"Don't call me 'babe.' "

Sai stuck his tongue out at her, grinning.

Emilia shook her head and picked up her cup of tea and led them back to the lounge.

Pari said urgently, to get them back to being focused, "There's a new boy and he's sitting outside in his back garden *with Jack.*"

"So?" said Sai, settling onto the sofa next to Emilia.

Pari for a second couldn't manage to say anything. How could Sai not see what a tremendous deal this was? "So?" she echoed. "*So? Are you mad?* How can Mum think you're

25

at the library all the time, when you're so thick?"

Sai frowned. "A boy and a dog are outside, what's the big—"

"Jack is supposed to be *my* dog," Pari said, pointing out the obvious.

"Jack isn't your dog," said Sai. "Jack is nobody's dog. Jack's the street dog."

"Right. But he's going to be *mine*. Once I can convince Mum and Dad."

Sai and Emilia both looked like they thought that wasn't going to happen, when it was *totally* going to happen. *Obviously*. Only not if this new boy stole Jack from her.

Pari sat cross-legged on the uncomfortable, fancy chair in the Pachutas' lounge. Clearly, this called for *strategy*.

Emilia glanced outside the front window, then sat a little straighter and said, "Uh-oh. Your dad's home. Might be time to sneak back. Don't start too much of a war over Jack, Pari. There's enough Jack to go around."

Pari rolled her eyes, because Emilia clearly just didn't *get* it.

Sai gave Emilia a kiss.

Emilia said, "See you tomorrow, babe."

Sai said, "Don't call me 'babe.' "

Emilia stuck her tongue out at him.

Arthur Tyler-Moss wasn't often home before Darsh Basak, which was why Arthur wasn't often witness to the flurry of activity provoked by the sight of Darsh at the top of the street. Arthur watched from his kitchen, where he was chopping herbs to add to the hotch-potch meal he had bubbling away on the stove, as the teenaged Basak boy and little Basak girl came squeezing through the tumbledown fence on the left, darted through the back garden, and then squeezed through the tumbledown fence on the right.

And Arthur said to Max, "We really must mend the fences."

"Nonsense," said Max. "Do you really care that our back garden aids the cause of young love?"

Jack, barking happily, came streaking through the back garden, froze at the sight of Max through the door, and then changed direction to come bounding over to him, tail wagging happily.

Arthur gave Max a look. "Why is Jack begging at our door?"

"I've no idea," said Max innocently. "It certainly isn't because I ever feed him."

Arthur sighed and leaned down to reach the very back of the cabinet under the sink, where he pulled out the box of dog biscuits Max had "hidden" there and shook it in Max's direction.

Max did not look chastised, because Max never looked chastised. He just said, "Thank you, darling," and took the dog biscuits and opened the door to give some to Jack.

Arthur said, "You know, other people's

27

husbands hide evidence of their infidelities. You hide dog biscuits."

"Lucky for you the only creature I'm having an affair with is a dog," replied Max.

"That sounds alarming," Arthur said. "Don't say that you're having an affair with a dog."

Max grinned as he closed the door, leaving Jack on the other side. Jack wagged his tail once more, then turned to bark at a squirrel, then followed the Basak children to their back garden.

Arthur said, as he chopped the herbs, "It isn't that I mind young love—"

"Oh, good, I was afraid you were about to say something dreadfully unromantic," said Max.

"—it's just that if something happens to them while they're on our property squeezing through ramshackle fences, then—"

"Hush," said Max. "That was dreadfully unromantic. You sound like an insurance agent."

"I *am* an insurance agent."

"We have new neighbors," said Max, changing the subject and coming over to stick a finger in Arthur's concoction and taste it speculatively.

"I saw the flamingo," Arthur said. "How is it? Good?"

"Adventurous," Max decided.

Arthur decided that was good enough to eat. He tossed his pile of herbs in and stirred everything together and said, "Did you go over to say hello?"

"To who?" asked Max blankly.

"The new neighbors," said Arthur.

"What?" said Max. "Of course not. Is that a thing we do now?"

Arthur shrugged. "I don't know. Maybe we should start. It would be polite."

"The politest thing would be for all of us to ignore each other and get on with our own lives and not interfere with theirs. The old man was already over there bothering them."

"How do you know that?"

"I spied on them, of course. I spy on everyone while I pretend to be home all day 'painting.'" Max put elaborate air quotes around the word.

"Ah, I knew the painting thing was all an elaborate ruse. Come, let's eat my adventurous food."

They sat at the table together and Arthur turned on the television to watch the news and decided Max had been right in his assessment that the meal was "adventurous."

Max said, after a moment, "Are you okay?"

Arthur said immediately, keeping his eyes trained on the television, "I'm fine."

Max, not to be deterred, said, "You were home earlier than usual today—"

"I'm fine," Arthur said again.

"I know that last week was—"

"I'm fine," Arthur repeated, as sternly as he could. And then felt mean, so added, "How are you? Are you okay?" and looked across at Max.

29

Who looked steadily back at him. "Fine," said Max, after a moment.

"Good," said Arthur. "We're both fine." He turned his attention back to the television.

Max said, "We'll just try again, love, it's bound to—"

"Can we not talk about it right now?" asked Arthur, hoping he didn't sound like he was begging, even though he basically was. "I would like to not talk about it right now."

And after a moment Max, bless him, agreed, "Yeah."

Outside the last house on the row, where Penelope Cheever lived alone and wrote freelance articles on a wide range of topics and where she'd carefully cultivated a herb garden after writing an article on developing a green thumb, and a small struggling beehive after writing an article on the importance of bumblebees to the environment, Pen was setting out healthy food for Jack. Because if she didn't do it, nobody would. She also shook out the bushy spring of her hair from the ponytail she'd trapped it in for her run, pulled out the ingredients for a protein shake, and then jotted on the notepad she kept by the fridge for just such occasions: *Flamingos. Why are they pink? What other animals are pink? Why do they stand on one leg? Are birds just weird? YES, BECAUSE DINOSAURS.*

Critically she studied what she'd written, decided to let it marinate a little bit longer in her head. One never knew where one might find a good idea for an article, and the flamingo that had just appeared in the handkerchiefsized front garden of the house down the street could turn out to be good inspiration.

In the meantime, she called out, "Hello, Jack!" to the dog, who had appeared to start eating the food she'd set out, enjoyed the tail wag she got in reply, and turned her attention to her protein shake.

The thing about moving, thought Sam, in a new house full of new sounds and old things that didn't really seem to fit, was that it never felt real until the first night.

Sam had done his fair share of moving, but there had been a while there, with Sara and Teddy, when he'd stayed put. He had been out of practice with packing, and he had forgotten how untethered one could feel in a house whose creaks and angles were still unfamiliar. He'd blithely sent Ellen home to feed Sophie and Evie, reasoning that surely he and Teddy would have to fend for themselves in the new house sooner or later, and sooner had seemed just fine to him. And now he was wondering if that hadn't been a gross miscalculation. He was missing Ellen's presence. He realized he'd been relying on her to buffer how painful it was that Teddy seemed so unhappy.

Sam had set up a small folding table in the dining area and had improvised using boxes as chairs. He had wanted this to seem like a grand adventure, but Teddy looked hardly interested in eating his pizza and definitely not at all like he was on a grand adventure.

Sam said this. "You don't look as if you're on a grand adventure."

Teddy looked dubious of Sam's sanity.

Sam wondered if other people's eight-year-olds looked at them this way. Sam hadn't really known any fellow parents of eight-year-olds in the States. Sara had been friends with some fellow parents, but none of Sam's friends had had children. It had been another point in favor of moving back home: start over, make new friends with the parents of kids in Teddy's class, not be labeled instantly as The One With the Dead Wife that everyone whispered about as he passed in the hallway.

Sam continued bravely in the face of Teddy's skepticism, "And this is indeed a grand adventure."

"So you keep saying," said Teddy, sounding unimpressed.

"What we are going to start doing," said Sam, arriving at this conclusion on the spur of the moment, "is we are going to start saying one adventurous thing that happened to us during the day, at dinner every night."

"Every night?" repeated Teddy.

"Every night when we eat dinner, which is . . . yes, every night."

Teddy lifted his eyebrows at Sam. "You think something adventurous is going to happen to us every single day?"

"I do, yes," said Sam. "Even if the adventurous thing is just . . . finding a really big spider in the bath."

"That's a terrible adventure," said Teddy.

"Or the adventure could be spilling chocolate milk all over yourself in the morning."

"That's another terrible adventure," Teddy said, but his mouth was twitching with the opening act of a fully-fledged smile instead of looking dour, and Sam would take that.

In fact, Sam wracked his brain for another terrible adventure. "Or the adventure could be accidentally brushing your teeth with mud."

Teddy gave in and giggled. "That's so gross," he said. "How would that even *happen?*"

Sam watched his son laugh and thought how he'd say all of the silliest things he could for the rest of their lifetimes if it kept Teddy laughing. He said, "I don't know. That's what makes it an adventure. You never know, afterward, how it all happened. That's how I know we're going to have an adventure every day. Because that's how life is: a series of things you can never quite explain afterward. All adventures."

Teddy gave him his typical dubious look, mirth vanished. "Like moving to England?"

"Moving to England is the greatest adventure we've undertaken in a long time," Sam said. "And that's a good thing. Don't you think that's a good thing? Don't you think that we needed to . . . find new adventures to have? We were just having the same adventures, day after day, and they weren't even *good* adventures, and . . . that's no good. That's not a life." Sam studied Teddy closely, wondering if Teddy was grasping what Sam was saying. He knew he had not been the only one trapped by the continual box of tragedy that the community wouldn't let them out of, even years later; he knew that Teddy had felt it, too. He just didn't know if Teddy was willing to admit it.

Teddy said, "But they were *our* adventures, back home."

"And whose adventures are these, that we're having here? It's still us having them. It's still you and me. They're still ours."

Teddy looked at his pizza, flicked at a piece of pepperoni, generally looked unconvinced.

Sam said gently, "Listen. This is going to be a good place, where we're going to meet nice people and make nice friends and have nice adventures."

Teddy looked up at Sam from underneath his sandy fringe. "How do you know that?"

"I'm very smart?" Sam tried.

"Not that smart," said Teddy without missing a beat.

"Ouch," said Sam. "You wound me. There was a time when that would have answered any question you had."

Teddy looked steadily at Sam with his blue-green eyes, and Teddy actually looked nothing like Sara at first glance, but sometimes Sam saw her in the tilt of Teddy's head and the weight of his stare when he was asking *more* of Sam.

Sam admitted, "I don't know. I just have a really good feeling." Teddy looked at Sam for a moment longer without speaking, and Sam tried to discern what he was thinking, but Teddy could be secretive about his emotions when he wanted to be. All Sam really knew was that Teddy said softly, "What was your adventure today?"

And Sam interpreted that as an olive branch. He said immediately, "Today my adventure was dropping a box of books directly on my toe and managing not to break it."

"Is it swollen and purple and disgusting?" Teddy asked. "Did the nail fall off?"

"No," said Sam.

"That was another bad adventure," Teddy said. "Why do you only ever come up with bad adventures?"

"Hey, my toe didn't break—I count that as a win," said Sam. "What was your adventure today?"

Teddy considered, then said, "I met a dog."

Sam was relieved to have Teddy engaging with him but surprised by his adventure. "Oh. I did, too. Where did you meet your dog?" He was curious about when this had happened, because Teddy had spent the entire day sulking in the back garden.

"In the back garden," said Teddy.

Sam supposed he should have expected that. He wondered if it was the old man's dog. "How'd it get into the back garden?" asked Sam.

"The fences are kind of a mess. You probably never looked at them because you never go outside."

"I go outside sometimes," Sam said automatically, even though it was fair of Teddy to point out that Sam's more usual pursuits were all indoor pursuits. He automatically added *fix fences* to his mental to-do list of unexpected problems he had encountered during moving that day. As if the electrics and the damp hadn't been enough to deal with. "So what happened to the dog?"

"I don't know. It went away somewhere."

"Through the broken fence?"

Teddy nodded, focused on his pizza. "Don't worry. It was a nice dog. It wasn't mean or anything. It was basically the best part about today."

Sam supposed that was a point in favor of Crotchety Neighbor and His Dog.

Jack had a good sense of time. Bill often thought that Jack had a better sense of time than most of the people Bill knew these days, who showed up whenever they felt like it and thought nothing of making you wait while they stared at their phones for a little while longer. But Jack was never late for dinner. Jack was *dependable*.

Bill let Jack in when he arrived and said, "How was your day, then? Did you learn what you needed to about the new neighbors? I see you didn't bother their plastic flamingo, and you really could have; that would have been no great loss. You could have chewed it up, just a tad."

Jack kept his head down, snuffling in the food. Jack was a dog with a good appetite. Bill approved. And he should have known better than to try to start a serious conversation about the flamingo when Jack was in the middle of dinner.

Bill left Jack in the kitchen and walked down the hallway to the front door, where he checked to make sure the bolt had been thrown, just as he did every night. Then he walked to the window in the lounge and looked out on the street. Just checking up on whatever madness happened to be underway. It was quiet, actually, now that the neighbors had moved in and the workers had departed. The Indian woman who lived down the street was just coming home. One of the cats from the Polish family's house was slinking through the front garden.

Bill twitched the curtains closed and turned away from the street. Jack, apparently done with dinner, came into the lounge, tail wagging happily.

"Well, Jack," Bill said. "I suppose it's telly for us. As usual. Let's see if we can find anything worth watching."

The movers who had handled the large pieces of furniture had set up the beds Sam had bought, so he and Teddy at least had somewhere to sleep.

The beds were not made, as Sam had no idea where the bed things might be in his sea of boxes. So he had borrowed some extra blankets from Ellen and made Teddy a makeshift cocoon on his mattress, and it seemed like one minute Teddy was complaining about the weird sleeping arrangement ("It's an *adventure*," Sam had reminded him) and the next he was sound asleep.

That was either the lingering remnants of jet lag, Sam thought, or exhaustion brought on by endless whining.

Sam left Teddy sleeping in his bed and wandered into his own bedroom, yawning. He was knackered himself. Maybe it was time to call an end to this first day in their new house. The first days were always the worst. *You'll feel better when you're settled,* Ellen had said on her way out the door that evening, and Sam agreed. Sam wanted it to be the second day in the house already, then the third day, the fourth day, the *eighty*-fourth day. Sam wanted it to be some time in the future when the house around them would feel like a home. When he would be used to the shadows on his bedroom ceiling, to the locations of the lights. They just needed to get through the first day, and they almost had.

Sam changed and brushed his teeth and crawled into his own cocoon on the mattress. And he had just closed his eyes when a cacophony began on the wall behind his bed. Not the wall that adjoined the old man's house— that was quiet as a tomb—but the wall that was shared with the neighbors he hadn't met yet.

These neighbors were playing the drums.

Granted, it was early still, so Sam understood that some noise was still to be expected. Nevertheless.

Sam turned and snorted helpless laughter into his pillow, thinking of Ellen's comment about the wild parties Sam ought to throw. Ellen would definitely approve of the non-old-man neighbors, he thought.

Chapter 2

Ellen: Need help unpacking? Can
bring two teenage girls over to help.
Only minor whining accompanied.

Sam: Not necessary! Don't mind us,
we'll bother you enough in the
future, I'm sure.

On Day Two of their New Life, Sam unpacked boxes containing Christmas decorations and Teddy's saved baby clothes and questioned his ability to label things properly, since the boxes had been labeled KITCHEN.

Teddy sat outside, visited at times by the dog he'd met the day before, who Sam verified was the same dog he'd seen with the old man next door.

"He belongs to the neighbor," Sam informed Teddy. "We should take him back to the neighbor."

"He'll go back when he's ready," Teddy said, stroking the dog, who was sprawled happily at his feet and watching the trees for squirrels. "I don't want him to feel like he's not welcome."

Since Teddy looked the happiest Sam had seen him since setting foot on British soil, Sam decided not to raise a fuss about the trespassing dog. In fact, he experienced a pang of envy for the dog. Dogs never had to unpack things. Dogs never had enough possessions to unpack. Dogs might be onto something.

Teddy's adventure that day was the dog showing it knew how to roll over. Sam's adventure that day was finally locating a relevant box of kitchen accoutrements under six other thoroughly irrelevant boxes.

On Day Three of their New Life, Sam unpacked an entire box of old wrapping paper and thought his packing skills would be less embarrassing if he'd been drunk while the packing had been going on. Teddy reported at dinner that the dog chased a squirrel and that had been very adventurous.

Sam said, "Don't you think you should get outside and meet some of the other kids on the street?"

Teddy said, "You want me to just go knocking on doors looking for kids to play with? What if one of our neighbors is an axe murderer? You don't know. They're all strangers."

These were very wise points, so Sam considered and then said, "My adventure today was surviving another day with a potential axe murderer for a neighbor."

Teddy grinned.

The fine weather turned gray and wet on Day

Four of their New Life and Sam dropped and shattered an entire box full of plates and Teddy kept fretting because he hadn't seen the dog all day. Sam decided to get them both out of the house and run to the high street to purchase more.

"We can't live without plates," Sam told Teddy.

"Why not?" asked Teddy reasonably, following Sam down the aisle. "It's not like we cook."

"I need something to reheat the takeaway on," Sam replied.

"We could just use paper plates," suggested Teddy.

"Someday we might have people over, and then I'll want to be able to offer them proper crockery," said Sam.

"Who?" asked Teddy skeptically. "Who would we have over other than Aunt Ellen and Sophie and Evie?"

"I don't know." Sam tried to decide if he wanted plain white plates or maybe something with a design. "Maybe if you make some friends."

"*You* haven't made any friends," Teddy pointed out.

"Good point," said Sam, because it was. Part of the reason he'd moved back home was to give himself an opportunity to make more friends. "Maybe I'll make friends."

Teddy looked his usual level of dubious.

"You don't think I can make friends?" said Sam.

"Making friends is hard, Dad," said Teddy. "You don't just . . . *do* it."

Sam looked up from his contemplation of plate possibilities, at Teddy standing in the aisle looking bored and lost and . . . very young still. Very young, in a world that exhausted Sam, and he had decades of experience dealing with it. Very young, in a whole new country, and with only his dad keeping all of the vast unknown of it at bay.

There were probably a million things Sam could say, none of which he was going to say in the middle of a shop, choosing plates.

He said, "You're right. Why don't I give it a try for both of us?"

Teddy looked away from the shelves, met Sam's gaze. "Give what a try?"

"Making friends," said Sam. "I'll sort the making-friends thing. It is hard, and the hard things are my job."

Teddy leveled his dubious gaze on Sam. "You're going to make friends?"

"You needn't sound so skeptical," said Sam, a trifle put-out. He knew Teddy was always very skeptical of him, but Teddy ought at least to have confidence in his dad's friend-making abilities.

"With who?" Teddy asked.

"I think it's 'with whom,' " said Sam.

"Really?"

"I don't know," Sam admitted. "But I will find people to be friends with."

"What people?" Teddy insisted, not to be deterred from his line of questioning.

Sam said the first thing that came into his head. "The neighbors."

Bill was frowning into his display cabinet, at what seemed to him to be an unusually small number of glasses. He supposed it was possible he'd broken one or two over the years, but the number in his cupboard now was impossible to believe.

"When Agatha and I got married, we had a full set of glasses," Bill told Jack. "I know we did. They looked so beautiful in this display cabinet. Agatha was so pleased when I finished it. She loved to show off the glasses and the crockery and whatever else we had in here." Bill peered into the shelves, dusty and much emptier now than he ever remembered them being when Agatha was alive.

Jack looked suitably concerned about the sparse interior of the display cabinet.

Bill said, "And I just can't imagine where those glasses went over the years. I just can't imagine where half the things I used to have went. I can't imagine they're being stolen. I mean, I know you can't trust people these days, but who would want to steal some glasses?"

Jack tipped his head and wagged his tail a little bit.

Bill sighed and said, "You're right, it's probably unlikely anyone's stealing my glasses." He took one out of the cupboard and filled it with water. "I've probably just misplaced them over the years. Probably misplaced a lot of things." Bill ran a hand over the finish of the display cabinet, remembering how much Agatha had loved it, how fond she had been of the simple carving ornamentation he'd added. *Art deco,* she'd called it, as if it had been as posh as all that. Bill said, "Everything feels like yesterday, except when you stop to take stock of how much has been lost."

Teddy hadn't seen Jack all day, and when he walked out into the back garden to look for him, he heard the girl next door obviously playing fetch with him.

Teddy, disapproving, marched back inside, where Dad was stacking the new plates into a cupboard.

"The neighbor has stolen the dog," Teddy announced, with the appropriate level of drama.

"The dog belongs to the neighbor," Dad replied.

"No." Teddy shook his head. "Not *that* neighbor. The girl next door. She's outside playing with the dog right now."

"Oh, good," said Dad. "Perfect opportunity for you to go and introduce yourself."

"*You're* the one making friends with the

45

neighbors," Teddy reminded Dad, because sometimes Dad forgot *everything*.

Dad gave Teddy one of his *looks*. "She's around your age and you both love that dog. You already have a connection."

"That's not a *connection*," said Teddy. "Everyone loves dogs. She's stolen the dog."

"Nobody's stolen the dog," said Dad. Because Dad just didn't *get* it.

Pari had hatched a brilliant plan. If she couldn't get Jack into her own house, she could get Jack into Emilia's house, which would be almost the same thing, since they spent so much time over there.

"One of us has to take Jack in before the winter comes," Pari informed Emilia.

Emilia lifted her eyebrows. "Winter's a long way away."

"Right. But we need to have our plan in place. For instance, do you have a bed for Jack?"

"A bed?"

"He probably likes a bed."

"Jack sleeps at the old man's, doesn't he?" Emilia pointed out.

"Yeah, but he can't possibly like that," said Pari. "I don't think he stays with that old man out of *choice*. Would you stay with that old man, if you had any choice otherwise? I mean, the old man smells. I bet his *whole house smells*. And I bet that really bothers Jack, because dogs have good noses."

"The old man smells?" said Sai, barely looking up from where he was glued to a documentary on Emilia's telly. "When have you ever even been close enough to the old man to figure out that he smells?"

Pari shot him a look.

Emilia said, "What are you *doing* over there?"

"I'm trying to learn about baby chimpanzees," Sai said, "but it's hard with Pari babbling on about stealing Jack."

"I'm not stealing him!" Pari protested. "He should have been mine after he got left behind!"

"Why do you need to know about baby chimpanzees?" asked Emilia.

"Because my mum and dad think I spend all day at the library."

"So they think you're learning about baby chimpanzees?" said Emilia.

"Well, I've got to be learning about something, don't I? Dad wants me learning about something that could be a career. Could baby chimpanzees be a career?"

"I guess if you're going to be a vet."

"I could be a vet. Almost like being a doctor."

"And if you're going to be a vet, then you need a patient to practice on!" exclaimed Pari. "Jack could be your first patient."

47

"Sai doesn't actually know how to take care of a dog," said Emilia.

"It's really easy," Pari said. "You just feed him and give him water and play with him a lot. So can he live here?"

Emilia blinked. "What? Jack? Live here?"

"Yeah. So Sai can practice on him."

"No," Emilia said. "We have cats. Jack won't get along with the cats."

"The cats almost always stay upstairs," said Pari. "Jack could stay downstairs. Your mum and dad are hardly ever home. They'd never notice you having a dog."

"They'd notice. The cats'd be fretful. Mum'd notice the cats being fretful. Mum notices everything about the cats."

"So that just leaves us," Pari said. "We have to take Jack in before the winter comes. Otherwise how will he survive outside in the winter?"

"The same way he survives outside now," said Sai. "We don't live in Antarctica."

"That is very cruel of you," said Pari primly. "Now, shh, I feel like this is an important point for me to remember about the baby chimpanzee."

Pari and Sai walked home in the afternoon, slipping through the gardens the way they always did. They could see Mum in the kitchen, putting the finishing touches on a few baskets full of welcoming gifts for someone who knew a bunch of families who were just coming over, or something. Pari couldn't keep up with all of Mum's goings-on.

Pari put a hand on Sai's arm, to stop him from going inside, and said, "Can you back me up on this?"

Sai looked blank. "On what?"

Pari whacked the back of Sai's head.

"Ow!" Sai exclaimed, rubbing it like Pari had hit it *hard* or something.

"Emilia always does that to make you be clever."

"Emilia barely taps me when she does it!" Sai protested.

"Can you back me up on us needing to adopt Jack to help you be a vet?"

"Pari," Sai sighed.

"I back you up on not telling Mum and Dad about you and Emilia," Pari pointed out.

Sai sighed again, rolled his eyes up to the sky, and then finally said, "Ugh, okay, fine, yes."

Pari, pleased, smiled at Sai. "If we can get Mum to agree, then we can get Jack."

"Dad won't want a dog, either, you know," Sai said. "He always blames it on Mum but he doesn't like dogs, either."

"We can hide the dog from Dad, if we have Mum's help," said Pari, and then tugged open the back door.

Mum looked up from her baskets. "Oh, good,

just in time! Tell Dad I've left dinner; you just have to heat it up. And I must run to Ananya's and drop off these baskets and then I'll be back. How are you both? Did you have a good day? Was the library good?"

"Mum, I want to talk to you," said Pari, trying to get her rushing mother to stay still for a second.

"When I get back, okay?" Mum put a kiss on the top of Pari's head. "When I get back, we will do all of the talking."

"Sai wants to be a vet," Pari blurted desperately.

Mum looked at Sai, that soft smiling look. Pari knew what came next.

"You're so handsome," she said to Sai fondly. "You would make a wonderful veterinarian."

"Right," Pari agreed. "So don't you think that—"

"Bye!" called Mum, already out the door.

Pari sighed.

"Better luck next time," said Sai.

"We might just have to hide Jack in here ourselves."

"How are we going to hide Jack ourselves?"

"The same way we hide that you're dating Emilia."

"That's different. Emilia doesn't live in our *house*."

"Well. I'm going to figure something out." Pari went in search of biscuits to serve as brain food.

· · ·

"She really is stealing the dog," Teddy reported at dinner that night. This was his adventure of the day.

Sam suppressed his sigh. He didn't understand how he'd ended up on a street with so much dog drama. In his head, Teddy was supposed to have already made friends with other children and be running around playing complicated games of tag. Sam was mostly unpacked by now, the house was mostly in order, and he was supposed to start his job next week. He had hoped Teddy would be more settled by this time. Granted, he was happy Teddy was apparently so engaged in the life of the street, but he wished it had been a less combative relationship.

Teddy continued stuffing pasta into his mouth. At least there was nothing wrong with his appetite. "I heard them plotting about it. The girl is going to take the dog and hide him in her house."

"Hide him?"

"Her mum and dad won't let her have a dog."

"Then I don't think the girl is going to be successful in stealing the dog," said Sam.

Teddy looked as if he couldn't believe how stupid Sam was to not realize how much children could hide from parents. A look Sam would have preferred not to be subjected to until at least Teddy's teen years.

Teddy said, "It isn't fair. The dog belongs to all of us."

"The dog belongs to the old man next door. The dog definitely does not belong to us," said Sam.

"Great. He probably senses that you don't want him and he'll start coming around less."

"He just spent all day in the back garden with you," Sam pointed out.

"Right. Listening to the people next door plot about kidnapping him. Dognapping him. Whatever."

"Your mother and I let you watch *101 Dalmatians* too much when you were younger," said Sam.

Teddy had been considering the situation from all angles. While Dad was locked up in his office working, Teddy had plenty of time to consider the best course of action. If he wanted to keep the girl from stealing the dog from him, he had to let the old man know what they were planning. After all, it was the old man's dog.

So Teddy knocked on Dad's office door.

"Come in," Dad called. He was sitting at his desk, which was fully unpacked and thus a total mess. Dad always made a mess when he worked.

"I am going to go see the neighbor," Teddy announced, deciding it was best not to say anything more than that.

Dad, who had been frowning at his computer,

looked up and smiled widely. "Really? That is excellent, Teddy. I'm so glad. Just be home for dinner, yeah?"

"Yes," Teddy agreed.

Then he walked outside and next door to the old man's house and rang the doorbell.

Bill was whittling. In his younger days, he used to whittle almost constantly. He had wooed his Agatha with gorgeous, intricate figurines of ancient queens, of elegant birds, of impossibly delicate trees. He still whittled when he could, but his hands gave him trouble these days and he couldn't seem to do anymore the things he had done without thinking so many years ago.

"Things just keep going away and not coming back," Bill remarked ruefully, stretching his cramped hand, and then realized Jack wasn't there to hear the comment. Wandering the street, was Jack. Keeping an eye on the neighbors.

Then the doorbell rang.

For a moment Bill was startled. And then he crystallized into grim determination. A *visitor*. Surely someone selling something or asking for money in some other way. This visitor must be fought off. Otherwise, Bill thought, an entire legion of people would start pointlessly descending on his doorstep.

Bill made his way over to the door and peered through the glass at a young boy. *Even worse,* they were now sending *children* in to do their dirty work.

Bill opened the door and said shortly, "Well?" as an opening salvo.

The boy, after a moment, squared his shoulders and tipped his chin up, and Bill respected that. He was, Bill had to admit, an intelligent-looking kid, with bright blue-green eyes and a head of wavy sand-colored hair. He needed a haircut, but who didn't these days?

"I'm Teddy," said the boy.

And then said nothing else.

"And?" barked out Bill.

"I live next door," said Teddy the boy. "I play with your dog."

"My dog?" said Bill. "You mean Jack? He's not mine. He belongs to the street."

The boy looked confused. "To the street?"

What was difficult to understand about this? "Yeah," affirmed Bill brusquely, because apparently this kid was the sort that needed to be told everything twice.

"You mean he belongs to everyone?"

"He just roams around the street," said Bill.

The boy chewed on his bottom lip, which was a terrible habit he really ought to break. Then he said, "That little girl is planning to steal him from everyone else."

"Steal who?"

"Jack. And I don't want anyone to steal him.

I want him to keep belonging to the street. I want him to keep belonging to everyone. Don't you?" The kid seemed very determined now, his stubborn posture back. And then his eyes sharpened on the little figure Bill realized he was still holding in his hand. "Is that supposed to be Jack?" he asked, peering at it.

Bill didn't answer. His instinct was to close the door immediately and end this conversation.

The kid said, "That's cool! Do you make other things?"

Bill wanted to say that he didn't. Bill wanted to say whatever would make this kid turn around and never come back. But he thought of all the wooden figures arranged through his house, all of which no one but he had seen in so many years. He thought of the one of Jack he was clutching in his hand. Of Jack himself, who stopped by every night.

And he noticed one of the gay neighbors, in his front garden, spying on the entire conversation.

Bill frowned and said gruffly to the kid, "Get inside." Nobody minded their own business these days.

Sam made scrambled eggs for dinner.

Well. It was supposed to be an omelette, but that had been too ambitious a plan. So it was scrambled eggs on toast with some cheese scattered on top.

Not that Teddy seemed to mind. He came inside and dropped down at the table and immediately began eating.

Sam said drily, "Well, hello to you, too. Did you have fun playing with the girl?"

"What girl?" asked Teddy around a mouthful of scrambled eggs.

Sam winced and said, "Let's remember table manners, please. Haven't you been off playing with the neighbor girl? You said you were going to meet the neighbor."

"Oh," said Teddy, thankfully swallowing his mouthful. "I meant the old man. His name is Mr. Hammersley and he used to make things out of wood. He has this whole shelf full of wooden dragons. It's pretty cool."

Sam, surprised, blinked at his son. "You've been with the old man all this time?"

Teddy nodded and took a large gulp of his milk.

Sam said, "The *old man* was the neighbor you intended to go and meet?"

"I wanted to talk to him about how the girl is trying to steal the dog. Whose name is Jack, by the way. Mr. Hammersley has lots of figures of him, too. Not as many as the dragon, though."

"Okay," Sam said slowly, still processing all of this. Although, now that Teddy was explaining it, it seemed like he should have realized immediately this was what Teddy meant when he'd said he was going to meet the neighbor. "So you told him that you think the girl is trying to steal the dog?"

"Jack. And I don't *think* it. She definitely is."

"Right," Sam agreed, because that wasn't a point worth fighting about at the moment. "What did Mr. Hammersley say when you explained the dognapping plot?"

Teddy, beaming with triumph, announced, "He said that Jack belongs to everyone!"

"What does that mean?" asked Sam. "Jack is, what, like air and the sun?"

"Mr. Hammersley's not Jack's owner. Jack just roams the street."

"So Jack is just a stray dog?"

"That sounds mean," Teddy frowned.

"Sorry," said Sam drily. "He's just a carefree wanderer, I suppose. Doesn't want to be pinned down."

Teddy scooped up another mouthful of scrambled egg and said, "Because he belongs to everyone, that means that the other kids won't be able to steal him. The whole street will turn out to prevent it."

The whole street? thought Sam. Now Teddy had managed to convert the stray dog situation into a glorious cause. Sam shook his head a little and said, "I suppose this whole thing is your adventure for the day."

"Of course," said Teddy, chewing on his toast enthusiastically. "What was your adventure?"

"I got the remote access software to work properly on the computer," said Sam.

"You don't have very good adventures, Dad," said Teddy, sounding sorry for him.

Sam chuckled. "I know."

"It's been utter madness," Ellen said when Sam called her that night, after Teddy had gone to bed. "I do not advise having teenage children, Sam. Keep them tiny and wee like Teddy."

"Is Teddy still wee?" asked Sam. "He seems impossibly old to me."

"I remember when I used to think that, too. Then they get *even older*."

"Do they get wiser, too? Teddy already thinks he is much wiser than me and laments my pathetic stupidity."

"Ah, but he has you for a dad, so he's not wrong about that," said Ellen.

"Aren't big sisters supposed to be supportive?"

"I must have skipped that day at Big Sister School," said Ellen. "Now. What can I do for you? You sound tired."

Sam was tired. He was exhausted. It was partly because he was trying to transition into a job working remotely with largely American clients, and the time difference was brutal. And it was partly nothing to do with that at all. "Just some long days. Unpacking is . . ." Sam decided there was no need to choose an adjective to finish that sentence. No adjective was suitable to describe unpacking.

"Sophie and Evie and I are coming by to help you this weekend and I will not hear you argue otherwise. It's not being a failure to enlist our help for this project."

Sam didn't want to bother Ellen too much, and at the same time he thought the help sounded good. And said that. "Good. Because I need to get the house set up so I can have a party."

"A party!" exclaimed Ellen gleefully. "I knew you would want to throw wild parties fairly quickly."

"Not a wild party," Sam said. "A very boring, staid, basically middle-aged party."

"Sam, haven't you heard? 'Middle-aged' is the new early twenties."

"That doesn't even make sense."

"So tell me who's on the guest list for your party. You need at least a couple of D-list celebs; they perk everything up."

"Just the street," Sam said.

"The street?" echoed Ellen. "As in your neighbors?"

"Exactly."

"The old man next door? You're going to throw a wild party and invite the old man next door?"

"No, I'm just going to throw a normal party and invite the old man next door. And all the other people next door. There are a couple of families and I'd like Teddy to meet the girl near his age and apparently the only way to make that happen is to literally sit her down right in front of Teddy. And even then I'm not entirely sure. They might just stare at each other dumbly."

"Making friends is hard," said Ellen.

"I know. But that's why I'm going to show him how it's done."

"At your wild party."

"Not a wild party," Sam corrected again.

"I hate to break it to you, Sam, but if it's not a wild party, then I'm not sure you're going to make many friends at it."

The weather had broken into a brief burst of bright sunlight, and this was Max's favorite type of evening—warm, endless twilight where the back garden seemed to hoard the daylight and glow back at him—and Max wanted to try to capture the scent of the air in the particular shade of violet he was using on his canvas. He procured a curry for dinner from their favorite takeaway and opened a bottle of wine and went out into the front garden to trim some roses to put in a vase.

Which was when he was treated to the entertaining sight of the new little boy who had just moved in marching determinedly over to the old man's house and ringing his doorbell. Max wasn't sure anyone had rung that doorbell in twenty years. The old man opened it, frowned at the little boy, and then, after a brief conversation, inexplicably invited him in. Max shook his head. "Will wonders never cease," he told the nearest rose, as he snipped it.

The woman from the other end of the street went jogging past, clutching her customary green protein shake, her black curls springing in their ponytail in time to her pace. She lifted up a hand in greeting, and Max returned it briefly, and then Jack came dashing out of the Basaks' house to joyfully follow her down the street.

The little Basak girl came running out of the house after him, shouting, "Jack! Come back!" And then stamped her little foot in a gesture of supreme annoyance.

Her brother, appearing in the front doorway, said, "See, Pari, I told you, Jack doesn't want to live here."

Max clipped another rose and thought that the street was an interesting place when you stopped to really pay attention.

Arthur arrived home to the scent of his favorite curry intermingled with the fragrance of the overflowing vase of roses and immediately said suspiciously, "What's the occasion?"

"No occasion," Max said. "I am alarmed. Can't I do something sweet and romantic for my husband without it being an occasion?"

Arthur regarded him warily. "Have you spilled paint all over one of my suits again?"

"No," Max said fervently. "I swear, I did that *once* and you've never let me forget it."

Arthur smiled, which made Max smile in return. "It was the early days," Arthur said. "It made a big impression on me. Life with an artist."

"It was a simple mistake," Max said. "I wasn't used to living with someone else."

"I know," said Arthur, still smiling, and sat at the table and pulled his curry over to him. "Thank you for my curry. You had a good day, I take it?"

"Lovely weather, lovely painting, lovely husband."

"You're effusive tonight," remarked Arthur.

"I meant me," said Max. *"I'm* a lovely husband."

"Wanker," said Arthur.

"Exactly," said Max.

"Where did you get the roses?" asked Arthur.

"Our garden. Put them to use. And so much happened whilst I was snipping them."

"Like what?"

"There is a plot to dognap Jack."

"Dognap Jack?" echoed Arthur, sipping his wine.

"Pari wishes to adopt him. Jack appears to be resistant."

"Well," noted Arthur, with his mouth in that tight, bitter line that Max hated, "adoption, as we all know, is a tricky thing to accomplish. Not as easy as all that."

There was a long moment of silence.

Arthur took a bite of his curry and said, "Sorry."

"No," Max said, because he'd allowed Arthur to avoid discussion of this topic for a fair while now, and he was calling a halt to it, suddenly, abruptly, now, on this beautiful summer evening when he had gone outside to extravagantly cut his husband *roses*. "See, you say things like that and it makes me think that we should give this whole thing up."

"We're not giving up," said Arthur.

"I used to be *excited* about it," Max said, ignoring him. "I used to hope every day that the phone would ring and they'd tell us we'd been chosen and there was a baby for us. And now I *dread* that because I just worry they'll take the baby away from us again and you'll get even unhappier—"

"I'm not unhappy—"

"—and I don't want that. I wanted to have a child with you. I didn't want to *lose* you."

"Stop it," Arthur said, sounding weary. "You're not going to lose me. No one's losing anybody. Unless you count us losing babies."

"I don't mean that you would leave me," Max said. "I mean that I *miss you*. And before all this happened, I literally never saw that horrible expression on your face, the one you get every so often, and I could happily have gone my entire life never seeing it, and I don't want to make it show up more often, darling. I want it to *go away forever*."

Arthur closed his eyes, took a breath, and then opened them. Max watched him closely, feeling that, if he blinked, Arthur would somehow squirm away from him, wriggle out of his grasp.

Arthur said, "I'm fine."

"You're not," Max countered.

"All right," Arthur said. "I'm not. How are *you* fine? It's bloody irritating, you know, that you're not the least bit—"

"If you think I'm not upset, or disappointed, you're wrong."

"You just hide it better?" asked Arthur mockingly.

"I just look at you and think that I've already won the lottery once in my life, so it's a little ridiculous of me to get stroppy over not winning it a second time," Max snapped.

Arthur looked across at him, his dark eyes wide and gleaming in the last of the dusk that was still clinging to the sky. He said finally, softly, "I know. I'm a spoiled brat."

Max shook his head. "That's not what I meant."

Arthur reached out, picked up Max's hand, pressed his lips to Max's knuckles and then leaned his forehead against them, breathing deeply.

Max, after a moment, turned his hand over to rest it against Arthur's cheek, to draw his head closer so he could plant a kiss on the top of it. "It's going to be okay," he murmured.

"Is it?" Arthur asked, head still down, pressed now against Max's shoulder.

"Yes," said Max. "No matter what happens. Yes."

Pen Cheever had a habit, in the last minutes of her day, before allowing sleep to claim her, of pulling her laptop into bed with her and calling up her blog.

The blog had started as just a way to keep herself honest with regard to her writing goals. Every night, she would post in her blog how much she had managed to accomplish that day. And then it had slowly, creepingly, expanded. She started putting up facts about her daily runs, and then recipes for her protein shakes, and then just interesting things she'd come across while working on whichever article had caught her attention at the moment.

And now, she had to admit, a large part of the blog was the goings-on of the street around her, which she saw a great deal of during her runs. Her street, she thought, was typical of most London streets. The neighbors all thought that they kept to themselves, exchanging nothing but polite waves when they encountered each other, but really each one of them told the most remarkable life stories if you merely paid attention. And

Pen was a journalist. Her job was to pay attention.

Tonight's blog entry was all about Jack, as they frequently were, because Jack was often one of the more extraordinary of the street's inhabitants, and the true common thread between them, house location be damned.

As you know, all of the children on the street are mad about our dog Jack, Pen wrote. The parents on the street all seem decidedly less enamored. But it does seem as if Jack may be the cause for an unlikely friendship between Grouchy Old Man and New Boy on the Street. An alliance one might not have predicted, but I witnessed it with my own eyes during my evening run.

Speaking of evening runs, it's time for a new protein shake recipe! Even Jack seems to approve of this one!

Chapter 3

Please join us for a backyard bar-b-q!

September 1, noon,
No. 4 Christmas Street.

RSVP to Sam (the new neighbor).

Teddy looked absolutely horrified. "What? No!"

Sam lifted his eyebrows. "Teddy, it's an invitation to a party. I'm not asking you to eat worms—"

"Eating worms would be easier! At least it's not embarrassing!"

"What is embarrassing about delivering invitations for a party?" asked Sam, exasperated.

"Can't you just put them in the mail like a normal person?" asked Teddy.

"Everyone who's invited lives right on this street. Why put them in the mail when we can just hand them to people?"

"What if everyone wants to *talk* to us?" complained Teddy.

"That's the general idea," remarked Sam drily. "We're trying to meet people."

"We wouldn't have to meet people if we'd just stayed in America," Teddy grumbled.

"I know," responded Sam equably. "And look at the adventure we would have missed out on. The adventure of ringing people's doorbells and handing them a party invitation."

"I still think it's embarrassing and weird," said Teddy. "I've never heard of anyone handing out party invitations like this."

"That's because we've only known boring people. Come on, let's go."

Teddy, moving approximately as fast as a snail, dragged himself toward the front door. Sam was counting this as a win. The past couple of days had been nothing but Teddy locked up in his room playing video games or sitting in the back garden, with or without Jack, frowning in the direction of the potential dognapper next door. Teddy's adventure of the day at dinner last night had been "another day without dog-related crime." Sam had had every intention of putting the invitations in the post "like a normal person," as Teddy said, except that he was looking for any excuse to break Teddy out of this rut. And if that meant they had to walk up and down the street knocking on doors and handing out invitations as if that was something people did, well, so be it.

Jack came bounding up to them as soon as they stepped outside, and Teddy brightened immediately and scratched behind his ears and said, "No one's stolen you yet, Jack? That's good."

Sam sighed and walked up to the old man's house and rang the bell. Mr. Hammersley, Teddy had said he was called. The one neighbor Teddy had managed to strike up a conversation with.

Sam and Teddy and Jack stood in front of the door and waited.

And waited.

And kept waiting.

"Maybe he's out," suggested Teddy.

Jack stood up, wagged his tail in apparent agreement, and then sat back down.

Sam's office looked out over the street and he spent a great deal of time spying. He hadn't yet seen the old man leave his house. Nor had he seen anyone go over there. Except, apparently, his son. His eight-year-old son, who was only friends with the old man next door.

Sam was annoyed because, frankly, he'd kind of been hoping to arrive in England to a new, appropriately aged best friend for Teddy sitting on their front step, ready to be played with, and instead Sam was walking door-to-door handing out invitations practically begging for friends and it *was* embarrassing and at the very first door he was failing, even though the old man was *always home*.

"Out where?" said Sam, a trifle shortly. "He's always home." Sam leaned forward to see if he could peer through the leaded glass on the door, leaning on the doorbell again as he did so.

Which was when the door opened, so that Sam was inappropriately close to the old man, obviously trying to spy on his house.

"What do you want?" snapped the old man.

"Hi, Mr. Hammersley," chirped Teddy happily.

Jack stood with a joyful bark and wagged his tail and went threading his way through everyone's legs.

"Careful," Sam said, trying to catch the dog before he tipped the old man over.

The old man said, "I can handle a dog!"

"Okay," Sam said, instinctively taking a step away from this scowling man. And his son had just headed inside for a cuppa here? Sam decided to just get down to business. "This is for you." He handed across one of their invitations.

The old man took it suspiciously and actually *sniffed* it, like it might smell of arsenic or something.

"Don't worry," Sam said drily. "It isn't poisoned."

"Poisoned?" barked the old man, looking as if he thought

Sam was daft.

Sam didn't blame him.

Neither did Teddy—who poked at Sam's leg in what Sam supposed was justified horror—or Jack, who actually stopped his boisterous greeting of the old man to tip his head at Sam, like even dogs understood what a git Sam was being.

Sam said, "Not that we would ever give you a poisoned envelope."

The old man's eyes narrowed.

"Of course," Sam heard himself say, as if he was no longer in control of his own voice, "you're right to be suspicious, because only somebody who had just handed you a poisoned envelope would protest so strenuously that it's not poisoned." He tried a jovial smile, like, *See, I acknowledge how ridiculous I am being.*

The old man thrust the envelope back at Sam. "Whatever this is, I don't want it," he announced gruffly.

"No," Sam said, harshly enough that it sounded very much like a command, which made the old man's expression grow more disapproving. Sam hadn't thought that was possible. "I mean"— he tried to correct himself, trying to sound placating—"it's just an invitation."

"An invitation? To what?"

"We're having a party. A backyard barbecue. You know, hot dogs and hamburgers and all that."

"I'm not going," said the old man, and swung the door shut in their faces.

Then it opened again, and Jack came bounding out, and then it slammed shut again.

Jack barked a couple of times, tongue lolling out in his delight at all the excitement.

Teddy said, "This is going really well, Dad."

• • •

The doorbell interrupted Emilia and Sai in the midst of a very important discussion about whether Sai ought to trust his girlfriend enough to cut his hair.

"It's just that my hair is very important," said Sai. "You know my hair is very important."

"You know your hair is very important to me, too," said Emilia, ruffling at it. "I just think you could change it up a bit, and you know that I am an *artist*. Look at my fingernails. Don't you think I'm an artist?"

"I don't doubt you're an artist," said Sai haltingly. Which made Emilia frown.

Which meant it was a relief to Sai when the doorbell rang. Emilia peered out the window and said brightly, "Oh, it's the new family from next door," and pulled the door open. "Hiya." She gave them a wide smile, because she saw nothing wrong with being friendly and welcoming to new people. Emilia had been about the new kid's age when they had moved onto the street, so she remembered well the feeling of intimidation of all these houses, crowded up against you, filled with *strangers*. The kid was stone-faced, no answering smile in sight, but his dad gave Emilia a smile in return, looking relieved by it. The dad and the boy looked a lot alike: same sandy hair with a flyaway tendency, same blue-green eyes. Emilia wondered what the mum looked like. Meanwhile, Jack stood between them, tail wagging.

"Hello," said the father. "I'm Sam and this is Teddy."

Jack barked.

"And Jack, of course," added Sam.

"Hello, Sam and Teddy," said Emilia. "I'm Emilia. And hello, Jack. Jack and I are old friends."

"Very nice to meet you, Emilia," said Sam. "I just wanted to stop by and give you this." He handed across an envelope.

"Oh," said Emilia, momentarily confused. "Did the post get mixed up?"

"No, no. It's an invitation. A party invitation. We're having a barbecue, in the back garden, just to get to meet everyone."

"Oh," said Emilia, surprised by that. No one had ever had one of those before. "Okay. Nice."

"So be sure to invite your parents for me," Sam said. "Everyone's welcome."

"Absolutely," Emilia said. "Are you inviting everyone on the street?"

"Yes," Sam said. "Of course."

"Ta!" said Emilia, and looked down at Jack. "On your way, then, before the cats get all stroppy about you being in their domain." Jack trotted outside and Emilia said, "Bye!" and closed the door and turned to Sai. "I guess we're all going to a party."

"Are we going to have to pretend not to know each other at this party?" Sai said.

Emilia laughed. "We'll be very polite and distant. I might think you're obnoxious. You have that look to you."

"What look?"

"That terrible haircut you have."

"Look, if you cut my hair, my parents will know I wasn't at the library."

"You could have just popped in to a barber's on the way back."

"With what money?"

"And the barber thought you were so dashing he cut your hair for free."

"That *is* believable," said Sai.

Emilia laughed again. "Fine. Whatever. Keep your hair. I'll make sure to comment on it at the backyard barbecue." She held up the invitation and grinned. "I think this is going to be fun."

"So that went well," Sam said, pleased.

"I guess," allowed Teddy grumpily.

"You are very difficult to impress," remarked Sam, as they walked up to the next house. "You're like Queen Victoria." He rang the doorbell. "Wait, I think she wasn't amused, not impressed."

Teddy gave him his usual not-impressed look. Yes, Sam thought, it was a very Victorian look.

The door opened, revealing a man about Sam's

age, blond-headed and blue-eyed and wiping his hands on a towel and shirt absolutely covered in . . .

"Oh," said the man, looking down at where Sam's gaze was fixed. "It's not blood. It's paint. Which I recognize is exactly what I would say if it *were* blood."

"Hey, I just convinced the old man down the street that I was giving him a poisoned envelope by assuring him that it was not a poisoned envelope," said Sam, "so I understand the dilemma here."

The man laughed, which was nice and made Sam feel like maybe he hadn't entirely lost the knack of interacting with fellow humans. He said, "You're the new lot who just moved in, yeah? I'm Max."

He offered his hand for Sam to shake, which Sam did, saying, "Sam."

Max turned his hand to Teddy, who looked at it and then shook it after a second, saying, "Teddy."

Sam was at least relieved that Teddy wouldn't be so rude as to directly refuse to shake a hand and introduce himself.

"And hello, Jack," Max said to the dog, who bounced about a little in joyful greeting, and Max scratched briefly behind Jack's ears before turning back to the humans. "Sam and Teddy. Very nice to meet both of you. Welcome to the street. I'm sure it's only slightly bonkers. No more so than any other street. Or so I tell myself. Was there something I could do for you?"

Sam handed across his envelope.

Max took it and said, "Oh, did the post get mixed up?" Which apparently was going to be a standard response. "No, it's a party invitation," Sam said. "Thought I'd save money on the postage by inviting everyone personally."

Max had opened the envelope and was studying the invitation. "How nice of you. Backyard barbecue, hmm?"

"I thought it would be a nice way to meet the neighbors," said Sam.

Max gave him a look he couldn't quite read and said, "I see. Well, lovely idea, thank you. My husband and I will appropriately RSVP." Max gestured to the RSVP request on the invitation.

"Great," said Sam. "Thanks."

"See you, then," said Max, and closed the door on them.

"He thought that was weird," Teddy said.

"He maybe thought that was a little weird," allowed Sam.

Diya Basak was sorting through her husband's old clothes, because Mayra Khatri knew someone in desperate need of some nice clothes for an interview, and Darsh certainly had enough to spare. The doorbell ringing surprised her, because they didn't ordinarily get visitors during the day.

Sai was at the library, as he usually was, but Pari was downstairs, so Diya shouted down to her, "Pari! Can you see who's at the door?"

"It's the weird new people," Pari called back up. Surely loudly enough to be heard by whoever was standing at the door.

Diya frowned, both at Pari's rudeness and at the fact that she had no idea what Pari meant by "weird new people," and walked down the stairs to answer the door.

Pari was staring out the window at the visitors.

"Get away from the window," Diya hissed at her.

Pari said, "He has *Jack* with him. *My Jack*."

"What?" asked Diya, far more concerned with how Pari looked than with whatever Pari was saying. "Did you even brush your hair this morning?" What were people going to think? She had a rude *and* messy-looking daughter.

Diya opened the door and smiled brightly at the people on the other side of it: a man, a boy, a dog. The boy looked very unhappy. In fact, he looked just as unhappy as Pari, whom Diya shoved behind her before Pari could be any more horrifyingly rude. The man looked uncertain. The dog wagged its tail and barked and immediately stormed into the house.

Diya shrieked and ran up the first couple of steps of the staircase, as if that would stop the dog from reaching her.

But the dog didn't look interested in her. It seemed to be attacking Pari.

"Help her!" Diya commanded the man, who was just standing uselessly in the doorway.

"Help her?" the man echoed.

"It's okay, Mum," said Pari, and Diya realized she was laughing. "This is Jack. You know, my dog Jack."

"Your dog?" Diya said. "You don't have a dog."

"Jack belongs to the entire street," said the little boy on the doorstep. "Jack belongs to *everyone*."

"Who told you that?" demanded Pari.

"Mr. Hammersley," said the little boy.

"And who is *that?*" responded Pari.

Diya said, "Pari, that tone. Be polite." She looked to the man on the doorstep. "And please could you control your dog? I don't like dogs."

"Er," said the man, looking at the dog, and then he whistled and said, "Here, Jack."

Jack left Pari alone to come running to the man and leap at him.

"Okay, boy," said the man to the dog, and grabbed at his collar to settle him at his feet.

The dog sat, his tail sweeping happily out behind him. Diya, thinking it was safe, descended the staircase slowly and walked over to the door carefully.

The man said, "Sorry. He really is the street dog. He's just been following us around."

"Following you around where?" said Diya,

glancing warningly at Pari, because Pari was grumbling under her breath.

"The street," said the man. "I'm Sam, and this is my son Teddy. We just moved in, a few houses down."

"Oh," Diya said, as the recollection vaguely came back to her. "You have the pink bird outside in the garden."

"Bob," said the man.

"What?" said Diya.

"Bob the flamingo. That's who the pink bird is."

Diya was beginning to wonder if she should have opened the door at all. "Oh," she said.

The man seemed to realize that he was behaving a bit mad, because he said quickly, "Anyway. We have just come to give you this," and held out an envelope.

"Oh," said Diya. "Did the post get mixed up?"

Which made the little boy—Teddy—give his father a look. The man called Sam said, "No. Sorry. We're confusing everybody. It's an invitation. We're having a little get-together. To sort of meet all the neighbors. Nothing big or extravagant, just a little backyard barbecue."

"Oh," said Diya, because that wasn't the sort of thing the street ordinarily did, and usually her days were busy enough without adding street socializing. But she didn't want to be rude. In fact, she felt she had to be extra-polite to make up for Pari's initial loud pronouncement that these people were weird.

Even if it was a little weird to show up on a doorstep with an invitation. Diya said, "Excellent. Thanks so much. And if you could just control your dog. I'm really not very fond of dogs."

"He's not my dog," said Sam, which made no sense, because the dog was currently slobbering happily all over the man's shoes.

"Thanks!" Diya said, and closed the door. And looked at Pari.

"And what was that, young lady?"

"That boy is trying to steal my dog," Pari fumed.

"You don't have a dog," Diya reminded her. "That is not your dog."

"He and I are *at war*."

"You're not at war. Don't be so dramatic. And there was absolutely no reason to be so rude when they came to the door."

"You can't be nice when you're at war."

"You're not at war," Diya repeated, slightly more emphatically. "Now. Come and help me sort through Dad's trousers."

"What?" yelped Pari.

But, at Diya's look, she did follow her upstairs.

"Do you know what I could really use?" said Pen to her goldfish Chester, who was swimming around his bowl looking unimpressed by

Pen's meager word count total for the day. "A distraction. Is it time to eat lunch yet?"

It was not, in fact, time to eat lunch.

Pen contemplated.

"Maybe time for a snack," she decided.

Chester, with a flip of his tail, approved.

Pen wandered into her kitchen and opened her refrigerator and contemplated its contents. One of the dangers in working out of one's own home was the constant access to food. At one time, Pen's kitchen had been full of as many sweet and/or salty snacks as she could stuff into it. Then she'd done the article on modern food practices and now she was all about healthy and sustainable foods, but sometimes you just wanted a Jaffa Cake.

Pen sighed, rethinking her snack plan.

Which was when the doorbell rang.

Pen practically ran to answer it, opening it on the new family who'd moved in down the street. The father and the little boy. Pen had seen a woman around the house around the right age to be the mother, but not regularly, and she certainly didn't live there, so Pen hadn't yet untangled that one.

"Hello," she said enthusiastically. "You lot are lifesavers!"

The man looked uncertain at this greeting. "We're what?"

"I was just looking for an excuse to not be working, and here you two are."

"Oh. Yes. Well." The man looked like he didn't know quite what to say.

"I'm Pen," she said. "And I'm a writer. But that's not why I'm called Pen. It's short for Penelope."

"I'm Sam," he said. "I work as a consultant for corporations striving to improve the communication infrastructure between information technology specialists and particular groups of users in order to promote a greater symbiosis between—never mind, it sounds horrible. This is my son Teddy."

Pen waved at the little boy, who looked dazed.

Jack barked and wagged his tail and nudged forward to be petted, the shameless hussy.

"And Jack," added Sam.

"Oh, Jack I know. I keep treats just here by the door for him." Pen leaned over to grab one of Jack's special dog treats.

Jack sniffed it and took it daintily, the way he always did, and then walked over to promptly bury it in Pen's front garden.

"He loves them," Pen said. "He keeps a whole stash of them in my front garden so he can get them when I'm not home."

"Oh," said Sam, turning from watching Jack's antics. "Anyway, we were just stopping by to give you an invitation."

"An invitation?" Pen pulled it over to her and

opened it enthusiastically. "To what? Ooh, a backyard barbecue? How fab!"

"We thought it would be a good way to meet the neighbors," said Sam. "Seeing as how we're new here."

"Oh, absolutely! Can't wait to go! There are people who live on this street I haven't spoken to the whole time I've lived here, so I am looking forward to meeting them!" Pen beamed.

"She was *really* excited," remarked Teddy, as they walked back home after delivering the last invitation to the writer at the end of the street. Jack trotted along with them, looking very pleased at how their adventure had gone.

"Yes, she was. So that's good, right? One excited person."

"I thought it was weird," said Teddy.

"Not everything can be weird," said Sam. "It can't be weird if they're excited *and* weird if they're not."

"Yes, it can," said Teddy wisely. "Life's just weird."

"Actually, I can't even argue with you on that one," remarked Sam, as they reached their house. "So there you have it. All the invitations delivered. Party forthcoming. Friends ahoy."

"Don't say things like 'friends ahoy,' " Teddy said. "Nobody's going to be your friend if you say 'friends ahoy.' I'm going up to play *Mass Extinction Event.*"

"Ah, yes, that perpetually cheerful and optimistic video game," said Sam.

Teddy didn't even appreciate the sarcasm, just ran up the stairs.

Jack stood at the door and wagged his tail.

Sam sighed and said, "Go ahead," and Jack barked his thanks and went running up the stairs after Teddy.

Sam thought he really ought to point out that Jack *wasn't their dog,* but it seemed like a lot of effort at the moment.

Bill was in the midst of heating some beans to spread on some toast when Jack's scratch on the back door came.

Not that Bill had been worried that Jack wouldn't show up—Jack wasn't his dog, after all, as he'd told that little boy from next door; Jack belonged to the entire street—but it was nice to see him.

"Hello, Jack," he said, as he let him in. "And where've you been all day? Roaming around the street handing out bloody party invitations?" Bill snorted, to show what he thought about that, as he greeted Jack with some patting as a reward for the nonsense Jack had had to spend the day engaged in.

Bill got Jack's dinner and then finished getting

his own dinner and then sat down at the table, to eat beside where Jack was noisily inhaling his food after his long, hard day.

Bill had tossed the invitation to the "backyard bar-b-q" on the table, where it sat, looking ridiculous, a hot dog smiling up at him.

"That sausage has eyes," he told Jack, just because he felt Jack needed to appreciate the absurdity of that.

Jack snuffled into his food bowl in clear disapproval.

It was simply the most ridiculous thing. Who had ever heard of it? Showing up on someone's doorstep just to babble at them about poison and then leave them with invitations with sausages with eyes. The last thing Bill would ever want to do is go to a barbecue with all of the odd people he shared this street with. Who knew what sort of food they'd try to get him to eat? And then they'd spend the whole time asking him if he was still okay living on his own, like he was a child who couldn't take care of himself, like he hadn't been taking care of himself before any of these people had even been *born*.

"The insult of the whole thing," Bill said to Jack.

Jack nudged his empty food bowl across the lino in reply.

Bill got Jack more food and thought that you let one new person into your house to talk about whittling and the next thing you knew people were knocking down your door thinking you were the sort who wanted to go to a "backyard bar-b-q."

No more of that, Bill decided firmly, and looked down at Jack.

"What do you think's on the telly for us tonight?"

Jack licked his hand, which seemed to indicate a happy optimism about the television schedule that Bill didn't share. But that was what was nice about Jack.

Arthur walked in with Chinese, to an empty house. Which meant that Max had lost track of time and was still painting. So Arthur stuck the food in the microwave—which in his head qualified as "keeping it warm"—and turned to make his way upstairs to Max's studio. Pausing when his attention was caught by the invitation on the kitchen table.

"Huh," remarked Arthur, and took the invitation with him.

Max's canvas was covered in reds and oranges and yellows.

It was both impossibly sunny and impossibly intense, and Arthur, looking at it, had the same feeling he'd had the first time he'd ever looked at one of Max's pieces: *What the hell is that all about, and I need to meet the artist.*

"Hi," Arthur said, and kissed the back of Max's neck deliberately to nudge him out of his artistic reverie.

Max started anyway, and then turned to him fully, his smile wide and beaming. "Oh, look, a handsome man has wandered into my house. I shall abandon my art forthwith."

"I like it," said Arthur, gesturing to the canvas.

"Do you? Thank you. I'm not sure where it's going next, or if it hasn't got there already. Must sleep on it. Did you bring food with you?"

"I did. Also." Arthur held up the invitation. "We've been invited to a party?"

"We have. I'm guessing the hot dogs will be edible and not anthropomorphic at this party, but one never knows. Let me change and wash the paint off me."

"There's some in your hair," said Arthur.

"Then I suppose I'm taking a shower," remarked Max ruefully, brushing at his hair, which left it in even wilder red spikes.

Arthur left Max to his shower and went downstairs and raided the fortune cookies because he was starving and they were there. *You have new invitations that could open new doors,* read his fortune. Arthur snorted and left it on the counter with the barbecue invitation to amuse Max.

It was a gray, wet day and the flowers in the back garden were shimmering with moisture

87

and there were no children dashing through, nor stray dogs.

Max came up behind him and settled his chin on Arthur's shoulder to look out the back door with him.

"Remarkably quiet in our back garden," noted Arthur.

"No untoward dangerous liabilities?" said Max.

"Sit and eat," said Arthur, and poured the Chinese food onto plates, because that made him feel more like they were competent adults.

Max had grabbed the fortune off the kitchen counter. " 'You have new invitations that could open new doors,' " he read out loud.

"And we do have a new invitation," Arthur said, sliding Max's plate of beef and broccoli in front of him and sitting down with his own plate of lo mein. "So are we going to that thing?"

"You were the one who wanted to start socializing with the neighbors," Max pointed out.

"I just thought it would be polite," said Arthur. "I don't know if I want to have to start having dinner parties."

"Oh, the horror," said Max. "Perish the thought."

"We don't cook," Arthur reminded him.

"But we order takeaway so brilliantly," said Max. "Anyway, he has funny ideas."

"Who does?"

"Sam. The new neighbor. Wanting to get to know all of us. He came round personally to drop off the invitation. Very keen on all of us being friends, apparently."

"Hasn't he got other friends?" asked Arthur. "Why does he need to be friends with us?"

"People who haven't met their friend quota yet are *so* tiring," said Max.

Arthur pointed a chopstick at him. "Don't pretend that you like meeting people. I am definitely friendlier than you are."

"You're an *insurance agent*."

"You're a tortured artist."

"Fair enough," said Max, and took a bite of beef and broccoli.

Arthur poked at his noodles and ventured, "Are you thinking it'd be good for us?"

Max looked up queryingly.

"To meet new people?" Arthur clarified.

Max considered, chewing, then said, "It might be."

Arthur tapped his chopstick against his plate. "How did he seem?"

"Fine. Not any more annoying than most other people are."

"Ringing endorsement."

"Well, I didn't want to be too extravagant in my praise, then you'd know I was lying."

"Then we'll RSVP for this backyard barbecue and be friendly neighbors."

"You have new invitations that could open new doors," said Max wisely.

• • •

"So," said Sam, as they sat down to a dinner of cheese toasties. "What was your adventure for the day?"

Teddy gave him his hopeless-dad look. "Clearly it was walking around the street handing out envelopes that everyone thought were poisoned or mixed-up post. What was *yours?*"

"Yeah, same," admitted Sam.

Anna Pachuta, hunting through the kitchen for her stash of chocolate, was listening with half an ear to her daughter's recap of the day, and then heard something that made her lift her head up and look at her more closely.

"We got a what?"

Emilia was sitting munching on a bowl of grapes set out on the table. She said, plucking a few more grapes off, "An invitation to a barbecue."

"Whose barbecue?" Anna asked in surprise. None of their friends struck her as likely to have a barbecue. They were too busy to even make cups of coffee these days.

"The new neighbors'," explained Emilia, popping the grapes into her mouth.

"The new neighbors," echoed Anna blankly. Her head hurt. She couldn't keep up with other people's lives; she was barely keeping up with her own life.

"Yeah, you know, they just moved in where the Thurstons used to be."

"Good," said Anna, pulling out some chocolate and sitting at the table with Emilia. "Have they got rid of that horrible dog?"

"No, Mum, it's the street dog now," said Emilia.

"Emilia, that's ridiculous. We can't have a street dog. It terrorizes the cats. Maybe we should go to this barbecue so I can have a talk with them about getting that dog under control."

Emilia rolled her eyes.

Anna frowned at the reaction but didn't say anything about it, because honestly she felt like she was home so seldom these days that she didn't want to spend what little time she had with Emilia fighting with her.

The kettle clicked and she got up to make herself a cup of chamomile tea—her customary treat at the end of the day, after the burst of chocolate reward—and said, "What did you do all day?"

"Not much," said Emilia. "Painted my nails again."

"It'll be better when the summer holidays are over and school starts up again," Anna said.

"Dad said maybe we could go on a proper holiday before school begins," said Emilia.

Anna couldn't help that she snorted. "Really?"

"Dad said maybe we could go to the seaside."

"Your dad is always saying ridiculous things," Anna said.

"How would you know?" asked Emilia. "Do you even talk to him anymore?"

Anna held her gaze and took an even sip of her tea. The tea was too hot for such a big sip but she wasn't about to let that show. She said, "Of course I talk to him. I'll talk to him when he gets home tonight, about going to the new neighbors' barbecue." And about how impossible a trip to the seaside was at the moment.

"Okay," said Emilia, sounding skeptical.

And Anna wanted to prove her daughter wrong, of course she did, but in the end she was too tired to wait up for Marcel and just left the invitation on his side of the bed, for him to see whenever he wandered in, and curled up in bed with the cats.

Darsh came home to find his wife there for once.

He said jokingly, "Is there no one who needs a curry somewhere? Have you exhausted the world's demand for welcome baskets?"

"Ha," said Diya, and he grinned and kissed her and looked down at what she was cooking.

"Is that for us, or destined for a friend of a friend of a friend?"

"For us," said Diya.

"Shocking," said Darsh. "Where are the children?"

"Upstairs. I'll call them down for dinner in a second."

Darsh, shifting through the mail on the table, paused on a picture of a smiling hot dog. "What's this?"

Diya glanced at it, then rolled her eyes. "Oh. Strangest thing. The new neighbors are having a *party*."

"And invited us?" asked Darsh, confused. "Do we know them?"

"No, they want to meet all of us."

"They must have heard that being your friend earns you a remarkable amount of free food."

Diya seemed caught between fondness and exasperation. She said, "Oh, and I gave away some of your trousers today," as she walked out of the kitchen down the hall.

Darsh heard her calling for the children, and then said as she came back into the kitchen, "My trousers?"

"Mayra had a friend who really needed some trousers, and you had extra." Diya shrugged.

Darsh, after a moment, shrugged as well, because it was no good trying to make sense of Diya's decisions on these things. He said, "I'm surprised you didn't give them away to the new neighbors."

"He's taller than you," Diya said, smiling. "He would have looked ridiculous. Sai! Pari!" she shouted.

Darsh winced.

"Go and threaten them," Diya said, organizing the food on the table. "I'm not walking over to the stairs again."

But before Darsh could stand, the thunder of their children coming down the stairs for dinner began.

Darsh said, "So are we going to this barbecue?"

"I don't really want to," said Diya, "because you know how busy I am, and the day of the barbecue I already have two other parties I'm supposed to be going to."

"Of course you do," said Darsh.

"But I have to go to make up for Pari's rudeness."

Pari had just walked into the kitchen, just in time for Diya to look at her meaningfully. Pari drew up short, looked at her mother, and then frowned and crossed her arms, ready to do battle.

Sai, behind Pari, took in her stance and said, "Maybe I should go back upstairs."

"Nonsense," said Darsh. "Come in and sit. You, too, Pari. And tell me what you were so rude about."

"I wasn't rude," said Pari sulkily, as she sat at the table.

"She shouted that they were 'weird.' While they were standing right at our door," said Diya, also sitting.

"He started it," said Pari.

"Who's 'he'?" asked Darsh.

"The new boy. He's trying to steal Jack."

"Jack the street dog?" said Darsh.

"Yes."

"How's he going to steal a street dog?"

"I was going to make Jack *my* dog," said Pari.

"Ah, so you were going to steal the street dog first."

Pari paused. "No," she said, and then seemed unsure what to say next.

Diya said, "Nobody is stealing any dogs. I don't like dogs, and that dog is very poorly behaved, and anyway, the dog seems to like the new neighbors and they like the dog, so let them have each other, I say."

"But, Mum," whined Pari. "We need the dog."

"We definitely do not need a dog," said Diya.

"We need the dog so that Sai can have a patient."

Sai started choking on his food.

Darsh glanced at him. "A patient for what?"

"Sai is going to be a vet," said Pari.

"Oh, splendid!" exclaimed Darsh. "Sai, that is just a brilliant choice! Veterinarian! Excellent career!"

Sai, recovered, took a sip of water and said, "I've been learning all about baby chimpanzees."

Darsh said, "So you're thinking of taking care of exotic animals? Working in a zoo, I suppose?"

"No," Pari said. "He might want to take care of dogs, too. That's why we need Jack."

"Diya, don't you know someone who's a veterinarian? Isn't Anika's cousin—"

"Yes! That's right! I'll see if I can talk to her about talking to her cousin about letting you work in the office a couple of days a week."

"Oh," said Sai. "Oh. Right. Okay."

Diya beamed at Sai and then at Pari, the earlier disagreement clearly forgotten. Diya was like that: naturally sunny, tending toward rosy thoughts. She looked at Darsh and said, "Don't we have beautiful children?"

The children looked like Diya. So Darsh took her hand and kissed her knuckles and said, "Yes."

Pen, settled in bed with the latest herbal concoction next to her, called up her blog.

Shocking new development on the street, she typed. **New Neighbors have decided to be friendly? And socialize? They are having a party. It's odd and I'm sure the rest of the neighbors are, like me, wondering how much small talk we shall have to make with each other now. But I remain excited. Opportunities to get to know the people on one's street are always exciting, and**

I have many questions to ask about the romance between Polish Teenager and Indian Teenager as well as exactly what it is Blond Gay Man does all day whilst Dark-Haired Gay Man is away at work. Perhaps he's a writer, too, and we can sit at home and procrastinate writing together!

Most important update: Jack helped to deliver the invitation. Looking forward to discussing the formal street status of Jack at the "backyard bar-b-q" as well. I do wonder what sort of healthy food options will be there. The invitation contains an illustration of a smiling frankfurter, so I'm not holding out too much hope, alas.

Chapter 4

**Hot dogs
Hamburgers
Buns
Other delicious foods that
people will eat??????**

Weekends on the street were odd, because Sam realized he'd already grown rather used to the rhythm of the street, to everyone going off to work. On the weekends most people stayed home and went out at disparate times in pursuit of various errands. The blond man—Max—came outside and cut some roses. Sam wondered if he ought to ask him for advice on taking care of the roses in his own front garden. The Indian mother came and went constantly, always laden down with stuff when she left and arms empty when she returned. Jack trotted up and down the street, wandering in and out of gardens. The black woman at the end of the street went for a run. The old man stayed shuttered up inside. The teenage girl next door, who must be the source of the drums, played every so often. Sam never saw her parents, but he presumed she had some.

And Ellen arrived with Sophie and Evie.

"Hello, Uncle Sam!" chorused the girls,

descending upon the house in a whirlwind of energy.

"The house looks great."

"You could use a little design help."

"Really, you haven't put a single thing up on the walls?"

"Everything in this house is beige; you could use a pop of color."

"Don't worry, we're here to help!"

"Just call us your brilliant interior decorators!"

"We even brought new cushions!"

Sam, bewildered by this onslaught, managed to say, "Oh, lovely," before the girls went dashing away, presumably to decorate.

"They are very excited to help you be less hopeless," Ellen informed Sam.

"Less hopeless?" echoed Sam, accepting Ellen's hug of greeting. "Setting the bar awfully high, aren't you?"

"Where's my favorite nephew?" asked Ellen.

"Upstairs." Sam leaned back and shouted for him. "Teddy! Your Aunt Ellen and the girls are here!"

"I know!" Teddy shouted back. "I'll be down after I die!" Sam looked at Ellen. "He's playing video games—he's not being *that* melodramatic."

"Good," said Ellen.

Sophie stuck her head out of the lounge. "Uncle Sam, what do you think about stripes on the walls?"

Sam blinked. "Did you bring paint?"

"No, but we brought *samples,* and stripes seem like a good idea."

"Okay," Sam said vaguely, because he'd never thought about stripes on his wall before.

"Aces," said Sophie, and disappeared back into the lounge.

Sam lifted his eyebrows at Ellen. "They paint?"

"Let's have a cuppa," suggested Ellen.

"Can we put something *in* the cuppa?" asked Sam, following Ellen into the kitchen.

Ellen laughed. "Something other than tea? That depends on the state of your drinks cabinet."

"It's dismal," said Sam. "I probably must rectify that before the party, hmm?"

"That depends," said Ellen, setting two mugs out on the counter. "Exactly how boring are you hoping this party is?"

"Ha ha," said Sam. "Not boring at all. Just not wild. I want to be in between. In the middle of the spectrum."

"Average. Exactly where most people aim."

"Less hopeless," Sam reminded her.

Which made Ellen laugh again. "You seem better," she said.

"You're funnier."

"Was I bad before?" asked Sam, surprised.

Ellen gave him a soft smile. "Not bad. Just overwhelmed, I think."

"You try moving yourself across an ocean. It isn't easy when you're no longer eighteen with all of your belongings fitting into a backpack."

"I didn't say it wasn't justified, Sam. No defensiveness necessary." Ellen poured out the tea.

"Sorry," said Sam. "This is why I need to be around people more, possibly."

"Possibly," said Ellen, handing him his tea and then turning back and snagging a piece of paper off the fridge. "What's this? 'Hot dogs, hamburgers, buns, other delicious foods that people will eat'?"

"Shopping list," Sam said, because he thought that was obvious.

"For your *party?* This is your shopping list for your *party?*"

"Yes?" Sam offered, blowing at his tea.

"Not very specific, is it?"

"I'm hoping inspiration strikes me in the supermarket."

"You need a proper list. With proper ingredients. To make proper food."

"Proper food?" Sam repeated. "I don't cook."

"How do you and Teddy eat?"

"Very, very poorly," said Sam.

"Samuel," Ellen said.

"You can call me by my full name all you like, it isn't going to make me any more of a bona fide, functioning adult."

"Uncle Sam?" shouted Evie from the lounge. "What about zebra print for an accent wall?"

"Do these girls know anything about design?" Sam asked Ellen.

"Do *you* know anything about design?" Ellen countered. No. He didn't. "Sure!" he called back, mentally shrugging.

"You need to know how to cook. Women love men who can cook. The way to a woman's heart is through her stomach."

"I thought that saying was about men."

"Don't be sexist," said Ellen. "Anyway, if you're going to invite people over, you should make them proper food. Be impressive. Don't you want them to be impressed with you?"

Well. Sam supposed that the alternative was that they think he was pathetic, and he had moved back home partly to get out from under being labeled pathetic. He said slowly, "Yes."

"Good." Ellen beamed. "Then it's settled. You'll make something impressive, and it will help you make friends."

"On the false pretense that I can actually cook."

"If you really do cook it, it won't be a false pretense. What's this?"

Because Jack the dog had appeared at the back door, tail wagging.

"Ah," said Sam. "Watch this. Teddy! Jack's here to play!"

That got an immediate response roughly

equivalent to a herd of elephants descending from the upper floor.

Teddy went racing through the house, shouting, "Hi, Sophie! Hi, Evie! Hi, Aunt Ellen!" and then, "Bye, Dad!" and barreled his way outside.

Ellen raised an eyebrow at Sam. "Teddy has a dog now?"

"Teddy definitely does not have a dog. As we have already established during this conversation, I can barely take care of the things it is already my responsibility to take care of, never mind adding a dog to the list."

"Then who is Jack?" Ellen asked, pointing to the back garden, where Teddy was visible getting an extremely enthusiastic greeting from Jack, including lots of licking and an entire wriggling back end.

"Jack is the street dog. We have a dog who wanders the street. Isn't that charming?"

"You don't sound as if you think that's charming," Ellen pointed out.

"I think it's rather odd, frankly, that I have somehow managed to inherit a part-time dog. But Jack is the only thing Teddy likes about this place, so I suppose I am eternally grateful to him."

"It's good, then," Ellen said, sipping her tea and watching Teddy play with Jack. They were chasing each other around the back garden. "Women like dogs, too, you know."

"I'm going to start pestering you about *your* love life," Sam said. "Dated many people since the divorce?"

"No," said Ellen. "I was thinking of trying Internet dating. Want to try it with me?"

"No. That sounds, in fact, like the absolute last thing I want to try in the world."

Evie and Sophie appeared in the kitchen doorway.

"Uncle Sam," Evie said. "We have a great idea."

"We are thinking"—Sophie spread her arms, the better to visualize—"spikes from the ceiling."

"Like a *cave*," added Evie, eyes sparkling.

Sam looked at Ellen. "I take it back. *That* sounds like the absolute last thing I want to try in the world."

Ellen had said that Sam would feel better when he got settled, and he was surprised to realize that was mostly true. Work was actually a welcome distraction, he had ready access to most of his important belongings, and he and Teddy were slowly developing a routine. He remembered, when Teddy had been a baby, getting lectures from Sara on the importance of having a routine, and Sam had believed it blindly, but now he believed it *fervently*, because yes, the routine helped.

And the fact that the rest of the street also had

a routine to it definitely helped. Sam didn't really know any of their names yet, but he recognized his neighbors by sight, and he was actually hopeful that the barbecue would be a success and he might make friends. Many of the neighbors seemed, like him, to be home during the day, and it would be nice to be friendly with them. And, of course, Teddy would be friends with the little Indian girl. Sure, they seemed to loathe each other now, but they would realize neither was trying to steal Jack from the other and then they could be best friends. Forget about this being an adventure, thought Sam. Maybe it could be a fairy tale with a happily-ever-after at the end.

Sam tried to come up with interesting daily adventures, hampered by the fact that, well, the usual adult life wasn't terribly adventurous and that was actually what made it *good,* in Sam's opinion. Teddy's adventures continued to revolve around Jack, to whom he was teaching tricks, and the fact that Teddy was confident that Jack liked him better than he liked Pari.

"It's not a contest," Sam said, which Teddy didn't seem to hear at all.

Sam got RSVPs from everyone on the street except Mr. Hammersley. Sam supposed Mr. Hammersley had given his RSVP when he had dropped off the invitation. Other than Mr. Hammersley, though, everyone else was coming.

And Sam hated the fact that he found himself

thinking, *I should make something impressive for this barbecue.*

Ugh, bloody Ellen putting this bloody idea in his head. Sam, unable to sleep, pulled his phone over and Googled *impressive barbecue foods*.

The first result suggested he roast a whole pig.

"Nope," he said out loud to his phone, and scrolled past.

And then considered: Brussels sprouts or aubergine? And what the hell was *burrata*?

The day was overcast, and Teddy was bored. Everything in England was *boring*. He sat at the front window and looked out of it and watched the lady from down the street go jogging past. What was her name? Pencil, or something. Whatever. She saw him in the window and waved cheerfully. Teddy sighed and waved back so as not to be rude.

Then he went in search of Dad.

Who was working, clicking away on the computer he'd set up in his office.

"What's up?" he asked distractedly when Teddy entered.

"I'm bored."

Dad lifted an eyebrow at him. "Bored? You have all day to do nothing but play. You can't be bored. What about all of your video games?"

"They're boring."

"Glad I spent all that money buying them for you, then."

Dad was always missing the *point*. Teddy frowned at him.

"Why don't you go introduce yourself to the girl next door?"

"I don't like her."

"You don't know her."

"I feel like I don't like her."

Dad sighed, as if Teddy was being difficult. And then he said, "What about the dog? You could play with the dog."

"I haven't seen him," Teddy said mournfully, because usually Jack wandered by at some point during the day. "I think the girl stole him."

"The girl didn't steal him," said Dad, who for some unknown reason was convinced the girl wasn't going to steal Jack when she was *totally* going to steal Jack. "He's probably at Mr. Hammersley's house."

"Can I go to Mr. Hammersley's house?" asked Teddy, because maybe that would be something interesting to do.

Dad sighed, again, like Teddy was being difficult. He said, "I guess. Don't pester him too much."

Teddy jumped up and raced out of the room. "Bye, Dad!"

"And see if you can get him to come to the barbecue!" Dad called after him.

• • •

There was a knock on the door.

Bill looked up from where he had been just about to pour himself a cup of tea and frowned. Jack, who had been curled up on the floor, went running to the door, barking joyously.

Bill muttered under his breath. Because, really, he'd never had so many people knocking on his door. He didn't want to talk to any of these people. Couldn't they just leave him *alone?*

Jack leaped about, tapping at the doorknob with his paw as if wishing he could open it.

"There's no need to be that excited about *people,*" Bill told him disapprovingly.

Jack had the nerve not to look the slightest bit ashamed of the way he was acting.

"Have a little *dignity,*" Bill told him under his breath, and peered through the door.

It was the new American boy from next door. Bill wondered if Americans were constantly knocking on people's doors, disturbing all their peace and quiet. Was this how it was going to be from now on?

Bill sighed heavily and, resigned, opened the door. "Well?" he prompted gruffly.

"Hi," said the boy, laughing a little as Jack bounded over to him and proceeded to lick him a lot.

Dignity, thought Bill, feeling ashamed for Jack.

108

"I was wondering if Jack could come out and play," said the boy, patting Jack enthusiastically.

"I don't own Jack," Bill said brusquely. "He does as he wishes."

"So are you making more cool little figures?" the boy asked.

"Whittling," Bill said. "It's called whittling."

"The little dragons were cool. I think you should make wizards to go along with them."

"Wizards," Bill repeated flatly. What was this child even talking about?

The boy nodded. "Dragons need wizards, I think. They can be the wizards' pets."

"Dragons aren't pets," Bill said automatically, and then wondered why he was even having this discussion. "Never mind. Take Jack." Bill went to go back inside.

"Oh," the boy said, causing Bill to pause. "My dad wants to know if you're going to come to the barbecue."

"I already said no," Bill replied.

"Yeah, but . . ." The boy shrugged.

"I'm not going to stand around with strangers eating hot dogs."

The boy frowned, lifted his chin, pushed his shoulders back. That stubbornness that Bill remembered. He said, "I think the barbecue is stupid, too, but my dad is really excited about it, so you're not allowed to be mean about it. Okay? He's just trying to be nice."

And with that the boy turned away from the door and walked firmly down the front step and through the front garden.

Jack stood on the step a second longer, looking between Bill and the boy, before letting out a bark and following the boy.

Bill frowned, thinking, *Mad Americans, we never had any of these issues before they showed up,* and slammed the front door.

Sam had a shopping list that now read: *hot dogs, hamburgers, buns, ingredients for beetroot salad (garlic, white wine vinegar, Dijon mustard, shallots, salt, pepper, hard-boiled eggs, beetroot, olive oil, pine nuts, salad leaves), lots of crisps, ALCOHOL.*

He considered it, then added at the end, *Also nonalcoholic drinks,* because he supposed he should have something on hand that was more appropriate for people like his eight-year-old son. And just because he thought he needed a lot of alcohol didn't mean he needed to assume on behalf of everyone else.

He found Teddy rolling over in the garden, while Jack sat and stared at him.

"What are you doing?" Sam asked.

Jack, seeing him, immediately came bounding over to give Sam a greeting more appropriate for a deity suddenly appearing on Earth.

"Yes," Sam said to him, trying to pet him while

Jack contorted all over in such ecstatic greeting that it was almost impossible to get a good head scratch in. "Hello. How are you?"

"I'm teaching Jack how to roll over," said Teddy, from his back on the grass.

"I thought Jack already knew how to roll over."

"He seems to have forgotten," said Teddy.

"Well, that's not what it looks like," Sam remarked. "It looks like you're rolling over and Jack is thinking you look ridiculous."

"Jack doesn't think I look ridiculous!" protested Teddy.

Sam walked over to look down at Teddy. "No, you're right, he's probably impressed at what a talented human being you are."

Teddy grinned.

Sam said suddenly, "But does Jack know about *tickling?*" and then dropped to the grass in a tickle attack.

Teddy laughed uproariously and Jack ran around them barking and Sam thought it was absolutely, by far, the nicest moment they'd had in England so far. Maybe the nicest moment they'd had in *years*.

Sam sprawled on the grass with Teddy and looked up at the gray sky over their heads. Jack flopped down beside them. Teddy's head was just brushing against Sam's shoulder and it was nice. Grounding. Sam had spent a long time feeling like he was running flat-out just to keep up with everything he had to keep up with. He couldn't remember the last time he'd stayed still and breathed and let sink into him the recognition of how miraculous it was to have a child and to have that child be Teddy.

Sam said abruptly, "I'm glad you're here with me."

"Where else would I be?" asked Teddy, sounding bewildered.

"Somewhere else, soon enough," said Sam, and kissed the top of Teddy's head before pulling himself off the grass. It wasn't as easy to do as it once had been. "We have to go shopping."

"Shopping for what?" asked Teddy.

"The party," Sam said. "The super-fun party we're going to host in this very back garden in a couple of days."

Teddy sighed extravagantly, but stood up and said to Jack, "You should go back to Mr. Hammersley's. Dad and I have to go *shopping*."

Jack wagged his tail, then slipped his way through the fence that didn't border the old man.

"He's probably going to see *that girl*," said Teddy darkly.

"Which is totally allowed," Sam said. "He belongs to everyone, remember?"

"I *guess*," grumbled Teddy, as they headed inside together. "So what are we going to buy at the store? Ice cream?"

Sam, tucking his shopping list into his pocket,

pulled it back out and scribbled, *Pudding?????* onto the end of it.

Sam had grown up in England, so you would have thought that he would remember where everything was in a British supermarket. For instance, he should have remembered that they didn't keep eggs refrigerated in British supermarkets.

He didn't remember, until he stumbled upon them.

Teddy said, "Why are they *here?* They don't put them in the fridge here? Is that safe?"

"It's perfectly fine. Would they do it if it wasn't safe? Since when do you care passionately about the temperature of eggs?" Sam asked.

"I didn't know I *had* to care about it," Teddy said. "England makes me have to care about weird things."

"Indeed," said Sam. "Now, where do you think they keep the beetroot? Produce, right?"

Teddy's eyebrows would have fallen entirely off his forehead if they could have. "Beetroot? What are you doing with that?"

"Making a salad."

"A salad? A salad requires lettuce. Not beetroot."

"I'm being impressive. A salad with lettuce is not impressive. A salad with beetroot, however—"

"Is hideous."

"It's going to be delicious. And healthy."

"Oh, exactly like all of the food we always eat," said Teddy.

"You're going to be insufferable when you're a teenager," said Sam.

"Does this have to do with Aunt Ellen? I bet she's behind the beetroot. I mean, who are we even trying to impress?"

"Our guests."

Teddy shrugged, like impressing their guests wasn't very high on his list. And probably Sam should be praising that lack of desire to conform and play pointless one-upmanship games with people. He wanted Teddy to grow up to be his own person, unafraid of what people might think of him. That was absolutely what he wanted.

But he also wanted to impress their new neighbors.

So Sam said, "See that?" and drew a circle in the air in front of Teddy's dubious face. "That is exactly the kind of negativity that we are working on getting rid of with this party."

"I just don't think beetroot is a good way to impress people. I mean, not the type of people you'd want to be friends with. Not *fun* people. I'm really only worried about you, Dad," said Teddy earnestly. "You're just so very bad at making friends."

"Cheeky," said Sam. "You are a cheeky child.

And I am making a grated beetroot salad, which I think sounds pretty darn impressive."

"If you say so," said Teddy, with his special brand of skepticism firmly intact.

"I do," said Sam, refusing to be rattled. "Run and pick out some chocolate biscuits for pudding and meet me in the produce section. And stop sulking. You can't sulk when you're on your way to chocolate biscuits. You have to smile."

Teddy gave him an angelic smile.

"Brat," Sam said, and gave Teddy a little shove on his way past him.

Teddy grinned and then took off in search of the biscuits.

Sam contemplated if he should offer something better than chocolate biscuits. Maybe some ice cream to go along with it. Baking a cake was probably beyond him. He should probably stick to just the one overwhelming ordeal: the grated beetroot salad.

Newly determined to tackle beetroot, Sam went to the fruit and veg section. Where he quickly discerned that beetroot, in its native form, was terrifying and looked as if it required effort to be rendered edible.

Sam stared at it and wondered if he should switch to the aubergine recipe instead.

Which was when a woman next to him said, "Excuse me, you're looking very angry at the beetroot and clearly have something to debate with it, but if I could interrupt for just a moment to grab some carrots . . ."

Sam said automatically, "Oh. Of course. Sorry. Totally my fault," and stepped back a little bit.

Not quite enough space for the woman to reach the carrots. She had to brush against him on the way past, which meant that Sam was aware of the perfume she was wearing, light and fresh. And then she turned to him, carrots retrieved, and gave him a smile. She had a radiant smile, bright eyes, and dark red hair that she'd tucked under a newsboy cap.

Sam, standing amongst vegetables clutching a useless recipe and contemplating the absurdity of beetroot, had a moment he'd experienced only once before in his life, an *oh, it's you* moment, as if they'd been scheduled to meet right here in this supermarket, as if he ought to say, *hello, remember me?* even though they were, theoretically, complete strangers.

The woman brandished her carrots in a little salute in Sam's direction and said, "Ta," and Sam thought that that was it, she would walk away with her carrots and he would turn back to the beetroot and the rhythm of the world would click into place again and Sam would find himself rushing again, desperately, just to keep up.

And for this one small moment in this supermarket looking at a ginger woman holding a bag of carrots, Sam felt like it was finally still enough to feel when he took a breath.

So he said, "The beetroot and I are engaged in a negotiation." Which . . . made some sense as a pickup line in some universe that was not this one, Sam supposed.

Except that it did what he had hoped it would, and kept the woman suspended in the moment, instead of rushing off into the normal pace of life. She said, "Are you? Over what?" and smiled at him again. She had adorable dimples.

For a moment Sam forgot what he was supposed to be talking about.

The woman said, "I hear beetroot is tough as a negotiator. Don't want to be facing it across the table when you're negotiating settlement terms." She looked very serious about this.

And this woman was either mad or delightful. Or possibly both.

Beetroot, Sam remembered, smiling back at her helplessly, and said, "Yeah, I am supposed to be turning that"—he gestured at the offending vegetable—"into something edible."

The woman looked at the beetroot briefly and then back at Sam, which Sam preferred. She was still smiling, which Sam also preferred. "The key is bacon," she said.

Sam glanced back at the beetroot. "And, presumably, removing the stalks, right?"

The woman laughed. Sam was not being

ridiculous in deciding that this woman's laugh was composed of puppy kisses and rainbows. She said, "Ah, I see, we're starting right at the very beginning."

"I don't make beetroot very often," Sam confided, leaning ever so slightly closer.

The woman lifted an eyebrow. "No? So why are you engaging with it now?"

"I'm trying to be impressive."

The woman's smile widened, one corner of her lips twitching. "Is beetroot impressive?"

"Isn't it?" countered Sam. "Would you not be impressed at someone managing to tackle that into submission?"

The woman glanced at Sam's trolley and said, "I am more impressed by people who have decided to stock up on every type of crisp this store carries."

"Yeah, but the beetroot balances the crisps," Sam said. "If you have some beetroot, you can have as many crisps as you want. And people with packs of spotted dick in their shopping trolleys shouldn't throw stones."

The woman smiled, dimples deep, and said, "Escalating the conversation, are we?"

"Sorry," Sam said innocently. "Should I not have brought up your dick preferences just yet?"

"Oh, no, *that* would have been fine," the woman replied. "It's my dessert choices you shouldn't have criticized."

Sam laughed. He stood in the middle of the produce section of a supermarket, on a Friday night, with a trolley full of hamburgers, hot dogs, and every type of crisp in the store, and looked at this woman with a carrot in her hand and thought, *Let's do this again sometime,* which sounded ridiculous even in his head. *Come here often?* also sounded ridiculous. He needed something smooth and charming. Surely *Come over to my place and I'll make you beetroot* stepped over the creepiness line.

Which was when Teddy said curiously, "Hi?"

Sam startled and looked at Teddy, who was holding chocolate biscuits and looking between Sam and the woman. Then he stared at Sam and lifted his eyebrows in his all-knowing eight-year-old look.

"Hi," said Sam. "Hi."

Teddy's eyebrows got higher.

"You got the chocolate biscuits," said Sam.

"Yeah." Teddy put them in the trolley and looked pointedly at the woman with the carrots.

Who said of the chocolate biscuits, "Good choice. My favorite."

Teddy said, "Better than beetroot."

The woman smiled at Teddy, and the terrible thing was that that smile at Teddy was the best moment of Sam's entire evening. Any woman might smile at Sam, but a woman who smiled at Teddy had smiled at the more important person.

She said, "Give the beetroot a chance. It drives a mean bargain."

Teddy looked perplexed.

The woman looked at Sam and said, "Good luck with your negotiation. I hope you manage to form an alliance. Remember the bacon."

"Yeah," Sam said. "Enjoy your carrots and your spotted dick." *Oh, my God,* he thought, *the supermarket can swallow me now.*

The woman smiled at him and said, "Thanks," and then moved off, pushing her trolley through the fruit and veg, over to the next aisle.

Sam watched her.

"Who was that?" Teddy asked.

"I have no idea," Sam said. "A woman who wanted carrots."

"Probably you were supposed to ask her for coffee," said Teddy frankly.

Sam, in the middle of pulling a beetroot out of the pile, promptly lost his grip on it and sent several bouncing to the floor of the supermarket. Sam ignored that. He looked at Teddy and said, "Why would I ask her for a coffee?"

"Because you liked her," said Teddy.

"I didn't like her," said Sam. "I just met her."

"You were smiling at her so much, it was embarrassing."

Oh, Christ, thought Sam. "You're exaggerating."

Teddy looked appropriately dubious.

Sam leaned down and gathered beetroot into his arms.

"What are we doing with all those beetroots?" asked Teddy. "Is that how many we need for the salad?"

"I don't know," said Sam distractedly, dumping them haphazardly into the trolley, where they probably crushed all the crisps. "So you'd be okay? With me . . . going for coffee with someone?"

Teddy looked across at him, and Sam was aware that they probably shouldn't be having this conversation in a supermarket. "Dad," he said, like it was obvious, as obvious as Sam being an idiot ordinarily was. "Why not? I want you to be happy. Of course I do. That's why I'm here in England, so you'll be happy."

Sam reached out suddenly and pulled Teddy into a tight hug.

"You're strangling me," Teddy croaked.

"Bloody vegetables," Sam muttered into Teddy's hair. "They make me emotional."

"*What?*" said Teddy.

"I want us *both* to be happy," said Sam, and released Teddy and then crouched down to be on his level. "I wanted to give you . . . a new start. And . . . more of a family. More than I could manage alone and . . . I know you feel like this was all me, but I—"

Teddy put a hand on Sam's shoulder and said, "It's okay, Dad. I know. I get it."

"I'm sorry you hate it here," Sam said, "but I really think that—"

Sam didn't know what he looked like, but it must have been pathetic because Teddy said, "I don't hate it here. It's okay."

Sam gave Teddy what he hoped was an older and more mature version of Teddy's dubious look. "Oh, really?"

"Yeah. At least we have a dog here."

Sam sighed. "We don't have a dog here."

"We kind of have a dog here," said Teddy.

It wasn't even worth the fight about it, Sam thought. Especially not if the dog was the first thing Teddy named when talking about good things about England. So Sam said, "Fine. Okay. Whatever. We kind of have a dog."

Teddy grinned, triumphant, and said, "Good. Can we get him some dog treats, then?"

Sam groaned and stood up. "Fine. Yes. You win."

"Thanks."

They walked side by side for a second. Sam thought he should consult his shopping list but it seemed like the least important thing in the universe at the moment. Too much else had happened at this supermarket.

Teddy said finally, "You'll probably see her here again."

"You think?" said Sam.

"Yes. Who only goes to a supermarket one

time? When you see her again, be cool and ask her for coffee."

"I'm not taking dating advice from my eight-year-old son."

"You should. Aunt Ellen says you're hopeless."

"Yeah, but I think I'm slowly climbing to be a little less hopeless. So there's that. Baby steps," said Sam.

"Wait until I tell Aunt Ellen about the woman in the produce section," said Teddy.

"Oh, God," said Sam.

Chapter 5

How to prepare beetroot

How to prepare beetroot salad with bacon

Getting beetroot stains out of shirts

How to stop eyes watering while
cutting a shallot

Is a shallot the same thing as an onion

What can I use for a grater if I don't
have a grater

Plane tickets to Fiji

"Teddy," Sam said as his son came into the kitchen. "We are moving to Fiji."

"We just got here and when we got here you told me to remind you that packing is horrible and the only thing worse than packing is unpacking and I was to remind you of that if you ever said we were moving ever again."

"I don't care," said Sam. "We're moving to Fiji. Fiji's nice. You'll like it."

"What's in Fiji?"

"*Sun,*" said Sam fervently, looking outside, where it was raining very energetically. Not even polite, wispy rain that Sam could have expected his guests to brave. But proper if-you-walk-outside-a-raging-flood-might-whisk-you-away rain.

Teddy stood at the window and looked out at the rain and said, "Maybe we should cancel the party."

"No," said Sam, determinedly chopping his beetroots into very fine pieces because surely that was the same as grating them. "We are definitely not canceling the party."

"But it's a barbecue," said Teddy. "We're supposed to be outside for it."

"We'll just be inside for it," Sam said. "It'll be an inside barbecue. It'll be an *adventure*."

There was a moment of silence.

Teddy said, "We probably should have put a rain date on the invitation."

"Yes," Sam agreed, chopping even more energetically. "We probably should have."

"What are you doing?" Teddy asked, watching him.

"I am grating beetroot. I am grating beetroot even though we don't have a grater. I have decided this is good enough. Who ever heard of grating beetroot, anyway?"

"I think you should give up on the beetroot salad," said Teddy.

"Not when I've come so far," said Sam.

"It stinks," was Teddy's assessment.

"You are not the world's most supportive son, you know," Sam informed him.

"It wouldn't help you for me to tell you not

to serve that to people you don't know," said Teddy, looking at the salad with his nose wrinkled. "You wanted to impress people, but I think this is the wrong way to go about it."

Sam looked at his beetroot salad. "Yeah, wrong type of impression, isn't it?"

"A bit," agreed Teddy.

Sam sighed. "Ah, beetroot salad, we hardly knew ye."

"You're so weird," said Teddy.

"I told you about this," Anna was telling Marcel. "I know I told you."

"That we have to go and socialize with strangers in the middle of torrential rains?" Marcel said. "You definitely did not tell me that."

Anna huffed impatiently. "Well, I didn't know it was going to rain at the time that I told you about the invitation."

"Who are these people again?"

"They moved in where the Thurstons used to live." Anna frowned at her shirt, decided to swap it for another one. Everything made her look fat lately; she had to stop eating so much chocolate.

"We never used to have to talk to the Thurstons," Marcel remarked.

"Would you stop whining?" Anna said, pulling a new shirt over her head. "You'd think I was leading you to a firing squad. Fine. If you don't want to go, you don't have to go."

"I don't want to go," Marcel said.

"Don't go," Anna snapped at him.

Emilia started playing the drums. Which was a thing she did whenever they argued.

Anna sighed and rubbed at her forehead, where a headache was lurking, and the drums weren't helping, and the fighting with Marcel wasn't helping, and the rain wasn't helping, and the bloody party next door wasn't helping.

Marcel said, "You're awfully keen to go to this party."

"I'm not. I'm really not," Anna said. "And don't even start. There's nothing suspicious going on." She considered her choices for shoes. What shoes would be best for standing around in mud and puddles?

"Well, it *is* a tad suspicious," Marcel said. "When I wanted to go away for a few days, you weren't nearly as keen as you are about wanting to go to this party."

Anna batted Socks out of her way as she reached for her perfume. "Because going away would have cost money, and we're trying to save money."

"For what?" said Marcel.

Anna, perfume still in her hand, looked at him and said blankly, "What?"

"What are we saving money for?"

"What do you mean what are we saving money for?"

"How does the saying go? 'A rainy day'?" Marcel gestured to the rain outside.

"It's not meant literally. And there's a lot to save for: Emilia's future. Our future. We don't know how long we'll have our jobs and how long they'll pay us for—"

"We also have no reason to think we're about to lose our jobs. You're making up scary troubles when there aren't any."

Anna put the perfume down with a sharp click and said, in a low furious tone, "Do you not remember running out of money before we could eat for the week? Counting every cent to try to pull together enough for milk for Emilia?"

Marcel walked over to her and caught up her hands in his own, as if that would be *soothing,* as if that could make her forget the endless driving panic of lying awake worrying over the child she'd brought into the world and how she would ever provide for her. "I remember that," Marcel said. "Of course I do. But it was a long time ago. Emilia's practically grown. She has plenty of milk, and whatever other food she desires. We cannot go back in time to give us money to get through those days. And we don't need to. We made it through."

Anna, after a moment, pulled her hands out of Marcel's. The house was quiet; Emilia had stopped playing the drums, although the rain against the window seemed like a lingering echo of the sound. Anna was safe and warm, but in her gut was the memory of being empty and hollow and hungry, and she didn't understand how Marcel could so easily forget that.

Anna said evenly, "I am going to meet our new neighbors."

Max, coming down the stairs and finding Arthur hiding literally within the curtains by the front window, burst into laughter. "What are you doing?"

Arthur, shrouded in his curtain, did not take his gaze away from the window. "I am watching to see who's going to be the first to go to the party."

"And you're wrapped up in drapery because . . . ?"

Arthur glowered at him. "Because I don't want anyone to see me, *obviously*."

"Darling, I am fairly sure they can still see you; you just look like a lunatic who likes to wear curtains now."

"They can't see me," denied Arthur. "I'm stealthy."

"My mistake," said Max, and walked over to the window to peer out it.

Arthur grabbed him and pulled him into the curtain with him. "You can't just stand there *openly*."

"This is very romantic," Max told him. "I do hope a good snog session is in our future."

"Currently I foresee no snogging for you," Arthur informed him primly.

"You are very cruel," Max said. "Go away and bring back my nice husband."

"Shut up," said Arthur, and maybe leaned over him to peer out the window again, but maybe also pulled closer because it was almost a snuggle.

Max decided not to point out they were snuggling, as he thought that would be less likely to get him a snog. "Has anyone gone over yet?"

"Not yet," said Arthur.

Max tried to look at his watch from within the confines of the curtain. "Well, it's early still. No one wants to be the first one at a party."

"Exactly," said Arthur. "That's why I'm waiting."

Max let silence fall, watching Arthur as he watched the window. Then he said, "What if we're all standing at our windows watching to see who's going to be the first person to go over there, and none of us are going to go until someone else goes, and therefore no one will ever go?"

"Don't be silly," said Arthur. "That's not what's happening." A pause. "No, hang on, that's probably exactly what's happening."

"Yeah," Max agreed.

Arthur was silent for another moment. "It's just . . . if we go over now . . . what are we going to talk about? What are we going to talk about *at all?*"

"Probably the weather," said Max.

"Okay. 'Wow, terrible weather we're having.' 'Yeah, just awful.' 'But I hear the sun might come out in a couple of days.' 'Oh, really? Lovely.' Then what?"

Max chuckled into the skin behind Arthur's ear. "Really, darling, your conversational prowess. How did you ever pull me?"

"I don't recall my prowess there having anything to do with conversation," replied Arthur.

Max laughed again. "Fair enough."

"Oh." Arthur leaned forward, closer to the window.

"Careful. They'll see you."

"The Basaks," Arthur said. "The Basaks are the first to go over."

"Should have put money on that," Max remarked.

"He's carrying something. I think they're bringing food. Were we supposed to bring food to this thing?"

Max considered. "I think we might have some Jaffa Cakes."

"They'll have to do," said Arthur grimly, like he was preparing for battle. "Let's go."

In the Basak house, Diya had a bowl bigger than her own head into which she was carefully arranging a vast amount of pakoras. Diya had a lot of bowls bigger than her own head. Diya spent a lot of time bringing vast amounts of food to people.

"Will they even want pakoras?" Darsh asked. "They're not Indian."

Diya stared at him. "*Everyone* wants pakoras."

"If you say so," said Darsh. "Are you sure they're still even having this party?" He looked outside at the driving rain.

"They're having it," Diya said. "If they're not, what will I do with all these pakoras?"

"I am confident you will find a use for them," remarked Darsh.

Diya thrust the bowl into her husband's arms and walked over to the stairs and shouted up, "Pari! Sai! Time to go!"

Sai came down the stairs, his hair flopping into his eyes.

"I wish you'd cut your hair," Diya said. "Darsh, you should take him to have his hair cut."

"*Take* me?" said Sai. "I'm not five!"

"Veterinarians need to have serious haircuts," Darsh said.

"It's true. I'm not even sure Anika's cousin will let you shadow her with hair like that."

"Shadow her?" Darsh asked.

"That's what Anika said you call it," Diya explained.

"You've already *talked* to her about it?" asked Sai, eyes wide.

"Of course," said Diya. "I know how very

keen you are on it. I didn't want you to miss this opportunity."

"Mum," said Sai, and then sighed heavily.

"What?" said Diya. "It'll be good for you."

"I think it will give you an opportunity to see if you like it," Darsh said. "You're very lucky to have an opportunity like this."

"Yeah," agreed Sai glumly.

Diya frowned at him, but instead turned back to the stairs and shouted for Pari again.

Pari appeared at the top of the staircase. "I'm not coming," she said, folding her arms.

Diya lifted her eyebrows at her. "You're what?"

"I'm not coming. The new boy and I are at war over Jack, and so I can't just—"

"No war," Darsh said, leaning past Diya so he could see his daughter. "There is no war happening. You have no idea what real war actually *is*."

"Don't be difficult," Diya said. "Your brother isn't raising a fuss over having to go to the party."

"Because Emilia will be there," huffed Pari.

Sai squeaked, "What?"

Diya said, "Emilia? Who's Emilia?"

"Is that the Polish girl from down the street?" Darsh said. "Is she going to be there?"

"Presumably," Diya said. "All of the neighbors are going to be there. But why would Sai care?"

"Well," said Sai, and pushed his hair out of his eyes.

"I understand she's someone Sai's age to talk to, and you of course should be polite to her. There is never any need to be rude," Darsh said.

"Right," Diya said. "Be polite. Try not to boast too much about how you're going to be a veterinarian."

"Mum," said Sai, "I'm not even in university yet."

Diya waved her hand to dismiss that ridiculous protest, because that was surely just a *formality,* and turned back to her daughter and said, "You are coming down these stairs right this instant and you are going to this party with us and we are all going to be very polite to all of the neighbors and then we don't have to talk to them again."

Pari, sulking with every step, dragged herself down the stairs.

Diya said, "Good. Let's go," and led the family out of the house into the rain.

The first ring of the doorbell made Sam realize that this was actually happening.

He looked at Teddy. "We're having a party."

Teddy gave him the why-are-you-so-daft look.

Sam didn't want to explain that he wasn't sure he'd ever had a party on his own. He had hosted them with Sara, of course, but that had been Sara's thing, mostly. The same way making friends had been Sara's thing. Maybe Teddy was feeling adrift in England, a place he knew only vaguely, and maybe Sam was technically back home, but *this* was where Sam was adrift, in the place of being two parents at once and having to excel at everything because there was no one there to complement the weak parts anymore.

Sam glanced around the kitchen, which was an absolute mess, and then decided, "We'll just keep everyone in the lounge and the dining room."

Walking down the hallway to get the door, he glanced in the lounge and dining room, both of which were only approximately operational and both of which were only half-decorated because Sophie and Evie hadn't had time to finish.

Probably they should have got decorations for the party. Sam opened the door on the Indian family from down the street: the woman he'd met, and the girl about Teddy's age, and then what he presumed to be her husband, and then a teenage boy.

"Hi," he said, with his very brightest smile intact. "Welcome!"

"Hello," said the woman, and Sam raked his memory trying to remember if he'd ever learned her name. "This is my husband Darsh."

"Hi," Sam said to the man, who was carrying the largest bowl Sam had ever seen. "Can I . . . take that from you?"

"Please," said Darsh, with a smile.

Sam took the bowl. Which was heavier and more awkward than he had anticipated.

The woman said, "They're pakoras. I thought you might appreciate some food."

"More than you know," Sam said. "Come in, come in." He looked at the teenager and said, "Hi. I'm Sam."

"Sai," the teenager said, and pushed his hair out of his eyes.

"So," said Sam, carrying the bowl back to the kitchen. "Can I get you something to drink?"

Everyone followed him into the kitchen, which had not exactly been Sam's intention, since the kitchen smelled of beetroot and also looked like a bomb composed entirely of beetroot had gone off in it.

I should have lit a candle, thought Sam. And then: *Do I own any candles?*

The family was taking in the kitchen. Sam thought he ought to crawl under a rock, except that he didn't know of any rocks big enough.

The woman said, "Getting settled, I see."

"Gradually," Sam said. "It's a lot of boxes." He looked at Teddy and the little Indian girl—what was her name? Sam wasn't sure he'd caught that, either—who were basically facing off against each other. "Do you play video games?" Sam asked, hoping for an affirmative response.

"Video games are stupid," pronounced the girl.

"Okay," said Sam.

"*Pari*," said her mother, which solved the question of the little girl's name.

"Sai plays video games," said Darsh.

"Oh, good." Sam looked at the teenager, who nodded. "Teddy's pretty good at some very uplifting games."

"Uplifting?" said the woman. Sam really had to find out her name.

"They're all called things like *Mass Extinction Event*," Sam explained.

"I love *Mass Extinction Event*," offered Sai.

And Sam had been hoping to find Teddy a friend but hadn't predicted it would be a teenager. At any rate, Sai and Teddy headed upstairs to play video games and Pari was commanded to join them by her mother and Sam was just trying to figure out if he ought to offer drinks again when the doorbell rang again.

It was the gay couple, who appeared to have chosen the absolute worst time to make the dash down the street, because they looked like a couple of drowned rats.

"Hi," said Max jovially. "Lovely weather we're having. This is Arthur. And we brought Jaffa Cakes."

"Oh," said Sam, and shook Arthur's hand and accepted the Jaffa Cakes. "Thank you. Won't you come in? I'm sorry about the rain."

"Couldn't be helped," said Max cheerfully.

"I like what you've done with the place. Is that going to be a zebra-print accent wall?"

"Oh," said Sam. "I have nieces who are . . ."

"Decorators?" suggested Max.

"No. They're actually not. Which is why I didn't finish that sentence, because I'm not sure how I ended up putting them in charge of decoration."

Max laughed.

Arthur said, "Max is an artist."

"Oh." Sam recalled the red paint that had covered Max when he'd met them. "Right."

"Which isn't the same as being a decorator," said Arthur, "but was a relief, because he handled all of the decoration."

"Because I had actual *opinions* on the decoration," said Max. "Arthur's reaction to everything was 'whatever.' "

"I don't care what color the walls are," Arthur said.

Sam smiled and said, "Won't you come back to the kitchen? The, uh . . ." Sam realized he didn't know the family's last name and he didn't want to say "the Indians" because that felt rude.

Luckily Max ahead of him saw the family and said, "Diya! Darsh! Nice to see you again!" Which solved the question of the woman's name, too, thought Sam in relief.

Sam put the Jaffa Cakes on the counter next to the bowl of pakoras and said, "Can I get anyone anything to drink?" and then opened his fridge to display the selection.

He was pleased when they all chose their own drinks, and he provided glasses and then they stood and looked at each other, and Sam thought, *This is the world's worst party.*

So he said, "Terrible weather, isn't it?"

Arthur said, "But we're supposed to see some sun in another couple of days."

"That's good, then," said Sam.

And that exhausted the topic of the weather.

This was going well.

Anna said nervously, trying to pretend she wasn't nervous, as they walked next door for the party, "I wish you'd dress better."

"Mum," Emilia said. "I dress fine."

"You *could* dress better if you lost a bit of weight."

"*Mum,*" said Emilia.

"I'm just saying. You know I'm only worried about you. I know how harsh teenagers can be."

"Mum," said Emilia, her ordinarily pale face red now. "Please stop."

"Fine." Anna reached out and rang the doorbell. "I'm just saying. It's a tough world out there and a little extra weight doesn't do you any favors."

"Ugh," said Emilia, and rolled her eyes.

The door opened on the man Anna had seen a couple of times now. Shaggy sand-colored hair, and a pair of light, bright eyes, and a welcoming smile, all dressed in jeans and a T-shirt, and Anna felt vaguely overdressed in the sundress she'd finally decided on and then decided to blame this man for not being better dressed considering he was the party's *host*.

Anna graciously extended her hand and said, "Hello. I'm Anna Pachuta."

"Sam Bishop," Sam said, shaking her hand.

"And this is my daughter Emilia," Anna said.

"Yes. We met when I dropped off the invitation. Hello again, Emilia."

"Hi," Emilia said.

"Come in from the rain," Sam said, stepping inside to let them in. "We were just discussing how horrible the weather is, and Arthur was saying that it's supposed to be sunny in a few days."

"Oh," said Anna, because she didn't know what else to say. "Good."

Sam looked at Emilia. "The other teenager, Sai, is upstairs with my son and his sister, if you want to join them. You don't have to. They're playing video games, if that helps you make your decision."

"I'll go upstairs," Emilia said, and shot up the staircase.

Anna didn't blame her. She didn't feel like facing all of these neighbors, either.

The Basaks and the gay couple from next door

were all ringed around the kitchen, drinking various things. They greeted Anna when she came in and Anna said hello in return and let Sam get her a drink and then tried not to feel too self-conscious about the fact that both the Basaks and the men were clearly *couples,* and her husband wasn't there, and that was, well, *embarrassing.*

Really, all Anna asked out of life was not to be *embarrassed,* and it was horrible how tricky it was to achieve that. Horrible and exhausting.

Diya Basak said, "And how is Marcel, Anna?" as if to rub in that Marcel wasn't there.

"Oh, he's fine," Anna said. "Feeling a little under the weather today, or he'd be here." She felt she needed to give some explanation for that.

"The weather is terrible today," said the one Anna was pretty sure was called Arthur.

"Yes," Anna agreed, as if she hadn't just had a whole conversation about the weather with Sam. "Terrible."

"And how is Emilia?" asked Diya.

Honestly, Anna thought she'd rather talk about the weather than all of these prying questions. "She's fine," Anna said.

"Still playing the drums?" asked Diya, apparently determined to bring up every humiliating thing about Anna's life.

"Oh, is she the one who plays?" asked Sam, from where he was fiddling around with the food in the kitchen.

Anna was alarmed and appropriately, well, embarrassed. "Oh, no, can you hear her over here? Of course you can. Is it terribly annoying?"

"Not annoying at all. She's quite good. And she doesn't play too late at night. Sometimes it can make conference calls interesting, but luckily listening to drums being played next door is generally more interesting than whatever's happening on my conference calls." Sam sent Anna a smile.

Anna sighed. "She is just determined to play those drums. Won't listen to sense. If she's bothering you, I'll just tell her she can't play anymore."

Sam shook his head. "She really isn't bothering me. Don't worry about it."

"And how are your kids?" asked the other man of Diya, who Anna was pretty sure was Max. Unless she had them confused. At any rate, she felt now like *she* should have been the one to ask about the Basak children, and now everyone was wondering why she hadn't.

Diya beamed with pleasure. "Oh, *so* good."

"Sai is going to be a veterinarian," added Darsh.

"Does Emilia know what she wants to be yet?" asked Diya.

Anna had demurred on something alcoholic and was now wishing she hadn't. "She's keeping her options open."

"Drummer," Sam said. "Obviously."

"Massive groupie future," added Max.

Anna looked between them, uncertain how she was meant to respond to that.

Luckily the doorbell rang at that moment.

Sam moved down the hallway, and they all sat in awkward silence listening to him greet Pen from down the street, who had apparently brought vegan brownies to the party.

Anna hadn't brought anything. She wondered if everyone else had brought something. Well, there was a big bowl of what looked like Indian food so obviously Diya had made something. Diya was *always* making something. It was a lot easier to do things like that when you were home all day instead of working desperately to keep enough money in the bank account.

"Hello, everyone!" Pen said, coming into the kitchen, practically bouncing.

Pen had way too much energy, thought Anna, always running around the street the way she did.

And then Pen went around hugging and kissing everyone, like *that* was necessary, like they'd met more than once or twice before in their entire lives.

Then Pen sat down and said, "Isn't this cozy? Your house is lovely, Sam."

"Thank you," Sam said. "That's nice of you to say."

"I am so excited about this party," Pen said. "I feel like we coexist with each other every day and never get to *talk*. How *is* everyone?"

Everyone stared at Pen.

Sam said eventually, "I'm fine," which provoked a chorus of everyone else agreeing that yes, they were also fine.

"Terrible weather," added Arthur.

"But sun in a few days," tacked on Max.

Sam said, "I think I am going to go grill."

"In the rain?" asked Pen.

"Yup," said Sam, and then, lucky devil, escaped outside into the storm.

Teddy was good at *Mass Extinction Event*.

Sai wasn't bad.

"You're not bad," Teddy told him.

Sai lifted his eyebrows and said, "I'm brilliant at this game."

Pari sat in the corner and refused to talk.

Emilia came in and said, "Hello, Teddy. Hello, Pari. Hello, Sai, I'm Emilia, nice to meet you," and, smiling, held out her hand.

Sai grinned and said, "Nice to meet you, too. I think I've seen you around the street before. What house do you live in?"

"Oh," said Emilia, "the prettiest one."

"Of course," said Sai.

"But you should know: I have a boyfriend."

"I bet he's a pretty great boyfriend."

Emilia lifted one shoulder in a shrug and said, "He's okay. He has a terrible haircut."

Sai laughed. "It's okay. I have a girlfriend, only she's very cheeky."

Emilia whacked the back of his head in that gentle, glancing way she had that was more like a caress. Not that Pari seemed to understand that.

The new kid, Teddy, said, without taking his eyes off the television screen, "I don't know what's going on with the two of you but I just killed fifteen of your species."

"Oh, bugger," said Sai, and remembered he was supposed to be playing a video game.

One thing Sam was confident of was his ability to grill properly. It was why he'd chosen a barbecue as the party theme. He'd thought it was brilliant until he'd found himself getting soaked as he flipped hamburgers. But, whatever, it gave him a reprieve from having to come up with conversational topics. He should have made a list of conversational topics when he was preparing for this party. He should have done that instead of working on the failed beetroot salad. It would have been way more useful.

Sam took a deep breath and went back inside with a plate piled high with hamburgers and cheeseburgers and hot dogs, and for a little while everyone happily raided them and topped them off with crisps. The children came downstairs and

Pari and Teddy appeared to still not be speaking, but they also weren't actively attacking each other, so Sam supposed that was a good thing.

Everyone perched wherever they could with their food and Sam thought again how this all would have worked out much better if they could have been outside, where there was actual *space*.

"So," said Max, and Sam was grateful at Max's apparent penchant for launching conversational topics. He'd saved the party a couple of times already by suddenly bringing up a new television show or one of the shops on the high street or the latest Bollywood film that he'd seen. Sam was incredibly grateful for him. If Sam were gay, he'd try to steal Max from Arthur, he thought. A person like Max was useful to have around. "What's it like living next to the old man next door?"

Sam would not have chosen that conversational topic, but he supposed it was something better than sitting around in silence staring at each other as they ate. He said, "Mr. Hammersley, you mean?"

Which made everyone look up at him like he'd said something extraordinary.

Sam blinked. ". . . Isn't that his name?" He could have sworn that was what Teddy called him.

"How do you know his name?" asked Pen.

"What?" Sam said, confused. "I don't know.

Teddy found it out." Everyone turned to look at Teddy, who looked startled at the sudden attention, and Sam immediately regretted dragging him into the spotlight like this.

"He never talks to *anybody*," Pen said. "I tried to take him some vegan brownies when I first moved in and he basically slammed the door in my face."

"You took an old man vegan brownies?" asked Arthur.

"They taste just like normal brownies," said Pen, and turned to Teddy. "So tell us your secret, Teddy: how did you find out his name?"

"It's because Teddy's trying to steal Jack from all of us," said Pari, suddenly deciding to speak for the first time all day.

Sam frowned at her.

At least Diya said, "Pari, that's not—"

"I'm not," Teddy said. "*You're* trying to steal Jack."

"Okay," Sam said, stepping in. "Nobody's trying to steal Jack—"

"Steal Jack from who?" asked Pen.

"Exactly," Pari said swiftly. "Jack belongs to all of us."

"Exactly," agreed Teddy, and they glared at each other.

"Jack doesn't belong to us," said Anna immediately. "We have cats, and Jack terrorizes the cats."

"And Jack doesn't belong to us," said Diya. "I don't like dogs."

"*Mum,*" complained Pari. "What about Sai being a vet?"

"He's going to be an exotic vet," said Diya. "He's going to work at a zoo. He doesn't need to have a dog in the house."

"It isn't safe to have that dog wandering around," said Anna to Sam. "You should really keep him on a leash, or inside, or something."

Sam said, "He isn't *my* dog."

"Dad," protested Teddy.

"This is his house," Anna pointed out. "That makes him your dog."

"Okay, hang on," said Sam, getting a little annoyed, because he didn't understand how he was now responsible for the family who'd lived there before him abandoning their dog. "I don't understand how he ended up here anyway. What sort of people leave their dog behind when they move?"

Everyone basically shrugged.

"We didn't really know the Thurstons very well," said Max.

"Having 'street parties' wasn't a thing until very recently," said Anna—rather pointedly, Sam thought.

"Well," said Sam, deciding he didn't really want to row with his neighbors over this, "I think the dog probably belongs to Mr. Hammersley.

To the extent he belongs to anyone," he added hastily, upon seeing Teddy's hurt look.

That was, of course, when Jack showed up at the back door and leaned his front paws up against it and wagged his tail to be let in.

There was a moment of silence, into which Jack barked happily, oblivious of the drama he was causing.

"We should let him in," Teddy said. "It's raining on him." Sam agreed, but glanced at Diya, who Sam knew really didn't like dogs.

Diya, seeing his look, said stiffly, "It's fine. I just don't want him attacking me."

"Jack doesn't *attack*, Mum," said Pari.

Sam walked over to the door and let Jack in.

Jack greeted him with a soaking wet rubbing against his jeans. *Lovely,* Sam thought. "Hello, Jack," he said to him. "Are you bringing Mr. Hammersley with you?"

"Mr. Hammersley is definitely *not* a party person," said Anna.

"Yeah, he didn't seem too delighted at the invitation," Sam admitted ruefully, watching Jack make the rounds of greeting everyone in the room like old friends.

"I feel bad for him," Pen said. "He's got to be lonely. I never see anyone go over to visit him. Except for Jack."

"Well, you invited him to the party," Darsh said. "You can lead a horse to water but you can't teach him how to fish. No, how does that saying go again?"

Sam was busy watching Teddy and Pari have a silent but furious battle over who got to have Jack's head in their lap. He decided the best thing to do at this point was fetch a towel to try to dry Jack off.

In the awkward lull between the hot dogs and hamburgers and trying to decide when he should put the biscuits and Jaffa Cakes and brownies out and maybe offer to make tea and coffee for everyone, Sam ensconced Teddy and Pari with Jack and a towel in the lounge and hoped that no bloodshed would result.

Generally you could hear them quarreling about who was doing a better job of teaching Jack how to roll over, and that was at least evidence they were both alive, thought Sam, so he left them to it.

Emilia said, "So, Sai, you're going to be a vet?"

Sai ruffled at his hair and said, "Yeah . . ."

"He's going to shadow a veterinarian we know," Diya said proudly.

Emilia looked at Sai. "Oh, you are?"

"Yeah . . ." said Sai again.

The whole interaction felt awkward to Sam, so he said jovially, as he started putting the food to the side, "Can I make everyone tea? Coffee?"

There were a couple of affirmative responses and then the doorbell rang.

"Maybe it's Mr. Hammersley," suggested Max.

Sam, curious at the possibility, went to the door and opened it.

It was not Mr. Hammersley. It was a blond-haired man about Sam's age, and Sam said uncertainly, "Hello?"

The man smiled and said, "Hello, I'm Marcel Pachuta. Anna's husband."

"Oh," said Sam, surprised, because Anna had given him the impression that her husband wasn't coming. "Hello. I'm Sam Bishop."

He shook Marcel's offered hand and tried not to feel like he was being sized up.

Marcel said, "Is my wife still here?"

"Yeah, we're in the back," Sam said, gesturing Marcel inside. "I was just about to make tea and coffee." He led Marcel into the kitchen.

Anna said in surprise, "Marcel."

"Hello, everyone." Marcel smiled and waved and sat down directly next to Anna.

There was a general chorus of hellos.

Diya said, "Are you feeling better?"

"Better?" echoed Marcel.

"Anna said you were under the weather," Diya said.

Marcel said, "Did she? Well. Yes. I'm better."

Sam didn't know what to make of that conversation, either, so he decided instead to say, "Anyone want any biscuits? Or Jaffa Cakes? Or vegan brownies?"

Marcel said, "So, Sam. You've just moved in."

"Yes," affirmed Sam. "Thought I'd have everybody over to say hi."

"It's just you?" asked Marcel.

"My son and me. Teddy. He's in the other room."

As if to prove his existence, Teddy's voice in the lounge shouted, "No, no, that is *not* how you roll over, Pari!"

"He feels very strongly about rolling over," said Sam.

Marcel said, far too innocently, "No wife?"

Sam paused and looked at him and felt his hackles rise a bit. Because, really, it was fairly rude to come into someone's house and start quizzing them on their personal situation. He glanced to Arthur and Max and said, "How do you know I don't have a husband?"

Everyone looked at him.

Sam confessed, "I *don't* have a husband. And I had a wife, but she died."

Which led to another awkward pause.

So Sam said, "Tell us, Pen, what made you decide to become vegan?"

Everyone seemed more than willing to let him change the subject.

Pen said, "Oh, I looked into it for an article I was writing. And once I looked into it, I never went back. Writing is like that. I did a piece on bumblebees and I had to go and replant my garden with bumblebee-friendly flowers. The plight of the bumblebee is *intense* and *worrying*. Did you know it takes two million flowers to make a single pound of honey? It is environmentally vital that we help the bumblebees out."

Everyone seemed impressed with Pen's level of passion.

Max said, "You must learn a lot of random facts in your line of work."

Pen said, "You have no idea. The last article I wrote was about the evolution of the penis. You lot are *weird*."

The Basaks were the first to leave. Diya had somewhere to be; it sounded very complicated. They thanked Sam for the party and refused to take any of their pakoras home with them. They did take Pari home with them, which Sam was a little relieved about. Teddy sat with Jack on the floor of the lounge and looked triumphant, but Sam couldn't help feeling a bit sorry for the little girl who loved the dog, too, but whose mother really hated him.

The Pachutas left directly after the Basaks, and Sam tried to pretend they didn't look relieved to be getting out of there.

Max was engaged in a deep conversation with Pen about the evolution of the penis. He kept exclaiming, "Really? Fascinating!" And "Darling, did you know that?" Arthur was nowhere near him, instead putting dishes away in Sam's kitchen, but he kept calling back to him, "Hmm, very interesting."

"Don't you want to go over there and hear about how your penis evolved?" Sam asked him, as he joined him in the kitchen.

"I do not," said Arthur. "As long as it works, I don't want to know anything more about it. What can I help you put away here?"

Sam smiled and shook his head. "Don't worry about it. Thank you for coming."

"Thank you for having us. It was very nice of you to do."

"I get the impression this was an unusual amount of socializing for this street."

"We kind of keep to ourselves," Arthur admitted. "I mean, we're friendly, and polite, and nice. But yeah. My husband feeds Jack, too. Just so you know. I'm fairly sure that dog eats at every house."

"Dogs are the most skillful con artists," said Sam.

Arthur smiled and glanced outside and then said, "Max, there's a brief break in the rain. I think we should make a run for it."

"If you think so," said Max, standing and saying to Pen, "This was fascinating and you should feel free to stop by anytime and distract me from painting."

Sam liked this. He thought maybe he'd done at least a little bit of good with this party.

"This is going to be dangerous," Pen said, "because I am always looking for something to distract me from writing."

"You can join us in the procrastinating work situation, Sam," Max said, shaking his hand as he prepared to leave.

"I can just send an eight-year-old boy over your way," said Sam. "He's a pretty effective distracting machine."

"I'll take off, too. Thank you for this lovely party." Pen gave Sam a warm hug. "We should talk more often. After all, we all have a mutual interest in Jack the street dog."

"Yeah," said Sam, and saw them off, and then turned back to Teddy and Jack. "Well?" he said. "What did you think? Success?" Jack barked and wagged his tail. Sam interpreted this as *Yes! Success!*

"Could have been better," Teddy said. "Could have been worse."

"Can't actually argue with that," said Sam. "But I prefer Jack's take. Jack thought it went well."

"Jack thought there should have been more squirrels for him to chase. Do you feel like you made any friends?"

Sam thought of the last interaction between him and Max and Arthur and Pen and said, "Maybe. Possibly. What about you?"

Teddy gave him a look.

"Sai seemed nice," Sam said.

"He's sixteen, Dad."

That was a fair point. Sam said, "What about Pari?"

"Pari kept telling me she's 'at war' with me."

Sam sighed. "I think it's hard for Pari. Her mother doesn't like Jack very much, and Jack was mostly hers before we showed up."

"She's trying to steal him. I think he should be everyone's."

The Pari situation might be an irreconcilable issue, thought Sam. "Well, at least school is starting soon. You'll make friends there."

Teddy looked dubious.

Sam left him to his dubiousness. And, because he was determined to stay hopeful about things, Sam, feeling beneficent, decided to take some food over to Mr. Hammersley and tell him how much he'd been missed. Maybe Pen was right and he *was* lonely.

So Sam made up a plate and then said, "Come on, Jack." Jack had been snoring loudly by Teddy but he got up immediately upon hearing his name, stretching extravagantly and snuffling.

Teddy said, "Where are you going?"

"I'm going to bring Mr. Hammersley a plate of food, and Jack."

"Dad," Teddy began to complain.

"We've had him all day," Sam said, heading off the protest. "And he's not actually our dog. He's the street dog. He'll miss Mr. Hammersley and Mr. Hammersley will miss him."

"Fine," grumbled Teddy.

"Come along," Sam said to Jack, and Jack obediently followed him out and over to Mr. Hammersley's house. The rain had let up. It wasn't exactly nice out but it seemed less far-fetched that there would be sun soon.

Sam rang Mr. Hammersley's doorbell and waited for him to open the door.

Which he did with a snapped out, "Now what?"

It wasn't exactly that Sam had expected a warm welcome, but, well, he'd really done nothing to merit outright rudeness.

Sam forced his face into bland pleasantness and said politely, "Hello. We missed you at the party."

"I didn't want to go to your party," replied Mr. Hammersley belligerently.

Which made it difficult to continue to be blandly pleasant, but Sam gritted his teeth and took a deep breath and then forced another smile. "Well, I've brought Jack back to you—"

"You don't need to keep bringing Jack back," Mr. Hammersley said. "He's not my dog."

Even though Jack had trotted into Mr. Hammersley's house and disappeared.

"No, I understand, he's the street dog. Belongs to everyone," said Sam.

"I don't want Jack to become my problem," Mr. Hammersley grumbled.

"He's not a problem," Sam said patiently. "He's a dog. Anyway, I brought you a plate of food—"

"I don't want any of your rubbish food," snapped Mr. Hammersley.

Which turned out to be Sam's tipping point. Because maybe the food *was* rubbish, but he was just trying to be nice, and he'd spent all day trying to make friends, and he was exhausted with the effort, and Mr. Hammersley not meeting him halfway was the last straw.

"You know," said Sam, taking a deep breath. "I'm just trying to be nice. I have tried to be nice ever since I got here. I am trying to be nice, and hopeful, and not worry that uprooting my son to move an ocean away was the worst mistake I ever made. And you are being rude and making it very difficult for me to pretend like this is a good place for us to be living."

Mr. Hammersley stared at him in shock.

Sam, feeling satisfied, turned and marched away.

Pari was crying on her bed when Diya finally got home from her commitments.

"Where have you been?" Darsh hissed when she got in.

Diya was confused. "I told you, I had to go to Shanaya's, and then Saanvi had a niece who really needed help setting up a nursery, and then I had to stop at Anika's to check about the veterinarian thing for Sai—"

"Pari is heartbroken over the dog thing."

Diya sighed. "Still? You know we can't have a dog. I hate dogs. And, anyway, it seems to me that street dog belongs to either the new people or the old man. It spends most of its time with one of them."

"I agree with all of that," Darsh said. "But our daughter is still upstairs brokenhearted."

"And what have you said to her?"

"That you'd talk to her when you got home," said Darsh hopefully.

Diya sighed and went upstairs to deal with Pari.

Who hiccuped when she saw her and said, "But it's horrible. That horrid boy is going to steal Jack and I'll never see him again." Pari buried her face into Diya's chest, sobbing.

"Surely not. I'm sure he'll let you see Jack." Diya smoothed down Pari's hair and felt terrible about the fact that she just didn't like dogs. "We can't have a dog, but what if I let you go and spend the day with Sai at the veterinarian's? Would you like that?"

Pari stopped crying. She looked up, her face tearstained and blotchy. "Could I do that?"

"Would you like to?"

Pari nodded.

Diya said, "Then I'll ask Anika to ask her cousin about it."

• • •

Mum and Dad were having a row, about the party, the new neighbor, the trip to the seaside, money, work.

Emilia put her headphones on and sat at her drums and played.

She played until she couldn't hear them arguing anymore. She played until her brain focused away from them.

Unfortunately, it didn't focus on the drums. It focused on Sai, shadowing a vet. Which was fantastic for him, if that was what Sai wanted, but it was what Emilia worried about: that Sai would wake up to life outside the street, to all the girls he could have who were prettier than Emilia, cleverer than Emilia.

That Sai would leave, too, and then it would just be Emilia, and a drum set, and her parents, arguing endlessly.

Emilia crashed her sticks against her cymbals and let the vibration carry through her body. She closed her eyes and imagined she could ride the vibrations directly out into the sky.

They got ready for bed in silence, which wasn't unusual for them. They were used to each other, and there wasn't always much to say by this point in the evening.

Max looked across at Arthur, who was brushing his teeth, and then said, finally breaking the silence, "Dreadful weather we're having."

Arthur spat into the sink and grinned and said, "But I hear we're supposed to get sun in a few days' time."

Max laughed and said, "It was an odd party, wasn't it? But I learned a lot about penis evolution."

"I don't want to know anything about that. It's weird that that was a topic of conversation at the party."

"Better than the bloody weather again, Christ," said Max.

"I'm glad we went, for the neighbors' sake, but it was painful in many places."

"It confirmed that, of all people on the street, I'm glad you're the one I live with."

"High praise, indeed," said Arthur.

Pen got into bed and pulled her laptop onto her lap and opened up her blog.

Well! she wrote. **First street party out of the way! It rained buckets, of course, and we all had to huddle inside. Much has been learned about the neighbors. There was mild drama in that Indian Family and Polish Family tried to each prove they're better at raising children. Polish Couple seems uncomfortable with each**

other. Not sure what's happening there. Indian Little Girl and New Neighbor Boy are fighting over Jack the street dog. No one seems to know Indian Teenager and Polish Teenager are dating. They pretended not to know each other. It was frankly hilarious and I enjoyed it. Found out Blond Gay Man is an artist. Definitely plan to bother him at least daily, as have been encouraged to procrastinate with him. Old Man did not come to the party, but Jack did. He was his usual charming self, except that Indian Woman doesn't like him. Poor Jack. I noticed that New Neighbor Boy slid him some crisps. I must explain to New Neighbor Boy that I have Jack on a strict all-natural diet.

Bill lay awake in his bed and stared up at the ceiling. He wasn't especially tired, but there was nothing on the telly and there was nothing else to do.

Which meant that he had nothing to do but contemplate how silent the house was around him. How silent the room was around him. He missed the time when there had been another person in the bed, breathing with him. He missed the time when the parties that happened on the street were ones attended by people he knew, and people who knew him, and not people who saw him as the old man who needed to be brought pity food at the end.

Jack didn't usually sleep on the bed, but Bill didn't argue when he suddenly came into the room, claws clacking on the wood, and leaped up beside Bill. He curled up next to him, warm and solid.

Bill put a hand on Jack's back and said, "Hello, Jack."

Jack did nothing, but Jack breathed, and that was enough.

It took Sam what felt like hours to right his house after the disruption of the party. He had just collapsed onto the sofa when Ellen rang.

"Hello," he answered.

"Hello! Tell me everything about the party! How was it?"

"It poured," Sam said.

"Please tell me you didn't make everyone stand outside in the rain."

"Of course I didn't," said Sam. "We all sat awkwardly around the kitchen making awkward conversation."

"Oh, dear. See, you should have had a band. Dancing would have solved that."

"Where would I have fitted a band in here? I could barely fit all the guests in here."

"A D-list celeb would have helped, too."

"I couldn't even get the old man to come."

Sam heard how glum he sounded and cursed himself.

Ellen must have heard it, too. "Oh, Sam. Don't be so down on yourself. I'm sure it wasn't as bad as all that."

"It wasn't," Sam said. "I'm just tired. And it was just . . . not quite what I expected. I mean, everyone came, but it was awkward and no one really knew what to do and I failed at making the grated beetroot salad. I was definitely not impressive."

"I'm sure you were impressive," Ellen said soothingly. "How did Teddy do?"

"Well, he played video games with the teenage boy who came, so I suppose that's something. But the little girl says she is 'at war' with him. It's very charming."

"At war with him?" echoed Ellen.

"Over Jack. That bloody dog, he's causing a lot of problems."

"He also makes Teddy happy," Ellen reminded him.

"Yeah, there is that."

"So what about you? Did you make any friends? Any available women?"

Sam thought about the woman with the carrots at the supermarket. He said, "It was a party, not a speed-dating event.

"I just thought I'd check. You do sound tired. You should get some sleep. Tomorrow the girls and I will come over and we can drink and they can finish up the spikes on your ceiling."

"I said no to the spikes on the ceiling," said Sam.

"Oh, did you?" said Ellen. "You'll have to tell them that tomorrow. Bye, love!"

Ellen ended the call.

"Cheeky," Sam mumbled under his breath. He was apparently getting spikes on his ceiling.

He sprawled on his sofa and closed his eyes and listened to Emilia playing the drums next door.

Chapter 6

Dear Mr. Bishop,

We invite you and Theodore to visit us at Turtledove Primary School! Theodore's form teacher, Miss Quinn, will be present to answer any questions, as will I. We look forward to assisting you and Theodore in smoothing Theodore's transition, and welcoming Theodore to Turtledove! Coo coo!

David Sullivan, Head Teacher

"What's this?" asked Ellen, pulling the invitation off Sam's fridge.

"Why are you always spying on what I put on my fridge?" asked Sam.

"If you didn't want me to spy on it, you wouldn't leave it out. 'Coo coo'?"

"Yeah, I think it's the sound that turtledoves make. Get it?"

"I think they should rethink that as a school sign-off," said Ellen.

"I think I will not say that in the meeting because I think that I want Teddy's teachers to like me."

"You were always like that, you know," Ellen said, brandishing the piece of paper at Sam like a weapon.

"Like what?"

"Always wanting to make sure people liked you."

Sam tilted his head. "You say that like it's a terrible thing."

"I guess it doesn't have to be. But it can be if you deny who you really are in order to please others."

Sam sighed as he finished emptying the dishwasher. "Ellen. It's a stupid cutesy sign-off. It has nothing to do with denying who I really am."

"Just making sure," said Ellen, as Jack showed up at the back door, tail wagging. "Oh, look," Ellen said. "Your dog is here."

Sam sighed again and let Jack in and called for Teddy. "Teddy! Jack is here for dinner! Hello, Jack."

"Jack comes for dinner every night?" asked Ellen.

"I'm fairly certain Jack shows up for dinner every night at every house on the street. But I've told Teddy if he wants to pretend Jack is his responsibility, then he has to feed him every night."

"How's that working out?" asked Ellen.

"He comes if I shout for him long enough. Teddy!"

"Coming, coming!" called Teddy, thundering down the stairs. "Hi, Jack!"

Jack bounced happily all over Teddy in his usual greeting.

Teddy went about filling Jack's dog bowl with Jack's food.

Ellen looked at Sam. "He has a dog bowl. And food."

"He does," Sam agreed.

Jack trotted over to the shelf where Sam kept a squeaky toy squirrel for him, because Teddy had insisted, and picked it up and trotted back to his food and put it next to him.

Ellen said, "He has a toy. On a special shelf."

"He does," Sam agreed.

Ellen looked back at Teddy and said, "So. Teddy. I hear you're going to meet your new teacher. Coo coo."

Teddy looked dark as he put Jack's food away. Jack meanwhile attacked the food as if he'd never eaten before in his life, even though Sam would bet money he'd just eaten at at least two other houses on the street. He said, "I don't know why I have to go *special by myself* to meet the teacher."

"I keep telling you: it isn't a punishment. They're trying to be nice and friendly."

Teddy gave him his why-am-I-surrounded-by-hopeless-grown-ups face. "I have to go to school, before it starts, and meet with a teacher. It's punishment."

"He has a point," said Ellen.

"You're not helping," Sam told her.

Ellen looked unrepentant.

Jack came running back over to Teddy, licking his face in gratitude for the food.

Teddy brightened, grinning, and said, "All done already, Jack? Maybe you can stay over, sleep here tonight?" He looked at Sam hopefully.

"No," said Sam. "You know Mr. Hammersley will miss him if he spends the night here."

Teddy's face fell and he obediently let Jack out, then trudged up the stairs back to his bedroom.

Sam remarked, "The sad thing is, I don't even know if Mr. Hammersley cares if Jack shows up every night, and maybe we should just take over responsibility for Jack, but also Jack is the street dog and I feel like I made enough waves trying to have a party and make everyone be friends."

"So everyone isn't friends now?"

"Well, we wave to each other when we see each other in the street. But we did that before."

"You should make friends online," said Ellen. "That's what most people do."

"I could hang out with Mr. Hammersley. He's home all the time, except—oh, wait, I kind of snapped at him when he insulted my party food."

Ellen blinked at him. "I thought Mr. Hammersley didn't come to the party."

"He didn't. I thought I would be a nice neighbor and bring him a plate of food. It didn't go over well."

Ellen gave him a sympathetic look and then said, "Aww, my little brother, do you need a hug?"

"No," denied Sam. Then, "Okay, I'll take a hug."

Ellen grinned and gave him a hug. "You've been here less than a month. You're doing fine."

"Thanks." Sam released the hug and put the kettle on. "I'm seriously considering getting Teddy a puppy, since the thing with Jack is weird and he seems to like dogs so much."

"A puppy? I thought you didn't even want Jack because it was too much to take care of."

"It's true," Sam said. "But, I don't know. . . . Did you see the look on Teddy's face just now when he saw Jack? I like that look. I'd like to get that look on his face more often."

Ellen smiled softly at him and said, "I don't blame you. It's a cute look. Now you know why I pester you about dating."

"What? No, that's a different thing."

"It isn't at all. He looks like you, and that look on his face is what you look like when you're happy, and I like that look on you, and I kind of miss it. You'd like that look on his face more often? Now you know how I feel."

Sam considered Ellen, and thought how, well, put that way, he had a hard time arguing with her. He took a deep breath and said, "I've been here less than a month. At least let me get Teddy into school before I start going on terrible dates."

"And when will you start going on spectacular dates?"

"Is that a thing that happens? I've never once been on a spectacular date."

Ellen gave him a look. "You were *married.*"

"Yeah, we didn't date."

"Of course you dated."

"Not like that. We were in the same group of friends and then we were like, 'Hey, we like each other,' and then we got married."

"Don't tell women that story. That makes you sound like the least romantic man on the planet. How did you ever get Sara to marry you?"

"Green card issues," deadpanned Sam.

"You're a horrible man," said Ellen. "No wonder you never had spectacular dates."

It wasn't that Sam was nervous about meeting Teddy's teachers. But it *was* that Sam wanted to make a good impression. It hadn't bothered him in years that his hair wouldn't lie flat—why would that bother a grown man?—but he felt suddenly the way he had when he'd been Teddy's age, with his mother futilely running a wet comb through his hair and despairing of his ability to look *serious.*

"Look serious," Sam told his reflection in the mirror. Maybe he needed reading glasses. That would help.

Sam wanted to ask Teddy if he thought a suit was overkill for meeting Teddy's teachers, and then he thought it wasn't fair to drag Teddy into Sam's ridiculousness, so he pulled himself together and decided on jeans and a shirt, which he thought walked the line of "I respect your station as teachers of my child, but I am also a chill, relaxed, fun person who won't be stirring up any trouble."

"Bloody hell, pull yourself together," Sam told himself under his breath, swiped at his hair uselessly one last time, and then went to collect Teddy.

Teddy looked roughly as enthusiastic as if Sam were coming to collect him to get a root canal.

"Let's pretend to be a child who knows how to smile," Sam suggested.

"I just hate this," Teddy complained. "We never had to do this at home."

"This is home now," Sam reminded him.

"No, it's not. It's just the place where I'm *different*. I'm so *different* I have to go talk specially to the teachers without any of the other kids. Everyone knows how *different* I am as soon as I open up my mouth. That's what this place is."

Sam looked down at him and took a deep breath. Because if he was nervous and he was the *parent,* he couldn't imagine how Teddy felt.

Sam crouched down to be on Teddy's level.

Teddy looked at him, mouth drawn tight in displeasure.

And Sam said, "You're amazing."

Teddy's mouth twisted in even greater displeasure. "Dad—"

"No. I'm not saying that because I'm your dad. I'm not even saying that because it's a pep talk. I'm saying that because I'm not sure I could have done at your age what you've had to do at your age. You're amazing. And good things are right in front of us, right? Right around the corner. I bet you are going to have a fabulous teacher and you'll go to school and everyone will find your accent super-exotic. And you'll get all the girls. Or boys. However you roll. It's all good."

"Dad, I'm eight," said Teddy, but he said it in his my-dad-is-so-ridiculous voice, and that voice was better than the deep displeasure that had just been creasing his expression.

"Oh," Sam said. "Right. That means I can still do this to you," and pulled him into a tight cuddle. And then he said, "How'd you like to get a dog?"

Teddy pulled away from the hug, eyes wide and bright. "Jack?" he asked eagerly.

"No. Jack's the street dog. A different dog. A new dog just for you."

Teddy looked confused. "But . . . Jack is my dog. I just want Jack."

"Jack's the street dog."

"Right. And that's what's great about him. Jack belongs to all of us. He's the only thing that belongs to all of us. I don't want to take him away from that. He *likes* belonging to the whole street. I just want him to get to stay at our house, too, sometimes, if he wants. I don't want to change him. I don't want something new. Everything I have is new."

Jack was new, too, but Sam didn't point that out. Sam supposed that, relatively, Jack was the oldest thing Teddy had right now. Jack and Bob the flamingo.

"Okay," said Sam. "I'll go talk to Mr. Hammersley about if we can keep Jack sometimes." He wasn't looking forward to it, but he'd go do it.

They met Pen on their way to the school. She jogged in place, her hair bouncing on her head, and panted, "Hiya, you two! Where are you off to?"

"Teddy is going to meet his teacher and take a tour of his new school," Sam said.

"Fun!" Pen said brightly. "Can't wait to hear all about it!" As if they got together for coffee all the time. She jogged off with a wave.

Teddy said, "*That* was embarrassing. Let's not tell too many people I'm doing this. I don't want the whole street to know."

Sam shook his head and rolled his eyes.

174

But that was why, when they met Diya Basak and her two children, he said preemptively, "Teddy and I are just walking around. No destination in mind. Just wandering."

Which made them sound like they were casing joints to rob or something equally suspicious. Teddy gave him a look that said that his stupidity had surpassed even the levels that Teddy expected him to achieve.

Diya Basak, after a second, said, "Well, I am taking the children to shadow a veterinarian. Sai wants to be a veterinarian."

Sai looked roughly as happy to be shadowing a vet as Teddy did about going to school.

Pari looked excited, though. She said to Teddy, "I am going with him and I am going to see *lots* of dogs and cats."

"Good for you," Teddy retorted.

"Lovely seeing you," Sam said brightly, and moved Teddy off before a brawl could break out right in the middle of the street. "You two really need to call a truce."

"We just don't like each other."

"Couldn't you make an effort? Be a little less belligerent?"

"Not everyone needs to like everyone else, Dad," said Teddy. Sam heard Ellen telling him that he needed to have everyone like him, and thought maybe there was truth to that, and maybe Teddy had a point.

They met no more neighbors and arrived at the school, where David Sullivan met them.

He was wearing a suit. *Damn it,* thought Sam.

"You must be Mr. Bishop," said David Sullivan, shaking his hand.

"Please, it's just Sam," said Sam.

"And this must be Theodore." David smiled at Teddy and held out his hand.

Teddy shook it and said, "Teddy, please," and didn't say it rudely, so that was good.

"Welcome to Turtledove," said David. "Coo coo."

Sam looked uncertain. Was he supposed to say it back?

"Yeah, I know, it's ridiculous," said David. "The teachers are always telling me I have to stop saying it. Anyway, let's walk down to your classroom and meet your teacher, and you can stay with her, Teddy, and she'll tell you a bit about the structure of the class, and you and I, Sam, can go over some of the information we need to know to ensure Teddy's smooth transition."

"Sounds good," said Sam, unreasonably panicking that maybe he wouldn't know all of the necessary information, which was ridiculous, but being back in a school was making him flash back to not having properly studied for exams.

The school was a lovely old building, and Sam liked how bright it was, how large the windows were, letting in light in every classroom they passed. It would be a pleasant place to go to school, Sam thought. He was happy with it. Teddy would like it here. He had a good feeling about this place.

It was just as he was thinking about what a good feeling he had about the place that they turned the corner into the classroom and David Sullivan said something like, "Teddy, this is your teacher, Miss Quinn," but Sam wasn't really paying attention anymore, because the woman sitting behind the desk, with her dark red hair pinned into place with a pencil, was the woman he'd last seen brandishing a carrot and walking away from him in a supermarket.

Sam had been to the supermarket since then, of course. He had always experienced a small anticipatory thrill that he might run into the woman again. He had also always experienced a sick feeling of dread that maybe he would meet the woman again and she wouldn't remember him. From the shocked look on the woman's face, she definitely remembered him.

They looked at each other and said, in perfect unison, "It's you."

David Sullivan looked between them, looking infinitely pleased. "Oh, good, you already know each other."

"Not really," said Sam dazedly. "She likes carrots."

"He was negotiating with beetroot," said

Teddy's teacher, not taking her eyes off Sam. Which was really rather nice, and it was really rather annoying that her *boss* was here and they were supposed to be doing something official and helpful relating to his son.

"I'm sorry?" said David quizzically.

Which seemed to break the woman out of the moment. She broke eye contact and shook her head and stood and said, "I'm sorry. Where are my manners?" And then she looked at Teddy and smiled brightly and held out her hand and said, "I'm Miss Quinn."

"I'm Teddy," Teddy said. He looked endlessly amused by this whole situation.

"Very nice to meet you," Miss Quinn said.

"I'm Teddy's dad," inserted Sam.

"I assumed." She offered her hand. "Nice to meet you as well." Sam would have liked to imagine that there was a spark as their skin touched, but actually they were standing in a primary school classroom in front of her boss and his son, which had a dampening effect on sparks.

David seemed to decide that he was just going to ignore how oddly they were behaving. "Well, Teddy, Miss Quinn will answer any questions you have about the classroom." David turned to Sam. "And you and I should go and do our boring paperwork now."

"Right," Sam said. "Yes. The paperwork. Let's do that."

• • •

Libby Quinn watched Beetroot Man walk out of her classroom. He glanced over his shoulder at her as he left. And she looked from him to his son, who looked a great deal like him: same unruly sandy hair, same eyes trapped between blue and green, slightly more freckles across the nose.

"Teddy," she said, deciding the best thing to do right now was to be completely professional and stop behaving like she'd never seen an attractive man before. "Welcome to Turtledove."

"My mum's dead," was how Teddy responded to that.

Libby blinked. "I'm sorry to hear that."

"In case you were wondering if my dad was single. He's, like, *very* single."

The thing about this conversation was that, unfortunately, it wasn't exactly *unusual*. She had lots of divorcees in her classroom parents. She was frequently the subject of matchmaking efforts. And she had a standard response to matchmaking efforts. She said, "That is very sweet of you, but my heart is too full of my students for anyone else." Which wasn't true. Which was a lie. But she usually didn't feel how much of a lie it was because she usually didn't run into the man she'd been unable to get out of her head in the middle of her classroom. She usually didn't meet men she was unable to get out of her head.

Teddy Bishop, as he was listed on her classroom roll, looked exactly as dubious at that claim of hers as he should have.

She cleared her throat, feeling self-conscious, and pulled at the chain she wore around her neck, twisting the charm on it. It was a habit she had, that she did constantly, and she knew it but she couldn't help it.

She said, "Well, we're here to answer any questions you might have about the classroom. So let's get to it, shall we? What can I tell you?"

Sai Basak could not remember a time before Emilia moved to the street. Their families didn't really talk, but Sai was aware of Emilia. And, of course, then they were in school together. And then they were friends. And then they were dating. And Sai knew this was not something his parents would look favorably upon. Sai knew he was supposed to focus on his studies and his future career, *exclusively*. That had been impressed upon him by his parents very firmly: no distractions like girls. But Sai liked Emilia. Sai *loved* Emilia. She was funny and clever and sweet. She was *brilliant*. So Sai had started dating Emilia, in secret, and he'd had the idea of saying he was going to the library and spending every day with Emilia, and that, too, had seemed brilliant, except that now it had ended up with him here, at the vet's office, surrounded by an enormous number of animals.

Pari was asking a million questions and the vet was answering all of them gamely, and then she said, "Actually, we're about to have a look at a sweet pup, if you'd like to see."

And so they were ushered into a small room, and there was a terrier in its owner's lap, and the vet pulled out the most enormous needle Sai had ever seen—

—and that was apparently, he was told later, when he fainted.

Sam forced himself to be serious and responsible and take his time answering all the questions David Sullivan asked him, because, after all, this was about Teddy's education, which meant it was also about Teddy's *future,* and so, really, Sam had to take this seriously.

So he took his time answering, and David gave him an enormous stack of papers that were supposed to be indicative of questions parents might have, and then said, "I'll take you back to Teddy now."

"That's okay," Sam said, probably too hastily. "I can find my way there myself."

David looked surprised, and then didn't. "I'm sure you can. It was nice meeting you, Mr. Bishop."

Which made Sam question momentarily how

many single fathers showed up thinking they had a chance with the lovely Miss Quinn. Probably every single father in London, he thought. So it was therefore unlikely she was about to be charmed by a man who had tried to flirt with her through the medium of *beetroot*.

When Sam reached the classroom, Miss Quinn was sitting on the floor with Teddy, and she had laid cards out between them, and she was saying, with one of those deep-dimple smiles, "No, no, your memory can't possibly be that good, you must be cheating."

Sam wasn't sure if he made a noise to give himself away, but they both looked up at him, so he must have. Miss Quinn scrambled to standing. She, at least, was wearing jeans, so Sam felt more appropriately dressed. And a pretty blue shirt and a necklace with a star pendant that her hand fluttered over as she said, "Oh. Mr. Bishop. All set with David?"

"It's Sam," Sam said. "And yes. Theoretically." He reflected upon the pile of papers in his hands. "I think he's concerned I might have a lot of questions."

Miss Quinn, smile restored, said, "Don't worry. If he's really concerned about your fitness as a parent, he gives you a whole three-ring binder with at least five hundred pages' worth of notes."

"Ah," said Sam. "Then I'm doing well." He looked from Miss Quinn to Teddy and wasn't sure what else to say. So *of course* he brought up beetroot. "I ended up surrendering to the beetroot."

Miss Quinn looked surprised. *Why* did he keep bringing up beetroot with this beautiful woman? She said, "Oh."

"You were right. They were very tough negotiators."

"Did you use bacon?"

"It turned out I didn't have bacon."

"Hard to make beetroot interesting without bacon," said Miss Quinn.

"It turns out, according to Google, that you can substitute feta cheese for bacon, but I wasn't sure it was going to have the same effect. And I didn't have any of that either." Sam thought it would be okay with him if he was just unable to speak from now on in Miss Quinn's presence. He would actually be more alluring if he would *stop talking*.

Teddy was looking horrified at him, which proved just how smooth he was being.

So he said quickly, "Anyway, it was very nice to meet you, and I'm sure we'll see you again lots, well, I mean, Teddy obviously will, he'll see you every day, and maybe we'll see you at the supermarket again, and I hope you enjoyed your carrots."

Miss Quinn looked stunned, and not stunned by his charm.

Sam gave her a quick wave and practically pulled Teddy out of the classroom and outside.

"What was *that?*" Teddy said, staring at him. "That was *horrible.* Why were you talking about *bacon?*"

"I don't know!" Sam said. "I panicked! She's pretty! I like her!"

"How did you ever pull Mom?" asked Teddy, with a pitying shake of his head.

It was Pen who found out that Sai fainted at the vet's, because Pari couldn't wait to tell *someone,* and Pen happened to be outside checking on the flowers she was tending for the bumblebees. And Pen mentioned it to Emilia when she came to bring the rubbish outside because Pen knew Emilia would want to know about Sai.

And that was how Emilia found herself, frantic with worry, knocking on the Basak door before she thought better of it.

Mrs. Basak opened the door and looked at her in surprise. Of course. Because Emilia had never been to this house while an adult had been home.

Emilia tried a nervous smile and tried to come up with a plausible lie for being there. She should have thought this through. "Hiya," she said.

"Hello," Mrs. Basak said, and pointedly waited for her to say something else.

"I, er." Emilia thought desperately of the new, friendlier street the new neighbors were trying to provoke with their parties and socializing. She blurted out, "Mum sent me over here to see if maybe you wanted to meet for coffee sometime."

Mrs. Basak looked even more startled, and then, which was worse, suspicious. "Why?"

Emilia thought of the only thing that her mum and Mrs. Basak had in common. "To talk about kids."

Mrs. Basak didn't look convinced. "And also the street dog," added Emilia, on a whim.

Apparently those were magic words. Mrs. Basak nodded sharply. "Ah, yes, the street dog. Your mother and I *should* discuss the street dog. It simply cannot be wandering around the street. Your mother said it terrorizes the cats, and that's the right word for it: *terrorizing*. I have seen it hunting squirrels."

Emilia thought that was unnecessary. She didn't think Jack terrorized anything, unless with frantic tail-wagging. And she was pretty sure the squirrels hunted Jack, not the other way around. But Emilia also had a more important reason to be at the Basak house. "So, was today the day Sai was going to check out the vet's?" she asked brightly. "That sounded so interesting!"

"He *fainted!*" shouted Pari, practically running to the door to share this news. "He saw the needle and he just *fainted*."

"Is he going to be all right?" asked Emilia anxiously.

"Well, I suppose he will never be a veterinarian now," answered Mrs. Basak. "Or a doctor. Or even a *dentist*. These are dark days indeed."

"Right," said Emilia. "But Sai's okay?"

Mrs. Basak looked suspicious again. "Yes," she said. "Thanks for your concern." And then she closed the door.

But not before Pari nodded and gave her a thumbs-up behind Mrs. Basak's back, so Emilia supposed she felt a little bit better.

Sophie and Evie were trying to solve the problem of getting spikes to hang from Sam's lounge ceiling. Apparently this was more complicated than they'd anticipated.

"They didn't consider that it would be difficult to turn my lounge into a cave?" said Sam.

"This is the first house they've decorated," said Ellen. "There's a learning curve."

"I'm so honored to be their very first client."

"You're very special," agreed Ellen, as Teddy wandered into the kitchen from the lounge. "Teddy! How's it going in there?"

"They might make the ceiling fall down," said Teddy seriously.

"Oh, good," said Sam. "That sounds like it's going well."

"Girls!" Ellen shouted to them. "Don't make the ceiling fall down!"

"We won't!" they chorused back.

"There," Ellen said. "All taken care of. Now. Tell me all about the school. Was it wonderful? Did you like your teacher?"

Teddy brightened. "My teacher's the carrot girl."

"The what?" said Ellen blankly.

Sam decided to become extraordinarily fascinated by the contents of his mostly empty fridge.

"You didn't tell her, Dad?" said Teddy disapprovingly.

"Tell me what?" said Ellen.

"Does mustard expire?" asked Sam, still looking determinedly into his fridge. "I'm afraid our mustard is about to expire."

"Dad met a woman at the supermarket," Teddy said to Ellen.

"Really?" said Ellen, drawing the word out until it had the same amount of syllables as *this is going to be tremendously embarrassing for my little brother*. "Sam, get your head out of the fridge and talk to me. You've been holding out on me!"

Sam, resigned, straightened out of the fridge and closed the door. "I haven't been. I didn't really meet anyone."

"Yes, you did," said Teddy. He looked at Ellen. "He smiled at her like *crazy*."

Ellen smiled at Sam. "Did he now? Tell me more."

"She was going to buy carrots."

"Fascinating," said Ellen.

"Oh, my God," said Sam. "You two are ridiculous."

"This sounds like the maddest first meeting I've ever heard of," said Ellen, "which frankly sounds exactly like your type."

"I don't have a type," said Sam.

"You do have a type. It's 'slightly mad but mostly delightful.' "

"And the carrot woman turns out to be my teacher," finished Teddy.

"Well, this is fantastic!" said Ellen. "This is the most exciting thing I've ever heard!"

"Is it?" said Sam. "Is it really? You have two children. Surely hearing the news that you were going to have children was more exciting than this news."

"That happened so long ago, the thrill has faded," said Ellen. "So are you going to date Teddy's teacher?"

"Not if it's up to him," Teddy said. "He is *horrible* at it, Aunt Ellen."

"So I've heard," Ellen agreed grimly.

"Look, I don't think an eight-year-old is in any position to judge dating abilities," Sam defended himself.

"He kept talking to her about *beetroot*," said Teddy. "Basically every word out of his mouth was about *beetroot*."

Ellen looked blankly at Sam.

Sam covered his face with his hands. "It's true. I just kept babbling about beetroot."

"Wha . . . ?" said Ellen, bewildered. "Is this a thing you do? I've never heard you talk about beetroot before."

"I don't know," Sam said helplessly. "We met in the fruit and veg section. There was this whole . . . *thing,* about beetroot. And now, I don't know, I just keep bringing it up. It's like I don't know what else to talk about. It's like I literally have no other topic of conversation to bring up except for beetroot."

"Good God," said Ellen. "This is serious."

"That's what I said," said Teddy. "It was embarrassing."

"Maybe she likes beetroot talk," said Ellen. "Maybe it's a thing she finds attractive in men?"

"I don't even think I want to date a woman who lists 'beetroot' as an attractive thing," said Sam.

"You'd better want to date a woman like that, since apparently it's the only topic of conversation you're capable of."

Sam dragged a hand over his face and muttered a curse into it. And then he looked at Teddy and Ellen, both of whom were regarding him like they were judging his performance on a reality show. A dating reality show that he was doing really poorly on. "What should I do?"

"I feel like there are only two things you

should do," Ellen said. She held up one hand dramatically. "Number one: Ask her out on a normal date like a normal person."

"She's Teddy's teacher," Sam said.

"So?"

"So, do you think she'll think it's gross?"

"Not if you follow the second thing you should do. Teddy, what's the second thing your father should do?"

"Stop talking about beetroot," said Teddy.

"Exactly," said Ellen. "Not your usual dating advice, but apparently vitally important when it comes to you."

Sam had a day in which he probably made a fool of himself in front of Teddy's head teacher—who no doubt thought he was pathetic for behaving like an idiot over Miss Quinn—and also in front of Teddy's teacher, which was made worse by the fact that he kind of liked Miss Quinn, even though he'd met her a grand total of twice, and both times he'd mostly talked about vegetables with her. *But still.* With the knowledge that he kept babbling about beetroot to a beautiful woman whom he found very attractive, Sam's self-esteem was not exactly at a high point.

So, when he walked over to Mr. Hammersley's, and Mr. Hammersley opened the door, he said immediately, "I've had a bad day, so let's skip over the part where you're annoyed that I'm bothering you and say rude things to me and pretend you don't care what happens to Jack and let's just discuss whether Jack can stay over our house every once in a while, because that would make Teddy happy."

Mr. Hammersley stood at the door, looked at Sam, and said, "You do look like you've had a day."

Great. Even the old man who talked to nobody was taking pity on him now. "It's okay," said Sam. "It's just been a long day. A long month." He laughed suddenly, without humor, and said, "A long *few years*. But never mind. It doesn't matter."

"Your boy wants Jack to stay over every once in a while?" asked Mr. Hammersley gruffly, not commenting on the fact that Sam was making no sense on his doorstep.

"Yeah," Sam said. "I know he doesn't belong to you, he belongs to the street, but—"

"Let me get him some food. Don't want him to go to bed hungry."

They already had food for Jack, but Sam was somewhat charmed by the fact that Mr. Hammersley clearly thought he was Jack's sole source of food, and Sam didn't want to disappoint him by pointing out that the whole street fed Jack. So Sam waited patiently while Mr. Hammersley shuffled off. He came back with a small bag of food and a small wooden figure that he handed across.

"What's this?" Sam asked, peering at it.

"It's a wizard. For your boy."

"A . . . Oh. Okay." Sam had no idea what to make of that, but the little figure was enchanting. "Did you make this?"

"Good night," Mr. Hammersley said, and shut the door. Apparently the conversational limit had been reached.

Sam shook his head at the door and sighed, "Weird bloody day."

Chapter 7

Welcome to Year 4 at Turtledove! We're going to have a wonderful year full of fun, learning, new challenges, and new friendships! You the parents can help your child by keeping abreast of what we're doing in the classroom. I'll keep you posted in periodic communications . . . and so will they! Your children will be working on a class newspaper this year, so stay tuned for tales of epic adventures!

Miss Quinn

On Anna's very long list of things to do, "have coffee with Diya Basak" was not very high. But Emilia had said that Mrs. Basak wanted to have coffee with her, to talk about the stray dog, supposedly. Anna suspected it was so she could brag about how perfect her children were, but Anna didn't want to be rude.

"I would just be rude to people," Marcel said when she told him. "You worry too much about being rude to people."

"That's why I have to worry about being rude to people," Anna replied, which effectively ended that conversation.

So Anna met up with Diya at her house one Sunday afternoon. Diya was making a batch of chai, and she offered some to Anna, and Anna didn't want to be rude so she accepted some.

Then they sat at the table in silent awkwardness. Finally Anna said, "Where are the kids?"

"A friend is having a party," Diya said. "Darsh took them. I stayed here to have tea with you."

Anna felt like there was a judgment in those words. She took a sip of her chai and said, "Anyway. About the dog."

"Yes. The dog." Diya nodded briskly. "I do not like the idea of that dog just wandering around the street. It's dangerous."

"It is dangerous," Anna agreed.

"We should talk to the new neighbors about controlling the dog."

"We should," Anna agreed again. "It's only right." She paused, then said casually, "Won't your daughter be upset, though? I mean, your daughter loves Jack."

"She'll be fine," said Diya darkly. "School has started now and she doesn't have all day to do nothing but think about the dog."

"If you say so," said Anna innocently. "I wouldn't want to cause an issue within your family."

"We're fine," said Diya challengingly.

"Us, too," replied Anna.

"I'm glad we had this discussion," said Diya.

"We can be united together when we confront the new neighbor."

"Yes," said Anna.

"But I have to run to the party now. We'll do it later."

"Of course," said Anna, and left most of her chai behind her. Strangest, most pointless conversation ever, she thought. Why had Diya even wanted to speak with her?

She said that when she got back to their house. Emilia and Marcel were embroiled in playing a card game, laughing at each other, and Marcel said, "That was fast. How was not being rude to the neighbor?"

He was kidding, and she knew he was, but she still felt self-conscious as she leaned over to turn the kettle on.

"I thought you just had tea," said Marcel.

"It was chai. And it was the most pointless conversation. I don't know why she even told you that she wanted to talk to me," said Anna to Emilia.

"Yeah," Emilia said, staring fixedly at her hand of cards. "So weird."

Marcel reached for her hand, and Anna knew this was a gesture of reconciliation, and she shouldn't turn it down, so she took it.

He said, "Would you like to play with us?"

But Anna was bad at card games, especially the card games Emilia and Marcel played.

When Emilia had been small, and the money had been so very tight, a deck of cards had been her main toy, and Marcel had taught her strange and complicated games late into the night, even though Anna insisted everyone should be sleeping. Cards were Emilia and Marcel's thing together, just like the drums were also Emilia and Marcel's thing together, and Anna didn't know what things were her and Emilia's, or even her and Marcel's.

It was easier, Anna thought, to just be at work than to try to navigate this family where she didn't have a place.

"No," said Anna, and managed a smile. "That's okay." And she turned to make herself a cup of tea.

There wasn't much else to do, so Bill had generally been in the habit of looking out the window to watch what the neighbors were up to, but he made a particular point these days to be at the window when the children came home from school. It was easy enough to remember, because Jack always went dashing up the street to meet them, barking the whole way and bouncing in such overexuberance that he was always half-tumbling over his paws. Jack served as a public announcement for most street events.

Bill had noticed that the Indian girl almost inevitably came home in a knot of friends, chattering away. Friends coming over to visit her house, or friends who lived a few streets away but close enough to walk together. It was a happy little bundle of children that Jack circled around, bouncing and barking.

The American boy—Teddy—was almost always by himself, almost always looked tired and grumbly and out-of-sorts, and brightened only when Jack made his way over to him and licked his hand in greeting. Bill might have got used to having Jack around the house, but he understood why the American wanted Jack sometimes, too. It wasn't that Jack was Bill's dog to share, but, well, all the same, Bill *would* share him, to the extent that he could.

Because Bill had to admit that he understood what it was like to be lonely.

Teddy had slipped a thank-you note into the mail slot. In large, precise writing, it had thanked Bill for the wooden wizard and said that he would call the wizard Mike. Which didn't seem likely as a wizard name as far as Bill was concerned, but who was he to argue? He did regret that he hadn't given the boy a dragon to go with the wizard, since the boy had said dragons could be wizard pets. Another unlikely thing, but again, Bill wasn't going to get into arguments about fictional fantasy people.

Which was why, when he saw the boy's father outside, frowning at a piece of furniture he was trying to get into his house, Bill decided to just take a little dragon over to him.

The man looked up in surprise when Bill walked over to him, and Bill raked his head for the man's name, came up empty, and decided that was fine. He didn't need to know his name. He cut off the man's greeting by thrusting out the figurine.

"It's a dragon," he explained, because he didn't know if the man would understand. "For your boy."

"Oh," said the man, turning it over in his hand. "This is so very lovely. Thank you so much. You don't need to be so nice—"

"It's nothing," Bill said. "I already had it carved. Don't make a big fuss."

The man said, sounding amused, "Yes, God forbid I call you 'nice.' I'll be sure to give it to Teddy when he gets home."

And Bill didn't actually *care* how the boy was doing in school, but, all the same, it stung that this young man was so sarcastic toward him, and so Bill said, "How's the boy doing in school?"

The man smiled in a way that was clearly a lie. "Well, you know," he said, "it's a process. I tell Teddy we just have to get through it."

Bill considered. "I suppose." And he should just leave it at that, he knew, and yet . . . "On the other hand."

The man lifted his eyebrows.

Bill shrugged. Because this wasn't being *nice,*

this was just being . . . old, and knowing things other people didn't know. "If you spend too much time just getting through things, before you know it, you blink and you're old and you realize you spent your life just trying to get through, and there's nothing on the other side you're trying to get through to."

Bill left the man with his furniture problem and went back to his own house.

Buying the bookcase had really seemed like a good idea. It was a gorgeous old piece of furniture, and it would look fantastic in Sam's office, where he really needed a bookcase, but he couldn't even figure out how to get it inside, never mind up the stairs.

And meanwhile his crotchety old neighbor had decided to suddenly give him advice about the fact that he was wasting his life by just trying to get through it instead of living it, and now he was contemplating a larger life failure than buying a bookcase slightly too big for his house.

"You look like you have a conundrum, mate," remarked Max, standing at the end of the walk.

Sam said, "I might have wasted the last few years of my life and also I'm encouraging my son to waste his life, too."

Max lifted an eyebrow.

Sam said, "Oh, I see, you were talking about the bookcase."

"I cannot help you with the existential crisis you're having there, but I can probably help you lift a piece of furniture," offered Max.

"You're sure?" said Sam. "It's a lot of trouble."

"This is a new, friendly street," said Max. "And anyway, probably if I throw my back out, I can sue you. My husband's an insurance agent; he'll figure out a way to get your insurance company to pay."

"Oh, good," said Sam, as Max said hello to Jack, who was watching all of the proceedings with interest, and set up on the other side of the bookcase. "A win-win for both of us."

Except that, no matter how they attempted to maneuver the bookcase, it seemed to be impossible to get it through the door.

Even Jack had lost interest in their incompetence and was now scouring the street for his nemesis squirrels.

Max and Sam finally stepped back to assess the situation.

"Will it even fit?" Max asked, lifting up his hand to shade his gaze from the sun, which had broken through the clouds in order to ensure that it was the hottest September day *of all time* for them to be struggling with a piece of furniture. "I mean, did you even measure?"

"No," admitted Sam. "It just *felt* like it would fit. I mean, it's just a bookcase. Who would make a bookcase too big to fit through a *door?*"

"I have a measuring tape," remarked Pen. "I could fetch it for you."

Sam hadn't even noticed that Pen was there, but she had stopped on the pavement, clearly just having finished a run. "How long have you been standing there?"

"Long enough to know that neither of you has 'furniture mover' in your future career prospects," she replied. "Let me fetch you the measuring tape."

Pen returned with the measuring tape and together they ascertained that yes, the bookcase *should* fit through the door.

"It's something with the angles," mused Max.

"Yes, and God knows I don't know anything about angles," said Sam. "I can barely do my son's maths homework with him."

"Well, *I* don't know anything about angles," said Max. "I'm an artist."

Max and Sam both looked at Pen.

"Have you," Max said, "by any chance, written an article about angles?"

Pen rolled her eyes. "No, but I'm Googling it. You two are hopeless."

Although, even with Pen's Googling and giving them impossible directions like "Make yourselves smaller" and "Put your hand on the other side of your body," they could not get the bookcase in the house.

"Shocking that we couldn't accomplish it,

even with maths and directions," remarked Max.

"You would have got it through the door if you'd been able to get your feet properly up on the wall," Pen told him.

"I do accept the full responsibility of this failure," said Max.

"I need a beer," Sam decided. "Beers for everyone?"

"Beers for everyone," Max and Pen agreed.

They settled on the front step, because, no longer struggling with a bookcase, the unexpected warmth of the day was no longer a trial to be endured but a pleasant bonus.

"It *is* a gorgeous bookcase," Max remarked.

"Well, you can have it, I suppose," said Sam. "Since *I'm* not going to have it."

"We have the same house," said Max. "How would I get it inside my house if I couldn't get it inside your house?"

Sam shrugged. "Magic?"

"Speaking of magic." Max picked up the little dragon figure Sam had forgot he'd put down and held it up. "This is cute. Did it come with the bookcase?"

"Oh, no," said Sam. "Mr. Hammersley made it."

Max and Pen both looked surprised.

"The old man?" Max clarified. "Who lives next door?"

"Yes. That Mr. Hammersley. He's an artist, too."

Max looked down at the little dragon figure reflectively.

"Really?"

"So you talk to him," Pen said. "Like, really talk to him."

"Not really. I don't know. It's weird. I think he's taken an interest in Teddy, for some reason."

"It's because they both love Jack," said Pen. "Jack bringing people together. The love of a good dog." She reached down and scratched behind Jack's ears.

"I suppose," said Sam, as Jack suddenly sat straight up, tail wagging, looking toward the top of the street.

"The children must be coming," Max said, and indeed a group of loud children appeared at the top of the street, dispersing in various directions.

Pari Basak and a group of chattering children walked past, followed by Diya Basak, who looked curiously at the trio of them ringed on the front step, and the bookcase. And then went out of her way to avoid Jack, who went running from Pari to Teddy in greeting. Teddy, bringing up the rear, feet dragging as they usually did.

"Hello," Sam said, as positively as he could, as Teddy came up to them. "Good day at school?"

"It was fine," Teddy said. "Here." He handed Sam a piece of paper.

Turtledove Chronicle! it exclaimed at the top.

There was a drawing of a swooping turtledove, with *Coo coo!* coming out of its beak.

"Thank you. You ought to walk around with Jack and see if there's anything for you to clean up," Sam suggested. It was part of his ongoing lessons about the responsibility of part-time custody of a dog.

Teddy thought everything to do with Jack was magnificently exciting, so he headed out to clean the streets, Jack trotting happily next to him, bouncing a little bit with excitement and keeping an eye out for squirrels.

"Having a street dog is much nicer now that he comes with cleanup duty," remarked Max.

Pen started to talk about an article she'd researched about the problem of horse manure in cities at the turn of the last century, and Sam perused the *Turtledove Chronicle*. There were several articles about what the class had been doing. They were using what they'd learned about angles to construct a city out of nothing but pasta (nothing about aiding in getting a bookcase into a house, however). They were writing a play for them to perform for Christmas entitled *Miracle Snow at the Baby's Birth in the Desert*. The article below proclaimed it to be *a stirring epic with a message about peace on Earth and climate change*. They were experimenting with different sounds in science; the school had concluded that the loudest sounds were henceforth prohibited.

And, at the bottom, was Miss Quinn's weekly column, *From the Teacher's Desk*:

> *Next month we will be taking the children on a field trip to the Natural History Museum. We are seeking volunteers to assist with chaperoning the children. Please send a note to school with your child if you are willing to chaperone!— Miss Quinn.*

Sam reflected upon the field trip request. He had done nothing with regard to Miss Quinn since school had started. Maybe he ought to chaperone the field trip. And use it to flirt with his son's teacher. That . . . might be untoward of him. And maybe a little creepy. He'd met her twice, and barely exchanged words with her, certainly nothing meaningful. But he found himself watching out of the corner of his eye for a glimpse of dark red hair, wherever he was. Sometimes he even leaned out of the window of his office, as if she might wander down the street when she was in actuality busy teaching his child. He suddenly, abruptly, for the first time in years, *wanted* to go on a date, but only with Miss Quinn. No one else appealed. He'd even poked around online just to make sure, although he would never admit that to Ellen.

Sam asked abruptly, "Do you believe in love at first sight?"

Whatever Max and Pen had been discussing, it hadn't been that. They both looked at him and said, "What?"

"I know," Sam said. "That's an out-of-nowhere question."

"Are you doing some sort of survey?" asked Pen, as if that would have been a normal thing to do.

Max just said evenly, "Yes. I believe in love at first sight. Arthur doesn't, though."

Sam looked at him. "So how did that work? You loved him at first sight, he took some convincing?"

"No. It's different definitions of 'love.' I asked him about it once, because I was a little offended. I wanted him, of course, to say he took one look at me and knew no one else would ever do. How devastatingly romantic, right? I told everyone that was how I felt about Arthur. I thought it made for a wonderful story. And I thought it was true. I still think it's true. But Arthur has a point, and his point is that I looked at him and I just immediately wanted to know more about him. And after I knew more about him, after I knew he was it, I went back and interpreted that first spark as 'love.' He looked at me, and he wanted to know more about me, but what Arthur would tell you—what he's told me—is he didn't fall in love with the *sight* of me, he fell in love with the *me* of me, later, and the initial look was what made him look again, and it was the second look that made him fall in love. That's Arthur's version of romance: eminently practical, and utterly disarming in that practicality. To me, anyway."

Sam considered. "I might be on Arthur's side," he said. "Let's say I met someone. At, say, the fruit and veg section of the supermarket."

"A very sexually charged place to meet someone," said Max. "Virtually everything is phallic in the produce section."

"We met over carrots."

"Phallic."

"And beetroot."

"Could be a sex toy," suggested Max.

"This conversation is gross," Pen said.

"Agreed," said Sam. "I'm just saying: I met her, and as soon as I met her, I thought, 'I want to know more about her.' And I've been sitting here, for a while now, thinking how ridiculous that is of me. How can I know I want to know more about her? I don't *know* her."

"So why don't you *get* to know her and find out?" asked Max. "The worst that happens is she's not for you. The worst that happens if you don't take the risk and get to know her is that she *was* for you and you'll never know it. That, to me, was always the bigger tragedy."

"I think," said Pen, "that meeting people that you want to know more about is . . . rare, frankly. In any sense. We all of us just exist in our own little bubbles, and don't venture outside them. Look at how long we all lived on the same street and barely spoke to each other. The things that happen on this street—the things we know about each other—and we don't ever *say* anything to each other, about anything. We don't get to know each other. We don't stop and help each other with furniture and end up talking about the nature of love. But look, when we do, how much nicer it is. I don't know if I believe in love at first sight. I think what I *do* believe is that every once in a while we, as humans, just want to reach out and get to know another human and not feel alone on the planet anymore. Romantic or otherwise. And I think that's important. Every relationship you make is important." Teddy was coming back up the street, racing Jack, who was moving so quickly and so enthusiastically, with his little half-bounces, that he was practically tripping himself. "Even relationships with dogs," she finished, smiling.

Jack went rushing past the front garden, stumbling to slow to meet Arthur, walking down the street, who greeted him with a pat on his head and then stopped in front of the house and said, "Hello."

"Darling," said Max. "Would you like a bookcase that wouldn't fit in our house?"

"Not especially," said Arthur. "Hello, Teddy. How's school?"

"Very long," Teddy said. "And we have to learn a *lot*."

"I see," said Arthur.

Max smiled and stood up. "Sorry about the bookcase," he said to Sam.

"It's okay," Sam said. "I'll find another bookcase somewhere."

"You can't get that in the house?" Arthur said. "I feel like it's just a matter of angles, no?"

"Human limbs are in the wrong place to accomplish it," Max said, as he walked over to meet Arthur. At Arthur's look, he added, "Don't ask. Good night!" He waved back to Sam and Teddy and Pen.

"Good night," they called back, and then Pen stood.

"Actually, I should be going, too. I was supposed to be writing today. Thank you for providing me with today's version of procrastination."

"Anytime," agreed Sam pleasantly. "Thanks for your help." Then he turned to Teddy, handing him the little dragon figure. "Look what Mr. Hammersley made for you."

Teddy smiled at it, turning it over in his hands. "A dragon to be a pet for Mike!"

"Exactly."

"Hang on," said Max, and Sam looked up, surprised to see Max had turned back and was now standing regarding the bookcase. "I *do* want the bookcase," he said slowly. "If you don't mind."

"I don't mind," said Sam. "I can't do anything with it."

"What will *you* use it for?" asked Pen. "We can't get it in the house."

"I think I'll be able to get it in the shed in the back garden," said Max. "And I'm going to use it for *art,* of course."

Sam, after the bookcase had been carted to Max and Arthur's shed, after he and Teddy had shared adventures over dinner (Sam's: buying an unexpected art bookcase; Teddy's: Miss Quinn taught them how to build the best paper airplanes), after he had helped Teddy with homework (massive amounts of which Sam himself did not understand although he tried not to admit that), after he had put Teddy to bed to the sounds of Emilia practicing on her drums (which he was sure meant that Teddy did not actually go to bed until Emilia finished but Sam didn't want to bother the Pachutas over it when Emilia always finished fairly quickly)—after all of this, Sam sat in his office ostensibly doing a bit of work and really considering the *Turtledove Chronicle.*

The thought of the fact that he didn't want to bother the Pachutas over Emilia's drumming made him think of Ellen saying he wanted everyone to like him, and Sam thought of how this tendency to want people to like him had somehow crystallized into wanting one person to like him: Teddy's teacher. In fact, he would prefer it if Teddy's teacher thought he was dazzling and fantastic. And he'd been worrying that this was irrational, but maybe Max and Pen were right: maybe this was a good thing.

Sam pulled out his phone to text Ellen, considered, then texted, **Am I supposed to be able to do Year 4 homework?**

Ellen texted back immediately: **Wait until the A-levels.**

Sam could, yes, happily wait a long time for that. He took a deep breath and texted back, hoping it sounded casual: **So. Too creepy to offer to chaperone the school field trip to spend time with my son and also my son's teacher?**

Ellen's response was again immediate: **Just creepy enough. Do it. Be charming. Don't talk about beetroot. Let me know if you need me to write down some appropriate conversational topics for you.**

Sam texted her the emoji that was, in America, the peace sign emoji.

Then he pulled over a piece of paper and wrote,

211

Miss Quinn—

I am happy to put myself at your service as chaperone for the museum field trip. Looking forward to seeing you.—Sam Bishop.

Then he thought, *No, maybe too creepy.*
He pulled over another piece of paper and wrote,

Miss Quinn—I would love to help introduce Teddy to the wonders of the Natural History Museum.—Sam Bishop.

He read that over. "What the hell is that, Sam?" he asked himself, and pulled over another piece of paper.

Miss Quinn—I can volunteer to serve as chaperone on the museum field trip.— Sam Bishop.

That, he thought, was much better. Except that his penmanship was horrendous and Miss Quinn taught handwriting and had beautiful writing herself, so Sam took another piece of paper and rewrote the note very carefully.

Chapter 8

Homework Journal of Teddy Bishop, ~~10/1~~ 1/10: Design technology: Worst. Modern language: Also worst. Information technology: Worst worst. Best: Miss Quinn is really good at ~~multiplacation~~ multiplication. Also best: Miss Quinn helped me with the Spanish vocabulary and didn't laugh at me. Final best: Miss Quinn let me choose the song to play over Getting Settled Time in the morning.

Teddy's homework journal was always, to Sam, a wealthy source of information. He was supposed to rank, every week, the three best and three worst things about the week. Teddy always started with the worst, which Sam found telling. And the worst were always consistently entire subjects that Teddy had not had in the American school system and so struggled with. He struggled with a lot of the differences between the school systems. So did Sam, who may have been educated in this school system but had never been a parent in it and had frankly forgotten a lot of what it was like to be a child in school.

Teddy's three best things invariably revolved around Miss Quinn in some way, shape, or form.

The truth was, if Sam had never met Miss Quinn, he thought he might be half in love with her just from Teddy's descriptions of her in his homework journal.

Miss Quinn almost always was part of Teddy's adventures of the day, too, when they went over them at dinner. Granted, people at work usually made up Sam's adventures of the day, so he understood that you tended to talk about the people you spent most of your day with, and for Teddy that was Miss Quinn. But Teddy seldom talked about any of his classmates, and basically never talked about having any friends. Teddy revolved exclusively around Miss Quinn, and Jack.

Sam pointed that out one night. "You talk a lot about Miss Quinn."

Teddy shrugged. "Miss Quinn's nice. You know that. I like her a lot."

"She's a good teacher?" said Sam.

"She's the best. She knows a lot, and she's nice to me. She helps me. She doesn't laugh at me."

"Do other people laugh at you?" Sam didn't want to say that he was prepared to sharpen weapons to start dealing with these people, but . . . well, maybe he was.

Teddy shrugged again.

Sam considered an approach to this. He settled for, "Well, I, for one, am looking forward to the field trip. And you can point out all the terrible children and I can be threatening at them."

Teddy looked unimpressed. "Dad, you are *not* threatening."

"I could be threatening," said Sam.

"I don't think you could."

Sam frowned. "Don't you find me threatening when I discipline you?" he asked.

Teddy actually started laughing.

These were Teddy's views on school: it was *so long*. Teddy felt like *every day* was an *entire lifetime*. And he felt like he never had an opportunity to catch his breath. He felt like he was underwater every single moment at school. It was like being in the ocean, unable to get away from the waves. Everyone spoke very quickly, using words that he only half recognized from Dad's vocabulary. They presumed a level of knowledge on things that he just didn't have. They learned math completely differently, and always called it "maths," which was just plain weird, because it wasn't like they called science "sciences." Teddy would have asked Dad long ago if he could just stop going to school, except for the fact of Miss Quinn.

Miss Quinn was basically the best person in the entire universe. Miss Quinn was so nice, and so kind, and so patient. Miss Quinn only laughed when he said something funny, never otherwise. Miss Quinn smiled almost all the time, except when she was perfectly serious. Miss Quinn knew the answer to every single question, but, better, she could explain those answers to Teddy in ways he understood. Miss Quinn even did a really good American accent, which always made Teddy laugh.

So it was lucky there was Miss Quinn, or he would just refuse to go to school. As it was, there was Miss Quinn, who maybe liked Dad, even though she never said it, and Dad, who *definitely* liked Miss Quinn, even though he liked to pretend she was just Teddy's teacher and nothing more.

There was Miss Quinn, and there was Jack, who met him after school every day and was basically the friend who walked home with him, since the other kids didn't seem interested in that. So the weather got colder and the days got shorter and the leaves swirled around them, and Dad insisted Teddy transition from a lighter coat to a heavier coat, and also assured Teddy that Jack didn't need a coat because he had a fur coat.

And every day Jack met him after school and walked back with him, even through the chilly drizzle, and nobody else talked to them.

Until the day one of the older boys decided for some reason to take notice and say, "What's up with you and that dog? That your only friend?" and then everyone else laughed like that was hilarious.

Teddy had been petting Jack hello, but he tensed at finding himself the object of all the kids' attention, and then Jack seemed to sense that and moved in a protective circle around Teddy, whimpering a little.

"It's not even his," said Pari. "It's the street dog. He belongs to *everyone* on the street."

"Not even your dog?" said the older boy who'd started all of this. "Why're you pretending that it is, then?"

"He is my dog," Teddy said staunchly, a hand on Jack's collar to keep him next to him. "He's everyone's dog, which makes him mine, too."

"Are you trying to steal this dog from everyone else?" demanded the older boy.

Teddy looked at the children ringed around him, and met Pari's eyes. Pari looked . . . horrified. Which was not how Teddy had expected her to look.

"Wait," said Pari. "He's not trying to steal him. He just helps take care of Jack."

"Seems like he spends more than his fair share of time with Jack," said the older boy. "Give us the dog."

"No," said Teddy, hand still on Jack's collar, although Jack chose that moment to start growling in the older boy's direction.

"Here now," said the older boy. "Stop him doing that. What do you think this is? He's not yours to make him growl at the rest of us."

Jack kept growling, and Teddy tried to decide what to do. He wasn't far from home, and if he

217

let go of Jack he could make a run for it. But would Jack follow? What if these older boys tried to steal Jack? They lived a few streets over, and Jack wouldn't know anyone on that street, and Jack's family was *here*.

And as Teddy was trying to decide, Mr. Hammersley said, "What's all this?"

The older boy, with an adult present, turned naturally angelic. "Oh, nothing, sir," he said. "Just admiring this lovely dog."

Jack kept growling.

Mr. Hammersley said, "Move along now. Move along. Get to your homes."

The children started moving away, including Pari, with one look back over her shoulder.

"I tell you, I don't know what this world is coming to," said Mr. Hammersley. "Children these days. Are you all right?"

Teddy . . . wanted to go home. *Home* home. But he clung to Jack's collar and nodded. Jack turned and pressed in against Teddy's leg, whining and snuffling kisses onto Teddy's hand.

Mr. Hammersley, peering at him, said, "Don't mind them, eh? Jack likes you and not them, and Jack is the best judge of character I know."

It was true. Jack was close against him, still licking at him.

"Run home," Mr. Hammersley said.

Teddy didn't need to be prodded to do that twice.

When he got home, Dad was in his office, still working, and he just said, "Did you have a good day?" and Teddy nodded and holed up in his room with Jack, curling up on the bed. Dad didn't show up to ask any more questions, so Teddy was free to put his face in Jack's soft coat and just breathe.

Teddy was being unusually quiet. Teddy could keep to himself a lot, but he usually was full of more words after a day of school, even if those words were mostly complaints. So Sam knocked on Teddy's door, once he was done with work, and when he received a "come in," poked his head inside.

"You okay?" he asked Teddy, who was sitting on his bed with Jack.

Teddy nodded.

He didn't *look* okay, thought Sam. "Something happen at school?"

Teddy shook his head. "No. School was good. Miss Quinn's good."

Sam lifted an eyebrow. "School was good?"

Teddy shrugged.

Hmm, thought Sam, and then said slowly, "Okay. You'd tell me if something was wrong, right? You know you can tell me anything like that."

Teddy nodded, but volunteered no further information. *Great,* thought Sam. How was he supposed to combat that? He said instead, "I don't know if Jack should be on the bed— he's filthy," but he didn't press that point and instead retreated downstairs to consider what they could have for dinner.

The doorbell rang, and Sam answered it to reveal the last person in the world he'd expect to see.

"Pari," he said in surprise, and then could manage nothing further, because he didn't know what else to say.

Pari's dark eyes looked wide and solemn. She said, "Is Teddy home? Could I see him?"

She didn't *seem* combative. So Sam said, trying wildly to think why Pari would suddenly have shown up, "Yes. Sure. He's upstairs with Jack."

"Thanks." Pari immediately bounded up the stairs with eight-year-old energy.

Sam considered following her to eavesdrop, then thought, No, a terrible parent would eavesdrop; then thought, No, wait, maybe a really *good* parent would eavesdrop, and because he couldn't make up his mind, he decided to just sit on the bottom step of the staircase, which wasn't as bad as listening at the door but maybe would enable him to hear *something*.

Teddy sat on his bed with Jack and just looked at Pari when she walked into his bedroom. At least Jack's tail wagged but he didn't get off the bed.

Pari, after fidgeting for a second, said, "I expect you're really angry with me."

Teddy said nothing.

Pari said, all in a rush, "Sorry. I didn't mean for anything to happen and I didn't want them to take Jack from you and I'm really sorry. I'm really, really sorry."

Teddy still said nothing. He didn't look like he believed her. But Jack got off the bed and came over to her and licked her face.

"Hi, Jack," Pari said, and then said to Teddy, "Can I sit on your bed?"

Teddy, after a second, nodded.

Pari sat on the bed and looked at Teddy, who looked miserable. The way Teddy had looked earlier, with Jack, had felt like the first time Pari had ever seen Teddy. Teddy was *unhappy* and *lonely*. That was why Teddy hogged Jack so much. Teddy didn't know anyone else. Teddy didn't have a big brother. Teddy didn't even have a *mum*. And Teddy knew no one at school. And Pari felt like she hadn't realized how much Teddy was alone until she'd actually been forced to *see* it.

And now she felt horrible.

She said, "I don't want to be at war with you anymore."

Teddy, after a second, said, "I don't want to be at war with *you*."

"So let's not be at war," decided Pari, shrugging.

Teddy looked suspicious still. "Are you still trying to steal Jack?"

Pari shook her head. "You're okay at sharing him. And I get to go to the vet's all the time now and see all sorts of animals. Yesterday I held *baby guinea pigs*."

"That sounds pretty cool," Teddy allowed.

"Yeah, and it works better because Mum doesn't have to see the animals. My brother doesn't go anymore because he fainted."

Teddy looked impressed. "He *fainted?*"

Pari nodded. "Yup. The vet showed him a needle and then he just fell right over onto the floor. Hit his head hard. I thought he was probably dead."

"Wow," said Teddy.

"I know. It was just a needle, right?"

Jack jumped up onto the bed between them and licked both of their faces in turn.

Pari said, "We should find a way for Jack to be in the school play."

"Good idea," said Teddy.

"*Brilliant* idea," said Pari, and smiled at him.

Sam could hear almost nothing from his perch at the bottom of the stairs, and he was just considering giving up and going to eavesdrop properly when the doorbell rang again. Probably, Sam thought, Diya, looking for Pari.

But it was Mr. Hammersley, all bundled up like

he was preparing to trek over Antarctica, when Sam swung the door open.

"Oh," Sam said, startled. "Hi. Is something wrong?"

"I don't want you to think that I'm going to get in the habit of knocking on your door all the time," said Mr. Hammersley.

"Okay," Sam agreed. "But was there something you needed?"

"Of course not," denied Mr. Hammersley. "I can take care of myself."

"Right," said Sam, not sure why else Mr. Hammersley would be on his doorstep.

"I just wanted to say that Jack can stay over here tonight and here's some food for him." Mr. Hammersley handed a bag of food to him.

"Oh," Sam said, bewildered. Jack stayed over at the house fairly frequently. They seldom communicated about it anymore.

"I thought your boy might need him tonight."

"Teddy?" Sam asked blankly.

"Yes. I think those children shook him up a bit, but he's tough, your boy. I wouldn't worry too much about it. And Jack did his part."

Sam stared at Mr. Hammersley. Clearly something had happened that Mr. Hammersley expected Sam to know about. "Right," he said. "Yes. The children." Because he didn't want to admit that Teddy had mentioned none of this.

"He's all right, isn't he?" said Mr. Hammersley.

"He's brilliant," Sam assured him, all false bravado.

And, as soon as he'd closed the door on Mr. Hammersley, he walked immediately upstairs and knocked on Teddy's half-open bedroom door.

Teddy and Pari were giggling together over something, Jack sprawled between them, still on the bed.

Sam stood for a second, staring, forgetting entirely his reason for coming to talk to Teddy, because there was Teddy, *giggling*.

"Dad!" Teddy exclaimed. "Pari and I have had the best idea! Can we give Jack a bath? Then he wouldn't be filthy anymore!"

Sam didn't have the heart to deny Teddy anything he desired when Teddy looked like that. *Keep that look on his face,* he thought. So he found himself setting up the kids and the dog in the bathroom and despairing for the mess they were about to make.

"Pari, what's your mum's number?" Sam asked. "I'll ring her that you're here."

"Oh, my mum's not home," Pari said, already laughing with glee over the wet dog. "She had to go to my uncle's house to help make some food for a party. But my dad's home."

"Right," Sam said. "Sexist of me. Let me ring your dad."

Pari gave him the number and Sam dialed it

224

and said, when it was answered, "Hi, Darsh, it's Sam Bishop from next door."

"Oh," Darsh said pleasantly. "Hello."

"I just wanted to let you know that Pari is here giving Jack a bath."

"How nice," Darsh said.

Yes, thought Sam. Wasn't it just?

After Jack had been washed and brushed and had made generally an enormous mess, Sam watched Pari run home and then decided not to have anything more taxing than cereal for dinner, because cleaning the bathroom had been taxing enough.

"Day's adventure," he said. "Mr. Hammersley coming over to check up on you after an incident with some other children." He had hoped to provoke Teddy into telling him what had happened, but instead Teddy just said, "My adventure today was I made a friend," and looked so pleased with himself that Sam thought this might be their most amazing day in London so far.

Chapter 9

Hi, everyone! We should make plans for Bonfire Night! It would be fun to go to see fireworks together. But, as Jack is our collective responsibility, we should also discuss what we can do with him whilst all the loud noises are happening! —Pen

For a while Max had been contemplating what to do with the bookcase he'd acquired from Sam. Multimedia was not usually Max's type of art, and while the bookcase was lovely, it wasn't exactly a unique piece of craftsmanship. It was just a striking piece of wood, but it had not been ornamented in any way, and it could do with a bit of personality. But Max was undecided about the personality that it should acquire. Every day he went out to the shed and regarded the bookcase, but every day the bookcase refused to speak to him. Sometimes Jack came and sat with him, and Max would say things like, "Do you know anything about the Japanese technique of Shou-Sugi-Ban?" and Jack would consider very intently.

Then Max read the note Pen slipped through his front door—everyone's front door, Max assumed—about Bonfire Night and taking care of Jack, and that day he walked out to the shed and the bookcase said exactly what it needed to be.

But the idea should involve the entire street, Max thought, and it should start, really, in fairness, with Mr. Hammersley down the road.

Which was how Max found himself knocking on Mr. Hammersley's door.

He didn't think Mr. Hammersley was going to open it, but he did, eventually, frowning. "What?" he demanded.

"Hi," said Max. "I'm Max. From down the street."

Mr. Hammersley looked very unimpressed by this. "What do you want?"

"I have a proposition for you," said Max.

"I'm not interested," replied Mr. Hammersley, and went to close the door.

Max caught it before it could entirely close, which earned him a glare that, thankfully, was not literally capable of killing him, or Max would have been dead. "At least hear me out," he said, striving for cheerfulness.

"Why?" demanded Mr. Hammersley.

"Because it has to do with Jack."

That got Mr. Hammersley's attention, as Max had thought it might. "What about Jack?" asked Mr. Hammersley grudgingly.

"I've an idea for a Jack-based gift. For the whole street. And I'd love your help on it."

"*My* help?" Mr. Hammersley looked astonished, and then wary. "Why?"

"Because Jack starts with you. Because any ordinary street could have got the dog off the street and taken him to the RSPCA to be adopted by someone else. But you were the first one to take him in and decide instead that the street ought to adopt him. So, with any Jack-based gift, I think it should start with you."

Mr. Hammersley looked like he didn't know quite what to say.

"And also," said Max, with a smile, "it's an art project. And you're an artist."

There was something living in his attic. Honestly, Sam did *not* have time for this. Work was busy and he was already taking a day off that week to chaperone the field trip. But he had to do something about it, because he and Teddy had both heard the scratching sound of something up there, and even Jack had taken to barking up toward the ceiling.

Teddy thought it was cool and hoped that it was a poisonous snake.

"Why would you want it to be a poisonous snake?" asked Sam. "What if it decided to bite us and kill us in our sleep?"

"It's stuck up in the attic," said Teddy, shrugging, unimpressed.

"The attic *is* connected to the house, you know," said Sam.

"We'd be okay," said Teddy.

"Especially because there aren't many poisonous snakes that live in the UK," Sam pointed out.

Sam told Ellen later, "There's something living in my attic."

"An animal?" said Ellen.

"Well, I hope not a person," replied Sam.

Ellen laughed like it was funny. "Relax," she said. "Just call someone about it. Get it taken care of."

So Sam rang an exterminator and followed him all around the house. The exterminator frowned and made notes. It was a bit like having a medical exam. Sam wanted to ask if the house had passed.

Instead the exterminator said, "Bad news. You've got bats living up there."

"Bats?" said Sam. "Bats plural?"

The exterminator shrugged, as if a herd of bats, or whatever the right collective noun was, was not alarming. "They tend to live in colonies."

"Okay," said Sam, trying to stay calm and not envision an attic crawling with bats. "So what can I do about it?"

"Well, it's tricky," said the exterminator. "They're protected, aren't they? So you can't disturb their roosts, really. Not without permission."

Sam stared at him. "So I just have to . . . live with a colony of bats in my attic?"

When Sam told Teddy that night over dinner, Teddy said, "That's cool! That's the best adventure you've ever had here!"

"So you've got bats living in your *house* with you," Pari said, looking appropriately impressed by this, as they enjoyed hot cocoa while huddled in their coats in Teddy's back garden. Pari had called it a "cold-weather picnic." Teddy thought it was brilliant.

"It's cool, right?" said Teddy. "It's a whole *colony* of them."

"What's a colony of bats?" Pari asked. "Like a family?"

"I think so, yeah. A really big family."

"A bunch of bats with a lot of brothers and sisters," said Pari. "They're probably rowing all the time."

"Rowing?" said Teddy.

"Like, you know, fighting," Pari explained. "Mum calls it squabbling. Lots of squabbling."

Teddy considered. "I guess. I don't have any brothers and sisters, so I don't know."

"You're just like Jack," Pari said. "He doesn't have any brothers and sisters, either. But that's why the street gets to be his whole family, which is pretty amazing."

Jack had been lying at their feet, ears back as he looked for squirrels in the growing-bare trees, but at hearing his name he picked up his head and barked a brief contribution to the conversation.

"See?" Pari said. "Jack totally agrees. Pretty amazing." She scratched behind Jack's ears just to set his tail wagging and his tongue lolling out.

Teddy said, "I wonder if Jack would want to make friends with the bats."

"I don't know," said Pari dubiously. "He doesn't like squirrels all that much. And I feel like bats are just flying squirrels."

"No, flying squirrels are flying squirrels," said Teddy. "Bats are totally different."

"I guess bats are more like flying mice, then?" suggested Pari. "And Mrs. Pachuta's cats go after the mice, and Mrs. Pachuta says Jack doesn't like her cats, so maybe Jack *does* like mice, and maybe he would like flying mice. Hmm." Pari looked at Jack thoughtfully.

Jack wandered off to investigate whether anything interesting might have wandered into the back of the garden.

"Doesn't matter," Teddy said. "We wouldn't even know how to get into the attic."

On the morning of the Natural History Museum field trip, Teddy and Sam left the house and almost immediately ran into Mr. Hammersley, heading down the street. Since Mr. Hammersley rarely left his house, Sam said in surprise, "Oh. Hello."

"Hello," Mr. Hammersley said, as if they ran into each other every morning.

"Hi, Mr. Hammersley," said Teddy happily. "We're going to the Natural History Museum today!"

Teddy was looking tremendously forward to this trip. Sam was so relieved and happy; it was like having his child back, frankly.

Mr. Hammersley said, "Well, have fun, then," and resumed walking down the street.

And Sam couldn't help it. He said, "And where are you going?" because he was too curious not to ask.

"I'm working on an art project," said Mr. Hammersley, and kept walking.

Sam started walking up the street with Teddy but he did turn around just to see where Mr. Hammersley went, which was to Max and Arthur's door. *Will wonders never cease,* thought Sam in astonishment.

The classroom was barely organized chaos, with a bunch of overexcited children all conversing with each other at top volume.

Miss Quinn came up to Sam and said, "Ah, Mr. Bishop, hello," and handed him a piece of paper and a laminated drawing of a fish with a safety pin through it. "These are the children you're responsible for. You are Team Barracuda. Pin it to your shirt, please."

"Barracuda?" echoed Sam.

"Don't read anything into it," said Miss Quinn with a quick smile, and then shouted, "Team Barracuda! Over here!"

Teddy and four other children obediently came to stand in front of Sam, all of them still chattering excitedly.

"Hi," Sam said to them.

They barely acknowledged his presence.

Teddy wasn't really participating in the chattering but he didn't look like he minded. He did wave across the room to Pari Basak, who was clustered next to her mother, also chaperoning the trip.

Sam glanced at the two other parents chaperoning, and noticed they were both men. Which was maybe sexist of him—he certainly hadn't expected to be the only father chaperoning—but he hadn't expected the majority of the chaperones to be men. And, as he watched, he noticed what seemed to him to be, well, an enormous amount of flirting with Miss Quinn going on. She seemed to parry everything gracefully and move on, but it struck Sam at that moment: how horrible and arrogant and rude he was being. To show up at Miss Quinn's workplace and assume that she wanted to be distracted with flirtation while she was trying to do her job.

Sam felt like basically the worst person ever for having had the idea.

Which was why he studiously avoided Miss Quinn as they moved to the coach and took their seats. She had a lot to deal with today, and she deserved to be allowed to do her job.

Diya Basak sat next to him on the coach and smiled and said, "Hello."

"Hi," said Sam, and was about to say that he was glad that Pari and Teddy seemed to have become friends.

Except that Diya distracted him by saying, "Did you see that the old man is doing something with the gay couple?"

Street gossip for the win, thought Sam. *"Yes,"* he said. "What do you think it is?"

"I don't know. We should ask that writer woman. She knows everything."

Further conversation was cut off by Miss Quinn, who stood at the front of the coach and said, "Okay, everyone is present and accounted for, and everyone has been given animal badges corresponding to their team. You now all know who you must stick with at the museum. Further instructions when we arrive. Next stop: Natural History Museum!"

The children cheered and the coach pulled away and Diya started telling Sam all about how busy she was with an extended network of friends and family but it was important to spend these little moments with their children, and Sam found that not much was called for on his part but nodding every so often. A bit bored, he happened to look up at the same time that Miss Quinn happened to glance his way, and she grinned at him, dimples in evidence. And he smiled back and thought later, after the field trip was over, when things were calmer, he would ask Miss Quinn to go for coffee, the way he should have done *ages* ago, and it wouldn't be weird and creepy; he would make sure it was just . . . *nice*. Because he liked her, and she acted as if she liked him, and if she didn't want to go for coffee, he would drop the whole idea.

And then, abruptly, the coach jerked and began slowing down.

Diya interrupted her monologue to say, "What's going on?"

Miss Quinn leaned over to have a conference with the driver.

Sam said, "I'm sure it's nothing," even as the coach came to a stop. Nowhere near the Natural History Museum.

Max had stretched a canvas across the back of the bookcase and was working on a painting, but Mr. Hammersley was carving along the front of it, and it was Mr. Hammersley's carving that fascinated Max. He spent so much time watching him carving that eventually Mr. Hammersley grumbled, "Stop staring at me."

"Sorry," Max said. "Sorry. It's just . . . amazing."

Max reached out and brushed his fingers over the swirling carving on the wood. "You're very talented. All I do is throw paint on things; this is . . . extraordinary."

Mr. Hammersley grunted.

Max looked at him, considered, then said, "Did you used to do it a lot? When you were younger?"

"I was busy when I was younger," huffed Mr. Hammersley. "Didn't have time for much of this. There wasn't much call for it." He stepped back and regarded his work, then admitted, "I used to do some of it."

"For fun," Max said. "I get that."

"You're all spoilt these days," Mr. Hammersley said. "You think everything is supposed to be fun. What do you do for fun, when what you do for work is for fun?"

Max laughed, but when Mr. Hammersley glared at him, he realized that wasn't the right reaction. "It's a good point," Max said. "That's why I was laughing, because . . . you make a point. I don't know the answer to that."

Mr. Hammersley moved forward, working on his carving again. He said, "Typical. You lot never think things through." Max wasn't sure which "lot" Mr. Hammersley was talking about, but he didn't even think it mattered. He was inclined to agree, no matter which "lot" it was. "That might be a fair criticism," he agreed, and went back to his canvas.

• • •

At first, when the coach stopped, Sam assumed that it was minor, or temporary.

It was beginning to feel permanent.

Miss Quinn was outside, on her mobile, dealing with the issue, while the driver was lost under the bonnet, and the kids were getting restless and starting to complain about being stuck on the side of the road instead of at the Natural History Museum. The other two chaperones seemed to be engaged in a heated football-related discussion, so Sam decided that it was up to him to help and stood up at the front of the aisle. "Hello, kids," he called. "Isn't this an adventure?"

The kids were still grumbling. They did not think this was an adventure. Teddy looked horrified that he was up there at all.

All Sam could think was that it seemed like a good idea to keep the children occupied with *something,* since it didn't look as if help was imminent.

"I hear that you're working on a play," said Sam.

"It's a Christmas play," a girl informed him.

"It has snow and babies," another girl said.

"And it's also about climate change," added a third girl.

"We've been writing it together," chimed in a boy.

"It's full of drama," the first girl said.

237

"Well, good," said Sam. "Sounds like just the thing to occupy our time. How do you work on the play?"

"We plotted it out," said the first girl again, "and then we're divided up into groups and each group has a scene we're supposed to be writing."

"Okay," Sam said, "well—"

Sam broke off as Miss Quinn appeared behind him, looking at him in surprise.

"Sorry," Sam said. "I just thought maybe I'd—"

"Have them work on their play," Miss Quinn concluded. "No. Good idea. Everyone, break up into your groups, work on your scenes, here we go."

The children scattered all over the coach, loudly finding their groups.

Sam turned to Miss Quinn. "I hope it's okay. I didn't mean to step on your toes, but you looked like you had your hands full, and the children were getting grumbly."

"No, thank you for that," said Miss Quinn. "It was a good idea. I don't suppose you also know how to fix coaches? Turns out the driver has no idea."

"Not one of my areas of specialty, unfortunately," said Sam.

Miss Quinn gave him one of her dimpling smiles. "No? Like beetroot in that respect?"

"I vowed not to bring up beetroot in our next conversation," Sam told her.

"Don't worry about it. I brought it up. So you're safe."

"Oh, good," said Sam, and then completely blanked on what else he could say to her.

Miss Quinn's smile widened. "You have no idea what to talk to me about now, do you?"

"All I can think about is beetroot," Sam admitted ruefully.

"Miss Quinn!" someone shouted, and she turned toward them, calling out, "Coming!"

As she walked away from him, down the main aisle of the coach, she said to Sam, "It's okay. The beetroot thing is working for you."

The beetroot thing is working for you. Sam thought that was a good thing. If it was working for him, surely it must be a good thing?

Sam settled back in his seat next to Diya.

Who immediately said, "So you like Miss Quinn."

Sam groaned and knocked his head lightly against the backseat. "Is it that obvious?"

"Yeah," replied Diya simply. "But I think she likes you back."

Sam leaned forward eagerly. "Do you think so?" And then: "Oh, Christ, I am literally sitting on a school coach asking if a girl likes me. I have made zero progress in the past twenty years of life on this planet."

Halfway through the day, Max suddenly stepped back from his canvas and said, "I could do with a cuppa. How about you?" Bill wanted a cuppa, of course, but he was not sure he wanted to have to socialize over a cuppa. Working together on the bookcase project was all well and good. Max was a keen worker, not given to babbling, and Bill appreciated that. But he didn't want to have a stilted conversation with Max where he would have to admit at least to himself that he had no idea what Max was talking about half the time. Talking with young people, Bill thought, was the surest way to remind yourself that you were old.

Max said, "I will not take no for an answer; tea is definitely needed to fuel further art," and went marching inside.

Bill, unsure what to do, thought maybe he could try to ignore Max and just get back to the wood-carving. Wood-carving was something he understood, unlike the rest of the world at the moment.

Max shouted, "Your tea is ready! Come inside!"

Bill wanted to just say *no*. Jack trotted out from the shed to stand beside Max's back door, not going in but stopping and waiting for Bill, tail wagging.

And Bill didn't want to disappoint Jack, who looked so excited at the prospect of tea with Max.

"Fine," Bill grumbled. He would have the tea. He didn't have to *like* it.

Max had set out tea and a pile of biscuits. He was now in the process of giving Jack some dog biscuits, in exchange for tricks. Jack was rolling over, which wasn't a trick Bill had known Jack could do. Not that Bill made Jack do tricks for his food. That was just cruel.

Max, now that there was no canvas in front of him, seemed to think it was time to talk. "You should carve an effigy for Bonfire Night. It could be added to a bonfire."

Bill shook his head.

"Why not?" asked Max. "It would be lovely."

Bill said, "I'm not going to any bonfires for Bonfire Night."

"And whyever not?" replied Max, as if he disapproved.

"Why would I go?" countered Bill.

"Because it's something fun to do," said Max. "Because we'd like to have you there."

Bill stared at him. " 'We'? You mean, you and your . . . what do you call him?" This was what Bill hated: he had no idea what to call the man Max lived with.

"What do I call who?" Max asked blankly.

Bill waved a hand awkwardly at the house, hoping Max would draw conclusions from that.

"Oh," Max realized. "Arthur. I call him Arthur. Or my husband, I suppose, if that's what you mean. But no, that's not who I'm talking about. I'm talking about the street. The street would like to have you at Bonfire Night. I imagine we'll all wander to see fireworks together."

Bill almost laughed. "The street?" he said. As if this street had cared at all about him in years.

"Of course. It is *your* street, after all. You're part of it. You should be there."

Bill shook his head. "Bonfire Night is for you lot, that all . . . know each other and share . . . green drinks or whatever."

"Really, only Pen does the green drinks," said Max. "The rest of us think that's disgusting. And we also all barely know each other. You know just as much as the rest of us do. In fact, you probably know more, because you know more about Jack, and Jack is the glue holding the rest of us together, frankly. You know Jack, and Sam and Teddy, and now you know me." Max popped a biscuit in his mouth. "So you really ought to come." As if that settled it.

Bill privately thought Max was absolutely mad. But Jack seemed to like him, and Bill supposed that counted for something.

Diya was, in her heart of hearts, a matchmaker. She was constantly alert to the possibility of romance around her. She was adept at pairing people up. She had found Darsh and had beautiful children and she thought the same should happen for everyone.

So Diya, on the pretense of needing to stretch her legs a bit, wandered up and down the coach until she found herself directly next to Miss

Quinn, who was helping a group of students with a scene.

"It is really up to you if you think the shepherd ought to be playing on his mobile while he tends to his flocks," Miss Quinn was saying to the children, but upon Diya arriving in her vicinity, she smiled at her and said, "Mrs. Basak, what can I do for you?"

"You should sit with Sam," Diya replied.

Miss Quinn's eyes cut over to where Sam was sitting in his seat, studying his mobile. She said, "Sit with Sam?"

"Yes," Diya said firmly. And because Miss Quinn looked as if she was about to make excuses, Diya added, "He probably has some ideas about our situation."

Miss Quinn lifted her eyebrows. "Ideas about our situation?"

Diya nodded.

Miss Quinn's lips quirked. She looked as if she was not fooled for a second by Diya's feeble excuse, but Diya didn't think she needed to be fooled. Diya just thought she needed some reason to go over there and talk to him. Sam liked Miss Quinn, and Diya was confident Miss Quinn would like Sam back, given the chance.

Miss Quinn said, "Well, then, perhaps you would like to help these children for a bit while I confer with Mr. Bishop about our situation."

"Yes," Diya agreed. "Good idea."

● ● ●

Sam looked up from the game he was playing on his phone when someone slid into the seat next to him. Diya, he assumed, until he looked up and it was Miss Quinn.

"Hi," said Sam, startled.

"Hi," said Miss Quinn. "You are like the shepherd tending his flocks. Playing games on his mobile."

"I'm like what?"

"The Christmas play. It's a retelling set in modern times."

"I see." Sam put his mobile away and glanced toward the back of the coach, where Diya was obviously spying on them and immediately turned her head when she saw Sam looking at her. Sam turned back to Miss Quinn. "Did Diya Basak send you over here?"

"She said you have ideas about our situation."

"What situation?" asked Sam.

"So," continued Miss Quinn, "I more than welcome any ideas you might have about our broken-down coach and our very slow rescue vehicle, but I would also accept ideas about beetroot as I know that those are your specialty." She smiled, giving the impression that she did not mind his inability to come up with better topics of conversation.

Nevertheless: "I have other topics of conversation that I stand ready and able to discuss," Sam said.

"Do you? I cannot imagine what these might be. No, wait: facts about quinoa?"

"I can prepare facts about quinoa for our next conversation, if you like," offered Sam gallantly.

"This makes me look forward to our next conversation with almost unbearable anticipation," replied Miss Quinn, eyes impossibly bright, even with a strand of hair falling over her forehead and half obscuring them.

Sam said, "I hope quinoa has some good facts for me to learn. I wouldn't want to bore you."

"I suspect that would be impossible," said Miss Quinn lightly, as if that were not a tremendous pronouncement to make, as if it didn't make Sam feel as if his head had been briefly knocked off his shoulders and might be floating overhead. "Now what were you planning to talk to me about today?"

"What?" Sam asked, aware that she was expecting a response from him but thoroughly unable to process anything in the face of Miss Quinn's . . . well, general existence.

"If your conversational topic wasn't quinoa, what was it?"

Sam looked at Miss Quinn, with her dark red hair caught up under a navy blue knitted cap, her smiling mouth, her teasing eyes, and heard himself say, "I have a bat—or possibly bats— living in my attic."

Miss Quinn laughed, and Sam decided that was

probably going to be his adventure for the day: *I made Miss Quinn laugh.*

He wanted to keep her laughing, so he said, "And I don't even mean that euphemistically."

"I should hope not. I don't even know what that would be a euphemism for, but I fear it might be something you might need a doctor to examine."

She was still laughing as she said it, looking relaxed and unguarded. He hadn't realized how tense she'd grown, over the course of this disastrous stranded coach scenario, and now that he was watching it slough off her, it made him feel bold. That, at least, was the only explanation he had for why he leaned in closer and lifted a single finger to push that fetching strand of Miss Quinn's hair out of her eyes. It could have been his imagination—but he was fairly certain her breath caught. She gazed up at him, and he experienced that moment, again, that he had experienced when he had first encountered her in the supermarket, that sensation of time slowly running down, halting all around him, to give him room to just *notice* and *live* and *breathe.*

It was a tactical error, he thought, dazedly, to be this close to her. This close to her, this close to the edge, it was so very easy to slip and fall entirely into those eyes.

He looked at her, his hand still lingering behind her ear, where he'd tucked her hair, and *of course* that was when the new working coach arrived. *Of course.*

There was an entire cacophony of "Miss Quinn!" and she blinked, and he moved backward abruptly, feeling embarrassed to think that he had been considering kissing her *on a school coach.* Christ, he really needed to stop behaving *literally* like a teenager, and she said a little breathlessly, "I have to—"

"Yeah. Yes," he agreed, as she slid out of the seat.

She glanced back at him as she exited the coach, one hand fiddling with her star pendant, her expression inscrutable.

Diya slid back into the seat and said happily, "Well? How'd that go?"

"That was unnecessary," Sam told her, even though, left to his own devices, he'd been doing a dismal job of having a conversation with Miss Quinn.

Diya gave him a look that said she knew that, and that her actions had been very necessary. "You probably should have kissed her," said Diya.

"I don't even know her first name," Sam pointed out.

Diya looked impressed. Impressed with what a terrible job Sam was doing of flirting, Sam thought. She said, "Wow. You need a *lot* of help. I might have to enlist the whole street."

"Oh, God, please don't," said Sam, horrified.

"You *should* use the dog," Diya said. "A lot of women who aren't me really like dogs."

"Are you actually going to sit and give me dating advice? Like I don't get that enough from my sister? This is the worst field trip of my entire life," Sam said, "and once when I was eleven we went to the British Museum and I tripped and fell down the stairs and broke my ankle. So I just want you to know where this field trip now ranks."

Diya snorted. "I saw what just happened in this seat. You definitely never went on any field trip better than this one."

Sam glanced out the window, where Miss Quinn was talking to the new coach driver. She had one hand fidgeting with her star pendant still, but the other one was near the ear Sam had lingered by, absently twirling a strand of hair. The one he'd tucked there, he liked to think.

"Okay," he allowed grudgingly. "Maybe."

Arthur spent a moment admiring the whorls of wood-carving on the front of the bookcase in his shed. "He did this?" Arthur asked.

"Mr. Hammersley," Max confirmed, relishing it. "My friend. We are old friends now."

"Are you now?" said Arthur. "That was quick."

"We had tea together and everything."

"Ah, that settles the question then," Arthur agreed. "Lifelong pals, you two are now."

"We are both artists. We understand each other's *souls,*" continued Max, really getting on a roll with his ridiculousness.

"Uh-huh," said Arthur. "Should I be jealous?"

"Always magnificently jealous," said Max.

"Uh-huh," said Arthur again. "Let's eat now, shall we?"

"You're so difficult to impress," Max remarked mournfully, following Arthur across the garden into the house.

"Hence why you were noteworthy," Arthur threw over his shoulder as he walked into the house.

"Ah, that stealth romance of yours," said Max. "Gets me every time."

Arthur chuckled, looking in the fridge and hoping that food might have magically appeared there. "I'm glad you had a good day with your artist friend."

"I think I convinced him to go to see fireworks with all of us for Bonfire Night."

"Are we all going to see fireworks?"

"Pen's note seems to assume there might be some concerted outing."

"And Mr. Hammersley will be accompanying us to see fireworks?"

"Well, if I haven't convinced him, I'll convince him eventually."

"And I *would* be impressed, except it's hardly surprising. You are the most bloody single-minded person alive."

"Quoth pot to kettle," remarked Max, as Jack showed up at the back door for his customary fourth or fifth dinner of the night.

Arthur ignored Max's statement, obediently handing him across some dog food to give Jack. He said instead, "I feel I ought to go speak to Mr. Hammersley. Maybe he and I could have a pint and commiserate over the pointlessness of trying to resist anything you wish done."

Max, completely unrepentant, merely grinned.

Street developments, Pen wrote in her blog, after a detailed recitation of her observations regarding resting heart rate. **Indian Girl and New Boy are now fast friends. Old Man and Blond Gay Man also appear to be fast friends now. I can't tell which is the more startling new relationship. Indian Girl and New Neighbor Boy run up and down the street with Jack at their heels. Jack patrols for squirrels; Indian Girl and New Neighbor Boy are on the hunt for bats, apparently. Old Man and Blond Gay Man hole themselves up in Blond Gay Man's shed, working on a secret art project, I am told.**

Meanwhile Indian Woman has added

New Neighbor Man to her list of People She Must Take Care Of. (Granted, her own family can sometimes be far down on that list, but she does mean well.) She frequently brings food to his house. Whether this is because of the new friendship or something else entirely, I'm not sure.

Chapter 10

The Year 4 Turtledoves will be celebrating Halloween! Please have your child wear his or her costume to school on October 31. Boo!
—Miss Quinn

"So," said Pari, "how many bats do you think there are living in your attic?"

They were supposed to be working on their Christmas play, but talking about the bats again seemed like a better idea.

"I don't know," said Teddy. "Probably a hundred."

"Wow," said Pari, suitably impressed.

"And they've got to stay there forever because you can't move bats without permission, or something."

"Is your dad going to ask for permission?" asked Pari.

"Maybe," said Teddy. "I guess it depends on whether he feels like being lazy or not."

"My mum is *never* lazy," Pari said. "I never see my mum sit still. Maybe she can ask about the bats for your dad."

"Does she know a lot about bats?"

Pari shrugged. "She says your dad likes Miss Quinn, though."

"Yeah, I think so," Teddy agreed. "She makes him smile a lot. Which is nice."

"She says he needs a lot of help, though."

"Help?" echoed Teddy.

"I overheard her talking to my dad, and she said your dad is *hopeless*."

Teddy snorted. "I feel like my Aunt Ellen would agree. Your mum and my Aunt Ellen should hang out sometime."

"Do you think any of the bats are vampires?" asked Pari, getting back to the more important subject.

Jack looked up from where he'd been snoozing on the floor, as if this was a very important topic of conversation.

"No," Teddy said wisely. "No such thing. They're just little flying mice."

Jack, reassured, put his head down and went back to snoring.

"Too bad," Pari said. "I was thinking we might use some of them for a costume."

Sam looked at the *Turtledove Chronicle*, read the message about the Halloween costume, and swore. *Halloween.* He probably should have been thinking about Halloween. Oops.

Over dinner that night, after they had relayed the day's adventures (Sam: Managed to get

253

Roger to stop sending every single e-mail with a high importance alert; Teddy: Remembered for the first time to add one of the UK's hidden *u*'s into a word without any prompting), Sam said, "You're having some kind of Halloween celebration in school and this reminded me that we haven't even talked about what you want to be for Halloween."

"I want to be a football player," said Teddy.

Sam blinked. "Football as in . . . ?"

Teddy rolled his eyes exaggeratedly. "*American* football, Dad. *Regular* football."

"Here football is not—"

"I know the *vocabulary*. But I want to be a regular, American football player for Halloween. And it's my Halloween costume. That means I get to be whatever I want. Isn't that the whole point of the day?"

Sam couldn't deny that. It *was* supposed to be a day to be whatever you wanted to be. If Teddy wanted to be an American football player, then Sam supposed he couldn't argue with it. "You're right," he agreed. Now he just had to figure out where he was going to *find* an American football player costume.

Sam decided it would be wiser to change the subject. "How are things going with the play? You and Pari getting your scene in order?"

"Yeah. Kind of. Pari said her mum says you're hopeless."

254

"Well," said Sam, a little offended, "I think *that's* uncalled for."

"I think she's going to try to help you out with Miss Quinn."

Oh, thought Sam. Well, he supposed in that context, he was fairly hopeless. But . . . "Define 'helping out.' "

Teddy shrugged. "I don't know."

Sam frowned.

"You're a lifesaver," Sam said, when Ellen arrived with her arms full of random detritus, some of which, Sam hoped, might become an American football player costume.

"Cutting Halloween a little close, aren't you?" she said, as she dumped everything in a big pile on the kitchen counter.

"Yes, yes," Sam said impatiently, digging through it. "I know. Can we skip the lecture? Haven't time for the lecture. Have to piece together an entire American football player costume from scraps of things that are definitely not American football uniforms."

"It would all be much easier if he just went as an actual football player. You know, a normal football player. A *real* football player."

Sam sighed. "Trust me, I do not want to get into yet another debate over which version of football is the 'real' version."

"Because there is no debate about that," said Ellen.

255

"Right. But his entire life before he came here had a different view and, frankly, no matter what my opinions on American football might be, his mum and I met for the first time at an American football game and he knows that story and I can't really fault him, Ellen, for making this costume choice."

"Of course not," Ellen said. "You're right. I didn't mean anything by it."

"I know," said Sam, still sorting through fabric. "I'm just feeling a bit stressed, given how late I've cut this."

"Hey, don't beat yourself up too much. One year I completely forgot Halloween and so I grabbed whatever I had handy and dressed Sophie and Evie as 'ladies of the evening.' "

Sam looked across at her. "You dressed your daughters as prostitutes?"

"It sounds bad when you say it like that."

Sam watched for a second as Ellen sorted through the stuff she'd brought before saying, "Also, the stuff you had hanging around your house just happened to be perfect for a prostitute costume?"

"I told you that story to help you feel better," remarked Ellen, "and now I'm regretting it."

Sam grinned, and glanced over at the door as Jack scratched at it. He walked over and opened it and said, "Teddy's at Pari's."

Jack wagged his tail in thanks and moved away.

Sam turned from the door to find Ellen looking at him with a soft, dreamy expression on her face, as if Sam had suddenly done something impossibly sweet.

"What?" Sam said warily. "I don't really speak Dog, you know, he's just . . . very clever. I'm not Doctor Dolittle."

Ellen's lips twitched. "I didn't think you spoke Dog."

"Then what's that look for, like I've done something that's going to make you weep?"

"Weep with pride. Good weeping. Because! Look how far you've come! You were so worried, when you first moved back here, and now look at you. Teddy has friends on the street, and a street dog, and it's Halloween and he's going to dress up and have fun and . . . you've just come a long way. And I'm proud of you and happy for you. It feels like it was just yesterday I was helping you move in and you were a wreck."

"I wasn't a wreck," denied Sam.

"You were a wreck. So. Let's talk about Teddy's teacher. Salad Woman, or whatever you call her."

Sam rolled his eyes. "Carrot Woman. Except that's not what I call her anymore."

"Oh? What do you call her now?" Ellen asked it with an arched eyebrow, as if the answer was going to be something delightfully, deliciously naughty.

So Sam had to say as casually as possible,

looking very closely at a sweatband in Ellen's pile of stuff, "Miss Quinn."

"Miss Quinn?" Ellen echoed, sounding like she was swallowing hysterical laughter. "Oh, yes, that is definitely progress."

"Stop it, okay?" Sam reached over and gave Ellen, now engaged in open hilarity, a minor shove. "It's . . . complicated. She's Teddy's teacher, and Teddy *adores* her, and what if it doesn't work out?"

"What if lots of things," Ellen said. "What if it does? She's not going to be Teddy's teacher forever. And presumably no matter who you start dating you would hope that Teddy likes her, so you're always going to have the issue of worrying about something not working out with someone Teddy likes. Yeah, it's complicated. That's life."

Sam sighed. "It's just that I had forgotten what complete *agony* this entire situation is. Like, falling in love is bollocks."

Ellen seized upon that immediately, eyes sharp on Sam. "Falling in love? Do you think you're in love with her?"

"No," Sam said. "But I don't know where it could go, you know? I . . . want to know more about her, I want to know the *her* of her, and meeting people you feel like you could have endless conversations with is a rare thing and a precious thing and—"

"Then don't complicate it," said Ellen gently.

"You're right, about all of that. So don't complicate it. Have you talked to Teddy about this?"

"Not explicitly," Sam admitted. "I mean, he
knows, about my interest, but we haven't—"

"I would talk to him, then. And I would stop
stressing out about it. Life's too short, Sam. Too
short for you to spend time second-guessing what
could be happiness."

Sam knew she was right. Sam knew that he, of
all people, should know that. He nodded.

Ellen said, "Right, then. What you *should* stress
out about is your last-minute Halloween costume
here."

On Halloween morning, when the doorbell rang,
Sam was in the middle of using his first cup
of coffee to approximate being a functioning
human being and Teddy was in the middle of
eating his cereal.

Sam looked blankly toward the front door.
"Was that the doorbell?"

It rang again.

"Uh huh." Teddy nodded. "The day's first
adventure."

"Like putting that costume together for you
wasn't adventure enough," mumbled Sam, and
went to answer the door.

It was Diya and Pari. Pari was dressed as a very
realistic zombie. Diya was carrying a tray.

Sam forced himself to be pleasant, even though

259

he thought it was a bit early for neighborly socializing. "Don't you look terrifying," he said to Pari.

Pari grinned and roared and grinned again. The grinning really undercut the effectiveness of the roaring. "Is Teddy here?"

"Yes, he's finishing up his cereal. Did you want to walk to school together?" They didn't usually. Because usually Sam was running incredibly late and just about getting Teddy out the door. He didn't know how Diya was so unruffled and organized, when getting a child ready for school was like having to forge a major international treaty on a daily basis.

"Cereal?" Pari wrinkled her nose. "That's what he's having for breakfast on *Halloween?* And not *brains?*"

"Well, he isn't dressed as a zombie," Sam pointed out reasonably. "Only zombies have brains for breakfast."

"I guess." Pari, clearly tired of the boring grown-ups, went running past Sam toward Teddy in the kitchen.

Sam looked at Diya. "I assume she didn't actually have brains for breakfast, but I suppose I shouldn't question Pari's commitment to her costume."

"If you put some green food coloring in some scrambled eggs, it looks like brains." Diya shrugged.

Sam stared. "You actually made her 'brains' for breakfast?"

"To stop her whining about it."

"Did it even taste good?"

"She didn't complain. Here." Diya handed across the tray.

"What's this?" Sam peeked underneath the foil.

"It's coconut chikki," Diya replied.

"Well, it looks delicious," Sam said. "It was very sweet of you to make it for me."

Diya scowled. "I didn't make it for *you*."

"Oh," said Sam awkwardly, and wanted to say, *You're on my doorstep offering me this tray. It seemed like a logical conclusion to draw.*

Diya continued, "I made it for the class's Halloween party today."

Sam blinked at her, horrified. "Oh, God, were we supposed to make something to bring? Was that in the *Turtledove Chronicle*? I didn't see it. Damn, I'll have to run to—"

"No," Diya hissed at him, and the *idiot* was only implied but it was very loudly implied. "They are for *you* to offer for the Halloween party."

Sam felt hopelessly confused, and he wasn't even entirely sure it could all be blamed on the lack of coffee. "For me . . . ?"

"Yes." Diya nodded, like he was finally grasping the concept.

He wasn't grasping the concept. "You . . . want

me to pretend to have made an Indian dessert? Why? No one would ever believe that. I routinely ruin *cereal*."

Diya rolled her eyes. "Which is exactly why you could never bring anything you had made to class. The food at your barbecue was really very sad."

"Wow," said Sam drily, "thanks."

Diya ignored him in favor of saying, "But *this*. My chikki is delicious and Miss Quinn will be impressed."

Finally, *finally* everything clicked into place. Maybe the coffee kicked in, too. Sam sighed. "Diya, she'll know I didn't make this—"

"But she'll appreciate the thought."

"But it's *your* thought."

"It's my thought I'm giving to you. It's fine. You are hopeless. I am trying to make you less hopeless."

"I'm not hopeless," Sam grumbled. Diya gave him a look.

"I am not *entirely* hopeless," he amended.

"No, if you were entirely hopeless, I would warn Miss Quinn away from you. But instead I think you have enough potential that she should give you a chance."

"You excel at damning with faint praise," remarked Sam.

"What does that mean?" asked Diya.

"Never mind. I suppose I'll escort the children to school and hand across the chikki?"

"Yes," said Diya. "Don't drop it on the way."

"Not *that* hopeless," Sam told her.

But then he almost dropped it carrying it back into the kitchen and reevaluated that assessment.

Bill watched Sam and Teddy and the little Indian girl leave for school, the children dressed absurdly, and it was only then that he realized the date. Halloween.

He was still standing at the window trying to discern what Teddy was meant to be when the black woman from up the street who was always running spotted him and waved enthusiastically. Jack, distracted from trotting behind the children, now came nipping at the woman's heels as she jogged up Bill's front path.

Bill wanted to just say *go away*. Or better yet, not answer the door. But she'd seen him standing right there and he felt compelled not to be rude.

That was the problem with talking to all these people now. Suddenly Bill felt like he couldn't just *ignore* them any longer. There was always something going on. Never a dull moment.

The woman rapped on his door and waved to him cheerfully through the window.

Jack barked.

How had he started talking to all of these people in the first place? He was now no longer clear on how he'd got to this point. He swung the door open and demanded, "What do you want?"

Jack barked hello to him and added a good morning lick for good measure.

"Did you get my note, about Bonfire Night?" she asked.

"Yes. I got it."

"So I've been thinking. The families with children will of course want to attend the fireworks. And Max is mad about fireworks; he always makes a point of dragging Arthur to a show every year. So I think it makes sense that I be the one to stay home with Jack, and I wanted to make sure you were all right with Jack staying at my house, or might you prefer that I stay here with Jack?"

Bill stared at her. "Stay here with Jack?" he managed finally.

"Yes." The woman nodded.

"Stay *here* with Jack?" Bill felt that suggestion was so absurd it needed to be repeated twice.

"Or I could take Jack to my house," offered the woman. "I wanted to know which you preferred."

"Why do you want to know that?"

The woman beamed at him. "Because Jack belongs to the street and you're part of the street. A vitally important part."

Bill lifted his eyebrows. This woman was off her rocker. "Why does anyone need to stay with Jack in the first place?"

"Because fireworks are very distressing to

dogs, and so someone ought to stay home with Jack and make sure he can feel comforted. And I think it makes sense for me to be the one to do that. I can take or leave the fireworks; they're not important to me."

"I'm not going to any fireworks," Bill said. "Jack can stay with me."

"Oh, but you must!" protested the woman. "Everyone is looking forward to going to the fireworks with you!"

"You're daft," was Bill's succinct pronouncement.

The woman laughed. "Maybe," she said. "You might be right. Anyway. Think about it." And then, with a cheerful wave, she went jogging off.

Jack stayed behind, looking after her.

"After a conversation with her, we deserve a nap, don't you think?"

It was early in the morning, but Bill had never known Jack not to be utterly delighted at the prospect of a nap.

Jack wagged his tail happily and trotted inside.

Pari and Teddy seemed happy enough as they walked to school, chattering away in their costumes. Other kids walking along the street toward school were also in costumes, and Sam compared them critically to Teddy's and thought that he hadn't done too badly.

Teddy's uniform was a little dubious. Sam had

managed to find an old jersey and the shoulder pads within it were created from shoulder pads from a hideous sequined jacket Ellen had owned ("I had to dress up as Cyndi Lauper once," she had explained. "Why?" Sam had asked. "Don't ask questions you don't want the answer to," Ellen had replied). But Sam had managed to track down a genuine US football helmet that fitted Teddy's head in a vague sort of way, and Sam thought that was all that was necessary to signal what the costume was.

Sam, feeling only a little like an idiot, followed the children into the school, carefully balancing his tray of Diya-made coconut chikki. Miss Quinn—he really *had* to learn her name at some point—smiled dazzlingly when she saw him. Or maybe it was just a standard smile for her, and Sam interpreted it as dazzling. Maybe Miss Quinn smiled at everyone in an equally dazzling way, and there was nothing particularly special about him.

"Hello, Teddy and Pari," she said, coming up to the knot of them. "Terrifying zombie. And what are you meant to be, Teddy?"

"A football player," Teddy said staunchly.

"An American football player," Sam clarified to Miss Quinn, who looked vaguely confused. "He insisted."

"Aw, that's sweet. So." Miss Quinn, hand fidgeting with the star charm on her necklace, looked at him and smiled. "To what do I owe the pleasure of this visit to my classroom?"

Was that an emphasis on the word *pleasure,* or was that Sam's overeager imagination? He wanted to read *attraction* and *infatuation* in every tiny movement of Miss Quinn's. Of course, there was also the fact that Sam was so attuned to every tiny movement of Miss Quinn's that he noticed this, and wondered if she was as attuned to his tiny movements in return, and if he was projecting *attraction* and *infatuation.*

"Dad," hissed Teddy, and Sam realized he was staring.

"Oh. Right." Sam cleared his throat. "I have brought you coconut chikki," he explained. He tried to offer the tray of chikki with a flourish but he probably just looked like an idiot.

Miss Quinn peeked under the foil and said, "Coconut chikki! How talented of you!"

"I didn't make it," Sam said, deciding it was ridiculous to pretend otherwise. "Pari's mother made it."

Miss Quinn looked up at him, dimples peeking. "I assumed. I assumed that the man utterly bewildered by vegetables hadn't suddenly started making coconut chikki."

"I can make plenty of things," Sam said, which was kind of a lie. He even felt Teddy give him a dry look that Sam ignored.

Not that Sam had a choice, because Miss Quinn

laughed, and Sam would have ignored a great deal if Miss Quinn was laughing. Sam would notice almost nothing in the face of Miss Quinn laughing.

Teddy, getting antsy, said, "We're going to go and play."

"Yeah," Sam agreed, forcing his attention back to him. "Have a wonderful day, both of you."

Pari smiled at him, as did Teddy, and then they rushed off together.

Miss Quinn said, "You will have to prove that eventually, you know. That you actually are capable of producing food that might keep you and your child alive."

Which . . . might have been a way of trying to lobby for a date invitation? Or might have just been a teacher expressing concern about the welfare of a student? Sam wasn't sure. Damn it, it had just been *so long* since he had had to do this. Had he ever even had to do this? It was different, meeting someone you were interested in as a university student rather than an adult. It was different trying to decide how you ought to pursue a relationship with your *son's teacher*.

So of course Sam said a ridiculous thing in reply, which was, "She thinks I'm hopeless."

"Who?" said Miss Quinn, not even questioning the *hopeless* part of Sam's statement, because clearly that was true.

"Pari's mum," Sam answered.

"Hopeless about what?"

"You," Sam heard himself say, as if from a great distance.

No, no, Clever Sam shouted in his head. *What are you doing? Why would you say that? You sound pathetic.*

But then Miss Quinn's smile widened, and her eyes were bright, and she didn't look away from him; indeed, if anything, Sam thought it possible she leaned closer to him.

Well done, said Foolish Sam who said whatever popped into his head. *Brilliant thing to say.*

"And what's *your* assessment on that particular front?" asked Miss Quinn.

Sam looked at her, definitely standing much closer to him, and was reminded that he'd fallen directly into those eyes the last time he'd been in near proximity with her and he still hadn't found a way of struggling out of them. He made a list of the things he wanted to do: tuck a strand of her hair behind her ear again; lean forward to press his nose against the soft skin beneath her jaw; taste that teasing corner of her mouth, the taunting invitation of her dimples. Sam couldn't decide which he would rather do first. "Oh, absolutely hopeless," he murmured, drinking in the sight of her, every incredible, amazing detail of her. "Absolutely."

The smile faded on Miss Quinn's face, replaced by a look that was intent, and expectant, lips parted and breath short. Her eyes left his to dart to his mouth and then back up again. Sam thought how easy it would be to cup his hand around her cheek, lean closer, press his forehead against hers and breathe, for just a second, in that world-falling-away stillness that Miss Quinn seemed able to provoke in him. Everything else—*everything*—seemed very far away. There was only the two of them, standing there, quiet and anticipating, and Sam inching himself closer to a decision, to that point where he would tip toward her and—

A gaggle of children suddenly came running up, having an enormous disagreement over something. Miss Quinn looked at them, breaking the spell, and Sam blinked and straightened away from her, shaking off the vestiges of the daze. And Clever Sam shouted at Foolish Sam in his head, *For God's sake, the only place worse than a school coach for a first grown-up kiss would definitely be a noisy, riotous Year 4 classroom.*

Miss Quinn gave Sam an apologetic look. "I must—"

Sam forced himself to say, "Yeah. Yes. Of course. Go," and make a pointless gesture with his hands, and call out, "Happy Halloween," as Miss Quinn moved into the pack of children, and she glanced over her shoulder at him with a little wistful smile.

Sam ducked out of the classroom and started the walk back home and that smile lingered with him, wrapped around his heart, and settled warmly in his stomach, like a gentle glow, and the feeling of quiet, contented stillness inside him never quite went away. The world hummed all around him, busy and bustling, and Sam felt a little bit like he floated through it, barely touching the pavement, barely registering all of the people jostling past him.

Maybe, Sam thought, it *was* like being in love.

"And what are you supposed to be?" asked Tommy Dower, with that usual *look* on his face.

Teddy had learned to *hate* Tommy Dower. Teddy had a list of things he hated in his life. It used to be that *England* in general was at the top of that list. At the moment it was Tommy Dower who occupied the first part of the list. The rest of England was improving in Teddy's view, but the corner of the country occupied by Tommy Dower was still horrendous.

"I'm a football player," Teddy said, and gave Tommy Dower an answering *look*.

"A football player?" said Tommy, and started laughing, and all of Tommy's annoying *friends* started laughing. Most of the time it seemed as if almost every person in the class was Tommy Dower's friend except for Teddy. "What sort of rubbish football player is that?"

Pari leaned over Teddy to insert hotly, "He's an *American* football player," because Pari never stayed out of an oncoming fight, in Teddy's experience.

"Oh, like, *fake* football?" sneered Tommy.

"It isn't fake—" Pari began, coming to Teddy's defense. Except that then Molly Wasserstein said, "I think it's kind of cool."

Teddy blinked, surprised.

So did Tommy.

Molly, ignoring all of them, came up to Teddy and picked up his helmet and said, "Can I try it on?"

Teddy and Pari exchanged equally confused looks. Was bullying right around the corner? Was this a trick?

"Sure?" Teddy said, not at all sure.

Molly put the helmet on, and it swallowed up her head, and Teddy could just about make out her eyes through the protective grille. She said, "This is aces in here!"

Which started a clamoring from the other kids—save Tommy. But everyone seemed to want a turn in the helmet.

Teddy watched the helmet get passed around the classroom and couldn't help but feel a moment of pure pleasure. Pari nudged him and smiled when he looked at her, like, *This is nice, isn't it?*

It *was* nice, and even better to have someone to share it with, thought Teddy.

● ● ●

Teddy and Pari walked home from school, Halloween costumes slightly bedraggled, and Jack came to meet them as usual, bouncing about in excitement at having them back, and chasing a few leaves around the street for their amusement, and otherwise telling them all about what they had missed while they were at school, which was generally, they assumed, standoffs with the street squirrels.

When Dad greeted him at the door and said, "How was your day?" Teddy replied enthusiastically, "It was an *awesome* Halloween. Everyone loved my helmet. They all wanted to try it on. It was great. Great costume."

"Oh, good," said Dad, as Teddy went running to the back of the house with Jack following, barking joyfully.

"Next year," Teddy said, opening the door to let Jack out and then preparing to follow behind him, "we should get Jack a costume, too."

"Have we thought through," Libby asked, "what might happen to someone who lives in a desert, like the manger owner in the class play, if climate change causes it to suddenly snow?" The class frowned intensely, all of them clearly thinking about this.

So Libby gave them some gentle prompting. "What do we do in our houses, when it gets cold?"

"Turn on the heating," said Marya immediately.

"Right. Do you think that the manger owner has heat?"

"In his *stable?*"said Pari, wrinkling her nose.

Libby was pleased. "Exactly. So what do you think will happen to all the animals?"

"They'll be cold," said Patrick.

"Wouldn't the baby Jesus make them warm?" said Edwina.

"The baby Jesus is just a *baby,*" said Molly. "He's not doing anything special yet aside from crying. Trust me. My baby brother does *nothing.*"

"Is your baby brother the baby Jesus, though?" asked Pari, very seriously, as if this was going to make a difference in the conversation.

Libby interjected, "Say the baby Jesus doesn't wander into your stable to be born. All of your animals are cold. You'll have to find some way to get them warm. And you probably don't even have useful heating in your house, because you live in the desert."

The children absorbed this solemnly.

"So you'll need to figure out something. And it's going to cost you money."

"Heating is expensive," said Misty.

"Very expensive. Very dear. So what do you think can be done for the poor manger owners?"

"Insurance," said Gilbert. "When my mum got in a car accident, the insurance helped us fix the car when we didn't have money to pay for it."

"Exactly," said Libby. "Insurance. So let's talk about what insurance is. Because insurance is going to depend on *probability*." She turned to the board.

Teddy and Pari were sprawled on their stomachs on the carpet in the lounge, working laboriously on their scenes for the Christmas play.

They'd been at it for a while, and Sam, curious, finally couldn't stand it any longer and wandered into the lounge and said, "So tell me about the school play."

"It's about the birth of Jesus," Teddy said.

"Do you know that story?" asked Pari.

Sometimes Sam couldn't tell if Pari would have asked these questions of anyone or if she genuinely worried that Sam had an appalling lack of knowledge. Sam said, "I know the story. What's your scene about?"

"Our scene is about the owner of the manger," said Teddy.

"Really?" said Sam. "He's not someone you hear a lot about in that story, usually."

"Right," Pari agreed. "But he has a lot to say. Considering that all of his animals are in the freezing cold probably dying because he doesn't have any heat."

Sam blinked in surprise. "That is a lot of stress for him to be under."

"Exactly." Pari went back to her piece of paper.

Teddy said, "His animals are dying because of climate change. He used to live in a desert, and now there's a blizzard."

"Baby Jesus is being born in a blizzard?" asked Sam.

Pari nodded.

Sam grinned. "I like this twist. Teddy was born in a blizzard, you know."

"You never said that!" Pari said to Teddy. "That's so cool!"

"It was in America," said Teddy, as if to remind Pari that it hadn't been a blizzard she had also got to experience.

"That's mostly where blizzards happen," Pari agreed. "These days. Climate change may change things."

"True," Sam agreed.

"And that's where insurance kicks in!" added Teddy enthusiastically.

"Insurance?" Sam had not expected that to be the next topic of conversation.

Teddy nodded. "Miss Quinn told us all about insurance, and how it's based on probability, and how you have to pay more based on how likely something is, and so it's not likely you'd have a snowstorm in the desert, so he probably wouldn't pay much."

"*Unless* climate change makes snowstorms likely *everywhere*," added Pari.

"And if it's *super* unlikely, then maybe the person who owns the manger doesn't even *have* insurance, and then what can they do?" finished Teddy.

"Sounds like this insurance situation is very intense," said Sam.

"It is," Pari agreed, nodding wisely. "It's going to be very dramatic."

"Jack is going to whine very pitifully," Teddy said.

"Whine about what?"

"The whole situation. He will 'provoke sympathy.' Miss Quinn says you want to 'provoke sympathy' in your audience if you want them on your side," Teddy announced grandly.

"This is true," Sam said. "I just didn't know Jack was in the play."

"Oh, we're writing him in," said Pari. "He's going to be one of the animals in the manger."

"Are you having other live animals, too? Live donkeys? Live cows?"

Pari and Teddy both gave him the perfect looks of despairing put-upon-ness.

"Dad," said Teddy. "Who has *live cows?*"

"Do *you* know anyone who has a donkey?" added Pari.

"No," Sam admitted.

"Dogs can be at the birth of Jesus," said Teddy.

"There's nothing that says dogs can't be there," said Pari.

"So Jack will be there because Jack's what we have."

"Jack and insurance problems," remarked Sam. And then, as it occurred to him, "Hey. You know who works in insurance?"

Max was getting out the Christmas decorations.

Max loved Christmas. Every year, Max was the first person on the street to put the decorations out. Every year, he hoped to persuade Arthur to let him do it before Halloween. He had not yet hit upon the magical means of persuasion that would make Arthur permit him to do that, but Arthur had stopped fighting him on anything post-Halloween. As soon as Halloween was over, Christmas decorations were fair game.

Max's approach to Christmas decorations was grand and artistic. Every year he worked intensely on a different vision. There was no need to be boring and routine when it came to Christmas. Every year, Max was determined to do something new and unique. Max's Christmas decorating schemes were *art*.

Max kept the Christmas decorations upstairs in the art studio, which was an expansive, airy attic with plenty of storage space. Arthur had suggested putting the decorations in the shed and Max had been appalled. Something as precious as Christmas decorations must be in the house for safekeeping. What if thieves broke into the shed?

"And stole Christmas decorations?" Arthur had said skeptically.

Arthur clearly didn't grasp the true value of their spectacular Christmas decorations. And Max had managed to win the storage space discussion, as the art studio was considered his sole domain.

So Max was standing in the art studio dragging out Christmas decorations and arranging them systematically over the floor, according to type, color, size and *artistic attraction,* which was difficult to describe, but Max knew its level instantly. When the doorbell rang.

"Darling?" Max shouted. "Could you get that?" He'd left Arthur in the kitchen, but Arthur had been talking about popping out to the shops, and Max had been too caught up in the Christmas decorations to notice whether Arthur had left yet or not.

Max, getting no response from Arthur, moved out of the art studio and halfway down the stairs. Arthur was still home, and had opened the door to reveal Teddy and Pari and Jack. Jack came bounding happily up the stairs to Max, tail wagging in greeting.

"Hello, Jack," Max said, responding with a scratch behind Jack's ears. "And hello, children. To what do we owe this visit?"

"We've come to ask Arthur about insurance," said Teddy happily.

Max looked at Arthur in amused surprise. "Oh, really?"

Arthur's ears were adorably pink with a pleasure that Max knew he would strenuously deny if asked. He said, "So they say."

"We have lots of questions," said Pari. "It's a very serious matter."

"Not too serious, I hope." Max glanced at Arthur. "I will leave you to your important clients."

"Thank you," said Arthur, looking torn between confusion and approval regarding the gravity with which Pari and Teddy were clearly treating this occasion.

Max went upstairs to occupy himself with the Christmas decorations again, normally an all-consuming task, but he was hopelessly distracted by the idea of Arthur, downstairs, with two children who inexplicably wanted to know about *insurance*. The idea of Arthur with children was irresistible in general. They didn't do much interacting with children.

Eventually, Max could resist no longer, and crept down the stairs just far enough to peek around the wall. Arthur was at the kitchen table, facing the children, whose backs were to Max, so Max could see the little frown of concentration on Arthur's face. He looked as if they were having a very serious conversation indeed. Max was fond of telling Arthur that his heart had fallen at Arthur's feet the very first time he saw him, and Arthur scoffed, but Max had felt it, and he felt it again at that moment, Arthur so somber and intent toward eight-year-old insurance issues, whatever those might be.

Pari was saying, "So if someone doesn't have insurance, there's nothing you can do for them?"

"Nothing the insurance company could do," Arthur said.

"But of course we would all try to pull together to help them out."

"But it would be better to have insurance," concluded Pari.

"It's always a good idea. Then you can stop worrying about it."

Max smiled fondly. Arthur was *such* an insurance agent.

"Sometimes it can be hard to stop worrying," said Teddy.

Arthur looked at him closely, and then said, "Yeah. It can be. And that's okay. It's just also good to sometimes make yourself take a deep breath and see what you have already, because if you're too worried about what could be, sometimes you forget to enjoy what is. You forget to appreciate the good stuff in your life. Sometimes you have insurance just to give your head some room to enjoy what it is you're trying so desperately to protect. It's your backup plan to keep safe the things that you love."

Max leaned his head against the wall and watched the look on Arthur's face.

"Yeah, like enjoying your stable with a baby

Jesus inside," said Pari, which made zero sense to Max.

And chased the reflective, thoughtful look off Arthur's face. "Yeah," he said wryly. "Like that."

"Dad makes us say adventures every night," said Teddy.

"Adventures?" echoed Arthur.

"Yeah. A fun thing that happened to us during the day. I think so we don't forget to appreciate the good stuff."

Arthur smiled. "That's a nice thing to do. It's a good idea. Your dad's clever."

"His adventures are usually pretty boring," said Teddy. "What would your adventure be?"

"Living with Max," said Arthur, tone desert-dry, which made Max laugh and reveal his presence.

The children turned to look at him. Arthur also looked at him, and Max winked at him, and Arthur rolled his eyes.

"Arthur gave us lots of information about environmental insurance," Pari announced as she stood.

"How kind of him," said Max. "Is that what you wanted to know about?"

Pari and Teddy both nodded.

"And what about you, Jack?" Max asked Jack, who had come bouncing over to be greeted again as if Max had not already greeted him before. "What did you learn about?"

"Jack learned about the Jaffa Cakes the children

kept slipping him under the table," replied Arthur. "Here, make sure you take them home with you," he said to the children, handing them the package that had been on the table.

"Thanks, Arthur," they chorused. "Bye, Max!"

They swept out the door, followed by Jack, who gave one last courteous bark good-bye, and Max watched them through the window as they went racing up the street.

Max looked back at Arthur, who walked to stand at the foot of the staircase, two steps below where Max was. Max lifted an eyebrow. "They wanted to know about environmental insurance?"

"For their Christmas play at school."

"This must be the only Christmas play in history with insurance as a major story point," remarked Max.

"And climate change," said Arthur.

Max chuckled and pulled Arthur in, the height difference imposed by the steps making Arthur even with Max's chest. He said, "This sounds like a Christmas play not to be missed." There was a moment of silence. "You gave them all my Jaffa Cakes, you big softie."

Arthur sighed. "Walk me through your Christmas Spectacle idea this year."

Which made Max brighten and forget all about Jaffa Cakes.

Chapter 11

Bonfire & Firework Display!

Gates open at **6:00pm**, Bonfire starts at **7:00pm**, Firework display starts at **8:00pm**.

Admission:
Adults £4. Children £1. Under 5's Free.
Limited parking available—car park £1.
Food available.

Children's rides.
For safety reasons—no fireworks or sparklers.

No alcohol allowed.
Under 14's must be accompanied by an adult.

Emilia was spying out the window, so she saw the exact moment the Basaks left their house to head to the firework display. Mr. and Mrs. Basak stepped out first, although Pari quickly skipped in front of them. Sai brought up the rear and looked up toward Emilia's window as he passed, lifting his eyebrows in silent invitation.

Emilia immediately turned from the window and sought out her parents, who were sitting in silence in the lounge, her dad watching TV and her mother reading a book.

Emilia said, "I want to go to the fireworks. Can I go? The rest of the street is going. I can just walk up with them." She spoke quickly, knowing that the Basaks would stop to retrieve the Bishops, but then they would all be on their way, and it might be difficult to find them again.

Dad looked up from the telly. "The fireworks? Actually, that's a good idea. Sounds like fun. We haven't gone to see fireworks in ages." He glanced over at Mum, who hadn't even looked up from her book. "Anna?" he said.

"Hmm?" Mum looked up at that, still distracted.

"I think I'm going to go to the fireworks with Emilia," said Dad. "You should join us."

It wasn't what Emilia had wanted—she had wanted to be able to slip off somewhere with Sai—and she was honestly shocked. She couldn't remember the last time her parents had done something like this, *together*.

So she looked at Mum, genuinely curious what her mother would say.

"That's okay," Mum said. "You two go."

Dad sighed. "Anna. Come with us, hmm?"

"Are they even having fireworks?" asked Mum

without looking up from her book. "It's not the best night for it."

Emilia glanced out the window, where the air was wet enough that it glistened with mist. Not that she cared, because the fireworks were hardly the point for her.

"It might clear before they start. Come with us, it would be fun." Dad walked over to Mum and picked up her hand and kissed it, and Emilia had to turn away at the naked emotional plea on Dad's face.

Apparently Mum was unmoved, because Emilia heard her reply, "It's been a long day. I don't feel like going anywhere. I'll just stay in here with the cats."

There was a long silence. Emilia risked a glance over her shoulder, to see Dad standing by Mum's chair, still and quiet, Mum still reading her book. As if he wasn't standing right there.

Emilia had wanted to go to the firework display by herself but suddenly she experienced a bolt of pure fury toward Mum, for doing this to Dad. She said loudly, "Come on, Dad. Let's get going. I could murder some chips."

She found herself holding her breath, but Dad said eventually, "Yeah, let's go."

"I just want to say," said Teddy, shrugging away from Sam when he tried to zip up his jacket a little tighter, "that having fireworks in *November* is a terrible idea. July's much better than standing outside in *cold rain*."

"I actually can't argue with you there." Sam handed Teddy a hat.

Teddy recoiled. "I'm not wearing that."

"It's cold outside, and rainy, and I don't want you to catch pneumonia."

Teddy said, "Whose fault is it that we're in a place where I'm going to catch pneumonia?"

"Your grandparents' fault, for giving birth to me in this country and not a warmer, drier climate," replied Sam, as the doorbell rang.

Sam opened it on the Basaks, who all chorused hellos, except for Sai, who was lingering in the back and glancing moodily up the street as if waiting for somebody. Arthur and Max and Pen were heading in their direction, but Sam doubted that was who Sai was looking for.

Everyone met up and exchanged general observations about the weather and whether the fireworks would actually happen. While they were debating it, the Pachutas' door opened and closed and Emilia and her father stepped out and walked up to the knot of people. Sam noticed that Sai, who had been basically sulking, brightened right away.

Emilia's father said mildly, "Mind if we join you?"

"Not at all," said Sam pleasantly, noting that Sai looked as if he agreed. Neither Marcel Pachuta nor Diya and Darsh Basak seemed to notice, however. Darsh was talking to Arthur about something and Diya was busy nosily nudging past Sam to ask Marcel where Anna was.

Pen said, "Hang on, let me dart in here to collect Jack and make sure Mr. Hammersley joins all of you."

Sam found himself standing next to Max and said, "Speaking of Mr. Hammersley, what exactly is this top-secret art project you're working on?"

"Top secret," replied Max cheerfully. "How's the environmental insurance Christmas play coming along?"

Sam chuckled. "Ridiculous, isn't it? But I think very well. I hope Arthur didn't mind that I sent them in his direction."

"Are you joking?" said Max. "It was the highlight of Arthur's year so far. He was tickled pink at getting to explain his beloved insurance."

"I think they're working on probability in school or something," Sam said, as Mr. Hammersley opened the door and Jack came bounding out.

Sam couldn't hear the conversation Pen and Mr. Hammersley had, but then Pen turned to all of them and called, "Mr. Hammersley doesn't wish to go to the fireworks! Tell him that's rubbish!"

"That's rubbish!" they all shouted obediently.

Teddy called out, "Please come, Mr. Hammersley. It's going to be so much fun!"

"Absolutely, Bill," Max shouted from beside Sam. "We can't go without you!"

Mr. Hammersley stood in the doorway, plainly bewildered.

"Oh, *do* come, Mr. Hammersley!" Pari exclaimed.

Mr. Hammersley blinked at them, and then said, after a long moment, "All right. I suppose I'll come."

And looked startled when they cheered in response.

Anna made herself a cup of chamomile tea and sat with her stash of chocolate and told herself she did not regret the decision not to join the others at the fireworks. It wasn't as if she had any great fondness for fireworks. Neither, frankly, did Marcel and Emilia. She didn't know why they had suddenly decided to go—why everyone on the street was suddenly deciding to do everything together. Pen Cheever from down the street walked to her house with that street dog and waved happily to Anna in the window like they were *friends,* when they had barely ever spoken.

Anna found herself reading the same sentence over and over, and tossed the book away from her in disgust. It was *ridiculous* to be this fixated over an event she hadn't wanted to attend in the first place. What had she wanted instead? For everyone to stay at home with her?

In the distance, fireworks began to thump and thunder. Anna checked her watch. It was far too soon for the firework display Marcel and Emilia were attending. She had hours yet to be alone. And she should have been rejoicing. It was blessedly quiet in the house, and she had her cats and her chocolate and her tea. What more could she want?

Anna looked out the window at the street, where all was quiet. Not even the street dog wandering about. Anna didn't realize until that moment how accustomed she'd become to the sight of that dog.

The fireworks kept pounding away *somewhere*. Anna checked her watch again, wondering anew if it could be the display Marcel and Emilia had gone off to. Her curiosity got the better of her, and she decided to just step outside to see if she could see the firework display. It wasn't the best night for it, but one never knew.

Anna went to the front door and opened it . . . and that was when Socks streaked outside.

And as she shouted after him, "Socks!" Tabby followed close behind.

Pen was sitting cross-legged on the sofa, her laptop cradled on her lap, staring at the latest article she was working on, which was about current trends in wine.

"Do you know anything about *terroir*?" she

asked Jack. She'd already asked the question of Chester, who, as usual, refused to share any vast knowledge he might have with her.

Jack didn't seem much more forthcoming. He looked at her and whined, tail wagging forlornly, and then walked over to the door and glanced back at her hopefully.

Pen shook her head. "Nope. No outside for you tonight. I read up on this, and during Bonfire Night you're supposed to keep dogs inside so they don't get too upset. And you might be a very special dog but you *are* included in the category of 'dog.' So even if you *do* want to update yourself on the current position of all street squirrels, you must stay inside for the night."

Jack looked unconvinced. He paced around the living room, plainly very unhappy with her.

In the distance, Pen could hear fireworks start up, which explained why Jack was so unsettled. She glanced at her watch. Early for any of the official firework displays to have started but probably some private parties getting impatient for the main event.

"They're fireworks," Pen informed Jack, who tipped his ears in her direction as if paying close attention to her. "Just a lot of noise and color, nothing to worry about. Actually, you can't see color, can you? No wonder dogs hate them so much. To you they're just a load of noise, aren't they? But don't worry. It's just a matter of . . .

celebrating something that frankly nobody cares about anymore. So really, it's just an excuse for us all to make a lot of noise, I guess."

Jack cocked his head to the side.

Pen shrugged. "People are odd. What can I say?"

Jack made a huffing sound and walked over to the front window and stood up on his paws to look outside.

Pen watched him for a moment, but he seemed a bit calmer, so she turned back to her laptop. *Which of these whites is all "white" with you?* her article read currently. Pen rolled her eyes at herself and opened her blog instead and started drafting an entry.

Hope everyone is having a lovely Bonfire Night! I am currently sitting here with Street Dog Jack, as I volunteered to stay home this year and soothe him about the fireworks. I'm not sure I'm doing such a good job soothing him, I confess. Having a difficult time explaining the point of fireworks other than to make a lot of noise, which Jack does not agree with! Anyway, everyone else on the street has gone off to view fireworks, including Old Man. The only one who stayed behind was Polish Woman, even though her husband and daughter both went. Again, don't know what—

Jack started whining again, and his tail began to beat back and forth more furiously.

"What is it?" Pen asked.

Jack turned in an anxious little circle, still whining.

"Jack, it's just fireworks," Pen assured him, but he seemed anxious enough that she stood and went over to the window and peered out. The street seemed quiet as far as she could tell.

Jack obviously disagreed with her assessment. He suddenly began barking furiously and practically flinging himself at the door in his eagerness to get out.

And Pen knew that she was supposed to keep Jack indoors to keep him calm, but in the heat of the moment, in the face of Jack's frantic barking, she opened the door without thinking, and Jack immediately shot out of it, into the street beyond.

"So, young American," Max said to Teddy as they walked to the park. "Are you bewildered by our Bonfire Night tradition?"

"Miss Quinn told us all about it," Teddy said. "It's basically like the Fourth of July only with more blowing people up."

"Well, actually, no one ended up blown up," said Arthur.

"Which is why we celebrate," added Pari.

"You know, the Fourth of July wasn't exactly a gunpowder-free zone," remarked Max.

"I think it's a strange reason for a celebration," said Darsh. "And at a miserable time of year."

"That I don't disagree with," Max responded. "The Americans had the right idea, plotting their treason in the summertime. Now, who's Miss Quinn? Your teacher?"

Teddy nodded. "She's basically the best teacher in the entire universe."

"She's behind the Christmas play involving environmental insurance?" asked Max. "Arthur approves of her."

"So does my dad. If he ever gets his act together." Teddy glared at him.

Sam became aware of all eyes turning to him and hoped it was dark enough outside to cover his blush.

"Oho," said Max happily. "Is this *romantic intrigue* I sense?"

"No," said Sam. "No romantic intrigue."

"Only because my dad is hopeless," said Teddy. "Isn't my dad hopeless, Mrs. Basak?"

"Absolutely hopeless," Diya agreed frankly.

"Thanks, everyone," said Sam drily. "Your support really means a lot to me."

"Aw, don't take it personally," said Max, and flung a casual arm over Arthur's shoulders. "This one here was also hopeless. You only have to be a little less than hopeless for a little while. It can be done."

Arthur rolled his eyes.

Max said, "What do you think, Bill? I'm sure you were rather the flash one in your day. Wooing with woodwork and all that."

"Don't be ridiculous," grumbled Mr. Hammersley. "That wasn't what it was."

"He made his wife all these little wooden flowers and stuff," Teddy said. "He showed me."

Mr. Hammersley basically spluttered in response to that.

Diya said, "Maybe you can make one of those wooden flowers for Sam. He needs all the help he can get."

"I really don't," said Sam. "I've got everything under control."

"How do you know all about this romantic intrigue, Diya?" asked Max. "You've been holding out on me. We should have tea more often."

"We chaperoned the same field trip," Diya answered. "He spent the entire time starring over her."

"Starring?" echoed Max.

"Mooning," Arthur suggested.

"Yes." Diya nodded energetically. "That's it. Mooning."

"Look," said Sam, "I am just waiting for the right moment."

"Oh, good," said Teddy. "Because there's Miss Quinn right over there."

Sam looked. They were near the park now,

close to where they were going to have to pay admission to get in, and there indeed, across a teeming sea of people, was Miss Quinn, her dark red hair trapped under a bright green woolen hat with a silly pom-pom on top, and even in a silly bobble hat, on a misty evening when everything else was muted around the edges, Miss Quinn shone bright and clear as a beacon. She was laughing, and Sam could almost fancy he *heard* that laugh, above all of the more earthly conversations that more boring people were having around him.

"Which one?" Max asked.

"The one wearing the green hat with the pom-pom on it," answered Teddy.

"Oh, well done, Sam," Max said. "She's lovely. Go and chat her up."

"I'm sure she's here with friends," Sam said, not because he was *nervous* but because yes, obviously she was there with friends—that's who she was talking to. "I don't want to interrupt her evening with—"

Which was exactly when Miss Quinn happened to look up and catch Sam blatantly staring at her from across the grass. Sam had no time to pretend that he hadn't been staring. He also had no ability *not* to stare. He didn't understand how everyone in the vicinity wasn't admiring Miss Quinn, wasn't feeling her gravitational pull the way he was.

Miss Quinn didn't look alarmed to find him

staring. She smiled at him and lifted her hand in a wave.

"Off you go, then," said Max. "We'll watch your child for you."

Sam tore his eyes away from Miss Quinn, looking at the knot of people all around him, at Teddy. "You're sure?" He wasn't sure whom he was asking. Possibly he was asking everyone.

But it was Teddy whose response he watched for. Teddy nodded and smiled and said, "Yes, Dad. I'm sure. Have fun."

"Be safe," said Max, managing to add a cheerful inflection to it.

Sam gave him a look and brushed a kiss over the hat covering Teddy's head. "I'll catch up with you later. You know my mobile number, right?"

Teddy nodded. "Go on," he said. "Before she thinks you're not interested again or something."

Sam nodded and waved to the rest of the group and told himself he definitely *wasn't nervous,* as he headed over to where Miss Quinn looked as if she was waiting for him.

He *wasn't* nervous, but Pari shouting out to him, "Don't eat anything that will make your breath gross, in case there's snogging later!" didn't really help his situation.

Pen went running into the night after Jack and nearly ran straight into Anna, also running down the street.

"Oh," Pen said, surprised. "Are you also chasing Jack?"

"Jack? No, I'm chasing my cats. Socks! Tabby! Come back! Oh, my God, that horrible dog is going to attack my cats!"

Pen glanced down the street, confused by what was going on, and then noticed that there were indeed two cats also streaking down the street, Jack in hot pursuit. "I'm sure he won't," Pen said, but she wasn't really sure about that. She didn't know how Jack was going to behave toward cats.

A car came around the corner, the headlights throwing the tableau of animals into dramatic sharp relief. The cats, apparently disoriented by the sudden flash of light, stopped running and huddled together, on the edge of the pavement, looking warily back to Jack. Jack also skidded his way to a stop. All the animals stared at each other in a tense showdown, before Jack took a cautious step forward, sniffing.

"Don't you dare touch my cats!" Anna shouted, still chasing after them.

Jack looked up, as if confused.

Pen said, "I don't think he's going to bother the cats."

And then, as another car came around the corner, Jack did the exact opposite of bothering the cats: he stepped out into the street, placing himself between the cats and the potential deadly weapon. The cats, startled, had no choice but to dart directly at Anna if they wanted to avoid Jack.

Anna caught both of them up in her arms and gave Jack a wary look, as Pen caught up to them.

"Good boy, Jack," she said enthusiastically, and Jack bounded over to be given a scratch behind the ears. "You managed to make sure the cats didn't dart out into the street in front of the car!"

"He didn't manage that," said Anna dubiously.

"He did," Pen insisted. "Jack is very clever, you know. He's probably part collie. Collies are very clever. The cleverest dogs. I wrote an article on them once."

Pen wasn't sure if Anna was even paying attention, because Anna was watching Jack sniff curiously at the cats in her arms, and the cats, in return, were pointing out their noses to sniff back.

"Look," Pen said happily. "They like each other."

"Maybe they do," said Anna cautiously, looking between the cats and Jack.

"Hey," Pen said after a moment of silence. "So, the street is basically you and me at the moment. Would you maybe want to . . . have a cup of tea?" Pen didn't know Anna very well, and it might be nice to get to know her better. And it would be an excuse to procrastinate writing even more.

Anna, after a moment, said hesitantly, "Yes. That might . . . be nice. Thanks."

• • •

Sam, having arrived at where Miss Quinn was waiting for him and still smiling, decided to start off the evening with the very scintillating choice of, "Hi."

"Hi," said Miss Quinn, smile widening.

"How are you?" asked Sam, continuing in his vein of making awkward small talk as an effective date strategy.

"I'm fine," Miss Quinn replied, luckily still looking amused by him rather than annoyed. "How are you?"

"Fine," replied Sam, and then paused to think of his next remark.

Miss Quinn said, "I fear you've lost your son. He just went in with a huge crowd of people."

"Yes," Sam said. "My neighbors. They're going to watch him for me."

"Watch him for you while you do what?" asked Miss Quinn, very deliberately, giving him the most perfect opening.

Sam took it, grateful. "While I ask if you would like to watch some fireworks with me."

Miss Quinn laughed. "See, that could be an incredibly flash line, but I suspect you mean the literal firework display that will be put on by others, not us."

Sam, in the face of Miss Quinn's laughter, felt the stiffness within him break loose. It was impossible for him to maintain any level of discomfort when Miss Quinn was laughing. It was as if her clearly relaxed state, her indication that she was having a decent time with him, reminded him of his ability to converse like a normal human being, inspired him to rise up to her level. He liked being in her presence, too. Surely he could find a way to show her that. "I like to start small," he said. "Set a low bar. Make sure expectations are reasonable. I don't want to promise too much. A bonfire and hopefully a literal firework display, if the weather holds. Maybe I'll even buy you some cotton candy."

"Ah, well, I was vacillating, but your mention of cotton candy has now convinced me in your favor."

"You were vacillating?" said Sam. "Shall I expect that as a vocabulary word for Teddy in the near future?"

"That was a special vocabulary lesson all for you," replied Miss Quinn, dimpling as she smiled at him. "I can be persuaded to give private lessons."

Sam said, "With or without fireworks?"

Miss Quinn's smile widened even further, until Sam thought that everyone around them must surely have stopped bustling about, then he remembered to take a breath and smile irresistibly in response. She said, "Let's see how the cotton candy goes."

• • •

Marcel had heard often from Anna that he was not the world's most observant person. But even he could observe that Emilia and Sai kept glancing at each other and looking away and making hand motions at each other that they thought no one could see, apparently, but were clearly attempts to communicate meeting up somewhere. Sai's parents seemed oblivious to all of this, chattering enthusiastically with the gay couple and the poor old man who looked dubious about being subjected to the conversation, and Marcel couldn't help but be proud that he had noticed when the rest had not. That, he thought, congratulating himself, was just how much he paid attention to Emilia. He couldn't wait to prove it to Anna.

"Chips?" he suggested to Emilia, wanting to get her alone so he could show off how clever he was being.

Emilia, who had been in the middle of trying to translate a series of increasingly intricate hand gestures from Sai, looked at him in surprise and said, "Uh. Yeah. Sure."

Marcel turned away, toward the chips, deliberately to give Emilia the ability to send some gestures Sai's way.

When Emilia caught up with him, he said, "You said you could do with some chips."

"Yeah. Definitely." Emilia smiled, not in

amusement. "Mum would say that I am always in the mood for chips, wouldn't she?"

"You can't let your mum get to you when she says stuff like that," Marcel said. "She had a rough time of it when she was younger. I think she wants to make sure that you don't have a rough time, ever, at all, in anything."

"By harping on about my weight?" asked Emilia sulkily.

"Most of the world your mother can't control," said Marcel, as he ordered the chips.

"So I get to be the one thing she tries to control endlessly?" said Emilia.

"Maybe," Marcel said, who had not thought of it in precisely those terms. "Possibly a little bit."

"I mean, that's what the drums thing is all about. *She* doesn't like the drums, so she doesn't want *me* to like the drums. But she can't control everything I like, you know? She just wants me to be just like *her,* and that's not fair. I'm *me,* not her."

Marcel took the chips and handed them to Emilia and said, "Is that why you haven't told her about you and the Indian boy?"

Emilia looked up, her face a picture of absolute shock. "What?" she stammered. "What are you— I'm not—What?"

Marcel could have laughed at how obvious Emilia's response was. "Well, if I wasn't certain before, I am now."

Emilia apparently decided it was no longer worth lying about, in favor of crowding closer to him and saying breathlessly, "You're not going to tell anyone, are you?"

"So his parents really don't know either?"

Emilia shook her head. "They won't like me because Sai's supposed to just focus on school, all the time. And Mum won't like Sai because Mum wouldn't like anyone I like."

Emilia seemed so sure of that, so earnest, that Marcel's heart broke a little. "Em." He reached out and cupped her cheek with his hand. "That's not true."

'Yes, it is," said Emilia, fighting back tears and swiping away at them impatiently. "And I really like Sai. He's a thing I really like that I just want to like without having to constantly *justify* it. I don't want to have her . . . rolling her eyes or . . . making little cutting comments about him. I just want to be able to enjoy him, you know?"

"She would let you enjoy him, Em. If you told her how important this was to you. She's not trying to hurt you. She's just trying to protect you. She loves you."

Emilia looked at him, eyes suddenly clear and sharp. "She has a funny way of showing that sometimes."

Which rendered Marcel speechless in response.

Emilia wiped the last of her tears away and tore into a chip.

Marcel watched her and then ventured, "How long has it been going on?"

"Since the end of school last year," Emilia said. "And we kind of got closer through the summer. We were both home all day."

"And how does he treat you?" Marcel asked.

Emilia looked at him. "What?"

"How does he treat you? Tell me about him."

"He's . . . nice," said Emilia.

"Good to you?" persisted Marcel.

Emilia nodded, with a reflective little half smile on her face. It made her look so strongly like Anna for a moment that Marcel's breath caught. Anna, twenty years earlier, young and unbothered yet by life, with nothing more pressing to worry about than a boy that she liked and the possibility that boy represented. That boy had been Marcel, and that possibility had been shining, and maybe there had been rough patches along the way, but Marcel didn't think they'd done that badly, to have an amazing and remarkable daughter standing there making the same little half smile, unbothered by life, with nothing more pressing to worry about than a boy that she liked and the possibility that boy represented. That, Marcel thought, was exactly what he would have wanted, if you had asked him twenty years ago: a daughter who looked the way Anna had looked in those days, absolutely enchanted by *possibilities*.

It seemed so long ago, and yet also just a moment ago, and all Marcel could think was that he wanted all of Emilia's possibilities to be the shiniest they could possibly be.

He pulled Emilia into a hug, which she jostled her chips to allow, and said, "I want you to be happy. So I won't tell anyone. For now."

"For now?" echoed Emilia.

"But you have to promise me that you'll at least consider the possibility that your mother, if you were honest with her, would be supportive of any choice you might want to make in life, because your mother really does love you. You have to promise me that eventually, someday, you might have a heart-to-heart with your mother. Maybe. Someday. That's all I ask."

Emilia was silent for a long moment, before saying, "Okay. Yes. I promise I'll think about it."

Cotton candy procured, Sam and Miss Quinn walked along the edge of the crowd, Sam very content to ignore everything that was going on in favor of watching Miss Quinn eat cotton candy.

Miss Quinn gave him a sideways glance as they walked. "So. Is this a date?"

Which caught Sam a little off-guard.

She continued, "It's just hard to tell, not being in the fruit and veg section of a supermarket, or on a school coach."

Sam laughed. "Come now. Didn't the school coach make you feel young again?"

Miss Quinn laughed in return. "I always wonder about people who are nostalgic for that time in their lives. I have no special desire to remember my time on school coaches. Do you?"

"At the moment, no," replied Sam honestly. "At the moment I am quite content to be a grown-up on a date on Bonfire Night."

"Ah, so it is a date,"said Miss Quinn wisely.

Sam said, "I think, at this point, before we count this as a date, I really ought to know your first name."

After a moment, Miss Quinn burst into more laughter, and this laughter made her double over with mirth, gasping, laying a hand on his arm as if for support. Sam stared at her hand on his arm and tried not to get too besotted over it. If he were a poet, though, he would definitely write odes to Miss Quinn's hands. If that wasn't too besotted.

Miss Quinn finally managed, "Oh, my goodness, do you really not know my name? Have I really never told you?"

Sam shook his head, still a little fixated on Miss Quinn's hand, which she had not removed from his arm.

Miss Quinn said, "So all this time you've been thinking of me as 'Miss Quinn'?"

"No, for a little while you were Carrot Woman," Sam said.

Miss Quinn smiled and took her hand off his arm, which left Sam momentarily bereft, except that then she extended it toward him and smiled and said, "Libby Quinn."

Libby, thought Sam; it suited her, somehow. He took her hand and shook it and said, "Sam Bishop."

"Very nice to meet you, Mr. Bishop," said Libby.

"And you, Libby," said Sam, and then, feeling bold, leaned over and kissed Libby's cheek. And tried to move away quickly, so it wouldn't seem creepy, but couldn't resist a moment of breathing, of cherishing the trick of letting the world swirl all around them, insignificant.

"Well," remarked Libby, voice low as he leaned away, as if to not break the spell of the moment, "moving closer to the fireworks."

The cats were both sitting on the sofa watching Jack. Jack was lying on the floor watching the cats.

It seemed like a cautious détente of relations. Anna nonetheless watched carefully, just in case Jack might decide to suddenly viciously attack. One never knew with a dog.

Pen came back into the lounge with two cups of tea, one of which she handed to Anna. "Too much milk?" she asked.

Anna took a careful sip. "No, just right," she said honestly. "Thank you."

Pen settled on the comfy, cozy chair across from Anna and sipped her tea and said, sounding amused, "You look so suspicious of poor Jack."

"I've always been a cat person," Anna admitted. "Not much of a dog person."

"Well, he's sweet," Pen said. "Very protective of the street. Even protective of your cats."

"Do you really think so?" Anna looked across at Pen dubiously. "I mean, it seems like a lot of planning for a *dog*."

Pen smiled a little. "I like to ascribe good motivations to as many creatures as I can. Isn't it nice to imagine a world where everything around you tries to be a little bit *good?* I even think good things about Chester." Off Anna's blank look, Pen said, "My goldfish," and gestured.

Anna glanced at the goldfish, then back at Pen, contemplating what she was saying. Finally she said carefully, not wanting to sound too dismissive but afraid she might not be able to help it, "It's . . . rather a rosy view of the world, isn't it? Everything being *good?*"

Pen shrugged. "People might have terrible motives sometimes. If I like to think a dog tried to save a couple of cats because it makes the world a little more hopeful, well, why not? Surely we ought to try to think rosy thoughts whenever we can."

Anna took a sip of tea to cover her scoffing

attitude toward that particular viewpoint. In her experience life was hard and tricky and thinking rosy thoughts didn't pay the bills.

Pen said, "Your daughter's very sweet. She always says hello if we run into each other on the street."

Anna blinked, surprised. Not that she thought Emilia *wasn't* sweet, but she supposed she hadn't thought about Emilia being involved with the life of the street. "Oh," said Anna, uncertain how she was meant to respond. She settled for, "Thank you."

"You must be very proud of her," remarked Pen.

Pen said it off-handedly, casually, like a platitude that you would say to anyone, and Anna went to respond to it in similar fashion, and then paused, hung up on the sudden realization that . . . she *was* proud of Emilia. She had never stopped to think of it in entirely those terms, and it was so hard to keep sight of that in the middle of all the fretting over everything horrible that might happen to the child you'd brought into the world, but the reason for all the fretting was Emilia, stubborn and bright and shining, and sometimes so different from Anna that she couldn't remember ever being so young, and sometimes so similar to Anna that Anna ached for the world that waited for her.

"Very proud of her," Anna said, and was

shocked to discover that she was choked up. She cleared her throat and said, embarrassed, "Sorry."

Pen said, "Not at all. Don't be sorry."

"It's just . . ." said Anna, feeling silly and that she ought to explain herself, "you have a child, and you work so hard to make a good life for that child, that sometimes maybe you forget to remember to stop and really see the child. You know? Oh, I must sound ridiculous to you."

"You don't," said Pen. "At all. You sound like a parent who loves very much and works very hard."

Anna chuckled self-deprecatingly. "And sometimes those things are at odds with each other and difficult to balance. And I'm not sure I've always done a good job of that."

"Nobody does a good job all the time, though," said Pen. "Thinking you can always do a good job, *that's* a rosy view of the world. It's just impossible. You do the best you can, and that's all anyone can ask."

Anna looked down at her tea and heard herself say, "I'm not always sure I've even done the best I can." She didn't know why she was saying these things. Except that . . . maybe she didn't have any close friends to talk to about this. She wasn't Diya, running off to socialize daily. She felt so isolated in her own life, surrounded by people whom she loved but couldn't find a way to reach across to *touch*.

Pen said gently, "I think you're being hard on yourself. I think, if you asked the people who love you, they would say that you're hard on yourself."

And Anna knew that was ridiculous, because Pen barely knew Emilia and knew Marcel even less, but there was . . . *hope* in the way Pen was talking. And maybe that was a rosy view of the world, but it was a view Anna wanted at the moment.

Anna said tentatively, "Maybe."

"Maybe?" echoed Pen. *"Definitely.* After all, if cats and dogs can get along, anything is possible." She nodded toward the floor.

Where Jack and both cats were now curled up, close enough to be touching, all deeply asleep.

"So, Sam Bishop," said Libby, as they wandered aimlessly through the crowd. The bonfire was burning away merrily and Sam could hear shrieks of laughter coming from that direction, but he could not have been less interested in that, being much more interested in the intriguing shape of his name in Libby's voice. "Short for Samuel?" she guessed.

Sam nodded.

"You were born here, judging by your accent, somewhat blurred though it might be, from your time in America. Was Teddy born in America?"

Sam nodded again. "His mother was American.

I met her when I went over there for university. And then I sort of stayed."

"What made you decide to move back here? Unless that's too prying," Libby corrected hastily. "Sorry, is that too prying? I don't do many first dates. Wait, I suppose I should say I don't do many *second* dates."

Sam looked at her in disbelief. "Who wouldn't take *you* on a second date? Are all the men in London mad?"

"Actually, yes," Libby replied seriously. "I know you asked that as if it were a joke, but really, honestly, yes. You would not believe the terrible first dates I have been on. One man brought his mother with him to approve the length of my skirt. I wasn't wearing a skirt, so I suggest that was the first strike against me. Another proceeded to explain to me at great length why I had chosen the wrong career. Imagine thinking that a first date was the appropriate time to reveal that you think educating children is pointless, to a *schoolteacher*."

"Wow," said Sam. "You make me very glad I have mostly avoided first dates to this point in my life."

"Well, you're on one now."

"Not at all," Sam said. "As you yourself pointed out, this is at least our third date. Fourth if you count meeting at the school that time."

"Surprisingly, I don't know if I'm going to

count your son's Year 4 orientation as a date," deadpanned Libby.

Sam smiled and stepped over a pile of discarded napkins, crumpled on the damp grass. He said, "But to go back to your original question: not too prying. My wife died a few years ago, and I felt like I'd finally . . . closed the door on that portion of my life. Which sounds harsh, and I don't mean it to sound harsh, but there was a lot of grieving and a lot of adjusting, and then Teddy and I came out the other side, and I felt like everyone around us just . . . wasn't going to let us. Like, everywhere I went there were all of these preconceived notions about how I ought to be behaving. And I realized suddenly that I'd neglected keeping up friendships over the years, meaning that the only people left around us were people I had known through Sara—my wife— and suddenly I wanted to . . . stand on my own? I guess you could say? In a way. I felt like I needed a chance to meet myself again. So I came home."

"I think that's very brave," said Libby.

Sam glanced at her, and she looked serious and kind, but with not a trace of pity in her face. More her face was shadowed with something like respect, Sam fancied. He said drily, "That's very kind of you. I think poor Teddy thought it rather foolhardy."

Libby shrugged. "Many worthwhile things look foolhardy in the beginning. Teddy's too young to realize how truly tricky life is. He thinks the right thing to do will always be obvious. Bless them. Sometimes, at this age, I think I'm catching them right at that last gasp of childhood, right before everything becomes complicated and swallows them up."

"I know," Sam said ruefully. "I'm trying desperately to enjoy it. I know I'll miss this in a few years. But honestly, having a child is like . . . a constant open wound." He heard himself say it, and then winced. "Wow, that sounds . . . horrible. But—"

"I get it," Libby said. "I may not have any children myself, but that means I have all of your children, basically. And I may not love to the absoluteness that a parent loves, I know that, but I know that that's what love does to you: it leaves this constant open, vulnerable area that can be so easily pressed against and injured."

And Sam thought that Libby was amazing, for understanding what he was trying to say, and wondered wildly if it was too early in all of this to say, *I think you're amazing.* What were the rules?

Libby went on before he could decide. "If it makes you feel better, Teddy's doing really well. Much better than at the beginning of the year. Not that he was doing poorly then, but there's always an adjustment period. Luckily Pari's taken him somewhat under her wing, and Pari is a force to be reckoned with. And I think he's finally getting into the swing of the schedule. He told me the other day that he's even starting to understand design technology. I can think of no higher form of praise, coming from Teddy."

"I can't thank you enough," Sam said seriously.

"Oh, it's really mostly Teddy," Libby said. "And the job you're doing raising him."

"You've made an enormous difference. You've made him feel safe and supported. He adores you."

"That's sweet," said Libby, smiling. *"He's* sweet. Takes after his dad."

Sam rolled his eyes and laughed a bit, a little embarrassed and unsure how to take the compliment. So he decided to change the subject. "Tell me about you. Libby Quinn. Short for Elizabeth?"

Libby nodded. "Indeed."

"And you were born here?"

Libby shook her head. "A little village outside Bristol."

"But you always wanted to live in London?" Sam guessed.

"I did," said Libby. "Plus my mum died, and she was the main reason I had been in Bristol. So, like you, I was looking for a fresh start and I came here."

"I'm sorry," Sam said, "about your mother."

"I'm sorry about your wife," Libby replied.

Sam determined not to let the awkwardness last more than a moment. He said, "Do you like it here?"

"I like it more now," Libby said, with a sly sideways smile. How many species of smile did she have? Sam wondered. He wanted to catalogue them all. "It's getting better."

Sam decided to play along. "Most places improve with my presence."

Libby chuckled, and then said thoughtfully, "You know how it is. You move to an entirely new place, it takes a little while to get your feet under you. I'd lived in my village all my life. I moved to London as an adventure, and it just . . . it's not as easy to meet people as I'd imagined it would be. Great, big, seething metropolis, I thought we'd all be bumping into each other endlessly. But the truth is, I think people react to being constantly surrounded by other humans by closing in on themselves. In the village, you bumped into people and you'd say hello. But here, you bump into people and you say, 'Excuse me.' It's taken me a little while to get used to it. I envy you, actually."

"Envy *me?*" echoed Sam.

"Your street seems very close, and I think that's lovely. You don't see that much in London."

Sam considered. "I guess so. I really wanted that. I liked the idea of it. After all, I came here because I wanted to make friends."

"And you just went out and did it," said Libby. "I admire that."

"Well, now that I reflect upon it, I suppose it was mostly Jack."

"Ah, yes, I have heard a great deal about Jack. Your dog, I gather."

"The street dog."

"The street dog?" said Libby. "What does that mean?"

"He's the dog who belongs to the street. We all share him. And at first when I moved in I thought it was as odd an idea as you do. I thought Jack would create all sorts of problems. I thought another creature to be responsible for was the opposite of what I needed. But now I . . . now I think Jack is really exactly what all of us needed. Jack brings all of us together. Jack does the opposite of creating problems. Jack *solves* them."

"He sounds like a remarkable dog," said Libby.

"He is," Sam agreed, almost surprised to hear how he felt about Jack. Then he said, "And how did I end up babbling at you about our street dog?"

"It's okay," said Libby. "It's charming.' " She stopped walking, forcing Sam to stop as well, to turn and look at her.

She had her collar turned up against the cold and her hair flattened around her head by the bright green hat she was wearing and she was so dazzlingly beautiful that Sam thought she looked like some sort of adorable wood sprite deposited in the midst of everyone.

Libby said, "I don't usually do things like this, and now I'm thinking that that might be what I've done wrong in London. I haven't been willing enough to step forward and say things to people, and maybe I've let things . . . Anyway. I like you. I like you more every time I get to see you. And I think you like me, too, but if I'm reading this wrong, if you could just—before it gets awkward for Teddy—"

Sam, with little forethought but with single-minded intention, stepped forward and curled his fists into the conveniently turned-up collar of Libby's coat and pressed his lips against hers. Once, then twice. And then she uttered a little sigh and lifted her hands, carding them through Sam's hair, and then Sam *kissed* her. The sort of kiss that reminded you why poets wrote sonnets about kisses, the sort of kiss that reminded you of the *point* of them.

He drew back the merest breath and murmured, "I think you're *amazing*," deciding it was definitely not too early to say that.

Libby's cheeks were pink and her lips were pink and her eyes were bright and she looked deliciously well-kissed and her hands curled into Sam's hair as if to keep him forever there, which was ridiculous because Sam was never going anywhere.

The booms and crackles and whooshes and rumbles of the firework display started, somewhere over their heads, casting Libby's green eyes in shades of sparkling gold.

Libby whispered, "Fireworks," and Sam was fairly certain she wasn't speaking literally.

It had been a very long time since Bill had gone on an outing for Bonfire Night. Normally he stayed home and made himself a nice cuppa and turned on the telly. If he was lucky, it was a night when Jack had decided to stay over, which meant there was someone there for him to criticize the telly to (and the telly always deserved criticism).

On the whole, Bill had always told himself, staying in for Bonfire Night was much the best way to celebrate Bonfire Night. Firework displays were noisy messes and bonfires were thoroughly unnecessary and it was, on the whole, much more sensible to stay inside where it was warm and comfortable and didn't cost one any money and didn't require one to be surrounded by dodgy strangers.

This was what Bill was reminding himself of, as he stood in the damp cold surrounded by—of all people—neighbors. He was reminding himself that being alone wasn't so bad. That there was no need to get used to having all of these people around him. That he most certainly did not need all of these people around him. He had, after all, passed many a pleasant evening without all of this fuss and bother and nonsense.

And yet.

And yet it *was* rather nice.

Max's young man or husband or whatever a person wanted to call him was a nice enough fellow, who spoke to Bill very politely about proper topics like the weather, and was solid and practical in a way that Bill approved of. Max was decent but he could be flighty. The Indian family had always seemed rather loud and chaotic to Bill, and his opinion hadn't changed on that front, but at least they appeared to be friendly in their own loud and chaotic way. Bill didn't know the Polish bloke very well, but he seemed steady enough, and the Polish girl had smiled at him in a pleasant way.

And then there was Teddy, who slipped close to him as the bonfire roared and said, "Hi."

Bill looked at him, this small American boy who had moved next door and insisted on . . . *talking* to him. Bill supposed he could talk back. "So," he said. "What do you make of your first Bonfire Night?"

Teddy smiled at him. "Pretty good so far. A little damp."

'It's England,' Bill said.

"It makes sense that you have to light a fire before the fireworks begin," said Teddy, smile wide.

Bill, out of practice with having a lengthy

conversation like this, smiled in a tolerant way (or at least hoped that he did, and also hoped that would serve well as a reply).

Apparently it served well enough, because Teddy kept talking (or maybe he didn't need any encouragement). He said, "I'm looking forward to the fireworks. I love fireworks. Do you like fireworks?"

Bill wasn't sure what to say to that. He wondered if it wouldn't be better to go back to not having to have conversations like this. He tried to consider the question seriously, to arrive at the right answer, and settled on, "I don't know. It's been a while since I've thought about it."

Teddy said, "Well, if you stopped to think about them, you'd probably like them, because they're pretty amazing."

Which was when the firework display started, with a huge series of bangs. Teddy turned his face toward the sky, his joy obvious.

Bill, after a second, looked toward the sky himself. Lights burst across it, showering down sparks of color. Bill, watching the show, wondered why he'd stopped going to them, wondered why he'd stopped thinking about fireworks.

Because fireworks were brilliant.

It was much, much later when Pen finally sat down with her laptop again. She and Anna had had another cup of tea together, and then she had helped Anna home with her cats, and then she had returned home to the waiting Jack, who had rolled over to display his belly for some scratches. Jack had seemed calm as the remainder of the firework displays played themselves out, even bored. He snoozed happily at her feet, and Pen leaned out the windows and tried to see if she could see the displays in the skies.

Then the neighbors began straggling back, chattering loudly and happily. Pen smiled, because it was a nice sound to have on the street. She sent Jack bounding out to all of them, and he danced around them barking in greeting and tripped over his own enthusiasm, and the kids basically fell on top of him in return.

Pari and Teddy, once they were done fussing over Jack, waved to her and said the fireworks were *so cool* and *amazing* when she asked, and then Teddy started to say something about someone—possibly Miss Quinn—but was silenced by Sam suddenly playfully capturing his head in a headlock and waving cheerfully at Pen as he did so. Darsh and Diya also waved, apparently still oblivious to the fact that Sai was lingering behind them near Emilia. Part of Pen wanted to stop Emilia and Marcel, tell them what she'd discussed with Anna that night, but the larger part of Pen knew that it was Anna's to share alone.

Max said, as he walked by hand-in-hand with Arthur, "Hello there, Pen. How'd our Jack do?"

"Oh, flying colors," Pen replied, and looked at Mr. Hammersley, who was walking along with them. "How was it, Mr. Hammersley? Have a good time?"

"It was all right," replied Mr. Hammersley gruffly.

Max threw Pen a wink.

Pen grinned and went inside and settled into bed with her laptop.

Where she found her blog still open.

She reread her last few sentences, about Anna. Anna who had just spent the evening with her, being kind and honest and . . . and who was Pen, to be writing about her in this way? To be writing about any of them? What had she been doing here? Treating her neighbors as if they were fictional characters in a story?

Pen deleted everything she had written for the blog that night and wrote instead: **Happy Bonfire Night, all! If you've been following this blog, I thank you, and I do hope you've enjoyed it. However, I've decided to bring it to a close. No more adventures of Jack the Street Dog and the street who belongs to him! You see, I think what I've learned is: those adventures belong to Jack, and to us. :-)**

Chapter 12

In honor of Remembrance Day, Year 4 will be visiting a local church, where we will pay a solemn tribute to those who have lost their lives for us. It will be a fitting way to impress upon the children the importance of remembering the past as we move forward into an exciting future.
—Miss Quinn

Max's Christmas decorations were complicated enough that they appeared in stages. At the moment, he was working on a detailed woven tapestry that he spent hours one day creating by the rosebushes in his front garden, watched over by Jack, who lazed on the pavement and contributed helpful suggestions by way of periodic barking fits. Sam spent the day procrastinating work in favor of watching the complex project.

He eventually remarked, as he went outside to wait for Teddy to come home from school, "That is quite a production." Jack came over to say hello, tail wagging, and Sam scratched behind his ears.

Max looked up and grinned. "Got to have impressive Christmas decorations. Who would want to buy art from an artist who has dull Christmas decorations?"

"I suppose you have a point," Sam agreed, even though he'd never given any thought to that particular subject before.

Max, stepping back to examine his creation with a cocked head, said, "Of course, it's difficult to judge how it's going to look during daylight hours. It may be gray and gloomy but that's no substitute for genuine night." Apparently satisfied, he turned from his front garden to face Sam. "When are you putting your decorations up?"

"I haven't thought about it yet," Sam admitted. "In America, we used to wait until after Thanksgiving."

"Well, if you want help, I am happy to help. Once I'm done with my own, I think I'm going to make Bill a display."

"Really?" Sam lifted his eyebrows. "And what does he say about that?"

Max laughed. "Oh, I think he'll come around. I'm ace at persuasion. Anyway, how are things with you? How's 'Miss Quinn'?"

Sam had only one complaint about the kisses he'd shared with Libby on Bonfire Night, and that was that he'd been teased mercilessly about them ever since. He had so far managed to keep the matter from Ellen, but he was sure that Teddy would tell her about them as soon as he saw her.

Sam said, with exaggerated patience, "Fine."

"And have you considered what you're going to do for a second date? How you're going to top the romance and mystique of Bonfire Night?"

"Ha ha," said Sam, and thought maybe life was easier when his neighbors didn't really talk to him at all.

"It's a tricky time of year to start seeing someone," Max remarked. "Christmas is right around the corner. You have to consider what level of gift you ought to get her. Very stressful."

"You could be a more supportive person, you know," Sam informed him.

Luckily, the children came down the street from school before Max could make Sam panic any further about the status of his relationship with Libby, and Sam greeted Teddy, who launched immediately into a hotly indignant complaint about school.

"Miss Quinn says we can't have Jack in the play! She says it's against the rules!"

"Well," said Sam, "I'm sure she knows what the rules are."

"Well, the rules are stupid," said Teddy. "The rules shouldn't apply to *Jack*. Jack's special. Does she know about Jack?"

"She knows about Jack's existence, yes."

"But she doesn't believe me about how special

he is," said Teddy. "Which is why I'm asking if *you* told her about Jack's acting abilities."

Sam blinked at him in surprise. "Jack's what?"

"He would be really good in the play. I mean, he is super well-behaved. Don't you think he's super well-behaved? He's not going to *do* anything. He'll just sort of be there. Pari and I have even written a whole role for him. He's going to be the manger dog, and he'll be very cold in the snow, and the insurance agent will talk about how the manger owner should have had insurance about the snow, only he didn't because of climate change, but everyone's going to help anyway because the manger owner was nice and helped out Mary and Joseph."

Sam said only, "Your school play has an insurance agent now? Arthur will be so pleased."

"Right, and how will the insurance agent have any point at all if Jack's not playing the manger dog who's cold in the snow?"

"You're right," Sam said. "Without a dog, an insurance agent has no place in a Christmas play."

"Then you'll talk to Miss Quinn about it?"

Sam looked reflectively at Teddy for a moment, then said, "We should talk about Miss Quinn, shouldn't we?"

Teddy shrugged. "What about her? She's the best teacher, and now you're dating her."

Sam studied Teddy closely but he looked

entirely unconcerned. "And that's a good thing?" Sam sought to clarify.

Teddy stared at him as if he were mad. "Why wouldn't it be a good thing? It's an *amazing* thing. No one else has a dad who's dating the teacher."

Sam lifted a dubious eyebrow. "Right, but that doesn't mean she's automatically giving you the best grades in the class or anything."

"No, I know," said Teddy. "She's too amazing for that. That's why you're dating her."

Sam continued to closely study Teddy. "So she's not going to give you the best grades necessarily, and I'm not going to talk to her to try to convince her to give you special treatment, for instance, by putting Jack in the school play."

Teddy sighed. "Fine. I *told* Pari it wasn't going to work."

Sam ignored that, preferring instead to focus on what seemed far more important to him. "What I really wanted to know, though, was if it's okay that . . . she's not your mum."

Teddy looked confused. "Mum is dead."

"I know," agreed Sam, trying to find a way around his words. "She is. And now I would like to see more of Miss Quinn. And she's not your mum. And is that strange for you?"

Teddy was silent for a long moment. Then he said, "No. It would only be strange if you wanted to see more of someone who wasn't awesome.

Because you're used to having awesome people around. Mum was one, and now Miss Quinn is another one. It's cool."

Sometimes it was easy to forget, in the day-to-day humdrum of just being sure to keep your child *alive,* how miraculous it was to have been responsible for another life entering the planet, and for that life to have spun away from your own to be its own person. But at this moment Sam was struck by that miracle, and by the even keener miracle of Teddy having spun away to become a person Sam *liked,* a person Sam would have wanted to spend time with even if he hadn't been his son. And maybe Sam was biased on that point, but Teddy *was* pretty amazing.

Sam said, "A good place to be is to be remembering the past but still being excited about the future. Thank you."

"For what?" asked Teddy.

"For being my daily adventure," said Sam.

The world seemed full of poppies, and to Teddy this was an unusual phenomenon. He watched Max threading some through Mr. Hammersley's now-hibernating roses and said, "Are they some sort of Christmas decoration?" Max was big on Christmas decorations. Max's house was slowly turning into a house composed entirely of twinkling fairy lights. Teddy thought it was cool and also obviously way too much work to even ask Dad to do something like that.

Max looked up from the poppies. Mr. Hammersley also looked up, from where he was standing in the doorway griping at Max whenever he did something with the poppies Mr. Hammersley didn't like.

Max said, "Do you not know about the poppies?"

Mr. Hammersley huffed out, "What do they even teach children in school these days?"

"Miss Quinn teaches us lots of stuff," said Teddy loyally. "I guess we haven't gotten around to the poppies yet."

"They're in remembrance," Max said, resuming his threading of the poppies. "For all the people we've lost in wars." He glanced at Mr. Hammersley.

So Teddy glanced at Mr. Hammersley, too. He looked frowny in a way he hadn't just a moment before, and he'd still been frowny then—that was generally Mr. Hammersley for you—but it was a different sort of frowny now.

Mr. Hammersley said briskly, "Too many people. Too many people lost. Too many people who never even made it to a graveyard. Too many people who are just poppies, and they don't even tell them about it in school."

"I'm sure they—" Max began, but Mr. Hammersley closed the door, disappearing inside.

Jack, concerned for Mr. Hammersley, got up from where he'd been keeping watch at the end of the path and stood in front of the door, whining a bit, tail wagging faintly.

Teddy said to Max, "I didn't mean to upset him."

"You didn't," Max said kindly. "It wasn't you. It's Remembrance Day coming up, that's all. He's been on edge about it. I asked him and he admitted he lost his dad in the war, so you can see how it's a tough time for him."

"Hello, you two," said Pen cheerfully, coming by in the middle of one of her many runs and pausing to look at Max's handiwork. "It's gorgeous. I'm glad Mr. Hammersley won't be alone this Remembrance Day. Ordinarily he goes to the church and just sits there, thinking about everything. He goes on the day itself, not even on Sunday, just making him more alone."

"He thinks about all the people lost?" said Teddy.

Pen smiled at him, but it was a sad smile. "Exactly. People lost in war, his friends he's lost over the years."

Teddy gave Jack a comforting pat on the head and thought about this.

"Poppies!" Miss Quinn said in school, handing out sheets of red construction paper. "That's what we'll be focusing on today. Remembrance Day, after all, is right around the corner. The day when we pause to remember all of the brave men and women who have given their lives to secure the lives we know and enjoy today. We will all be making poppies in remembrance, and then your assignment will be to give these poppies to a person of your choosing, who you think might need a reminder that they're remembered, as a symbol of the fact that you're thinking of them. Sometimes, as people grow older, it's easier for them to imagine that no one cares about them anymore, that the sacrifices of their past have grown obsolete."

Brian raised his hand. "What's 'obsolete' mean?"

"It means pointless. Lacking in relevance any longer."

Everyone started cutting up the red construction paper and Miss Quinn walked around the classroom, making comments and *ooh*-ing and *aah*-ing over everyone's work. Teddy thought hard as he worked on his own poppies.

Miss Quinn, as she arrived at his desk, said, "Those are lovely poppies, and you look very deep in thought."

"Does 'obsolete' mean not thinking you have any friends anymore?" asked Teddy.

Miss Quinn looked at him closely. "Well. I suppose if you think that all of your friends are behind you, yes. Maybe. It could make you feel obsolete, to have lost everyone you started out with. But you can always make new friends."

"Exactly," said Teddy. "My neighbor, Mr. Hammersley, he lost his dad in the war and he's old, so he's lost a lot of friends and stuff, too, over the years. He doesn't really have anyone around anymore. And I guess usually he spends Remembrance Day by going to the church, all by himself, to remember them. But wouldn't it be nice if we could go to the church to remember them *with* him? So that he would know that maybe he lost a lot of friends, but now he's got some new friends, and we can remember the past but still be excited about the future. You know?"

Now Miss Quinn looked thoughtful. "I do know. And I think that's a really lovely idea, Teddy."

Sam read over the latest *From the Teacher's Desk* column in the *Turtledove Chronicle* and said to Teddy over dinner, "You're going to a church for Remembrance Day?"

"Yeah," said Teddy. "We learned all about it in school, and I told Miss Quinn that it would be nice if we could go and sit with Mr. Hammersley while he sits all by himself and thinks about his dad who died in the war and all his friends he's lost."

"Is that what Mr. Hammersley said he was going to do?"

"It's what Pen says he does. Pen knows basically everything everyone does."

"That doesn't sound alarming at all," said Sam, contemplating the permission slip that had accompanied the *Chronicle*, for the church trip in a couple of days.

He had not, since Bonfire Night, contacted Libby in any way. It had only been a few days, after all, and he seemed to recall there being complicated rules about who could ring whom and when. He had her number now, programmed into his mobile, and he could call it at any time. But she also had *his* number, and she hadn't rung him, so they seemed to be in a mutual stand-off over communication, from Sam's point of view. Which didn't seem a good way to start a relationship.

He couldn't decide if he was supposed to be the first one to get back in touch. And he was surrounded by people he could ask for help now, but he was embarrassed to ask any of the neighbors and thus betray how pathetically out of practice he was with all of this, and he was trying not to ask Ellen out of a sense of self-preservation. Ellen would immediately squeal at a pitch that would likely knock out Sam's eardrums and possibly the rest of the street's, too.

Sam mulled it over, and then realized Teddy was talking to him. "What was that?" he asked, forcing his gaze away from the permission slip.

"I asked when you think we should put our Christmas decorations up," repeated Teddy, with exaggerated patience, to emphasize what a trial his dad could be.

Sam said, "Oh. Yeah. I was thinking about that."

"In America," Teddy said, "we always waited until Thanksgiving. But they don't have Thanksgiving here and everyone's putting stuff up all over the street."

"To be fair, Max is responsible for almost every Christmas decoration that's up right now. So the definition of 'everyone putting stuff up' is mainly Max."

"Still," said Teddy.

Sam looked across at him, and thought how Teddy had said *In America*. Not *back home,* the way he might have mere weeks earlier. Sam said the idea he'd been considering for a few days.

"I was thinking we might have Thanksgiving."

"What do you mean?" asked Teddy.

"They might not have it here, but *we* could still have it. I could make us a turkey, and we could invite the rest of the street, and we could have a tree-trimming party."

Teddy lit up. "Really?"

Sam was pleased. "Yes. Do you like that idea?"

Teddy nodded. "Will you invite Miss Quinn?"

Sam laughed.

• • •

That night, after Teddy had gone to bed, Sam contemplated the permission slip again. He gave his permission and signed it, that being the easy part, and then he turned it over and considered what to say.

In the end, he really could think of nothing to say. Should he ask her out again? On the back of his son's permission slip? Should he just leave it alone? But how would she interpret the ongoing silence? How *was* she interpreting it already?

Frustrated, Sam eventually settled for picking up a pen and drawing a series of cascading lines on the paper. Then he looked at his handiwork and said out loud, "Oh, hell," because they looked terrible.

So he scrawled at the bottom, *These are meant to be fireworks.—S*

And then he thought, horrified, that this had been a *terrible* move on his part, and what was he thinking? But it was too late now: it was Teddy's only copy of the permission slip and it had to be handed in so Teddy could go. Otherwise Teddy would be monumentally disappointed.

Sam banged his head gently on the desk in frustration.

But two days later, the edition of the *Turtledove Chronicle* that Teddy brought home had the back covered with much more artfully drawn fireworks, these in bursts of color because Libby had been clever enough to use crayons.

"That's a message from Miss Quinn," Teddy said, when he noticed Sam smiling at the fireworks. "Are you using me to date my teacher?"

Sam grinned at him. " 'Using' is such a harsh word."

It used to be that Bill had felt the hollowness of all he had lost heavily, on a daily basis. These days, for unclear reasons, he found himself thinking less of his old friends.

But on Remembrance Day, he got up and dressed very carefully, in the finest clothes he could muster. His mother had always made him dress up in his best clothes for Remembrance Day; he had always kept up that tradition. Jack had stayed over the night before—Teddy had brought him by specially—and he watched Bill's unusually detailed bathroom activities with interest.

Bill turned to him finally, fastening his poppy on. "How do I look? Pretty smart, right? I bet you didn't know I could clean up so nicely." He leaned over carefully to scratch behind Jack's ears, which made Jack's tail wag madly. Bill said, "I used to spend much more time dressing myself up, in the old days, when there was a reason for that." He glanced at himself in the mirror, at the glint of red where his poppy was fastened, and then took a deep breath. "All right, Jack. Time for you to go on patrol while I go on my way."

Jack tried to follow Bill up the street, and Bill had to stop and shoo him away. Sometimes the dog could be daft, Bill allowed. Eventually—and every year it seemed like the walk took longer and longer—Bill reached the local church and sat himself in one of the pews. He took a deep breath of the church-scented air and closed his eyes for a moment, then opened them and looked around him. The church was, as usual, deserted. Everyone had been there for services on Sunday, but no one was there today.

But then, even as he finished having the thought, a slight scuffling started, and then got louder and louder, and then Bill watched, astonished, as a solemn, serious, silent group of children marched into the church and slid into pews and bowed their heads. The teacher at the front of them, a pretty ginger who looked vaguely familiar to Bill, although he couldn't place her, smiled at him.

Bill looked back to the pews of children, and recognized with a start Teddy and the little Indian girl, sitting right next to each other.

Bill stared at the pair of them, and then the larger group. All of these children, here on Remembrance Day. *Remembering*. Where he was normally alone, the only person in the dim and dusty church, there was now an entire *group* of people keeping him company. Bill had no idea what to make of it.

Eventually, in response to a signal Bill didn't see, the children rose and began filing over to him, each of them handing him a paper poppy. Teddy came last, beaming a smile at him and winking as he left, and then, just as suddenly as they had come, the children marched out of the church.

Bill listened to the scuffling sounds of the small army of children marching out of the church, and stared at his hands full of poppies, and realized that, for some reason, he was crying.

Chapter 13

Please join us for a
traditional American
Thanksgiving feast! I will even
make a turkey!

Sam and Teddy

Sam, in the end, broke down and rang Ellen. Who basically screeched in response that *yes,* it was appropriate for him to ask Libby to at least *coffee* after sticking his tongue down her throat at Bonfire Night. Which was rather more graphic a description of the kissing than Sam would have liked—and not at all accurate—but he decided to trust Ellen's assessment of the situation. So one night, after putting Teddy to bed, he took a deep breath and pressed *send* on Libby's number in his mobile.

Anticlimactically, she didn't answer, and Sam wondered wildly if she'd seen that it was him calling, and didn't want to talk to him, and then her voice mail clicked on, and Sam considered hanging up, but it was far too late—she would see that he had called, so Sam just said, after the beep, "Hi. It's Sam. Bishop. And I . . . didn't know if maybe you wanted to go for coffee sometime. Or something."

Libby rang him back an hour later, saying cheerfully, "Sorry. I was at yoga," which made Sam feel like a lazy slob who had basically not exercised since moving back to England. "Coffee sounds wonderful. When were you thinking? Next weekend?"

"Yes," Sam agreed, although he hadn't even thought far enough ahead to consider that question. He was really and truly rubbish at this.

They settled on Friday at 7 p.m. and Sam, in preparation, went to the Basak house the next day.

Diya was standing outside, frowning critically at her house, and she gestured to Max and Arthur's house as he walked up. "They're showing off. Look at that house. It's lit up like a Christmas tree."

"Well," said Sam. "It *is* Christmas."

"And now he's going to turn the old man's house into another Christmas tree."

It was true. Max was whistling away in Mr. Hammersley's front garden, happily ignoring all of Mr. Hammersley's suggestions as to where the lights ought to go. Jack was lying on the front step next to Mr. Hammersley, watching the proceedings with interest. For the moment, it was apparently more interesting than the squirrels.

"I might have to put up some lights," grumbled Diya. "This is ridiculous."

"We *do* live on Christmas Street," Sam pointed out. "Maybe we should go all-out for Christmas."

"You don't have any lights up," Diya retorted.

"I'm waiting until after Thanksgiving," Sam replied. "Speaking of, did you get my invitation?"

"Oh. Yes. I'm slightly concerned."

Diya looked earnest, and Sam was confused. "Concerned about Thanksgiving?"

"Are you really going to make the 'Thanksgiving feast'? You're going to make a turkey? And everything else?"

Diya looked supremely skeptical, and Sam frowned. "Yes. There's really nothing to making a turkey. I've watched lots of them get made. You just stick it in the oven and then the little timer thing sticks up eventually and boom, it's done."

Diya said, "I will make something for this feast, too," clearly not convinced a turkey was easy enough for Sam to handle.

And because Sam had come over to discuss other things, he decided not to debate the point any longer. He said politely, "Yes, thank you. That would be nice. I wanted to ask you if you could just keep an eye on Teddy for me on Friday night. He and Pari are usually hanging out together anyway."

"They have been spending rather a lot of time together," remarked Diya.

"They're working on the class play," Sam said. "The class play starring Jack."

343

"Starring Jack?" echoed Diya. "Jack the dog? Why would Jack be in the class play?"

"Because our children are determined," said Sam.

"Hmm." Diya frowned.

"Anyway," Sam said, feeling they were being sidetracked, "can you watch Teddy for me?"

"I can," said Diya. "Is this because you're going on a date with Miss Quinn?"

Sam opened and closed his mouth.

Diya made an excited gesture with her hand that ended up having the effect of shoving Sam a little bit. She said, "You are! I didn't expect that to be true, but you are! I am so proud of you! Where are you taking her?"

Sam had barely thought far enough ahead to answer the question of when the date should happen, never mind where.

"Oh," he said vaguely. "I don't know yet. Coffee somewhere, I guess?"

Diya's jaw dropped in abject horror, as if Sam had just said his idea of a date was making her wax his back hair or something. She said, "You cannot just take her for *coffee*. This is your *first date*. You want to make a good impression! You want to sweep her off her feet! *Coffee* never swept anyone off their feet!"

"Maybe if it was really good coffee . . . ?" Sam offered hopefully.

Diya gave him a withering look and said,

"I will watch your child for you, but you must come up with a better date than 'coffee.' "

In the end Sam, inspired by their first food-related meeting, ended up texting to Libby, **How would you like to make a gingerbread house?** Libby texted back, **As long as it doesn't have to be structurally sound.** Sam replied with, **Collapsed gingerbread pile also counts as a house.** Libby's response was, **Brilliant!** And then, after a pause, **Wait, you're not going to insist the gingerbread house has beetroot, are you?**

Sam fell a little bit more in love.

On Friday, with an address tucked on the mobile in his pocket, Sam left Teddy with Darsh and Diya and Pari. Teddy, apparently unbothered by the entire affair, told him to have fun and then immediately ran off into the back garden with Pari in search of Jack.

Diya looked Sam up and down and said, "You'll do."

Darsh called from the kitchen, sounding amused, "Leave him alone!"

Sam decided Darsh was his favorite.

On the way to Libby's, he stopped to buy her flowers, settling on bright daisies because they seemed happy.

Libby's flat was in a building that had reached an air of benign age, saggy in spots but charming nonetheless. She answered the door for him, already tucked into a bright blue coat with a matching beret perched on her head, and lifted her eyebrows at the daisies.

"Look at you," she said. "Angling for bonus points, are you?" She gave him such a delighted smile that he thought he'd already won the bonus points.

"I'm hoping for an A-plus grade at the end of the evening," said Sam.

"Expecting me to hand you a report?" She was busying herself in the small kitchen, filling a vase with water, and Sam was striving to be polite and not spy openly at all of her decoration choices as if they might be keen insights into her psyche.

"I've never taken a teacher on a date before. I assume you must grade all social occasions."

"So I should expect best behavior, then?" asked Libby, daisies in a vase and keys in her hand, as she stepped back through the door.

"Mmm," said Sam, following her, watching her lock the door with those hands that seemed to so frequently become the object of his fascination. "Or my worst behavior, I suppose. It depends on which sort of date you want."

Libby looked at him for a moment, and then grinned and leaned forward and brushed her finger ever-so-lightly down his nose. "These freckles," she murmured. "They rather kill me." Sam had never had anyone say that about his freckles before. He said breathlessly, "Oh," and wondered if it was too early in the evening to kiss her, since she was standing close enough now that he could sink happily into her eyes.

She closed the distance, leaned up to press her lips gently against his, a sweet and brief kiss that felt exactly like the best sort of *hello,* a warm welcome that made you forget how many of the people in the world were strangers because the people you knew were just *lovely*.

Then she leaned back and said, "Shall we make ourselves a gingerbread house?"

Sam had chosen the class somewhat at random, because making a gingerbread house sounded like it would afford more opportunity for talking than cooking classes that involved the making of a whole feast. How difficult could a gingerbread house be?

It turned out to be incredibly difficult. If their roof wasn't caving in, then their walls were tipping over. Their windows were dangerously crooked, their door was far too small in proportion to the rest of the house, and their gingerbread began cracking, letting in what Libby said would be a fierce chill for the poor gingerbread inhabitants.

And Sam couldn't remember the last time he'd laughed quite so much. Libby was raw, pure joy, blithe about their errors, steadfastly optimistic about their futures as gingerbread architects, in the face of all evidence to the contrary. She gamely piped tiles onto their roof while it lay in pieces on the parchment paper. The instructor at the front of the room was explaining to the more competent participants in the class how to pipe garlands around the eaves, to serve as a Christmas decoration.

Sam remarked softly to Libby, "This assumes the gingerbread house has eaves."

"We have eaves," Libby replied, laughter in her voice. "They are horizontal eaves."

And Sam couldn't help but say, "You are so delightful."

Libby glanced up from her piping, a charming blush spreading across her cheeks, and then leaned back over their destroyed gingerbread pile.

In the end, they were allowed to collect their gingerbread pieces into a bag and they walked along the pavement, munching on destroyed gingerbread with random icing accents.

Libby said, "I thought you'd be better at gingerbread house construction. Surely you'd built some with Teddy before?"

"I've definitely *bought* some, premade, at a store," Sam responded.

Libby laughed, head thrown back a little. It was a crisp, cool night, but the gingerbread house class had been warm, so Libby's coat wasn't fastened, and the star pendant around her neck glinted in the city lights all around them.

Sam said, "Your necklace is beautiful," because it was, although maybe what he meant was *It suits you,* because that was perhaps truer.

She reached up to rest her fingers on the pendant and said, "Thank you. It was a gift. From my father. When I was younger, I was going to be an astronaut." Libby smiled as she said it, playfully, as if sharing a secret. "I was going to go up into space and see the stars from right next to them."

"That sounds lovely," said Sam. "All I wanted to be was a rock star, for no poetic reasons at all."

Libby laughed. "Do you play any instruments?"

"No," confessed Sam. "I can't even sing. I have no idea what I thought I was on about."

Libby laughed again. "And I get carsick, which pretty much put an end to any fantasy about orbiting the Earth. I'd never be able to handle G3 when I couldn't even handle the M4."

Sam chuckled.

"But I became a teacher instead, and, without being too terribly embarrassing about it, I still get to see stars up close. Just a different sort of star. Oh, God, that sounds horrible, doesn't it?"

"It sounds sweet," said Sam. "My job is just something I do that makes me money. But I think you love your job."

"I do," agreed Libby. "And also, it allows me to meet all sorts of interesting men." She flashed a coy smile at him, dimples just visible.

"I bet you heartlessly collect us, don't you?" rejoined Sam. "Slay us all with that smile and the way you laugh and then move off to the next crop."

"Normally, yes," replied Libby, still smiling. "But none of them ever demolished a gingerbread house with me. I might keep you around a bit longer, see how badly you can destroy chocolates for Valentine's Day."

Sam laughed.

At the time, it had made perfect sense to put Max's number down as the main contact for the adoption agency. Max didn't have an office job. Max was reliably with his mobile. Max didn't silence it for random middle-of-the-day meetings. Naturally the adoption agency should contact Max first.

Except that what this meant was that it was Max who received the call about being chosen for another baby.

What this meant was that Max sat in his studio, drinking in the middle of the day, debating whether or not to tell Arthur, debating whether or not to ring back and turn down the baby, debating whether or not he was the world's worst husband for even thinking about this, debating whether or not he could go through losing another child at the eleventh hour.

Which was when his doorbell rang.

Max swore and pressed his glass to his forehead and debated now whether or not to answer the door, and then decided that maybe it was a good idea to break himself out of this. Of course he had to tell Arthur about the baby. *Of course* he did.

Max opened the door on Sam, who looked slightly frazzled.

He said immediately, "Have you ever made pastry before?"

"You're making pastry?" said Max.

"Yes. For a pumpkin pie. For the Thanksgiving feast. I accidentally invited Libby to the Thanksgiving feast. So now I need to look as if I can cook. I really can't cook. As you may have already noticed."

Max looked at Sam, obviously in the middle of some kind of minor crisis, and thought how he couldn't handle someone else's minor crisis, because he was in the middle of his own rather major crisis at the moment, so he blurted out, "Arthur and I have been matched with a baby to adopt."

Sam blinked, and then grinned widely. "Have you? That's wonderful—"

"It isn't wonderful." Max shook his head.

"Don't you want a baby?" Sam asked hesitantly.

"I want a baby, yes. Arthur wants a baby, yes. Arthur would be *so amazing* with a child. Arthur would raise this incredibly serious little insurance agent of a child. We'd be good at it. I think we'd be really good at it. Don't you think we'd be good at it?"

"Yes," Sam said. "I do. Because you want to be, and that's important. Because you'd try really hard. Because you'd *love*. Why don't you sit down? You look as if you—"

"But we get matched with children and they take them from us. The first time it was before the baby had been given to us, so it was all in the abstract, and it was hard but we dealt with it. The second time, Arthur had *held* her, and his face was—and her face was—and then we couldn't have her anymore because—and I don't know if I can do that again. I don't know if I can."

"Take a breath," Sam said, stepping through the door and closing it behind him. "Have you talked to Arthur about this?"

"Yes," said Max. "No. I don't know. I think I've tried? But when the possibility of another baby was still in the abstract, I didn't realize the extent to which I was going to panic. Now they've rung me about a baby and I've plummeted directly off a cliff like a lunatic."

"Stop it. You are not a lunatic," said Sam. "Trust me. You're just under a lot of stress at the moment."

"Right. And if I can't handle this amount of stress, how can I handle a *child?*"

"Nobody thinks they can handle a child, once the reality of it really hits. You'll be fine. You really will be. But I do think you need to talk to Arthur about how you're feeling about the possibility of losing another child."

Max did not want to do that at all. Max did not want to bring up how concrete a new baby had become. Max did not want Arthur's rising hopes, Arthur's careful preparations, Arthur's measured excitement, because Max did not want the flip side of all of these things. Half of Max wished they'd got the first or second baby, and the other half of Max wished they'd never brought any of this up at all.

There was a knock on the back door, and Max said, "Oh, Christ, everyone on the street is coming to visit today."

It turned out to be Bill, who said, "Weren't we supposed to work today? Your shed is locked. What's the matter with you? You look like hell."

Which meant Arthur would definitely know something was up with him. Max said, "No working today. Only drinking today."

"And making pastry," said Sam.

"Making pastry?" echoed Bill, sounding extremely disapproving of this.

"Sam's going to make the pastry," said Max. "We're going to mock him whilst we drink."

• • •

Pari came home from school in a good mood. The class play was just going to be *amazing*. Miss Quinn had let them start running through lines, and Pari got to deliver dramatic pronouncements about insurance and climate change, and she even got to rest her hand against her forehead at one point in an almost-faint.

She told Mum, "Our class play is the *best*."

"Oh," Mum said, and pointed a wooden spoon at her, where she was stirring something in one of her gigantic pots. "I heard about your class play."

"Did you?" asked Pari happily. "Who told you? Did Miss Quinn say how fantastic it's going to be?"

"No, Sam Bishop told me that you expect that street dog to star in it."

"Oh, yeah," said Pari. "Isn't that a great idea? We're working on it. I feel like we can get Miss Quinn to agree."

"She shouldn't agree," Mum said. "She should definitely not agree. In fact, I am going to ring her and tell her that I think having the dog involved in the play is a terrible idea."

Pari . . . stared. Pari felt she could do nothing but . . . stare. Because . . . Because she'd had a good day, such a good day, and she loved her play, and getting Jack in the play would be the best thing, and . . . and . . .

Mum was stirring the contents of her pot and saying, "I have to go over to Anika's because her niece's friend's mum just found out she's having another baby and I said that I'd bring some rogan josh over for the celebration."

And she didn't even *notice,* thought Pari. She didn't even *notice* how she was saying something *so horrible.*

Pari said hotly, "Jack would be the best. The whole thing would be the best. You don't even know. Because you never pay attention." And then she stormed out of the house.

Tears were hot in her eyes as she stood in the back garden, blinking furiously. It was cold outside, and she'd forgotten to put her coat on, and there was no way she was going back inside now to fetch it. She could have gone over to Teddy's house, but she didn't want to be there, blinking back tears, explaining how her mum was going to ruin *everything.* Because her mum just didn't care. Her mum cared more about Anika's niece's whatever, whom she didn't even *know.*

Pari ducked out of her back garden into the garden next door, and from there into the street.

Jack came to greet her, looking as happy to see her as he always did.

"Go away," Pari said angrily as she marched up the street.

"Just go away, Jack. Everything is a mess and I don't need you jumping around me like it's all brilliant. Mum's only ever home when she wants to do something to ruin my life, and it's horrible. She doesn't even look at me. She doesn't even see the things I like. She doesn't care what I like. And everything is just the worst and *go away*." Pari shouted this finally, and Jack halted. His tail wasn't wagging, and Pari had never seen him without his tail wagging. He stood in the middle of the pavement and whined at her a little, and she said firmly, *"Stay,"* and then whirled on her heel and marched down the street.

It would probably be *hours* before anyone noticed, she thought. She'd probably be able to walk halfway to the Tower of London by then. She might as well.

Max, luckily, seemed unable to resist the adventure of making a pie from scratch. Before Sam knew it, he had basically taken over the entire project, and Sam's kitchen was full of flour and butter that was refusing to combine but that Max was trying to smash into submission. Considering that Max had looked on the verge of a full-fledged nervous breakdown when he had opened the door for Sam, Sam was relieved that he'd bounced back. He was fairly sure that, given a moment's reflection, Max would see that he should talk to Arthur about all of this.

So Sam sat with Bill, who looked dubious about the pie escapade and indeed, Sam suspected, would really have preferred to flee.

Sam said, "Are you coming for Thanksgiving tomorrow?"

"I don't celebrate Thanksgiving," Bill answered gruffly.

"None of us do," contributed Max cheerfully. "Doesn't mean we can't enjoy Sam's attempts at cooking."

"Hey, I'm blaming you for however that pie turns out," said Sam.

Max shrugged.

Sam turned back to Bill. "Come to Thanksgiving. Really. We're going to decorate the Christmas tree."

"Finally, your house will cease to be the black hole of no-Christmas cheer," remarked Max.

"It's not a black hole of no-Christmas cheer. We are going to unleash all of the Christmas cheer at the proper time," Sam said loftily.

Teddy came in and said, "Hi, Dad. Hi, Max. Hi, Mr. Hammersley."

They all said *hi* back and Sam said, "How was school?"

"Our play is so great," Teddy said enthusiastically. "Pari got to act out her scene today, and she was amazing. She talks all about insurance, and it's so dramatic. She even goes like this at the end." Teddy struck a pose, head thrown back and the back of his hand against his forehead, like he was about to faint.

"That's exactly what Arthur looks like when he talks about insurance," Max said, and then frowned a little bit at the mention of Arthur.

Teddy said, "What are you doing?" looking curiously at the mess Max had made.

"Making a pie," Max answered.

"We should probably just buy pastry," suggested Teddy.

"O ye of little faith," said Max.

"He's always of little faith," said Sam. "He's a doubter. Always dubious, with the expertise of a Year 4 student."

Teddy shrugged and said, "I'm going to go play *Mass Extinction Event*."

"Sounds uplifting," remarked Max.

"Exactly," said Sam. "What about homework?" he called after Teddy.

"Let me make something extinct first!" Teddy called back.

Sam let Max knead and roll at the mess he'd made of the dough and looked at the time and eventually said, "You know, you can't avoid Arthur forever."

"I'm not avoiding him," Max said.

"Did you two have a row?" Mr. Hammersley asked. "You should buy him flowers."

Max gave him a dry look. "Are you dispensing relationship advice now?"

Mr. Hammersley shrugged. "Always worked

for me. And I was married for forty-seven years. That's nothing to sneeze at."

Diya Basak knocked on the back door, and Sam opened it for her. At the same instant, Jack came bounding up at a dead run, tripping over his own paws in that way he had.

Diya flinched and said, "Get control of your dog."

"Shh, Jack," Sam said to him. "Take it easy."

"I'm here to take Pari home," Diya said. "She's had her ridiculous strop, but now I have to go to a friend's house and her father almost has dinner on the table."

"Pari?" Sam echoed blankly. "Pari's not here."

Diya said, "What? She must be here. She went running out of the house."

"Teddy!" Sam called up the stairs, going over to the foot of them. Jack kept barking and bouncing, almost tripping him now. "Quiet," Sam told him. "Calm down."

"Yeah?" Teddy called down, and then appeared at the top of the stairs. "Hi, Jack."

Jack barked at him.

"Pari's not up there with you, right?" Sam said.

Teddy looked confused. "What? No. She's not here. We walked home from school together but then she went to her house. Why?"

Sam glanced back at Diya.

Who looked annoyed.

"She must be hiding outside somewhere," said Diya. "She's probably trying to prove a point."

Diya turned around and shouted into the darkness that was gathering thickly all around them. "Pari! You've proved your point! Come out now!"

Sam peered out into the darkness with Diya. Nothing moved, except for leaves being scattered by the brisk wind that was blowing. And Jack, who ran in circles around the pavement, barking furiously.

"Pari!" Diya shouted, and then said, "She must be in our garden. I'll just go and check."

Sam watched her walk back to her house.

Max said, "That . . . doesn't sound good."

"Pari!" shouted Diya, in her otherwise still and silent back garden. She was letting herself be angry, because if she stopped being angry she would have to be worried. "Stop this at once and come out right now!"

Nothing moved. On the street, Diya could hear that dog still barking.

Darsh came to the door and said, "What are you doing?"

And then Diya had to admit it. "I'm looking for Pari."

"Why?" asked Sai from behind Darsh. "Where is she?"

"Why isn't she home?" asked Darsh.

"I thought she went next door, but she didn't," said Diya, and now she was starting to really fret. "Call for her. She'll listen to you—she's angry with me."

Darsh gave her a curious look and then stepped out into the back garden with her. "Pari! Come home now! I've made your favorite for dinner."

Silence still, all around them. Except for that stupid dog on the street.

"Pari!" Darsh shouted again.

"Where is she?" Sai asked from the house. "Do you think she's been, like, kidnapped or something?"

"No, she hasn't been kidnapped," Diya snapped automatically, even as the idea settled heavily in her stomach. Pari had been so upset, and Diya had been making rogan josh and had barely even looked up, and what if that was the last time . . . ? No, it couldn't be the last time—she was being silly. Pari was just sulking somewhere—

"Diya, why did you say Pari was angry with you?" Darsh asked.

"I think . . . She wanted that ridiculous street dog to be in her class play and I told her that was a horrible idea and I was going to talk to her teacher about it but it wasn't—"

"Mum," Sai said. "She loves that dog so much. She was so excited about that. Why would you say that?"

"Because it *is* a ridiculous idea," Diya said shrilly, hysterically, "and I was busy making rogan josh for Anika's niece's—"

"Of course you were," muttered Sai, and Diya's stomach plummeted even further. "We need to go look for Pari."

"It's going to be fine," Darsh said. "We'll find her. She can't have gone far."

"But what if we can't find her?" Diya asked. "What if she really has been kidnapped? What have I *done?*" Why hadn't she run after her, why hadn't she *looked* at her to realize how upset Pari had been?

"We'll find her," Darsh said. "Let's go."

Diya collected herself enough to follow him and Sai out of the house, pressing her hand against her mouth because otherwise she felt like she might have to scream with fear and worry. Her daughter was missing—*missing*—had run away, all because she had been making *rogan josh*. What was she doing? The street dog was still running in circles on the street, barking. Pen, clearly on her way out for a run, and Arthur, clearly just coming home from work, were both standing looking at him curiously.

"Hello," Pen said cheerfully as they approached. "There's something wrong with Jack. Maybe the squirrels have finally driven him mad."

Darsh said, "We're looking for Pari—"

"We've lost her!" Diya interjected, because she wanted to get the important point across. "She's missing!"

"What?" said Pen, sounding concerned.

362

"She ran away because I wouldn't listen to her," said Diya, wiping away furiously at her tears, because those *weren't going to help,* "and now we have to find her before anything horrible happens to her, and how do we even *start—*"

Darsh put a hand on her shoulder and Pen came up to her and took her hands and said, "We'll all help. Of course. We'll fan out and canvass the streets."

Arthur said, his mobile already to his ear, "I'm ringing the police."

Diya was dimly aware, through the haze of her panic, that Sam and Max and Mr. Hammersley and Teddy had stepped out of the Bishop house, and that Emilia had stepped out of the Pachuta house, and she felt like they were all staring at her and judging her for *making her child run away,* but they were also saying things like, "Yes. Yes. Of course. We'll help."

"We'll take Jack," Teddy said suddenly. "Jack probably knows where she is."

"How would Jack know?" asked Darsh, sounding bewildered.

"He spends a lot of time with Pari. He probably knows her smell. Dogs are good with smells."

"Jack's not that kind of dog," Darsh said, sounding dubious. "I think we'd be better off just—"

Teddy broke away from the knot of men in his front door and came into the street and crouched down beside the dog. He looked very seriously into the animal's eyes and said, "Jack, can you help us find Pari?"

And the dog barked once, then took off down the street, with his ridiculous stumbling run that made him look comical. He did not look at all like a serious rescue dog to Diya and yet, at the same time, she found herself taking off after him.

"Diya!" Darsh shouted after her.

But Diya didn't stop. Diya couldn't stop. Diya had to find Pari and make sure she was okay and make sure she knew how much she was loved. Diya couldn't believe Pari could have felt otherwise, could have *run away*.

The dog ran for what seemed to Diya like a long time, but Diya hadn't run anywhere in a while, and by the time the dog turned down a particular street, barking wildly, Diya was holding a hand to her side and gasping for breath.

But there was Pari, huddled into a ball in the corner of a bus shelter, shivering and cold. She said, confused, "Jack?" as the dog bounded up to her and licked her face, and then, sounding even more confused, "*Mum?*"

And Diya fell on her and pulled her against her and she was cold, so cold, and Diya said, "Oh, Pari. Oh, Pari. What were you *thinking?*"

"You noticed?" said Pari against her. "You noticed I was gone?"

"Oh, *Pari,*" said Diya, and held her tighter and

364

tighter, and the street dog came and licked her face.

Diya tucked Pari into bed. Pari seemed absolutely fine, like it hadn't been an ordeal at all, and in fact seemed to be enjoying being the center of attention. But Diya couldn't stop fussing. She couldn't stop reliving Pari cuddling into her, her voice full of wonder at her absence being noticed.

Pari said, "Do you think we'll be in the news?"

Diya said, trying to be brusque, "No."

"The police were here. We'll probably be on the news."

The police had been there, briefly, because Arthur had called them. Diya doubted it would make the news.

But she looked down at Pari, shining-eyed with this adventure, and Diya felt like she was actually *seeing* her for the first time. Her daughter, who liked all of these adventures, who wanted a dog in the school play, who was *so excited* about her school play.

Diya looked at Pari and said, "Tell me about the play."

Pari told her all about the play, and climate change, and the insurance agent, and Jack's starring role. "And you can't say anything bad about Jack anymore; he *found me*," she finished solemnly.

Diya smoothed a hand over Pari's hair and marveled at her and said, "Yes. He did."

"It was a good thing Jack was there," said Pari wisely. "A good job Jack is our street dog."

"A good job Jack is our street dog," Diya agreed.

Pari bounced with delight at Diya's statement.

"Pari ran away," Emilia announced, as soon as Anna walked through the door.

Anna, focused entirely on getting out of the clothes she'd been wearing all day, getting into pajamas, curling up with her camomile tea and Socks and Tabby, said wearily, "What? Who?"

"The little girl," Emilia explained impatiently, "who lives next door. Ran away. We all had to go looking for her. The police came and everything."

Now Emilia had Anna's full attention. "Did they find her?"

"Yeah, she's fine now, but it was super-scary."

"You went out looking for her?" Anna said, going back to that detail. "At night? By yourself? Wasn't it dangerous?"

Emilia gave her a look. "Mum. They're our *neighbors*. Shouldn't we help them when they need it? Wouldn't you want them to help you if I'd gone missing?"

Anna looked at Emilia and felt like a terrible person. What was wrong with her that she was so heartless? She said, "Yes. Yes, I absolutely would. And I should go and see Diya Basak. See how she's holding up. I should . . . take her soup, or something."

366

"Do we have soup?" asked Emilia quizzically.

"I don't know. We must have *something*." Anna opened a cupboard and looked into it, shifting through random boxes. She pulled out a box of pasta and said, "I could make pasta, I guess."

Diya stood and looked at the rogan josh that she had prepared to take to Anika's niece's friend's mother's house. It felt like that had been a lifetime ago.

Darsh said, "Who was the rogan josh for?"

Diya answered, feeling almost hysterical, "I don't know. I actually *don't know*."

Before Darsh could ask her anything further, there was a knock on the door, and Diya took the opportunity to collect herself and answer it.

Anna Pachuta was there, holding a casserole dish.

Diya forced a bright smile on her face and said, "Hello, Anna. How nice of you to come by."

"I brought some pasta," said Anna, indicating the casserole dish she was holding. "I thought you might . . . I don't know, I heard what happened, and I thought maybe you might . . . be in need of some company for a cuppa."

It was ridiculous, Diya thought, staring at Anna. Because they had never been friends. Why would she want Anna there for a cuppa? And at the same time, she suddenly *did* want the company, because then maybe she could . . . take a breath, and find a way to think of the whole evening without panic.

"That's so lovely," Diya said. "Won't you come in?"

Darsh greeted Anna politely and then excused himself to go upstairs to check on Pari.

Diya set about making tea.

Anna said, a little awkward-sounding, "How's Pari?"

Diya said, "She's fine, thankfully. She's just fine."

And then Anna said, "How are you?"

And Diya kind of crumpled a little bit. She stared at the teacups in front of her and said, "I . . . I don't know. I'm . . . My daughter ran away from home today. She *ran away*." Diya braved a look over at Anna.

Who didn't look disapproving or even pitying. Anna looked so exhausted that Diya felt all of her emotions mirrored. Anna said, "She came back. She's fine. She's okay."

"But . . ." Diya began, feeling helpless.

"Being a mother can feel like such an impossible task," Anna said. "Being . . . *everything*."

And Diya came and sank down into the chair opposite Anna. "*Exactly*. There's . . . so much, every day, that needs to get done. And who's going to do it, if not you? It's not going to happen magically."

"I know," Anna agreed, and they lapsed into a comfortable and thoughtful silence. After a moment, Anna ventured, "I'm just saying . . . we can't be perfect. We can only do our best. And learn. I guess."

"Yeah," Diya said, and thought again of Pari, curling into her, happy to be noticed. Learning, she thought. The best she could do was learn. "It's funny," she mused, "I feel like I forgot, for a little while, just how much you can learn from the people you love."

"The people you love," echoed Anna. "Yeah."

Anna, curled up with chamomile tea in the bed, cats purring next to her, was supposed to be reading but was really staring at the dark sky outside the bedroom window without really seeing it, thinking hard about the conversation with Diya, about being home, about *life*.

Marcel came into the bedroom and looked a little surprised. "Hello," he said, not unpleasantly. "You're awake."

"I'm awake," she said, and wondered when she had started to be asleep more often than not when Marcel got home. When had they fallen into that habit? She thought of . . . staying still. Of using her time and energy, maybe, more on the people she loved. And looking at Marcel, as he took off his watch and ruffled at his hair, she thought how, amazingly, she *did* still love

369

him. It had been so long since she had had that thought. It felt as if it had been years since she had actually looked at Marcel. Be with someone long enough, and it became like failing to appreciate that you could breathe the air around you, thought Anna. Maybe you didn't appreciate it until you tried not to breathe for a little while.

Anna said, "How was work?"

Marcel, on his way into the ensuite, paused and looked at her. He looked as surprised that she was speaking to him as he had been to find her awake. Had it really been *that long* since they'd had a conversation? "It was good," said Marcel, and turned fully away from the ensuite to face her. "Long, as usual. How was it for you?"

She made room for him on the bed. It disturbed the cats but it was worth it when Marcel accepted the wordless invitation.

"Also long," said Anna. "And then I came home to hear that Pari Basak ran away from home."

"I know," said Marcel. "Mad story, that, isn't it? Glad it turned out okay."

"How do you know?"

"Emilia rang me. To tell me she was running out to help search."

"I wonder why she didn't ring me," mused Anna.

"She probably wasn't sure you'd let her," replied Marcel, giving Anna a knowing look. "You can be a bit . . . *protective,* shall we say?"

Which Anna had to admit. She sighed and said, "I know, and I don't know why I let myself get . . ." She looked at Marcel, swallowed thickly, and told the truth. "I think I envy Diya Basak. With too much on her plate but a little less than me. Staying home all day. Being able to *afford* staying home all day."

"Anna." Marcel reached out and took the hand not cradling her cup of tea. "I keep telling you that we could—"

"But it turns out that I don't want to stay home. It's just that . . . I always feel stretched too thin. Like there's too much to do and I never get to see you or Emilia. And then I went tonight to see Diya and I realized that . . . she feels the same way. That there's always something else that could be done, and it occurred to me that maybe what I need to do is . . . ignore the things that could be done. For just a little while. I got caught up, but I miss you, and do you think that—"

She was cut off by Marcel leaning forward and kissing her fiercely.

He drew back briefly and said, "Yes."

And she found herself giggling, trying futilely to balance her tea, while the cats, yowling, fled off the bed. "You didn't even hear my question."

"The answer's yes, Anna. The answer's always yes to you, Anna. You never even have to ask," said Marcel.

And Anna put her tea aside.

Chapter 14

LOCAL DOG TRACKS DOWN
MISSING CHILD!

"The turkey says it's done already," said Sam, peering suspiciously at the bird itself, still settled in his stove.

"Then it's probably done," said Ellen with a shrug, pouring herself a glass of wine.

"It seems too fast," said Sam, and closed the oven door. "I don't believe it."

"You've decided not to believe a dead turkey." Ellen pointed at him with her wineglass. "You have trust issues."

"When it comes to food I'm cooking, yes, I have massive trust issues—it never does anything it's supposed to do."

"You know what else isn't doing what it's supposed to be doing?" asked Sophie, as she drifted into the kitchen, followed by her sister. "This spike." She held up what looked to Sam like a stumpy papier mâché rhinoceros horn. Sophie had walked in with it and had immediately disappeared into the lounge with Evie, and Sam hadn't asked questions because he assumed it was best not to when it came to his teenage nieces.

But now he decided it was time to ask. "Yeah, what *is* that?"

"The spike for your ceiling," answered Sophie.

"We made a prototype," added Evie. "But it's not working the way we predicted."

"It may be back to the drawing board," finished Sophie.

Sam said, "It really isn't necessary for you girls to add spikes to my ceiling."

Sophie and Evie both gave him the teenaged-girl equivalent of Teddy's *how thick can you be.*

Sophie said, "Your lounge is *tragic,* Uncle Sam."

"*Tragic,*" agreed Evie.

Sam looked at Ellen. "I thought it wasn't that bad."

"Don't argue with their taste," replied Ellen. "It's impeccable."

Sophie and Evie gave him looks that said, *So there!,* and then drifted back into the lounge.

Sam said to Ellen, "I am rethinking the blanket decorating permission I granted earlier."

"Too late," Ellen responded blithely. "You'll just have to take your schoolteacher into a house with spikes coming from the ceiling."

"She isn't 'my' schoolteacher," said Sam. "She's her own schoolteacher."

"No, she's your son's schoolteacher."

"Okay, that *is* more accurate," admitted Sam.

"Well, I for one cannot wait to meet her."

"You're going to behave yourself, right?"

Ellen looked offended. "I *always* behave myself."

Teddy and Pari were playing Double Fetch with Jack, which was a game Pari had invented that allowed both of them to play equally with Jack and have limited arguments between them, which Dad had said was always a good thing.

Pen Cheever came out of her house carrying a box and waved to them. "Happy Thanksgiving," she called cheerfully to Teddy.

"Thanks." Teddy smiled widely. It was nice to have it be Thanksgiving. It felt like a special, out-of-the-ordinary day, and to have everyone coming over for Thanksgiving was pretty awesome, as Dad had never done Thanksgiving on his own before.

"I have an apple pie here," said Pen. "That's traditional, right?"

Teddy nodded happily and, as Pen walked off toward Teddy's house, looked at Pari. "We are going to have so much good food."

Pari said, "I hope so. Mum made all of my favorites."

"Teddy!" Dad called from down the street, his head sticking out the door. "Check to make sure Mr. Hammersley's coming to dinner!"

"Got it!" Teddy called back, and then he and Pari agreed to race each other to Mr. Hammersley's door.

Jack won, of course. He was pretty fast. He was even faster than his own legs sometimes.

Mr. Hammersley answered very grumbly but he was always like that, so Teddy didn't mind him.

"Are you coming to dinner, Mr. Hammersley?" asked Teddy.

"What does it look like?" retorted Mr. Hammersley.

He was wearing a tie, so Teddy supposed that meant yes.

"Even though it's a rubbish American holiday," continued Mr. Hammersley sulkily.

Teddy squared his shoulders and said staunchly, "It isn't rubbish. It's important. Dad says it has sketchy beginnings but it's a nice opportunity to think about what we're grateful for."

Mr. Hammersley was still grumbling but he did step out of his door and close it behind him, locking it.

Pari said, "What about the fact that Jack's a proper hero now, Mr. Hammersley?"

"Jack was always a hero," replied Mr. Hammersley dismissively.

"Right, but now he's a *real* hero," said Teddy. "He found Pari. That's pretty cool and amazing, right?"

"She was only a few streets away," said Mr. Hammersley.

As they reached Teddy's house, Pari's front door opened and her mum and dad stepped out.

Pari and Teddy both waved.

Teddy called, "Happy Thanksgiving!"

Jack went bounding over to them to also say "Happy Thanksgiving."

Sai came out of the house, following Mr. and Mrs. Basak, and Teddy said, "I can beat Sai at video games again."

Sai grinned at him. "I've been practicing."

"We can't play video games all day," said Pari. "You told me we were going to get to decorate your tree."

"Oh!" said Teddy. "That's right! Dad and I already put the lights on; it's ready to go!"

"I'm not decorating a tree," said Mr. Hammersley.

Mr. Hammersley was helping to decorate the tree. Mostly by telling all of the younger set what they were doing wrong. Diya was also giving directions. Sometimes their directions clashed. Teddy and Pari were ignoring all of the directions anyway, so that didn't really matter to them, and Sophie, Evie, Sai, and Emilia were between them all only putting one or two ornaments on the tree every ten minutes, so they clearly weren't very receptive to the directions either. Arthur seemed to be the only person vaguely paying attention to the directions, and getting frustrated when he was being given contradictory ones. Even Anna and Marcel, who were also helping, seemed wrapped up in their own little world together. Pen was sitting on the floor between Diya and Mr. Hammersley, looking vastly amused by the entire operation, and Jack was curled up with his head in her lap, also watching the tree-trimming.

Ellen and Max were standing off to the side watching the proceedings as well and drinking wine.

Sam said, "Don't you two want to go and help?"

"You would have to pay me money to get involved in that," said Max pleasantly, gesturing to the tree tableau.

"Amen," said Ellen, and clinked her glass against Max's.

"That is not the true Christmas spirit," Sam berated them lightly, and then the doorbell rang.

"Is that your teacher?" asked Ellen.

"Not my teacher," Sam reminded her.

"Oh, have you met her yet?" said Max. "She's lovely."

"Have you met her?" asked Ellen with interest.

Max shook his head. "Just spotted her from across the way. If I went for women, I would have swooped in and stolen her from Sam."

Sam rolled his eyes and moved off to the door and opened it on Libby.

Libby . . . who was decked out today in winter white and carrying a small, gaily wrapped box, which she held out to Sam. "Hi," she said, with one of her dimpled smiles. "Happy Thanksgiving."

"You don't give gifts on Thanksgiving," Sam said, amused, accepting the box.

"Oh," said Libby innocently. "I had no idea; it's not my holiday."

"Come in," said Sam, "but please brace yourself for all of the horrible people I know."

Libby laughed, and Sam stepped aside to let her in.

At the time that he had invited Libby to Thanksgiving, it had seemed like a brilliant idea. Their date had gone incredibly well, they exchanged increasingly cheeky texts with each other, and it seemed odd for Sam to be hosting a party and excluding her from it. It had, in fact, seemed only natural to invite Libby along. Sam wanted to take the opportunity to spend every moment he could with Libby, and this was a lovely long day with her, decorating the Christmas tree together. In Sam's head, it was going to be a day full of bonhomie and merriment. Now he was just hoping Libby didn't get teased too badly.

But she really didn't. Pari and Teddy called, "Hi, Miss Quinn!" but were both far too interested in how they were arranging the mouse ornaments on the tree in the most effective formation to really be paying attention. Sam introduced Libby around, and everyone was very polite to her, including Mr. Hammersley, who was surprisingly gracious and almost charming to her in a very old-fashioned way.

And Ellen—darling, amazing, wonderful Ellen—just hugged Libby and said, "I've heard so very much about you, and it's so nice to meet you."

Libby said, in that playful way people responded to that, "All good, I hope."

"So good that I couldn't wait to meet you."

And Libby smiled.

And then she said something that should have been totally innocent but that ended up being the beginning of All Bad Things.

She said, "And is this the famous Jack?" because Jack had come up to say hello to her, tail wagging. She scratched behind his ears.

"The famous Jack," Sam confirmed.

"Yeah, who should be in our play!" shouted Pari, suddenly paying attention to the grown-ups again.

"He really should be," Teddy said. "We should take a vote. Who thinks Jack should be in our school play, *Jesus and the Climate Change Manger*? Raise your hand."

"*Jesus and the Climate Change Manger*?" repeated Ellen.

"That's the name we've decided on," said Teddy.

"It's a Christmas play," Pari added, as if that explained everything.

"It stars an insurance agent," said Max.

"I wouldn't say that's the *star*," said Pari.

"Jack should be the star," said Teddy.

"Well, I do admit I'm finding myself less able to resist adding Jack to our play, given that now he's basically a local celebrity," said Libby.

Sam looked at Libby in confusion. "What do you mean?"

"Well, I read about him online, didn't I? 'Local Dog Tracks Down Missing Child.' "

Everyone was now looking at Libby, even the teenagers.

"It was *online?*" Diya said. "A story about Pari?"

"Yeah. I mean, I assumed it must be him. How many dogs called Jack live on Christmas Street?"

"But . . . how did anyone know about this?" Diya asked, sounding confused. "I didn't give any interviews to anyone. Did anyone talk to anyone about this?" Diya looked all around the room.

Libby said, "I think it was on a blog or something . . . ?"

Pen said in a small voice, "Oh, no," and then all attention was on her.

"What 'oh, no'?" asked Diya, eyes narrowing.

"So." Pen scratched her head and said slowly, "You know how I'm a writer?"

No one said anything, because there was no need to answer that question.

"I've been keeping a blog," said Pen. "A blog . . . about the street."

And now there were responses. Lots of responses. Spilling all over each other.

"What, about us?" said Diya.

"What about us?" asked Anna.

"I knew it!" said Mr. Hammersley.

Max looked at him. "You knew Pen was keeping a blog?" Sam was equally surprised; he would have said that Mr. Hammersley didn't know what a blog was.

"No, but I knew that you can't trust anyone," said Mr. Hammersley.

"Look, it's no big thing," Pen said, although she sounded a little desperate. "It was a way for me to procrastinate what I was working on. I was just noticing what was going on around the street and I just . . . wrote about it. I actually gave it up, but the thing with Jack and Diya was so amazing, I just had to use it for an epilogue—I didn't use your *names* or anything."

"What's the address?" asked Arthur, with his phone out.

Pen, sounding miserable, gave the URL, and everyone whipped their phones out.

Anna suddenly screeched. "What is this! What is this that you're writing about my *marriage!* Right here where anybody can see it! About my *life!*" She held the phone up.

"Wait, what is *this!*" screeched Diya, and then

looked up at Emilia and demanded, "Are you dating my son?!"

Emilia, looking startled, blinked and started stammering a response.

But Anna jumped into the fray by exclaiming, "*What?* You're dating *him?*"

"Mum, it's not—" Emilia began.

"We just like each other," Sai finished.

"Not another word out of you, young man. How many times have we talked about how important it is for you to focus on your studies?"

"But, Mum—" Sai began.

"Hang on," Anna interrupted hotly. "What's wrong with my daughter? You think she would automatically make him bad at school?"

"Oh, don't pretend you're happy to have her dating my son," Diya snapped. "You know you've always hated me."

"I don't hate you," Anna retorted.

Jack, alarmed by all the shouting, started circling the two women, barking.

"Maybe we should all just calm down," suggested Sam, trying to step between Anna and Diya.

Anna turned to Marcel, saying, "Marcel, do you believe—" and then gasping and exclaiming, "Wait, you *knew* about this!"

Marcel looked sheepish. "Well, I knew Emilia was dating Sai."

"You've been reading this blog?" said Anna. "And didn't say anything?"

Marcel shook his head. "No, I didn't know about the blog. I just knew Emilia was dating Sai."

There was a moment of silence.

Sam tried again, "Why don't we—"

"She told you?" Anna said, and her voice sounded so small and raw and hurt that Sam felt like he ought to usher everyone out of the house. She turned to look at Emilia, who was still standing rather stunned. "You told him? And not me?"

Emilia looked helplessly to her father.

Marcel said, "I figured it out for myself. When I saw the two of them together. At Bonfire Night. You would have realized it, too, if you'd gone to Bonfire Night."

"So you found out and you kept it a secret from me?" said Anna.

"You kept it a secret from *everyone,*" added Diya.

Anna turned abruptly and mumbled some sort of excuse and ran out of the house, followed by Marcel calling her name. Emilia turned to Sai and made some sort of explanatory gesture before also running out of the house.

Diya announced, "Come on. We're going."

"Mum—" Pari began to protest.

"We are all going," commanded Diya, in a terrifying tone of voice that made her whole family fall in line.

Sam said, "But really, you don't need to—there's a whole turkey dinner—"

"Good-bye," said Diya brusquely, and led her family out of the house.

Sam looked at the remainder of his guests, including Pen, who looked crushed.

"I didn't mean to—it was just—"

"It's okay," said Sam, seeking desperately to salvage something from his party. "Let's focus on something exciting and positive. Something to be grateful for. Arthur! Max! Tell us all about the new baby!"

Max looked up so quickly, with such alarm in his eyes, that Sam immediately wished he'd never got out of bed that morning. He should have just canceled the entire occasion of Thanksgiving.

Arthur said, "What baby?" and looked over at Max, who instantly looked so guilty that Sam actually cringed in sympathy.

Max said, "Er."

Arthur said slowly, not taking his eyes off Max, "Maybe we should also go."

"Yes." Max nodded, and then glared at Sam.

Sam mouthed, *Sorry?* Although he knew it wasn't nearly good enough for breaking Max's confidence so utterly.

Pen said bitterly, "I guess that was one thing going wrong that I can't be blamed for."

"I'm going, too," announced Mr. Hammersley, standing.

"What?" said Sam. "No. Please don't. Stay. We'll still—"

"I need some peace and quiet," Mr. Hammersley said, and waved his hand around as if that indicated *peace and quiet,* and walked out of the house, followed by Jack.

Pen said, "I hope you don't mind, Sam, but I'm going to go, too."

"Pen—" Sam began.

Pen said, "No, really, as you might imagine, I am *definitely* not in the mood to pretend to be grateful for things."

"Pen, you shouldn't—" Sam was cut off by the smoke detector suddenly blaring. Swearing, he raced back into the kitchen, where smoke poured out of the oven as soon as he opened it and pulled out a fairly charred turkey and stared at it. He had been trying to give Teddy a perfect Thanksgiving dinner, and *look at it.* "Damn it," he exclaimed with feeling.

Libby said cautiously, "Is there anything I can do to help?"

"Yeah," Sam said, exhaling in frustration. "You could have not said anything about reading about Jack online."

Libby said after a moment, "Right, but I didn't know—"

"I know you didn't know, but everything was going pretty well until you had to go and mention that."

"Okay," Libby said. "First, let's dial back the tone. Second, this whole thing here was not my fault."

"I'm not saying it's your *fault*," Sam said, "I'm just saying that if you hadn't *said* that—"

"That does seem," remarked Libby evenly, "like you're saying it's my fault, and still with that tone, so this doesn't sound like it's going to be a productive conversation, and I think I should say good night." She said it in a clipped tone of voice, plainly displeased, and although she did call to Teddy, "Bye, Teddy, see you in school!" when she left the house it could be something said to be related to "storming."

Sam huffed in frustration.

"Well," remarked Ellen. "You handled that very poorly."

"I am aware," Sam sighed. "I am adding it to the list of things I handled poorly today, on Teddy's Thanksgiving. I maybe ruined my neighbors' relationships with each other, ruined my relationship with Libby, and ruined the turkey. I am declaring this Thanksgiving to be *canceled*."

Ellen stood in the doorway, Sophie and Evie behind her, and watched him, then said, "You should probably go after her."

Sam laughed humorlessly. "No. She's right. It wouldn't be productive right now. I need a second."

386

"Okay," Ellen allowed. "Maybe not." And then she walked over to him and hugged him. Because that was the kind of thing Ellen was always able to do: give him a hug, even when he was radiating the opposite of embraceability. "Don't be so hard on yourself," she whispered, and then kissed his cheek. "Let's go, girls. Say bye."

"Bye, Uncle Sam," they chorused, unusually reserved in the face of the absolute disaster of Sam's Thanksgiving.

"Bye, girls," Sam made himself say, and listened to them leave, and then swore again as he turned back to the turkey.

Teddy said in a small voice from the doorway, "Dad?"

Sam took a deep breath and then forced himself to sound as jovial as possible. "Well. The turkey is a lost cause but maybe we can salvage some pumpkin pie for dinner."

Teddy, after a moment, came up to him and gave him a hug. *Sometimes you're a lot like your Aunt Ellen,* thought Sam, dropping a kiss to the top of his head. *Or maybe your mum,* as it occurred to him, because the times of Sara's hugs were so distant now.

"I had a good Thanksgiving, Dad," said Teddy against him.

Sam was startled into a chuckle. "Oh, Teddy, it was rubbish and you can say it."

"A lot happened," Teddy allowed, "but it's still

not as bad as it was. Still things are better than they were. We have a lot to be thankful for, and everything else is going to work out. Isn't that what you said, when we were moving here? That things would work out, and so far they have, and I'm sure they'll keep doing it. Everyone'll make up. They won't stay angry. That would be stupid. That's not how it is here. It's turned out really good here, Dad." Teddy looked up at his father.

And there, in his eyes: no dubiousness or skepticism. Now Teddy was looking at him with eyes that shone with trust and adoration, one of those moments when Sam fully understood what it meant to be a dad. Because in the midst of everything else, Teddy, underneath it all, had a steady belief in Sam's ability to fix things. Even when he was fighting against, struggling with Sam's vision of things, Teddy really had no choice but to *trust* him. Sam, in spite of everything, could do no wrong in Teddy's eyes; much as Teddy might doubt, it was impossible for him to truly believe that Sam could lead him wrong. Given any other choice of any other person, Teddy would turn to Sam and follow his lead. And maybe that would fade eventually—Sam's level of influence in Teddy's life—but it was there now, and Sam felt a fierce responsibility for it.

Sam cleared his throat past the choked

sensation and said, "I'm glad, Teddy. I'm so glad. That's all I want. That's really all I want."

"Me, too." Teddy beamed. "For things to be good for us."

For us, Sam thought, when he had been thinking, *For you. I want things to be good for you.*

Sam said, "Tell you what. Why don't I help you finish trimming the tree?"

Teddy nodded, and Sam followed him and forced himself to focus on the ornaments instead of the rest of the disasters of the day: Pen sharing everyone's secrets on the Internet, Diya and Anna angry that their children were involved, Max being less than truthful with Arthur about the baby, the disastrously burnt turkey . . . and Sam unjustifiably taking everything out on poor Libby, who would probably never speak to him again.

He forced himself to open the box Libby had brought and left behind her when she'd stormed out, which turned out to hold a lovely gingerbread house ornament.

"Put it on the tree," Teddy said brightly. "Then when you make up with Miss Quinn and you have her come over here, she can see it."

So easy, Sam thought. It was just that easy for Teddy. *When you make up with Miss Quinn.* No "if" about it.

Sam hung it on the tree and let Teddy pull more

ornaments out of the boxes, and he told Teddy stories about all of the ornaments, until Teddy was giggling helplessly over all of them, and he finally lifted Teddy up to put the star on the top of the tree, as the final touch.

"Ta-da!" proclaimed Sam, and they took a step back to look at the twinkling tree.

And, actually, although it had been an incredibly terrible day in many respects, there was a Christmas tree Sam had just got to decorate with his son, and it *did* make things seem better.

"You know what's left?" said Teddy.

"What's left?" asked Sam.

"Bob's Santa hat." Teddy held it up.

Sam laughed. "Bob's Santa hat. Let's go put it on him."

It was crisply cold outside, and oddly dark. The street had been growing cheerful with Christmas lights but no one had any turned on, including Max and Arthur, which Sam thought was a terrible sign. He wondered if he should go over to try and apologize, or if that would make everything much worse. And, because he couldn't decide what he should do, he ended up deciding to focus on Teddy, as he positioned the Santa hat onto Bob.

"It's officially Christmas!" said Teddy.

Sam looked at the flamingo with the Santa hat and tried to drum up Christmas cheer.

∙ ∙ ∙

Jack walked down the dark and silent street, and
no one called to him, and no one came running,
and no one offered him any dinners at all.
Jack scratched at all the regular doors, and all
he heard was shouting that sent him skittering
backward, or an oppressive silence that made
him flatten his ears.

Sam let Jack in and sat with him on the couch
and said, "What a day," and stroked at his fur
and seemed generally so sad that Jack spent a
little while just resting his head on Sam's knee,
because Sam seemed like he needed it.

Sam remarked, "Thanks. I probably need the
company. You know, it's odd, but I think I'd
actually begun to get used to the idea of . . .
not being alone. There was a feeling of . . . that
maybe fresh starts did exist. And maybe they
were ginger." Sam sighed heavily. "Or maybe
not? Who knows?"

Jack didn't, so Jack just wagged his tail and
hoped that was enough.

Chapter 15

When you find a street full of people who really seem to want to care about each other, cherish that.

Emilia had locked herself in her drum room, but she wasn't playing. Anna had made herself a cup of chamomile tea and was determinedly not speaking to anyone.

Marcel said, "So you're just going to sulk?"

"I'm not sulking," Anna retorted. "It would be sulking if it wasn't justified. And it is definitely justified."

"Anna." Marcel had the gall to *sigh*. "You're overreacting."

Anna lifted her eyebrows. "Overreacting?"

"She isn't getting *married*."

"Yet," Anna said. "She isn't getting married yet. That's the next step."

"They're just kids."

"So were we. And I can't believe you would keep me in the dark about this. I can't believe you would know and not—"

"You're hard on her, Anna," Marcel said, sounding frustrated. "And I know that it comes out of love, because you want nothing but the best for her, but you can be hard on her, and so I promised her that I would—"

"I'm not hard on her, I just don't *spoil* her."

Marcel just looked at her, as if that assertion was too ridiculous to even rebut.

Anna frowned. "I think we should go back to not talking," she announced, and then was distracted by lights flashing outside on the street. She glanced at the window, and then said in surprise, "There's an ambulance out there."

Pari was sitting silently in her bedroom, feeling dramatically, poorly done by. She was supposed to be helping Teddy decorate his Christmas tree. And celebrating *Thanksgiving,* which she'd never got to do before in her *life.* And convincing Miss Quinn to let them use Jack in the school play, which Miss Quinn had seemed almost convinced to do, until everything had fallen apart.

And then she had had to be dragged home where Mum and Dad and Sai had managed to have a ridiculously long and boring row over the stupid Sai-dating-Emilia thing. Pari had never understood why the Sai-dating-Emilia thing was such a big thing. When she said it was stupid now, basically everyone told her she was too little to understand what was going on, which was *extra* stupid, because she understood *lots* of things, and she was tired of being treated like she *didn't.*

She could have run away again, but that had been cold and she didn't feel like being cold, so Pari had gone up to hide in her room and now Mum and Dad and Sai had all gone quiet, after much slamming of doors.

Pari sat in her window and pulled her knees into her chest and thought how everything was just *so stupid,* no one had even turned any of their Christmas lights on. It was basically the world's most boring street that she lived on.

And that was when the ambulance turned down it.

Max, after explaining, let the silence stretch for as long as he could bear. This was a trait of Arthur's, that he wouldn't immediately react to something that had upset him. Max thought Arthur thought this was a hallmark of how civilized he was, that he wouldn't react in a flash of anger, but Max would much have preferred a flash of anger over long-term silent treatment, and it was honestly one of Max's least favorite things about Arthur and made all quarrels between them much worse, in Max's opinion.

Arthur was unloading the dishwasher in the kitchen but he'd been doing that for so long that Max was fairly sure he'd loaded it back up and was now unloading it again. Max sat in the lounge and looked out the window at the dark street. He should really go out and turn the Christmas lights on, but he didn't feel right about it.

He sighed and called, "When do you think you're going to talk to me about this?"

"Sorry," Arthur called back. "Are you feeling angry that I'm not handling your betrayal well enough?"

Max sighed and rubbed his eyes and thought this was why he hated the silent treatment thing, because he found it impossible to confront.

Arthur appeared back in the lounge and said, "Were you going to tell me at all? Or were you just going to let the baby opportunity lapse?"

"Of course I was going to tell you," said Max. "After the weekend. I'd decided I'd just let us have this one last weekend—"

"Before ruining our lives with a baby?"

"Before ruining our lives with the *possibility* of a baby that you would go and fall in love with and then I would have to clean up all of the pieces of our broken hearts, *again*."

"First of all—" said Arthur, and then cut himself off.

"First of all?" prompted Max, who would much rather they have this out than lapse back into silence.

Arthur said, "There's an ambulance out there."

Pen was trying not to feel sorry for herself. She wasn't really achieving it.

"I think I've really messed everything up," she confided to Chester, who looked like he swam a little more mournfully than usual out of deference to her mood. "Am I a terrible person? I don't *want* to be a terrible person. I want to be a *better* person. But it was so stupid of me. I knew I shouldn't be doing it and yet I . . . went ahead and did it anyway, and that's probably the definition of a terrible person. I'm a terrible person. Probably everyone on this street hates me and they'd be totally right to do that." Pen fell silent, watching Chester swim around and around his bowl, and wished she could go back in time and never start the blog. Why had she *done* it?

Filled with self-loathing, she went online and deleted the blog, all of it, top to bottom. And replaced it with a single entry.

When you find a street full of people who really seem to want to care about each other, cherish that.

Pen turned from the computer to look at Chester. "*You* don't hate me, do you?"

Chester was silent on the matter, but Chester seemed to want to turn his back on her, so maybe Chester hated her, too. Damn it. Even her *goldfish* hated her. That was how terrible a person she was.

Pen got up and went to her window, considering whether she ought to turn her Christmas lights on. The street looked incredibly dark from her vantage point. Her actions had even managed to destroy *Christmas*.

And then the ambulance turned down the street.

Sam let Jack out without really thinking too hard about it. The street was still dark and quiet and suffocating and Sam thought maybe he ought to share Jack's ability to comfort. Probably Mr. Hammersley would be waiting for him.

Teddy came back downstairs from taking his shower and said, "So. Should we talk about your plan to make up with Miss Quinn?"

And then Jack showed up at the door, barking and bouncing.

"Oh," Teddy said, letting the dog in. "We have a whole burnt turkey. Maybe we could give Jack the turkey. It would be like a Christmas gift to him."

"Maybe," said Sam, but he wasn't really paying attention, because Jack was still barking, and kept darting toward the door like he wanted to go back out. It was weird. Was Jack just going through a frantic phase? "What's up, Jack?"

"He's being strange," Teddy said, also watching Jack's display now.

"Yeah," agreed Sam slowly.

Jack literally began tugging at first Sam's shirttails, and then Teddy's, and then back to Sam's, trying to tug them along. So they followed Jack, around the side of Mr. Hammersley's house, to the back garden. Where Mr. Hammersley was sprawled in between the rosebushes, right by the outlet where his Christmas lights plugged in. And he was completely unconscious.

Sam rushed to his side, leaning over him. Luckily, he was still breathing, but he was unresponsive.

"What's the matter with him?" asked Teddy, sounding fearful.

Sam looked up at him, even as he struggled to reach the mobile in his pocket to dial 999. "Nothing," he lied, breathlessly and automatically. "Nothing. He's fine. Take Jack into the house with you."

Teddy didn't listen. He started to cry. "He's all right, isn't he? He's going to be all right?"

Sam said to him, "Yeah," just as 999 connected, and then Sam said to the operator, "Ambulance, please."

Sam tried to keep Teddy back, away from the medics as they worked, loading Mr. Hammersley onto a stretcher and then onto the ambulance. Teddy was silent as he watched, and he was clinging to Sam, and Sam wished he wouldn't watch. Sara's death had not been at all like this. Sara's death had been a long time coming and had happened almost calmly, as serenely as Sara had wanted it, and without Teddy having to witness.

But Mr. Hammersley wasn't dead, Sam reminded himself. He had still been breathing, and the medics were certainly behaving with a sense of purpose, so all must not be lost.

"What happened? Can I help?"

Sam realized it was Pen talking to him, and also realized that the rest of the street was outside, gathered in a tense, nervous knot, watching.

"I don't know," Sam said, because he *didn't*.

Pen said, "You should go in the ambulance with him."

Sam hesitated.

"I'll take Teddy and follow and meet you there," Pen offered.

"We all will," added Arthur.

There was a general murmur of assent from everyone else.

Sam looked at Teddy.

Who nodded firmly and said, "Go with him, Dad. We'll meet you there."

Sam nodded back and kissed the top of his head and then climbed into the waiting ambulance.

Chapter 16

Sam found a waiting room entirely full of his neighbors, as well as Teddy, all of whom looked at him expectantly.

Sam gave a helpless little shrug. "They won't tell me anything. He's still alive, because they were working on him, but I don't know anything more than that."

"They'll come out and give us an update?" asked Diya.

"Yeah, that's what they said. But you don't all need to stay here. That really isn't—"

"Of course we all need to stay here," said Anna. "He's part of our street, isn't he? He's one of ours."

Sam noticed Diya glance at Anna and then look away. Really, the levels of tension in the room were so much more than Sam could handle, but he understood why everyone also felt they needed to be there.

"We should have brought Jack with us," said

Teddy. "Mr. Hammersley would have really liked to have Jack along."

"I don't think they let dogs in hospitals," said Pari. "Hospitals are stupid."

"Jack's going to wonder what happened, though."

"We'll be sure to let Jack know," said Pen, giving Teddy a small smile. "As soon as we get home."

"How long did they say it would be before we heard something?" asked Anna.

"Somewhere else you need to be?" countered Emilia, with some amount of bite.

Anna looked at her. "No. I already said I want to be here. I was just wondering."

"I don't know," Sam said. "They didn't say."

Emilia said, "Well, if we're going to be here for a while, I guess I'll go in search of some tea."

Sam watched her walk away. He also felt the stiffness of Diya and Darsh, who both looked at Sai as if he might follow.

But it was Anna who followed, standing and saying, "I'll help her get tea for everyone. We'll be right back."

Everyone in the room watched them walk away.

Max said, "They'll need more than four hands for all the tea. I'll help, too," and then made his escape.

Sam looked at the knot of people left in the room. Diya looked as if she would have happily made her own escape, too, if she could have worked out a graceful way to do it and if it wouldn't have forced her into fetching tea with Anna.

Marcel said abruptly, "You know, there's nothing wrong with my daughter. She is a sweet and good kid. Which is exactly what I think about your son. It's why I'm the only one not all tied up in knots about all of this." Then he got up and left, too, leaving Diya and Darsh sitting stunned in his wake.

Pari said, "He's right, though. Emilia's cool. She's always super nice to me."

Diya looked at Pari. "When did you ever talk to Emilia?"

"Oh, please, she and Sai spent all summer together. Emilia basically watched me all summer. She was always nice, to all of us. I don't get what the big deal is, but I like her."

Sam didn't know if it would help the situation or not but felt compelled to keep the room from lapsing into awkward silence. "She's very good at the drums."

Pen added, "I know that I started all of this, so you probably don't care what I think, but they seem like two kids who just like each other and make each other happy, and that's rare enough in this world."

"That's what Max thinks, too," said Arthur, sounding exhausted but also firm.

402

Diya looked at Arthur. "You knew Sai and Emilia were dating, too?"

Arthur lifted knowing eyebrows in Sai's direction. "They used to use our back garden to get back and forth between the houses."

Sai looked a little chagrined at that.

"And Max would tell you that finding people you want to spend time with is hard enough. When you find them, you hold on to them. Isn't that why we're all here?" Arthur stood.

"Now, if you'll excuse me, I have to go and find my husband and say nice things to his face instead of behind his back."

"Emilia!" Anna called, chasing her down the hallway. Damn, why was she so fast? It made Anna feel extra-old when Emilia finally stopped and Anna caught up and Emilia wasn't even breathing hard.

"What?" asked Emilia sulkily. "Now I can't even go and get tea?"

"No, you can . . . I wanted to talk to you."

"About what now, Mum?" demanded Emilia. "I think it is crystal clear to me what a huge disappointment I am to you—"

"Huge disappointment?" echoed Anna, bewildered. "What do you mean?"

"—and how I don't like the right things, including the right boy, and how basically you wish you had any other daughter but—"

"That is *not true,* Emilia," Anna said fiercely, and grabbed hold of Emilia's shoulders to force her to face her. "Look at me. That is *not true.* Do you hear me? I think you're amazing. I think you're so amazing that you're terrifying. You are anything but a disappointment. You are more precious than anything I ever expected to be put in charge of, and I'm making such a huge mess of it, oh, my God."

Emilia stared at her, mouth open, looking so shocked that Anna's heart ached. How, *how,* had she ended up with a daughter shocked to see how beloved she was? How had Anna done this so *wrong?*

"I am going to be better," Anna vowed.

"Better at what?" asked Emilia, sounding confused.

"Better at being your mum. Better at showing you how much you're loved. Because I love you, so very much. Your happiness is the most important thing in the universe to me." Anna thought of Marcel's accusation and said, "If I'm hard on you, it's because . . . because I want so badly to make sure you don't make my mistakes. I want so badly to make sure that you—"

"Your mistakes, Mum?" interrupted Emilia, sounding anguished. "But how can they be mistakes? I would be happy to make every mistake to be like you. Dad loves you so much, and we live on this fabulous street, and I'd love

404

to be a mum someday and . . . You realize that I don't see your life as being a *failure?* You realize that it shouldn't be a huge tragedy to you to see *you* in me?"

Anna, for a moment, could manage nothing. She felt as if she'd been looking through a kaleidoscope all this time, and things had suddenly tumbled into a new configuration. She put her hands on Emilia's cheeks and looked into Emilia's blue eyes and yes, saw her own, looking back at her. All along, Anna had wanted to save Emilia from Anna's mistakes, but, Anna realized abruptly, what she really needed to do was save *herself* from the mistakes her own mother had made.

So Anna licked her lips and said, "I need you to know this. Are you listening?"

Emilia nodded, a short little jerk, looking tearfully transfixed.

Anna said, "You're the most important person in my life. It's you. Everything I do is for you. Everything I've done wrong has been for you. And I'm sorry for all of it. But please try not to forget that there's nothing you could do that would make me turn my back on you. Nothing. I will always be your mum. And I will always be *here*." And oh, what Anna would have given for her mum to have said that to her; to have felt like there was a support system in place just to protect her, just to fall back on, instead of feeling

405

cast out so alone, so flailing, so lost, that she had almost ruined everything good in her life in her fierceness to try to keep it.

Anna, she thought, had to learn the lesson she hadn't yet learned, which was to trust the people she loved.

Emilia nodded again and said in a small voice, "Me, too, Mum. Me, too. Always."

Anna pulled Emilia into a hug, and Emilia buried her face into Anna's neck, the way she had when she had been small, her cheeks wet with tears, and Anna smoothed her hand over Emilia's familiar blond hair, so dear and so loved, and wondered when she had stopped giving comfort like this, vowed to do it from now on, for the rest of their lives.

She looked over Emilia's head, at where Marcel had paused in the corridor.

And she smiled at him.

"Hey," said Arthur, to Max's still back, where he was standing looking out a hospital window.

Max glanced over his shoulder and said merely, "Hi," before looking back out the window.

Arthur remarked, "You got lost on your way to the tea, I see," and leaned up against the window so he could see Max's face.

Max said lightly, "This place is a maze."

"Mmm," said Arthur noncommittally. "Max—"

"I've already apologized, you know," said

Max. "I can't keep apologizing hoping that the fiftieth time is the time when it will be enough for you—"

"Do I make you do that?"

Max sighed. "No. But I don't know what else to say—"

"This is me apologizing to you right now, if you would stop talking long enough to listen."

Max did stop talking. He regarded Arthur curiously. He said, "Apologizing for what?"

"You're right. And you've been saying this to me for a long time and I didn't hear you. Not properly. And I'm sorry for that."

Max didn't say anything. He furrowed his eyebrows together and studied Arthur.

So Arthur kept talking. "I let you do all of the emotional heavy lifting—"

Max started to protest. "No, you don't—"

Arthur talked right over him. "Yes, I do. I always have. And I thought that's okay because you're better with emotions and I'll run the numbers side of things and we'll work out okay. But we've had a lot of emotions over the past few months and not nearly enough numbers and we're out of balance and you're drowning and you tried to tell me and I didn't hear you. So I'm sorry."

"Arthur," said Max, but then didn't say anything else, as if he didn't know what else there was to say.

Arthur inched a step closer, because he thought it would be allowed now, and it was true that Max didn't flinch away. He said, "I am going to pull more of my emotional weight in the next few weeks. And I'm going to start right now. Do you remember when we first started dating?"

"Of course I remember. We aren't that old, darling; it isn't *that* ancient history."

"On our one-week anniversary, you proposed marriage. Do you remember that? Our *one-week* anniversary."

Max smiled a bit. "I was being . . . exuberant. I liked to watch your ears blush at how appallingly charming you found me."

"I know. I was horrified. And also, yes, of course, charmed, because you were right, from the very beginning, that I was always going to be charmed by you. You were right, all along. You knew, right away, and it's always taken me longer, and at every turn you've always asked me to take a leap of faith, to trust you to catch me if I fall, and I always have. I know you think I'm cautious, but I'm not, with you. You've always pulled me much faster than I ordinarily want to go, and I'm *fine* with that, but this is me, here, asking you to take the leap of faith for me. Jump with me, and trust that I will catch you if we fall. I *promise* that I will. I'm paying attention now. I promise."

Max looked at him, his eyes flickering over the features of his face, and Arthur held his breath.

And then Max tangled his hands into Arthur's hair and kissed him hard enough that probably it shouldn't have happened in a hospital corridor.

Which made it, of course, the best kiss of Arthur's life.

Emilia and Anna and Marcel returned to the waiting room, decidedly without cups of tea and looking teary-eyed. Max and Arthur also returned without cups of tea but holding hands with each other.

Sam remarked, so relieved at the release of some of the tension, "I've never seen so many people go to fetch tea and not come back with tea."

Which made everyone laugh a little and dispelled even more of the tension.

Diya said, a little shyly—and that in and of itself was astonishing—"So, Emilia. Sai was telling us how you play the drums."

Emilia looked surprised and then looked at Sai and gave him the most brilliant smile. "Yes. I do."

"She's really good, too, Mum," said Sai, smiling besottedly at Emilia.

"Ah, young love," said Max jovially, and pressed a kiss into the top of Arthur's head that Arthur didn't even roll his eyes at.

Sam smiled at them and said, "Should I apologize? I feel like I should."

Max shook his head a little. "You thought I was telling him, and honestly I should have. I should have warned you that it was still a secret. I'm getting very bad at lying to him. I really must improve in future."

Arthur did roll his eyes at that. "You're a cock."

"There are children present," said Max.

"Given all of the détente," remarked Sam, "perhaps we should address the last outstanding matter of disagreement."

Which caused everyone to look over at Pen.

Pen looked as if she were trying to shrink in on herself where she was sitting in the chair. She said, "I am so, so sorry. *So* sorry. It started out just because . . . I didn't know any of you lot. And I sat at home, every day, and watched all of these goings-on about your life, and didn't know any of you, and was curious, and wanted to know more, and was too cowardly to take the step that Sam did to get to know all of you. So I suppose I . . . made you all into characters, like this was all a story instead of your real life, and in that way I managed to be able to detach from the knowledge of what I was doing to all of you, but I *know* it was wrong, and I don't know what to do except to say that I am so, so, so sorry and I'll never do it again." Pen looked at each of them in turn, eyes wide and cajoling. "Now that I know all of you, I . . . feel so lucky to share a street with such wonderful people, and I can't believe I ever treated any of you as if you were just *characters,* when you're all so much more than that, so wonderful and complex and *lovely,* and I'm so honored to know you, and I hope you want to continue to know me."

Silence fell over the waiting room, which was broken only by a doctor coming through the door, and looking surprised at the number of people there.

"Well, then," he said. "I didn't expect an entire committee."

"How's Mr. Hammersley?" asked Teddy anxiously.

The doctor smiled at him kindly. "He's quite all right. Had a bit of a scare just there with his heart, but he's come through it. Of course, he'll have to adopt a more healthy diet and better careful exercise and take it easy, but . . . he's quite all right. He'll be home in plenty of time for Christmas. Now. Are you the family?" The doctor looked from Teddy to Sam.

Before Sam could say anything, Anna said, "Yes," and glanced at Pen, and smiled.

Diya also looked at Pen before looking back at the doctor and saying, "We're *all* the family."

Bill woke in a hospital room, which had always been a great fear of his. He looked up at the ceiling over his head, dull and white, and thought, *This is it. The beginning of the end.* There was nothing left to look forward to. It had caught up with him at last, old age, and uselessness, and he would fade away, alone and forgotten, pathetic, in a home somewhere.

Bill was ashamed of the fact that tears gathered at the corners of his eyes, made the ceiling over his head shimmer in a watery fashion.

The doctor was talking to him. Something about his heart, and it being merely a scare—a good one, but just a scare, with no reason to think that he didn't have many years ahead of him, provided he made a few small "lifestyle changes."

Bill didn't pay attention to the doctor. Making "lifestyle changes" required more energy than it was worth. It was easy to think there was a point to a "lifestyle change" when you were as young as this doctor was.

The doctor said something that sounded like, "Now I'll go make the report to your family. Are you up for them to visit?" Bill tore his gaze away from the ceiling, sure he'd heard incorrectly. "My family?"

"Ah, you'd like to see them, wouldn't you?" The doctor smiled at him.

Bill made some noise that he couldn't tell meant *yes* or *no*. Really it meant *what family?*

And then Teddy came running through the door, followed by the Indian girl, followed by Teddy's dad, and by Max and his husband, and by the constantly running girl, and the Polish bloke and his wife, and the Polish teenager hand-in-hand with the Indian teenager, and the Indian couple taking up the rear. There were so many people crowded into the room that they basically didn't fit.

Bill gaped at all of them.

Teddy came up and picked up his hand and squeezed it and said, "I'm so glad you're feeling better, Mr. Hammersley."

"Oh," said the little Indian girl frankly, "you're *covered* in tubes, aren't you?"

"Pari!" scolded her mother, sounding horrified.

"We heard you're going to be absolutely fine," said Sam, and smiled at him, as if . . . as if he actually *cared*. As if it actually *mattered* to him.

"But we did hear you have to adopt a healthier diet. Don't worry, I have many ideas about that," said the black woman, and Bill imagined being given green drinks. It sounded horrible. It sounded not at all like anything he would ever want. All this fuss. All these *people*.

Bill looked around at all of them and found himself thinking that he could accept the green drinks, he could accept this terrible crowd all around him at all times. It . . . might not be that bad.

He said, in amazement, "What are all of you doing here?"

"Max was very persuasive at convincing the

doctor we all had to be allowed in here," said Max's husband. "We all know about Max's power of persuasion."

Max winked at Bill.

That wasn't the question Bill had been asking. He tried again. "No, I mean . . . what are all of you doing here?"

Sam said gently, "Why wouldn't we be here?"

"We're here because we're your family," said Teddy.

Bill looked at all of them and felt ridiculously emotional again. It had to be the medication they'd given him.

Sam said, "Don't worry about Jack. We'll all take care of him until you can come home."

"We'll see if we can smuggle him into the hospital," Teddy stage-whispered.

Everyone laughed.

Except Bill, who just kept staring at all of them. "I thought you were all quarreling."

"Not anymore," said Anna. "We've all made up."

"We all had really good conversations," added Diya.

"And we're having a baby," said Max, which made Arthur smile and look at him.

"Having a baby?" echoed Bill. "How does *that* work?"

"Someone else has it for us," said Max. "We don't have the right parts."

"I didn't think the world had changed *that* much," remarked Bill, and everyone laughed again.

"So it's all settled," Sam said. "The only thing left to do is get you back home."

"And fix you and Miss Quinn," said Teddy, and then announced to the room at large, "Dad and Miss Quinn had a fight."

There was a general chorus of *oh, no*.

"Well, we have to fix that," said Diya.

"Absolutely," said Max. "We shall turn the power of the street onto your romantic entanglements."

"Soon you're going to have a new baby and be much too busy to deal with my romantic entanglements," said Sam.

"Which is why we must work quickly. And also I will, of course, leave the situation in Diya's capable hands."

"Do I need to bake something again?" said Diya.

"I can help," said Anna.

"I'm so very glad that we're all being united in worrying about my love life," said Sam, "but I'm sure I can sort it myself—"

To his chagrin, everyone shook their heads and made negative comments about that.

Even Bill felt he had to correct that. "You're very bad at women," he said. "If you feel like you need to borrow some of my wood carvings, that might help."

"Oh, Christ," said Sam.

"How do you think we might fix you and Miss Quinn?" asked Teddy.

"Well," said Max, "all I have to say is: it's going to be Christmastime, on Christmas Street. So I think it ought to be something incredibly good."

The day of the Christmas play was also the day that Mr. Hammersley came home.

It also happened to be the day that Arthur and Max brought home the tiny baby boy they had met three days earlier.

Sam helped Mr. Hammersley on with his coat and said, "Before we go to the play, I thought we'd stop at Arthur and Max's to meet the baby."

"Going to a Christmas play," grumbled Mr. Hammersley as he buttoned up his coat. "I never heard of anything so foolish in all my life."

But Sam noted he didn't ask to stay home, and Sam had been present when Mr. Hammersley had got the all-clear to attend the play.

It helped that Libby had agreed to allow Jack to star as "Manger Dog in Environmental Crisis." He was wearing a special festive red collar for the occasion and practicing his part with Teddy and Pari outside. Considering that his part consisted entirely of "lying still in the manger," Sam hoped he would excel and not be thrown off by the audience.

When Sam stepped outside with Mr. Hammersley, Teddy said eagerly, "Is it time to go?"

"In a bit. Would you like to go and see Arthur and Max's new baby quickly before we go?"

"Yes!" said Teddy.

"I've already seen him," said Pari. "Mum took me earlier."

"Not interested in seeing him again?" asked Sam, amused, because Pari's little nose was wrinkled at the prospect.

"He doesn't do much," said Pari.

Sam laughed. "Not yet anyway. Before you know it he'll be walking and chasing Jack around."

Sam and Teddy and Mr. Hammersley walked to Max and Arthur's and knocked on the door.

It was Arthur who answered, looking magnificently pleased with the state of the universe.

Sam smiled and said, "Have you had a constant stream of visitors?"

"Yes," called Max from the other room. "But come in. We never tire of showing him off."

Mr. Hammersley said, "He's just a baby. You lot all started out that way, too."

"Surely," Max responded, "none of us were half as beautiful as this baby is."

He *was* beautiful, too. Although not as beautiful as Sam remembered Teddy being, he was a lovely baby. And this one was impossibly tiny.

Sam couldn't remember Teddy being that small. He looked absolutely swallowed up in Max's arms, nestled comfortably in the crook, sleeping with the steady exhaustion with which the newly born greeted the world. Max leaned down and held him out a little bit so Teddy could look.

"You must remark upon how beautiful his nose is," Max said. "Arthur can't stop talking about the beauty of his nose."

"Shut up," Arthur said, sounding vaguely embarrassed but also, still, very pleased.

"He's lovely," said Sam. "The second most beautiful baby I've ever seen."

Max eyed Teddy with mock seriousness and said, "Hmm, I suppose I'll allow the possibility that Teddy was a handsome baby."

"What's his name?" asked Teddy.

"Jack," answered Max.

Teddy's eyes widened. "Really?"

"No," said Arthur. "It's Charlie."

Sam laughed.

"In the end," said Max, "we decided Jack probably wanted to keep his own name."

"In the interest of the street's sanity, we thought we wouldn't want to have lots of shouting for two beings named Jack," added Arthur. And then, after a pause, "Also we like the name Charlie."

"Charlie's nice," said Teddy. "And pretty soon

he'll be running around with Jack, so it'll be nice to have a different name."

"Let's not rush it," said Arthur. "I'm going to savor him being not-mobile for a little while."

"What do you think, Bill?" asked Max of Mr. Hammersley, who had been silent so far. "Approve of him?"

Mr. Hammersley looked down at the baby, and Sam thought he was going to say something gruff, but instead what he said was, "He's a lucky little boy."

Sam could tell Max had been completely caught off-guard by the way he blinked in reaction. Then he said, "Thank you," with genuine pleasure.

Arthur said to Teddy, "I'm sorry to be missing the Christmas play about insurance agents."

"I guess Charlie's too little to go?" said Teddy.

"A bit," said Arthur. "But I expect you and Pari to act it out for me tomorrow."

"Arthur is very keen on seeing the heroic insurance agent," said Max.

Teddy said, "Pari and I will act it out for you with Jack. Jack's the real star of the whole play."

"And what about everything for *after* the play?" asked Max, giving Sam a meaningful look.

"Hopefully it will work," said Sam. "Libby and I have been texting, and she's somewhat accepted my apology, so I think the rest of this will work."

"Of course it will," said Max. "It's brilliant."

"It's too bad we didn't know you were going to have Charlie before," said Teddy suddenly. "He could have played the baby Jesus in the manger."

"Maybe next year," said Arthur.

"This year he's very busy being the best Christmas gift in the whole world," said Max.

The entire street walked together to the school, save Arthur and Max and Charlie. And maybe it was a bit much, this large group of people all attending the Christmas play, but it also felt absolutely right. Sam sat in the middle of a crowd of people he hadn't even known a few months earlier, and watched his son in his first Christmas play, and it suddenly struck him, all at once, that they'd done it, he and Teddy. They'd embarked on a grand adventure and they had ended up here, surrounded by a support system Sam could only have dreamed about. All of these people, all of whom cared about his son, all of whom had made their lives so much richer. Sam thought of how lonely the pair of them had been before, with only each other to lean on, and thought now of how each person on the street had, in their own way, brightened their lives.

Teddy stood, an angel in a snowfall in a desert, and announced great tidings, and Sam looked at the people all around him—none of them strangers, all of them unexpectedly and remarkably dear to him—and thought, *Great tidings indeed.*

Jack comported himself remarkably well by basically following Teddy and Pari all around the stage. Pari played the insurance agent and relished every single phrase of her delivery. She was dour about climate change but she had a lovely line about how the purpose of insurance was to give you room to enjoy the things that you love. "Like our climate, and the baby Jesus," she finished.

The audience gave them a standing ovation when it was over, and Jack stood and looked out at the crowd and wagged his tail as if he had been responsible for all of it.

"What did you think?" Sam asked Mr. Hammersley.

Mr. Hammersley said, "Was the little girl— what's her name? Pari?—really playing an insurance agent?"

Sam laughed.

"Sam!" squealed Ellen, coming up to him and giving him a tight hug. "Teddy was *brilliant.*"

"Do you think he has a future on the stage?"

"No. But he was brilliant all the same. Now, are you going backstage to talk to Miss Quinn?" Ellen gave him a stern look.

"I am not."

Ellen sighed. "Sam—"

"Now, now, no lecture necessary. I think we've mostly made up the fight. I've apologized at least, and she seems to have accepted the apology, but she also seems a little wary."

"But we have a plan," said Diya, immediately inserting herself into the conversation. "We have a *very good plan* to win her back."

Libby, when the last parent had finally been small-talked with, thought maybe she would go home and treat herself to a large glass of wine and a very long bubble bath. The play had been exhausting to achieve, requiring the negotiation of multiple personalities, and of course through it all had been an annoying lingering lack of satisfaction with Sam. It was ridiculous to have been that affected by a row so early in the relationship, ridiculous to feel off-kilter as a result, as if Sam had already been such a regular feature of her life that he could be so *missed*. It was ridiculous, and maybe partly the problem was how much Teddy could remind her of him. At any rate, Libby was relieved to have got through the play, and was hopeful that maybe, with a little more mental space, she could decide what she wanted to do about Sam.

Maybe she could decide if she wanted him more than he wanted her, which seemed that it could possibly be the case. He had given no impression, through the series of texts they'd exchanged since their last meeting, of missing her nearly as much as she had been missing him.

And then, backstage, she came upon Jack, sitting by the coat she was going to grab on her way out the exit.

"Jack," she said in surprise. "What are you still doing here?" She glanced around, but there was no one backstage with her, and she knew the hall had been empty, as she'd just come from there.

Jack wagged his tail at her and showed off the fact that, pinned to his red bow collar, was a piece of construction paper with a curlicue instruction on it. *Follow the stars*. Libby looked at Jack, at the note, and then back at Jack.

"What's this? Are you in on the secret?"

Jack just wagged his tail again.

"I see," said Libby. "Not telling, are you?" She could, she knew, tuck the note in her pocket and just ignore it. She could go home to that bubble bath and bottle of wine.

. . . But she didn't want to. She wanted to see Sam. She wanted him to make her laugh by saying something silly. She wanted to feel the way she felt when he looked at her. And it was Christmas. Shouldn't you get the things you wanted at Christmas, at least?

So Libby stepped outside, with every intention of following the stars. She had no idea it was going to be meant so *literally*. But directly in front of the door had been placed a scattering of gently glowing plastic stars, and there was another pile a few meters away, and another pile a few meters away from that. Libby did indeed find herself *following the stars,* Jack wandering beside her, sniffing at the stars as they approached, all the way to Sam's street.

She probably would have simply gone to Sam's house, except for the fact that he was clearly standing at the other end of the street, lifting his hand in greeting, under a little garden archway.

So Libby began walking to him. And, as she began walking, the dark houses along the street began slowly to light up as she passed them, thousands of twinkling fairy lights arranged in the shape of stars that followed her progress down the street. It was . . . enchanting. Utterly absolutely enchanting. She paused as she got to Sam, to turn back to look over her shoulder, at the twinkling stars all over the houses on the street, and then she did turn to Sam, who stood under the archway watching her, his hands in his pockets.

"Hi," he said, with a little half smile, and Libby had been very inclined to forgive Sam entirely prior to following stars to a street with lights that turned on just for her, and even more inclined to do so after all of that, but it was the little half smile that did it, that made Libby close her hands on his jacket and lean up to kiss him. A soft, sweet, lovely, perfect kiss; a kiss composed of stars.

Libby, eyes closed, stayed close to Sam and breathed him in.

"Damn it," Sam whispered. "I didn't even get to use the mistletoe in my pocket."

"You didn't need to," Libby said, and opened her eyes to look at him. "You didn't need to. This might be too much for me to say," she added, suddenly fearful of the intensity of all of this.

"I just lit up a street with lights for you. I mean, all of the neighbors helped—a *lot*—but still: Libby. *That* might have been too much to say."

Libby said, "I moved to London, this entirely new place, and nothing about it felt like home until I met you."

Sam smiled at her, so soft and sweet, and Libby thought how she wanted to just sit and keep track of years' worth of his smiles. He said, "I moved to London, this entirely new place, and I found this incredible home, and I want you to be part of it. Now, I don't think I'm very good at dating—"

"Nobody's good at dating," said Libby.

"—but I do know that I don't feel like you take my breath away. I feel like you give it back to me. I feel like you make me feel as if I can take a deep breath for the first time in a very long time, and I would like to keep that. If you would like to have me. Even if I'm an utter prat sometimes."

"I can deal with utter pratness," said Libby, "as long as it's only sometimes."

"Yes," said Sam, laughing. "I really hope it's only sometimes." Libby was going to lean up and kiss him again, except that she was distracted by the fact that there were snowflakes suddenly catching in Sam's sandy-colored hair. She didn't kiss Sam; she leaned her head back and looked up at the sky, where snowflakes were falling, catching the twinkling of the street's fairy lights and gleaming like tiny diamonds against the black velvet of the sky over their heads.

It was, Libby thought, her breath caught in her throat, like standing in a sky of stars falling all around them.

She looked back at Sam and asked, her voice hushed to match the snow, "Did your magic street make it *snow?*"

"I wouldn't put it past them," said Sam, and kissed her until her cheeks were rosy and the snow was thick on her eyelashes.

Epilogue

If Jack had to tell you this story, he'd tell you:

On Christmas morning, on a street called Christmas, a dog called Jack was presented with a bookshelf that had been carved and painted by some members of his family. The bookshelf, he was told, had his name carved into the front by the man called Bill. It had his likeness painted on the back by the man called Max. And the purpose of the bookshelf was for the whole street to collect and keep treats and toys for Jack.

The bookshelf sat in a back shed, and its shelves gathered buckets of treats, gnawed pieces of rope perfect for playing tug-of-war, beloved tennis balls, and ragged stuffed animals that could be torn and thrown and chased. The members of Jack's family stopped to add to the shelves, or to pull new toys off when they wanted to play with him, and Jack loved the bookshelf.

Jack also loved his new bed, in the house of the boy called Teddy and the man called Sam. He loved how they tore down the fence between their garden and the man called Bill's garden, so Jack could move back and forth at will. He loved when the woman called Libby was at Sam and Teddy's, because she was the best at scratching his back. He loved when Bill was also at Sam and Teddy's, and it was all of his favorite people in one place.

Jack was less sure about the tiny human who had just begun to crawl around and kept pulling at Jack's fur. But Jack thought maybe he'd get better.

Things always seemed to get better.

Jack lost one family and gained so many more families. Every day for Jack was Christmas.

Jack's a special dog.

Acknowledgments

To the small army that helps to create a book, thank you! With special thanks to:

Thalia Proctor and Maddie West, for giving me this great opportunity, letting me share this lovely story world with all of the characters, trusting me with this amazing project of theirs, cheerleading along the way, and generally making this creative process so much fun;

The entire team at Little, Brown, for embracing this book and nudging it into shape to be the best it can be;

John Scognamiglio, Robin Cook, and the team at Kensington for shepherding the U.S. edition.

My agent Andrea Somberg, for tireless belief and support;

Sonja L. Cohen, for always being willing to read drafts and tolerate frantic writing, even when we're supposed to be at Harry Potter World;

Larry Stritof, for also tolerating such things;

Kristin Gillespie, Erin McCormick, Jennifer Roberson, and Noel Wiedner, for being bright spots;

Aja Romano, for teaching me about narrative structure, even if I ignored all of it;

All the Internet folks, through fandom and

Twitter and Tumblr and Slack, who have been willing to indulge my love of Christmas romances and who teach me daily, in all the best ways, how to be a better writer, and who remind me daily, in all the best ways, how much I love writing;

And Mom, Dad, Ma, Megan, Caitlin, Bobby, Jeff, Jordan, Isabella, Gabriella, and Audrey, for always being my favorite kind of chaos. I love you all dearly.

Books are
produced in the
United States
using U.S.-based
materials

Books are printed
using a revolutionary
new process called
THINKtech™ that
lowers energy usage
by 70% and increases
overall quality

Books are
durable and
flexible
because of
Smyth-sewing

Paper is
sourced using
environmentally
responsible
foresting methods
and the
paper is acid-free

Center Point Large Print
600 Brooks Road / PO Box 1
Thorndike, ME 04986-0001 USA

(207) 568-3717

US & Canada:
1 800 929-9108
www.centerpointlargeprint.com